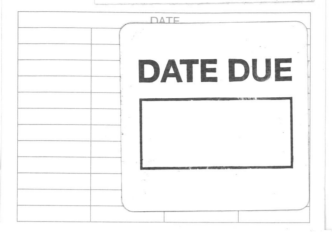

DATE

DATE DUE

FRIDAY NIGHTS
AT HONEYBEE'S

THE DIAL PRESS

FRIDAY NIGHTS
AT HONEYBEE'S

ANDREA SMITH

THE DIAL PRESS

FRIDAY NIGHTS AT HONEYBEE'S
A Dial Press Book/January 2003

Published by
The Dial Press
A Division of
Random House, Inc.
New York, New York

Book design by Lynn Newmark

Library of Congress Cataloging-in-Publication Data
Smith, Andrea.
    Friday nights at Honeybee's / Andrea Smith.
        p.   cm.
    ISBN 0-385-33428-1
        1. African American women singers—Fiction.
    2. African American musicians—Fiction.   3. Harlem
(New York, N.Y.)—Fiction.   4. Female friendship—Fiction.
I. Title.

PS3619.M54 F75 2003
813'.6—dc21

                                                  2002031443

Manufactured in the United States of America
Published simultaneously in Canada

10 9 8 7 6 5 4 3 2 1
BVG

For Nee and Nana, Aunt Margaret and Toni

FRIDAY NIGHTS
AT HONEYBEE'S

PROLOGUE

A bit of moonlight shone through the half-opened blinds. But for the soft sound of Bobby Timmons' "Moanin' " coming from the living room, the apartment was hushed. Forestine stood in the doorway and let her eyes adjust to the darkness. She could hardly see the figure draped across the bed.

"Vi," she whispered.

The girl didn't move. Forestine made her way through the room, nearly tripping over an open horn case and scattered clothing. She sat on the edge of the bed and clicked on the lamp atop the nightstand. The bulb glowed amber under a Chinese paper shade.

Viola lay sprawled on her back. Thick hair blanketed one side of her face. The ends were matted in the sparkle of her collar. Forestine bit the inside of her cheek to control her anger as she smoothed the tangled locks from her friend's face.

"Viola," Forestine said, gently shaking her. "It's me, baby . . ."

Viola's face, usually eager and innocent, was now vacant and dull. Her lips looked puckered and ash brown. Except for an occasional labored breath, her body was still. This stupor wasn't sleep induced. It was Eddie Bishop induced. And the saddest part was that Forestine had expected this. They all had. Honeybee, especially, had warned the girl time and again.

Forestine took Viola's purse and the sweater that lay on a chair across from the night table. She pulled Viola to the edge of the bed, lifted her up, and helped her stand. It pained Forestine to have to carry her friend home this way. But then, she considered her own choices in life. Though she wasn't as naive as Viola, she was just as obstinate and had fallen just as far.

Forestine struggled to guide Viola across the carpeted floor. Her body felt like dead weight. Forestine tightened her grip. "I'm here," she said, holding Viola closer. "I'm here and I've come to take you home."

Willie and Hattie Bent only had two children. Lilian, "that pretty child with the bright eyes," and Forestine, "the big, thickset one with the nappy hair." In 1958, this was how neighbors in the Kings County projects referred to the Bent girls. Lilian, at nineteen, was petite with eyes a shade lighter than her deep-brown face. Church members commented on her grace and beauty. They admired her glossy, paper-bag curls and the way her poofy poodle skirt cinched a waist the size of a large man's fist. Forestine, on the other hand, was a year younger, three shades darker, and already over six feet tall.

"Sometimes I think a grizzly took me in the night and nine months later Forestine was born," Hattie would say to friends of her younger daughter.

No matter how much he loved her, Willie couldn't quite find the courage to come to Forestine's defense. She was the spitting image of him, and for a woman, that wasn't a very good thing. But he liked the way she laughed, especially about herself. He enjoyed how she would make up little songs and sing them just for him. Willie had recognized Forestine's gift for singing at an early age and always encouraged it.

The two were inseparable. At the end of working a full day as a doorman at the St. George Hotel, Willie would hang out with

Forestine at old man Nick's apartment or Lester's Pub, where she'd stand in the back near the door watching the singers onstage, while Willie sat at the bar and got toasted. At dinnertime they'd climb into his car and she'd drive them both home.

One night, Phyllis Chubbs, a first-floor neighbor, had seen Forestine get out of the driver's seat and literally carry her father to the front door. Of course she called Hattie. Hattie decided not to raise hell right away. She'd wait until Willie's head was clear.

The next afternoon Hattie was straightening Lilian's hair in front of the stove. Forestine, trying to avoid her mother's glare, sat in the adjoining living room next to the window. Hattie had been unusually quiet most of the morning, and now her face was as hard and blank as a slab of concrete. She slammed the hot comb onto the jet and tiny flames rose up.

"You okay, Mama?" Lilian asked, pulling a fraying blue towel onto her shoulders to protect the collar of her cotton blouse.

"I'm fine," Hattie snipped.

Forestine could see by the way Hattie waved the smoking comb in the air that she wasn't fine. She could tell by the way her mother kept glancing at the closed bedroom door that she was waiting for Willie to come out. She yanked a patch of Lilian's hair and set the comb in it. Forestine could hear the sizzling of pomade.

"You sure you okay?" Lilian repeated as her head jerked back again.

"If folks do what the hell they supposed to be doin' 'round here," Hattie argued, "then maybe things be alright."

"What you do, Forestine?" Lilian asked.

Forestine continued to watch the late afternoon traffic pass through the fourth walk. Their apartment was on the third floor, so she could see straight down the walk in front of her building. Over the years she had witnessed muggings, teenagers feeling each other on the benches, fights, and drug exchanges of all sorts.

Just then, the bedroom door opened and Willie walked out. He was dressed for work in his navy uniform pants, his jacket slung over one shoulder.

"Mornin'," he mumbled.

"It's damn near evenin'," Hattie spat.

He went to the stove and filled a coffee cup. Usually Hattie would start in on him about what errands he had needed to do for her today or what he forgot to do yesterday, but instead, she just went about straightening Lilian's hair. Willie eyed her suspiciously.

"How long you been lettin' Forestine drive the car?" she asked calmly.

"Forestine drove the car?!" Lilian asked.

Willie turned away and shut his eyes. Forestine braced herself.

"I said, how long?" Hattie repeated.

"I don't know," Willie stuttered. "Couple years . . . maybe . . ." Then he quickly added, "But jes' a little ways."

"Are you out yo' mind," Hattie barked. "She ain't had license the first, ya damn drunk-up fool."

"Well," he halfway yelled back. "Leastwise she was big enough to reach the wheel."

Hattie cocked her head to the side and pursed her lips. "You know, Willie," she started, "there ain't no excuse for a man yo' age acting as stupid as that daughter of yours." She smeared thick grease on another section of Lilian's hair and gently pulled the smoking comb through.

"Forestine yo' daughter too," Willie said.

"Don't remind me." Hattie's insults were as common as the sun rising in the morning, and had been since Forestine was old enough to understand.

"I never have so much as a worry 'bout Lilian." Hattie placed the steel comb back on the flame and waited. "Lord know she don't give me a worry. But yo' daughter Forestine . . . did you know she cut two classes last week?" Willie shot Forestine a surprised look. "That's right," Hattie went on. "Runnin' 'round out there tryin' to sing something." Hattie grabbed the comb from the flame. The odor of singed hair permeated the whole apartment. "I tell you, Forestine, you got yo' priorities all messed up." She ran the comb through the section of frizzy hair. "Never did know what was important. Need to take yo' ass on to school, 'cause a girl look like you better have some sense."

Forestine leaned in toward the windowpane. She felt like she was crouching in a foxhole during an ambush.

"And she don't *ever* fix herself up none. Look just like a man." Hattie stopped talking to focus on pulling straight the small tight hairs around Lilian's ear. "Somebody ask me the other day how my son was doin'. I say, my what? Like to embarrass me to death. Runnin' in them streets and worse, goin' up there to see that nasty ole man..." Then like a staticky radio that finally clicked into a station, Hattie's words were crystal clear to Forestine. "Oh, I know 'bout that old man."

"Nick? What you know, woman?" Willie blustered.

"Seventy-some-odd years old and sniffin' after young girls like a dawg in heat. An old-ass dawg...hold yo' head down, sweetie...I tole you to stay away from that old man, Forestine. I heard things about him."

"The old man cain't even see," Willie mumbled. "How he gon' do something? 'Sides, Nick ain't big as a minute and Forestine beat the shit out of 'im if he try something."

"I heard things too," Lilian jumped in.

"All two of you ain't heard nothin' but yo' own voices," Willie said, waving them away.

Hattie wiped her hands on the towel hanging around Lilian's neck. She combed through the two sections of straight hair, stood back, and admired her work. "Always wished I had hair this long. Mostly wo' wigs when I was yo' age. But I had the body...Lord knows I had the body." She shook her head sadly. "That was years ago."

"Not so long ago, Mama," Lilian said.

"Been long as I can remember," Willie put in.

"Just get the hell outta here, ya fool," Hattie mumbled.

Willie slipped into his uniform jacket, but before walking out he shot Forestine a quick look. One that apologized for leaving her in the trenches alone.

"And you bring yo' ass straight in here tonight," Hattie went on. "Don't let me have to come lookin' for you."

She unclipped the next section of Lilian's hair and dotted grease in the scalp between the parts.

Hattie had always fashioned herself a woman of beauty. She came to Brooklyn in the forties from Pulpwood, Louisiana, with countless other colored folks. At just twenty, she started working at the Bush-wick Cab Company as a dispatcher, but Hattie never saw herself as any kind of a career woman. Jobs were for men, and she'd only support herself until she found the right man. That wouldn't be long, because Hattie was a stone head-turner and enjoyed every glance her chestnut face afforded her. She was considered a *whole* package, with straight white teeth, pensive almond eyes, and lips naturally shaded like dark cherries. Her chest was small, but her other parts more than made up for it. Hattie felt no compunction about dropping her purse or hankie in front of a possible suitor so that she could turn, bend over, and reveal her true blessing from God.

There were plenty of men, but Hattie never considered any to be deserving, so she always held out for the next. It wasn't until she was twenty-five that a local player caught her attention. She was sitting at her usual table at the Night Owl, a Brooklyn social club, right beside one of the red paper lanterns that she tilted in such a way as to give her face a bit of mystery. The bar was in the opposite direction from where she sat, but men usually took the long way around, just to pass her.

His name was Searle Watson and he was a Brooklyn numbers man. He sported a high conk, and had a heart-shaped face and velvet black skin. Hattie knew right away that this was the man for her. He had money and was as pretty as she was. She quit her job at the cab company because Searle gave her everything she needed: clothes, jewelry, and a furnished apartment on Flatbush Avenue. She did without his time, his babies, and his name. Searle had let her know from day one that these things already belonged to his wife. After a dozen years, though, Hattie needed more.

At thirty-seven, she left Searle Watson. With no husband, no family, and no home, she had to return to the cab company. Then came Willie Bent. Hattie and Willie Bent: a union that even God scratched his head over. Willie wasn't a singer, swinger, or numbers runner. He wasn't a tire salesman or even a butcher who could shower a woman in prime rib or pork butt. He wasn't any kind of a poet or preacher man; he never even went to church. In fact, at the time they met, he didn't have a job at all. He was tall and so thin that he looked fragile, but there was a tenderness in his eyes that Hattie had never seen in Searle Watson or any other man.

Hattie first heard of Willie Bent at the cab company. He'd tried to stiff a cabbie by making a dash for it after riding from Eastern Parkway to Willoughby Avenue. Cab number 862 had been headed down Ralph Avenue and saw number 477 in distress. The two drivers jumped from their cars and ran Willie down. They trussed him up, hands behind him, heels brushing the back of his thighs, and took him into the cab station, thinking this was the worm that had recently hit up some of the other drivers. Some cabbies had been cheated out of as much as a twenty-dollar meter. They called dispatch on their way in and told Hattie to round up as many of the drivers as she could find.

"Children, come on back to the bush," she droned into the radio. "Eight sixty-two wit' a weasel by the toe. Get back if you can."

They brought Willie in, his hair dented and his green polyester suit hanging from his shoulders like wilted lettuce. They untied his feet, then shoved him into an aluminum chair set beside the dispatch desk. Then one at a time the cabbies filed by and identified him as the little skunk who had stiffed them and run.

Hattie sat at the dispatch desk, cigarette in hand, smoke shimmying above her red wig. Folks who had never even filed a complaint pointed their fingers at this pathetic creature. She knew poor Willie would end up out in the back lot with a good old-fashioned Bushwick Cab Company ass-beating. Hattie phoned the police. She couldn't recall a time when someone in Bed-Stuy was happy to see the cops, but Willie cried tears of joy.

On the second day of Willie's stay in jail, Hattie went to see him. She wasn't a softhearted woman. Somehow, though, Willie and his pitiful self touched her. Maybe because she knew that he wasn't responsible for *everything* they accused him of, or because he had a sad face, or perhaps it was because Hattie was thirty-seven years old, lonely, and needed a man.

She sat at a long wooden table and waited for them to bring Willie out. She had gone to see Searle in jail when the numbers house was raided, but that place was different. Hattie had traveled all the way to New Jersey to visit with Searle behind clear glass. Here at the Twenty-seventh Precinct, prisoners were lead into an airy visiting room and allowed to sit right across the table from their family.

Hattie took a nervous breath and rested her hands on the wooden

table. Her thumb dropped along the bottom, but she pulled it back quickly when she felt the wads of gum plastered underneath. The side door opened and Willie Bent came out. He wore that same green suit, only the jacket was unbuttoned down the front and his white undershirt soiled with tea-colored spots. He stood by the door with his hands shoved in his pockets, searching the table for a familiar face. He walked past Hattie twice before she called to him.

"You remember me?" she asked.

He moved a little closer, but didn't sit down. "JoMarie's sister-in-law?"

"No, I am not."

"You ain't no kin to JoMarie? Name is . . . ?" He leaned in a little closer. "Bev'ly . . . yeah Bev'ly. That's yo' name. Work up at the rib house, right?"

"No, I'm not no Beverly."

"Damn," he said, rubbing his stubby chin. "If you ain't JoMarie's sister-in-law then I don't know who you is." Hattie grabbed her purse to her chest and lowered her head. She had made a mistake. A desperate woman's mistake. "Whoever you is," he said, "you got the prettiest eyes the Lord ever made." Hattie looked up from her lap and saw the gentleness in his smile. He sat down across from her.

"I'm from the cab company," she said. He drew back. "No, wait," Hattie said. "I'm not here to hurt you. Just wanna know how you gettin' along."

Warily, he settled back into his seat. "Why you wanna see me, woman?" he asked.

Hattie nervously ran her fingertips over the chipped wooden table. "Them men at the cab company . . ." she started. "Sometime they like a pack of dawgs, you know. All one mind. Run together, do they business together, and Lord, don't let nobody drop a piece of meat." Willie chuckled, and Hattie laughed with him. "I believe that's what happened to you. Went at you like a raw steak. You prob'ly ain't done half the things they say you did."

"I ain't done none of 'em," he insisted.

"I ain't stupid, Willie, and you sho' ain't no saint."

"Hey, Bent," a guard called. "Come on, man, time to go."

"It ain't no half hour yet." Willie jumped up. "I gets me a half a hour."

"I'll wrap this stick around your damn neck," the guard yelled. "Now, if you'da let me finish, man, I woulda told you that you gettin' outta here for good."

Willie jumped up from his chair. "Miss," he said awkwardly, "I thank you kindly. And hey, maybe I'll see you again one day."

"Yeah, maybe," Hattie said, watching the guard lead him through the door.

Three days later, she saw him crouched in the shadows outside the Bushwick Cab Company, waiting for her to leave. He was wearing that same gentle smile. One that said he needed her, and wanted a family. One that assured her he'd always come home and always take care of her.

For the next nineteen years, Hattie would never regret a trip more than the one she took to the Twenty-seventh Precinct. Living with a drunk was more than she could bear. Lilian was the only joy from their pathetic union, born six pounds, three ounces, and after only eighty-four minutes of labor. Caramel brown and as pretty as a picture, she was Hattie's chance to start over. Hattie was overjoyed when a month after Lilian's first birthday, she discovered she was pregnant again. Forestine was born ten pounds, two ounces, and after eighteen hours of labor. There was nothing pretty or cute about her, even as a little girl. Forestine was a cruel rebuke from birth, and Hattie regarded her as the physical sludge of a desperate relationship.

Lilian got up from the chair in front of the stove. Her hair was shiny and swinging just below her shoulders. "Your turn, Forestine," she said.

"The hell it is," Hattie said, turning off the flame. "I ain't about to fool with that mess."

Out the window, Forestine saw the Puerto Ricans passing through the third walk, lugging burlap bags and wearing crisp cotton shirts in bright Caribbean prints. They settled on the benches in the fifth walk every Saturday evening. Soon they would uncover a huge pair of conga drums, cowbells, and maracas nestled in their own little sleeves.

Their music would mix with the Brooklyn twilight along with the scent of salt pork and cilantro.

Forestine looked over her shoulder at Hattie and Lilian fussing about headbands and barrettes. Their voices often became white noise, like a drip from the faucet or the whir of the fan. Forestine slowly moved toward the door.

"Where the hell you goin'?" Hattie barked.

Without turning, she answered. "Out, ma'am."

"Did you hear a word I said 'bout priorities and such?"

"Yes, ma'am."

"Look at me when I'm talkin' to you," she snapped. Forestine turned. She waited patiently while Hattie lit a cigarette, puffed several times, and then pulled a piece of tobacco off of her tongue. "You a goddamned caution, you know that, Forestine?"

"Yes, ma'am," she answered blankly.

"Get on outta here." Forestine flew through the door. "I want you to check back in here at seven, you understand me? And you stay 'way from that old man..."

That was the first place she was going. She was sure that Nick was sitting in his window listening to the Puerto Ricans tuning up. He would know just when they were about to start playing, because he could tell when the conga skins were supple enough and the kalimbas were in perfect pitch.

Forestine took the stairs down two at a time. When she stepped out into the late afternoon sun, she saw Willie sitting on the bench. He was leaning with his forearms on his knees, smoking a cigarette.

"I was wondering how much of that bullshit you was gon' take." He smiled.

"Thought you had to work," she said, sitting beside him.

"I do, but I knew you'd be out soon." He got up and shook his cuffs over his shiny black work shoes. "I just wanted tell you that... yo' mama, you know... she don't think when she talk."

"I know, Daddy." Forestine wondered why, after all these years, he still felt the need to explain Hattie.

"The woman jes' open her mouth and have at it," he went on.

"I know."

Willie sat back down and put his arm around her shoulders.

Sometimes Forestine wished he would leave Hattie and the two of them would strike out on their own, but Willie would remind her that a young woman needed an older woman in her life. Forestine was seventeen and had to learn woman ways, proper ways.

"Don't take yo' mama's words to heart. Fact is," he said, "I think she got some envy over you. Lilian got some too." Her father saw the incredulous expression on her face. "Swear fo' God, Forestine. They hear the way folks talk about your singin'. You special. Got you some talent. What them two got? Lilian, she cute, but as bright as a wickless candle." Forestine held her head down and chuckled. "And Hattie, well she just old now and cain't accept that." He leaned over, kissed her forehead, and got up. "But I'm gon' tell you somethin'. That woman is right about one thing. She's right when she talk 'bout priorities. You always was a lil' fuzzy 'bout what's important. You know it's the truth."

"No it ain't." She shrugged.

"Remember when you was about eight and brought that mangy old dog to the apartment? I know you recall, 'cause Hattie nearly blew her top. She say, Forestine, either you sleep here or that dog. Cain't feed the both of you." Forestine turned away. "Next mornin' we found you sleeping outside in the hall by the incinerator and that dog was layin' up in yo' bed." Willie placed one leg on top of the bench and wiped a spot off of his shoe with a spit-moistened hankie. "You a strong girl but you want what you want and don't think sometimes. Music ain't s'posed to come fo' school. Just like me, I swear fo' gawd, I want a drink right now bad as anything. But I gotta work. You understand?"

"Yes, sir."

He nodded toward the fifth walk. "Puerto Ricans 'bout to play. Don't stay out here all damn night, you hear?"

Forestine watched him weave his way through the crowd that had gathered to hear the music. She knew that Willie needed a drink. He was an alcoholic, plain and simple, and living with Hattie Bent made his problem even worse.

Forestine could feel her shoulders begin to move to the sound of salsa. Brownsville was always filled with music, especially in the summer. She could walk down one block and hear calypso, then on another, merengue. On Atlantic Avenue the sounds of the Bethel Baptist choir poured out onto the sidewalk. But the best sound of all was at old man Nick's place. Right before she turned onto the next walk, the Puerto Ricans lifted their hands high, then struck the conga skins with hollowed palms.

"Evening, Miss James, Mrs. Ellis." Forestine waved at the two older women sitting on a bench enjoying the twilight. About this time of day, when the sun began to set, the seniors gathered outside. They had fought hard for these splintery benches and the street lamp right above. This was their place. A decent spot for the babies to play and for the older people to rest without dread.

"How's your mother, Forestine?" Mrs. Ellis asked.

"She's okay, ma'am."

"Send her my regards."

"I will."

Forestine entered Nick's building and took the elevator up to the fifth floor. All buildings in the projects looked the same, inside and out. If she closed her eyes and opened them quickly, she would swear she was in her own. Today there was a broken bottle in the hall right outside of Nick's apartment. Forestine carefully picked it up and put it in the incinerator, then walked back to Nick's door. He would be able to tell just by the sound who was knocking. Forestine liked to test the old man, so she varied her beat now and then. Today she tried to duplicate the salsa rhythm. Forestine listened at the door, and smiled to herself. She knew she had thrown the old man a curve.

"Come on in, Forestine," he yelled.

She walked in shaking her head. Nick was looking out of the window through a pair of binoculars, his usual cup of sassafras tea in front of him. "What do you think you see through them things?" she asked.

"Puerto Ricans been out there at least a half hour," he said, still looking out. "What took you so long to get here?"

"I was talking to Daddy."

"Oh? Trouble wit' Hattie again?"

"Yep."

Nick got up from the chair as suddenly as he could, given the steel rod in his hip. For as long as Forestine had known him, he'd had this bad hip, a result of diabetes.

"What is it?" Forestine moved into the window next to him.

"Damn," he gasped.

"What, Nick?" she yelled. "What do you see?"

He lowered the binoculars slowly and turned to her with a big grin on his face. "I cain't see a thing, remember?" he laughed. Nick's finger found his cup and lifted it to his lips. He grimaced a little before he placed the cup between his thighs, took a pint bottle of Old Crow from his back pocket, and poured the whiskey into his tea cup. "Where Willie Bent go this evening?"

"Work," she said, sitting on the sofa across from him. Forestine always sat on the left side of the wooden framed sofa. The right side was held up by a 1952 encyclopedia.

"Mean he ain't got himself right yet, huh?" Nick asked. "That Willie Bent is a good guy. I would've left that bitch of a wife a long time ago, but he knew that you girls needed him. Yep, Willie Bent know what's important." Nick looked up toward the ceiling when he talked, and his steel-gray eyeballs quivered in their sockets. Thick white hair stuck out from the sides of his head like cotton candy.

Forestine was only twelve when Willie brought her here for the first time. She had taken one look at Nick and decided that the old man was a monster. She remembered clutching her father's hand as he led her through the clutter of the old man's home: shoes, tattered and worn, ashtrays full of cigarette butts, suspenders and frayed ties flung over the top of a lamp. Old reeds, instrument mouthpieces, cuff links and ladies' earrings were strewn everywhere. His blinds had been closed against the morning sun, and the two-room apartment was dark and heavy with the odor of tobacco.

That day, he had been sitting in the same chair he sat in now, his saxophone beside him like an old friend. He'd been drinking tea from a cup that rested on a busted wicker stand in front of him. He had worn a pinstriped suit (one of the four he owned) with a vest and tie, as if he was waiting to go out.

"That you, Willie Bent?" A cigarette dangled from his bottom lip when he talked.

"What you know, Nick?" Willie yelled.

"I know some. Who's that you got there?"

Forestine edged a little closer to Willie. "Daddy, I wanna go home," she whispered.

"Daddy?!" Nick said. "That yo' lil' girl? Come over here, sugar, and let me get a look at you." Even then Nick liked to pretend that he wasn't as blind as a bat. Willie always fell for the trick.

"Go'n, Forestine, and let Mr. Nick see you," he said, pushing her toward the old man. "He a famous musician. You heard me talk about Mr. Nick befo'. Used to play wit' all kinds of folks. Go'n, baby, he won't hurt you." Forestine moved toward the old man hesitantly. She wasn't frightened of much, even at twelve, but when she saw Nick's eyes fluttering like Christmas lights, she ran back behind her father.

"What's the matter with you, Forestine?" Willie said. "Mr. Nick is a good man . . . a good friend."

"He's scary," she said.

"No, he ain't baby, he jes' blind."

Nick picked up the saxophone and pressed it to his lips. Forestine still couldn't look at him. Then the old man baited her with a quick riff. The charging brass was loud and stirring. Slowly she stepped to Willie's side. Nick kept that saxophone resting against his mouth until she stopped moving. Until he could hear a pin drop. Until he could feel her breath about to leap from her young chest in anticipation. He blew again. It was only scales, but Forestine was mesmerized. Then he stopped as suddenly as he had started.

"You know any songs, young lady?" Nick asked.

"Well . . ." she whispered shyly.

"Girl, you gon' make me think I cain't hear either if you don't talk louder."

"I say, I know some songs," she said.

"Like what, sugar?"

"I know 'C.C. Rider.' "

Nick rested his sax on his lap. "That damn Chuck Willis," he mumbled. "I forgot mo' about music than that cat'll ever know. Well, come on then. Stand over here and face this way." He moved his hand slowly up her arm and rested it on her shoulder. "How old you say this chile is?" he asked Willie.

"Twelve."

"She gon' be tall as you," Nick said. Forestine looked down at her feet. "Hold yo' head up, girl," Nick snapped as if he could see her. "Got to always stand up tall and confident when you sing. Every somebody that sing *good* is beautiful." He made his way across the room, dragging his left leg behind him to the rickety piano propped up against the wall. He felt his way onto the bench and played a few chords. "Can you sing this?" he asked her.

Forestine smiled shyly. "No."

"Why? You say you know somethin' 'bout Chuck Willis," he said, still playing. "You say you know it."

She shrugged her shoulders and looked down again.

"Hold your head up, Forestine," Willie whispered.

Nick stopped playing and turned around on the piano bench. "What you bring her here fo', Willie Bent?" he asked.

" 'Cause Forestine sing good," Willie answered.

"She cain't even talk, how she gon' sing?"

"Daddy, I want to go home."

"Daddy, I wanna go home," Nick mocked.

"Mr. Nick can help you, baby."

"I'm ready to go now," she said.

"Sing something first and show Mr. Nick," he pleaded.

"Willie Bent, take the girl home. She ain't ready."

"But she sing like a grown woman, I swear fo' God. She sing bet-ter'n any chile I know."

"Even Lilian?" Forestine asked.

Willie pulled her into his chest. "Much better'n Lilian," he said. "Way, way better. Lilian couldn't even dream about singing like you, Forestine. Couldn't even dream! Now go on and sing that song 'bout the blues."

Willie's faith gave Forestine the courage to begin. Nick didn't re-spond when he heard her voice. He didn't move at all, even when she finished "Amazing Grace." It wasn't until Forestine started "For Senti-mental Reasons" that he started to accompany her, and for the next four years Nick taught Forestine Bent everything he knew about blues and jazz. Together they listened to recordings by Robert Johnson, Alberta Hunter, and Betty Rawlins, as well as Dizzy Gillespie, Hazel Scott, Billie Holiday, and Miles Davis. He taught her how to play a harmonica, a little on the saxophone, and as much as he knew on the piano. He taught her about personal style, not only in the way she sang but in the way she walked and talked. After Willie, Forestine had come to think of Nick as her only friend. She could even abide Hattie's talk as long as she knew that he was in her life.

Nick cracked the window, and the salsa music poured in. "You singin' at the club tonight?" he asked.

"This is Saturday, Nick."

"And?"

"And you know Lester don't let me sing on Saturday."

"Girl, you blow the roof off on any old day, and besides, that's when you need to be singin' up in there. When somebody that *should* see you, *will* see you. Fuck a Wednesday night! Ain't nobody there but the lunkheads."

"How you know so much about Lester's place? You haven't been there in . . . what, over five years?"

"Don't need to go there to know 'bout Lester's place. That's just a lily pad, Forestine. Frogs don't get too comfortable on a lily pad. They set for a minute, catch a few flies, and move on. Don't you get too comfortable there."

"Lester won't let me get too comfortable."

"Lester is a fuckin' asshole wit' no vision. He should be holdin' on to you for dear life. Oh, I know Lester and his place. I don't have to go nowhere to know that. 'Sides, where I have to go? Miss Stanley buy my food, Willie get my clothes clean, git me reeds and things. Got everything I need right here." He thought for a moment and his voice got low and bawdy. "Well . . . almost everything."

Every once in a while Nick got strange like this, and it made Forestine uncomfortable. She would know when the strangeness was on him by the way he shifted in his chair, crossed his legs, or sipped his liquor-laced tea. She would know by the timbre of his voice, by how he paced the room, dragging his bad hip along. He was beset by a blues, a pitch-black and lonely blues. Sometimes this mood of his was so strong that she found a reason to cut her lesson short and leave, but today he wasn't so bad.

"What's it like to be blind, Nick?" She had asked this question many times over the years in order to change the subject.

The curl in his lip straightened, and just that quickly he seemed to settle down. "Well, since I don't know what it's like *not* to be blind, I guess I cain't say."

Forestine puffed her cheeks with air, as she often did when she was pensive. Hattie hated it. She'd tell Forestine, "It's not ladylike and besides you ugly enough as it is."

"I wouldn't mind being blind," Forestine said suddenly.

"Girl, you talkin' pure-d nonsense. Nobody wants to be blind, just how it is sometimes. Why you say something like that?"

"If I was blind," she said, "I wouldn't have to see nobody and then I wouldn't have to see nobody seeing me."

Nick turned toward her. He struggled for a moment, then rose to his feet and moved across the room, familiar with every bit of clutter. He found the dilapidated couch and lowered himself slowly onto the cushion beside her. She watched him curiously. Nick was a man of few moves, but each had purpose. He reached up and found Forestine's face. He moved his fingers around her chin and across her cheek. Then he slapped her so hard that it whipped her head back. Forestine was stunned. Tears sprang to her eyes. Nick rose, crossed the room, and sat down as if nothing had happened. He picked up his saxophone and started to blow.

Forestine held her face in her hand. She lay back on the old sofa and closed her eyes. Willie had put her onstage at Lester's Pub when she was just thirteen years old. The audience gasped at the sight of her. Nick had tried to warn Willie that she wasn't ready for the stage then. Not because she couldn't sing the songs, and sing the hell out of them, but because she wasn't mature enough. Willie Bent, being the proud father that he was, persisted, and now she sang at Lester's place every Wednesday night.

Forestine pulled herself up on the couch. She wiped her tears with the collar of her shirt. She knew why Nick had slapped her. At thirteen, Forestine could sing the blues like a woman twice her years, and now at seventeen, she was seasoned and ready. Although it still hurt when she heard a remark about her looks, Forestine was coming to understand her unique power. The power to quiet the snickers, the "po' chiles," and to fill the empty stares of men with just a few simple notes. "And none of that blues *or* jazz bullshit," Nick would say. "Blues or jazz, his'n or her'n, girl, it's colored folks' music. Just ask what the song is and sing it. If the band fall into a bluesy groove, fine. Jazz, cool. Ain't no blues *or* jazz . . . them is white folks' labels. Just sing the damn song, Forestine."

She hummed softly, her voice blending with his sax like another instrument. After a while she had no choice but to sing. Nick stopped playing in the middle of the song, but kept the beat with the tapping of his foot.

"Stretch it out, Forestine," he yelled. "Gon' stretch it out. You ain't no damn baby, so don't gimme bullshit."

CHAPTER 2

Miss Rosalee's Dress Shop was a jumble of old and new clothes, from hoop skirts and ball gowns to tops trimmed in lace or rabbit fur. Viola Bembrey loved the small store that sat on the corner of Main Street. Everywhere she looked, there was something frilly and colorful. To the left of the front door was a lady mannequin decked out in a yellow linen dress. One lifeless hand perched on her hip, and the other, with its chipped red nail polish, rested just above her waxen blue eyes. To the right of the door was a coat stand layered with chiffon and silk scarves. Rolling racks in the middle of the shop were packed so tightly with clothes, you could barely see the dressing area in the back. Miss Rosalee had fashioned the changing room herself by placing a full-length mirror against the wall and a Queen Anne chair beside it, then boxing the area with three white, wooden screens dotted with tiny red carnations.

Viola thought the lack of order in Miss Rosalee's shop made it all the more interesting. Her mother, Nell, was a little put off by the clutter, but always seemed to leave with at least one bag and sometimes a hatbox.

Miss Rosalee was wrapping a half slip at the counter for Sister

Trench when the shop bell tinkled and Nell and Viola walked in. Miss Rose peeked over the top of her cat-eye glasses and smiled.

"Y'all early," she called. "I was just about to lay out a few things for Viola."

"How are you, sweetheart," Nell said, kissing her on the cheek. "And good day to you, Sister Trench." Nell squeezed the old woman's hand. Most folks in Jasperville never knew if Sister Trench was having a good day or whether she was lost in a senile fog. When she looked at Nell and Viola as if she hadn't seen them in church every Sunday for the last dozen years, Viola figured she was lost. "Viola, say hey to Sister Trench," Nell whispered.

"How do, Sister Trench," Viola said. The old woman looked at Viola blank-faced and wandered toward the back of the shop.

Nell rested her pocketbook on the counter. She removed a silk kerchief from her jet black hair, then smoothed a strand that had escaped from the loose bun resting at the nape of her neck. "Sister Trench isn't here alone, I hope," Nell asked.

"Her husband next do' at the tackle shop," Miss Rosalee whispered.

Nell nodded and looked toward the back, where she could see the top of the old woman's head.

On this pretty spring afternoon, Miss Rosalee's shop had fewer than a handful of customers. Lois Hobbs and her daughter Chickie browsed sweaters on the side racks. Orenthia Mays and Lucy Penn from Juniper County waved as they left.

"I do declare," Miss Rosalee said to Viola, "you lookin' jes' like a calendar gal . . . pretty as you can be."

Viola could feel her face heat up with embarrassment. Whether Miss Rose uttered these words at Sunday service, a church dinner, or here at the shop, they always seemed to make Viola feel self-conscious.

"What do you say to Miss Rose?" Nell asked.

"Thank you, ma'am," she whispered.

"I have a few dresses here that I know Viola is gon' love," Miss Rosalee said, moving to an armoire just a few feet away.

"Spring colors, Rose," Nell urged.

Viola left Miss Rosalee and her mother to their business. She was soon bored, browsing through a wicker basket filled with embroidered handkerchiefs, and was headed toward the racks when she caught sight of herself in the princess mirror. Viola studied her face, trying to imagine her deep brown cheeks dusted with plum powder and her eyelashes swept up with a bit of mascara. Her lips were full and naturally red, but she would love to wear a bit of lipstick. That's how a calendar girl would look, she thought.

Suddenly Miss Rosalee shrieked and threw her hands up. "Gracious a lie!"

"What is it, Miss Rose?" Viola asked.

"It jes' come to me," she exclaimed.

"What?" Nell replied.

And then, as if Viola weren't embarrassed enough, Miss Rosalee started to sing Happy birthday. Her shrill voice made the hairs on Viola's arms stand up. Most would've ended the song after the first verse, but Miss Rosalee didn't, and was soon joined by all the ladies in the shop, including Sister Trench. "*How old are you now?*" Miss Rosalee opened her arms to Viola, rocking her body from side to side. Miss Rose had been hugging Viola this way since she was a little girl. "You pick the dress you want," she said, "and I'll gi' you the kerchief of yo' choice, on the house, okay?"

"Thank you, ma'am," Viola said.

"That's very kind of you, Rose," Nell added.

Embarrassment aside, Viola admired Miss Rosalee. She was different than most women in Jasperville. Though well over fifty, Miss Rosalee had never married and never looked like she missed it. She drove her own car, cut her own grass, and if someone needed something fixed, sometimes they just called on Miss Rose. She was one of the few colored business owners in town and the only woman business owner, colored or white. And she was pretty. Simply, softly pretty. Everything about Miss Rose was soft, including her face powder, which was a shade too light for her skin and caught in the feathery lines at the corners of her smile.

Viola quickly moved to the side rack where the spring linens hung. Miss Rosalee meant well, but what with Viola's father, Reverend Bembrey, her mother, and the entire congregation of the New

Pilgrim Baptist Church, Viola was worn out with the hoopla. There had even been a couple of lines written in the Jasperville *Bugle* announcing Viola's seventeenth birthday. The more prominent men of the cloth, Reverend Baines, Reverend Dr. Morgan, and even the Reverend Lightfoot, who had one of the biggest congregations in South Carolina, had sent their blessings. Presents arrived all day Thursday, Friday, and most of this Saturday morning. Pretty handmade gifts like a pink bed jacket from Miss Goodwin and walnut-banana bread from Sister Gladys. Mrs. Baker, the choir director, sent a bottle of Jean Naté. Donald Hinson left a freshly slaughtered hog, and in its mouth was a velvet box containing a string of pearls. Nell thought the gift a bit familiar from a church member, but after running the pearls across her teeth and taking into consideration that Donald Hinson was a good man, even if in search of refinement, she placed the necklace on Viola's chest and added him to the list of thank-you's.

"Viola look to be gettin' over that bashfulness a little," Miss Rosalee whispered to Nell. She selected several dresses from the armoire and laid them across the counter. As Viola shuffled through the linens, she could still hear the two women. "I 'member she couldn't even walk 'cross a roomful of people without shaking like a leaf."

"Viola's coming into her own, alright," Nell said, pulling on a straw hat. She looked into the mirror, then quickly removed it. "Coming into her own too fast, if you ask me, especially now that she's graduated high school. Sassed her daddy the other day."

"Sassed the *Reverend*?" Miss Rosalee was taken aback.

"Indeed she did," Nell replied. "And it wasn't the first time, either."

"What the Reverend say 'bout it?" Miss Rosalee waved at Sister Trench as she left the shop and joined her husband outside.

"After he prayed with her," Nell answered, "he sat Viola down and talked to her about her future . . . again. You would think it was a crime, Rose, an ugly old crime asking a young woman what she want to do with her life," Nell insisted.

"She at that age now, Nelvern," Miss Rose said. "We just oughta be thankful that she finally coming into her own."

The problem was that the "new woman" had no plans. Yes, Viola would go to the teaching college in Charleston, even though she didn't want to. Reverend Bembrey felt it was a "proper vocation for a young woman," and it was time that she made some decisions. Viola didn't feel that her whole future had to be decided just because she graduated from high school. And she told him as much.

Nell placed another hat on her head and looked at herself in the mirror.

"That one becomes you, Nelvern," Miss Rosalee said.

"You think so?"

"I do."

"The Reverend won't like it, though," Nell said. "A little too bright for his taste." She placed it back on the mannequin.

"What about yo' taste?" Miss Rosalee asked.

"His taste *is* my taste," she replied.

Miss Rose smiled tactfully, then she turned and laid a few more dresses across the counter. They all started to look alike to Viola, at least the ones she was allowed to have: soft cottons in pastels and muted checks or button-down A lines, same as the dresses she had hanging in her closet at home.

Miss Rose reached into the armoire again and this time took out a little crepe dress, just a shade cooler than hot pink. Viola was immediately drawn to it. The pink dress flared at the bottom where the hemline fell just above the knee. There were flirty little ruffles around a plunging neckline and a thin chiffon train attached to the shoulders in a softer pink than the dress itself. "Who this dress make you think of, Nelvern?" Miss Rosalee smiled.

"No one in this world except your sister," she answered.

"Got Honeybee's name written all over it." Miss Rose hung it on the door of the armoire.

"Can I see it?" Viola asked.

"You cannot," Nell answered.

"Cain't hurt to look, Nelvern," Miss Rose said as she lay it on top of the cottons.

"Your sister would wear this dress?" Viola asked as she ran the back of her hand under the pink chiffon.

"Her closet is filled with lil' numbers like this," Miss Rose replied.

"Where in the world would she wear it?" Viola asked.

"Chile," Miss Rose smiled. "My sister Honeybee live up in New York, and the woman stay on the go."

"Hasn't slowed down in all these years?" Nell asked.

"Not fo' a second. Her husband was a musician," she said to Viola. "He passed some years ago, but Honeybee still stay gone. Lord, that woman is a mess," Miss Rosalee went on, "but that's my baby sister, jes' three minutes younger than me. This lil' thing here," she said, referring to the pink dress, "chile, this ain't nothin' compared to some of the gorgeous things that Honeybee wear."

"She always had the shoes and accessories to match," Nell put in.

"Honey had shoes gon' to bed," Miss Rose laughed. "And don't let her purse be a little lighter or darker..."

"Scandalous," Nell laughed.

Viola rarely saw her mother this animated. Her amber face was beautiful when she wore a natural grin, which was rarely. Nell placed her hand on top of Viola's as she laughed, and her touch felt as soft and cool as butter. Viola wished her mother would laugh more often.

"Think you'll send this dress to Honeybee?" Nell asked.

"I don't know," Miss Rose replied. She moved closer to Nell and playfully whispered, "Might have to save it fo' myself."

"Lord, Rose," Nell laughed. "Don't tell me you're getting just as fresh as that sister of yours."

Miss Rosalee blushed at the thought. She took the pink dress from Viola and hung it back in the armoire, then gestured to the selection of cotton dresses that lay on the counter. Viola looked through them, as she did on Christmas, Easter, and every year around her birthday, and pretended she was trying to decide.

"I think these two," Nell said, draping two cotton shirtdresses, one blue, one mint green, over Viola's arm. "What do you say, Rose?"

"That green'll be pretty with Viola's coloring."

"Try that one on first," Nell said as Viola made her way toward the changing room. "And, Viola," Nell called out. "Keep your slip on."

Viola passed Lois Hobbs, who was lost in the task of trying to find a sweater that fit. Viola squeezed between two racks and stopped in front of the party dresses. Each outfit, sequinned, glittered, or feathered, was as bright and exciting as the little pink crepe dress. Viola pulled out a lavender one with sequins around the cuffs and collar. She was about to walk behind the screens when she saw a pair of legs back there. She thought it might be Chickie Hobbs, but Chickie would barely fit in the small changing room. These legs were seamed and shapely. The woman moved behind the screen like she was dancing. Viola watched as her feet pirouetted in their black spiked heels and as the hem of an orange satin dress twirled against her legs. Viola couldn't think of a soul in Jasperville who would wear a pair of shoes like that.

The orange dress suddenly fell to the woman's ankles, then she stepped out of it and slung it over top of the screen. Next a tent of black taffeta dropped around her calves. Viola watched for the pirouette again, but this time the woman walked right out. Viola quickly stepped behind a rack full of long dresses dripping with plumes. She couldn't clearly see the woman's face, but she didn't look like anyone Viola had ever seen in Jasperville. She was as fair as Nell, with wild crinkly hair, but it was the way she walked that caught Viola's attention. She looked at herself in the mirror outside the dressing room, smoothing her hands over her small chest and smiling at her own self. This woman had a confidence . . . an arrogance that Viola had never seen in *any* woman and especially one so young. When she turned in front of the mirror, the sound of brushing taffeta felt like ice against Viola's teeth. And then there were those shoes. Those skinny little spike-heeled shoes.

Viola kept her distance as the woman browsed the rack of party dresses. She turned to the side, and Viola could finally see her face. It was different from what she expected. Younger. Viola couldn't help but stare at this woman with her boy-flat chest and corn-colored face painted like a china doll.

"What you followin' after me fo'?" the woman called.

Viola froze.

"I see you back there and I know you followin' after me. I know you are."

"I'm shopping," Viola said, stepping in full view. She rifled through the dresses like she had been browsing all along.

"Shoppin', huh," the woman said doubtfully. "So what's them things you got on yo' arm?"

"Nothing special." Viola shoved the cottons into the rack with the party dresses.

"Ain't you Bembrey's gal?" the woman asked.

"Yes, ma'am."

"Ma'am?!" she said with half a smile. "I ain't nobody's ma'am." She held up an emerald satin dress against her body. "What you think?"

"Me?" Viola asked.

"Yeah, you! You like it?"

"It's about the prettiest thing I've ever seen."

The woman looked at Viola's blue cotton dress with its Peter Pan collar and then scanned the brown penny loafers on her feet. "I believe that's prob'ly true."

Her voice was husky for such a young woman. The Reverend might call her a low-land gal, born in the marsh with little money and no education. Viola rarely met anyone who knew the Bembrey name and seemed unimpressed by it. This woman seemed like she couldn't care less. She flung the green satin over her arm and without so much as a good-bye walked to the front of the store. Viola followed.

Nell was trying on a pair of white gloves at the counter when the woman walked up. Viola could see the shock on her mother's face as she took in the black taffeta and spiked heels. Nell glanced at Miss Rosalee, who was trying not to laugh.

"I'm gon' take this one, Miss Rose," the woman said.

"Fine choice," Miss Rose replied. Nell's mouth had dropped wide open. "But before you decide, I got one mo' you need to see." Miss Rosalee took the pink crepe dress from the armoire and held it up.

"It's pretty," she said. "But I don't know . . ."

"Look different on the hanger," Miss Rose said. "Try it on and it'll be a whole 'nother story."

The woman looked at Nell, then again at Miss Rosalee before she took the dress and walked toward the changing room. Viola was still transfixed by her shoes, black and shiny, clicking against the wooden floor. She tried to picture what her feet would look like in a pair of those shoes. She wondered if her legs would look as long or her feet as small.

"Viola," Nell called. "Where are the dresses you were supposed to try on?"

"I left them on one of the racks," she answered. "I'll get 'em."

"You'll stay right here, young woman," Nell snapped. She turned to Miss Rosalee at the counter. "What in digger's name does that woman have on her feet?"

"What they calls po' de soir," Miss Rosalee whispered to Nell, leaning into her talkin'-'bout-folks posture. "That mean, fo' the night," she went on. "Them the kinda shoes fo' a dance or a special affair and that mean you ain't s'posed to be walking 'round in 'em at no noontime on a Sa'urday."

"Who is she?" Nell asked.

"You know who she is, Nelvern," Miss Rosalee insisted. "Live out there in the Bluff."

"I've never seen that woman before in my life," Nell insisted.

"You know exactly who she is." Miss Rosalee handed Viola a white cotton dress, but Viola was too riveted to be distracted. "Maybe you ain't never *seen* her, Nelvern," Miss Rosalee whispered, "but you know who she is." Miss Rose looked toward the changing room, then clicked on a small transistor radio that she had behind the counter. "Unchained Melody" played softly. "You 'member Etta Daniels, died a few years ago . . ."

"Etta Daniels . . . ?" Nell said, trying to recall. "Isn't Etta Daniels the one that lived out in Camden County. She did day work . . ."

"You talkin' 'bout Etta Jordan," Miss Rosalee said. "She that nice lady live out near the onion field. I'm talkin' 'bout Etta Daniels, and she ain't live nowhere." Miss Rosalee was always glad to be the one to tell the story. "I mean she ain't live nowhere but out in the middle of the woods."

"In the woods!" Nell exclaimed.

"That's right," Miss Rose replied. "Had that tent set up outside the Bluff, way deep in the woods."

"Mercy me," Nell gasped. "Now I know who you're talking about. I know just who you're talking about."

"Miss Rose!" the girl called out, "I have another one I'm fixin' to try on."

"You go on, sweetie, take yo' time!" Miss Rosalee called back.

Lois and Chickie Hobbs passed the counter and walked toward the door. "Nothing for y'all?" Miss Rosalee asked.

"Not today, Rose," Lois called. "Call us when you get some sundresses in."

"Okay, dahlin'."

"Size eighteen," Chickie added before they left.

"I haven't heard about Etta in years," Nell said, letting her voice drop below the music. "I just assumed she moved on."

"Etta moved on, alright," Miss Rosalee said. "Etta moved on to her grave."

"My word," Nell gasped. "And that woman is her child?"

"Yes, ma'am," Miss Rosalee confirmed. "Name is Isabel."

Nell looked up to find Viola listening to every word. "Why don't you go on over and pick out a skirt or two," Nell said.

With the white cotton dress still on her arm, Viola sauntered to the side rack of linens and planted herself there, at the very edge of the rack. Each time Miss Rosalee's voice got lower, it seemed Viola had to stop breathing to hear the conversation.

"Isabel was only ten when all the mess started," Miss Rosalee said. "And as I understand, her and Etta did everything like most mamas and daughters did, 'cept they didn't have no house, exactly." She glanced toward the changing room again. The little pink dress was suddenly slung over the side of the screen. "They woke in the morning, bathed in the creek, and then ate. Sometimes Etta made fried catfish that she caught herself and sometimes she couldn't afford mo' than the frost on her breath. That sort of depended on how the previous night went."

"Ha' mercy," Nell exclaimed.

"Every morning Etta took a stroll," Miss Rosalee explained. "She either walked past the men working to pave the road or down to the rail station full of porters and yard men. Well, by late morning there'd be four or five of them men lined up outside her tent . . ."

"Shut up, Rose."

"I ain't even lyin'," Miss Rosalee went on. "During that time, Isabel, she just roamed the woods. Well, this one day, Etta had a line of men out there waitin'. This particular fella started getting a little fretful. Wadn't too right in the head to begin with and he started to feel that he might not get in to see Etta 'cause there were two other men in front of him and the mercury was already climbing past a hundred.

And see, Etta didn't like this fella in the first place. Say he smelled like a polecat, had that cheesy kinda skin, was over six-foot-five, two hundred and eighty pounds, and his thing was relative to his height..."

"Rosalee," Nell blushed.

Viola looked tentatively toward the back where Isabel was trying on clothes.

"But worse," Miss Rose went on, "Etta ain't liked the fact that this fella never had enough money to pay. Up 'til now she took pity on him. But Etta was in no mood that day. She say, 'I'm sorry, baby, but you gon' have to come back another day.'

"Well, this fella got mad. He turned on his heels and took off like a black bear through them woods. He dropped to the ground so hard that his knees made two dents in the earth, and like a mad rabbit he started burrowin' in the soil. Dug a small deep hole in that ground and then he commenced to spittin' and pissin' in it until it was warm and soggy."

"Why?" Nell asked.

"I nearly don't wanna say," Miss Rosalee said shamefully. "But just as this fella was about to...ram his thing in that hole, he looked up and saw Isabel skipping her way through the woods."

"No," Viola whispered to herself.

"Lord, if he didn't grab that little girl and commenced to nearly rippin' her in half." Viola took a deep breath to stop her eyes from welling. "Then after contemplatin' on whether to put the child outta her misery, he made a decision to let her be. He let that chile live just in case Etta ever turned him away again."

Viola found it difficult to look toward the back now. She didn't know this woman Isabel, but somehow felt the need to protect her.

"You would think after all that," Miss Rosalee went on, "Etta would've taken her girl away, but she didn't. Nope. Etta set up another tent for Isabel."

"No, she didn't," Nell gasped.

"Set that tent side by side to her own and the men lined up by the dozens. Then after years of working, they found Etta dead. Say she had one of them filthy sex diseases and died in a lot of pain. Fo' days Isabel worked that tent, paid fo' a nice funeral for Etta, and moved on. Folded her tent and bought that little house on the outskirts of the woods. Now she a singer up there at Snookie Petaway's."

"Miss Rose," Isabel called.

"Yes, dahlin'."

"Y'all sell any brassieres?"

"What size?"

"I don't rightly know." Isabel walked up to the front with the pink crepe dress on her arm. One too many buttons were left undone on her taffeta dress. "Ain't owned no brassiere in—" She glanced at Nell. "Well, you might say, in some time." Nell began to fiddle with the gloves again, but Viola was drawn to this woman, whose manner was as out of place as her po' de soir shoes.

"What you think of that pink dress?" Miss Rose asked. "Hot lil' number, huh?"

"It's pretty," Isabel agreed, "sho'ly got some danger . . ." She smiled. "How much you askin', Miss Rose?"

"Forty-seven dollars."

Isabel whistled like a man. "Too dear fo' me," she said. "I'll take this green satin one, though. My friend here seems to like that one." Isabel winked at Viola. "And gimme French Vanilla Number One."

Miss Rosalee rolled her finger down a row of flat boxes on the wall behind her. She pulled one out and placed it on the counter. "Seams, right?" she asked.

"Yes, ma'am."

Miss Rosalee opened the box, separated the soft white tissue, and removed a pair of stockings the same color as Isabel's skin. Viola watched as Isabel pulled the stocking over her clenched fist. "Two pairs, please," she said, and then turned to Viola. "Maybe one day you'll come and hear me sing."

"I would love to," Viola stuttered.

"I be down to Snookie Petaway's every Friday and Saturday night."

"I'm afraid that's something she wouldn't be interested in," Nell put in.

"She's old enough to come," Isabel said. "Can't drink no liquor yet, but she can come."

"I don't think so," Nell sniffed.

"She's seventeen," Isabel said. "I seen it in the paper with my own two eyes."

"Did you indeed?" Nell asked.

"Maybe you and the Reverend like to come down one day," she said. "I'll have Snookie set you to a fine table and everything."

"That's very kind of you," Nell said, "but his isn't a place we like to frequent."

"I see." Isabel opened a small silk purse, pulled out some bills, and placed them on the counter. "You know," she said to Nell, "I been meaning to come to yo' church. I declare, every Sunday I wake up and I say, Isabel, maybe you should go on over to the New Pilgrim Church today. Then every Sunday, I just turn back over and go to sleep."

"Well, maybe one day you'll wake up," Nell answered.

"Maybe I will," Isabel said. She picked up her package. "Bye, bye, baby," she said to Viola. "And . . . happy birthday."

"Bye."

The door closed behind her with the tinkling of the bell. Miss Rosalee gathered the bills and pressed them into a cigar box on top of the counter. "I feel bad fo' the chile, but if she stay on that path, she gon' meet wit' a worser end then her mama . . . if you ask me."

"Amen," Nell whispered.

"Got that same attitude as Etta." Miss Rosalee began to hang the rejected dresses back on the racks.

"I'll say one thing for her," Nell added. "She got it honest. Probably don't know any other way of being." Viola watched out of the shop window as Isabel strolled down Main Street.

"Well, that's the Christian way of looking at it," Miss Rosalee said. "But she over twenty-one and that's old enough to make her own decisions. Just 'cause she was dropped in that pit don't mean she got to stay there. Now as fo' you, young lady," she said to Viola, her tone brightening, "why don't you go in and try on that pretty white dress." The cotton paled next to Isabel's bright satin. "That dress come from Charleston, you know," Miss Rosalee said. "Say Miss Dorothy Dandridge wo' one jes' like that in one of her movies."

Viola knew Miss Rosalee was lying. Dorothy Dandridge wouldn't be caught dead in a dress like this, because Miss Carmen Jones wore dresses like Isabel's.

"We have to get going, Viola," Nell said. "Hurry and try it on."

Standing in the tiny room, Viola saw the orange satin dress flung over the top of the screens. Isabel's face flashed through her mind. She wasn't much older than Viola, yet she seemed as mature as Nell or Miss Rosalee. What could it have been like for a ten-year-old girl to have to entertain men? Viola had never even kissed a boy. Did Isabel like it? Viola sat in the Queen Anne chair behind the screens and closed her eyes. This time she saw an image of Isabel in her green satin dress, singing on a curtained stage in those po' de soir shoes.

"Viola," Nell called. "We can't stay here all day."

Viola slipped out of her dress. She was about to step into the white cotton, but picked up the orange satin instead. The thought of even trying it on seemed brash. Viola held it to her body and for a moment caught the fleeting scent of sweet perfume.

Isabel was truly a sight to see. She stood in the middle aisle of the New Pilgrim Baptist Church, watching the choir sing like she had come to see a picture show. Viola didn't notice her until she felt a stir in the church—a low but steady rumble like far-off thunder. When Viola looked out from the choir box to see about the commotion, there was Isabel in a pair of chunky-heeled shoes the same color lavender as her dress. Viola knew that this dress was probably modest for Isabel. It had a simple tie that stopped just below the crease between her breasts. Her hair was still wild, but a straw hat with a purple band kept it from flying in her face.

Viola covered a big smile with both hands. In the two weeks since they had met in Miss Rosalee's shop, Isabel had stayed in her mind. Viola couldn't help but imagine what it would be like to see the woman onstage. Dancing and singing the blues. Sometimes Viola saw the show in her mind as clearly as if she sat in the club watching.

New Pilgrim was completely put off at the sight of the girl. Isabel inched into a pew to sit. Rena Davis used her wide hips to push the girl back into the aisle. Isabel tried to sit beside Senior Brother Clark, Donald Hinson, and then Sister Gladys, but pocketbooks and valises were suddenly lifted from the floor, making slivers of each empty seat. She finally spied the kind face of Miss Rosalee, who moved herself over. Isabel sat, removed her black-lace gloves, then smoothed her church-going dress over a tiny scab on her knee.

The choir was singing "Were You There," a song that Viola had known since she was a child. Cynthie Nettles had just finished her solo, and Viola's was next. She had never before felt nervous singing in the choir, because New Pilgrim was family. Mrs. Baker, the choir director, insisted that when a song was meant for Jesus, there were no wrong notes. But now, with Isabel, a real live singer, sitting out there watching, Viola was tense. She reached down and squeezed Cynthie's hand. Viola liked singing beside Cynthie. They had been best friends until Cynthie got pregnant in their junior year of high school and the Reverend thought it best that they go their separate ways.

Viola stepped forward. She could feel her hands trembling.

"Knock it out, girl," Cynthie whispered.

Viola focused on the four panels of modest stained glass in the skylight above the pulpit. When the sun shone just the right way and her heart was full, Viola thought she saw images in the blue glass. She couldn't say if it was Jesus, her grandmother, or just the hot Carolina sun, but the impression of a tall, thin figure, with arms embracing itself, always kept a good feeling inside of her.

Were you there when they hung him to the cross,
Were you there when they hung him to the cross . . .

She kept her eyes closed as her voice, throaty and resonant, bounced from the walls of the small wooden church house. Anyone who heard Viola sing for the first time was surprised that such a deep and rotund voice came from a small, young woman. By the time she opened her mouth for the next verse, Viola had forgotten about the amens, Isabel, and everyone else in the congregation.

Oh, Lord, it causes me to tremble,
Were you there when they hung him to the cross . . .

The voices of the choir then covered her own like a warm blanket. When the organ finished the last chord, Isabel applauded in the quieted church and only stopped when Miss Rosalee grabbed both her hands.

Reverend Bembrey moved to his pulpit. "Let us be still," he said, removing a hankie from the top pocket of a starched white shirt just under his robe. He wiped his oily eyelids and forehead and dusted specks from the lenses of his thick-rimmed glasses. Then he placed both hands on the dais and lowered his head until the congregation had settled back into their seats.

"Hell," he started. "Everybody got their own idea of what it's like. Their own definition." Cardboard fans fluttered throughout the room like large white butterflies. "Mr. Webster of the Webster Collegiate Dictionary say it's 'the nether realm of the devil and the demons in which the damned suffer *everlasting* punishment.'" He stopped and shook his head. "Mr. Webster also say it's '*unrestrained* fun or sportiveness.'"

Viola's attention wavered from her father on over to Isabel. She looked so different from the young woman in the shop with the po' de soir shoes. Her ankles were crossed and her feet rested in the center aisle. She sat there in the pew, smiling like a child and waving at Viola with her fingertips.

"I say that hell is whatever *you* fear the most!" The Reverend's words echoed through the quiet church. "I once asked my daughter," he said, pulling Viola's attention back to the pulpit. "She couldn't have been no mo' than five or six at the time. I say, baby, what you afraid of?" A few amens rippled through the church. "Well, she looked up at me," he went on, "and with all that child innocence, she said, 'Daddy, I'd be afraid if you didn't love me no mo'.'"

A collective *ah*, especially the ladies. Isabel puckered her lips at Viola like it was the most adorable thing she had ever heard.

"Then she shock the juice outta me when she asked, 'Daddy, what *you* scared of?'"

"Take yo' time," Senior Brother Clark called.

"I say, well . . . and it kinda made me take pause because that's one of the worst things to have to face—your own fears. Your own hell." The Reverend shook his head slowly, as if coping with the thought. "I told her that I was afraid of two things. I say, 'Being hungry.'"

"Yes, sir," Sister Goodwin called.

"Being without home or family... dirty with no clothes and no place to live..." He pushed his glasses on his nose and skimmed two fingers across his thick mustache. "But more than that—" He paused again. "I'm afraid of falling out of God's favor."

"Praise 'im," Miss Rosalee yelled.

"I'm talkin' about me or any of my loved ones not walking a proper Christian path. For me, that would be hell! But for each person, hell is a different place. For Brother Clark here, it might be one thing. To Donald Hinson, another, to my wife, Nell, something else still—but take my word, y'all, it'll be something mean and odious that will perpetually slap you upside yo' head for ever and eternity. *Hell is our worst fears come to pass.* But you see, friends"—in the quiet, Viola could almost hear fans pushing the moist air—"I no longer fear hell."

"Preach!" Mrs. Baker yelled. She was so filled that she gripped the back of the pew in front of her.

"I no longer fear hell," Reverend Bembrey went on, "because I take comfort in knowing that my steps were ordered by God."

"Amen," Isabel yelled out.

Once again, a soft thunder rippled through the room. Even Nell turned in her seat to look at Isabel.

"Who is that woman?" Cynthie whispered to Viola.

"Just someone I know."

"You *know* that woman?" Cynthie's hair was pulled back so tight that tiny bumps rose at her temples. "Well, you best tell her not to come back here."

Viola hadn't expected that reaction. When Cynthie got pregnant, Viola was one of the few who tried to stand up for her. She convinced the teachers at the high school to let Cynthie finish out the school year.

The organ started low under the last words of the Reverend's sermon. As always, he ended with, "Let's all go with God." Mrs. Baker raised the choir, and the Reverend stepped away from the pulpit. He dropped his head and clapped as they sang "On Our Way."

The congregation began to rise from the hard pews. The Reverend walked somberly down the aisle and took his spot at the front door. Nell stood beside him as the departing congregation paused to shake their hands.

Viola would usually take her time after service. She'd gossip with Cynthie for a while, put her robe away in the rehearsal room downstairs, and then make her way to her place beside the Reverend and Nell. But today, she needed to find Isabel. Viola saw the girl heading toward the line to greet the Reverend. Part of her wanted Isabel to keep on walking out the door. She knew that Reverend Bembrey wouldn't appreciate her presence. Viola also sensed that Isabel wasn't the type of woman who left a place without meeting the top man himself.

Isabel waited patiently while those in front of her gave their parting words to the Reverend. When it was her time, she stepped up to him as if his arms were wide open.

"I enjoyed yo' sermon, sir," she said, extending her hand.

He reluctantly accepted it. "Don't think I caught yo' name, miss," he replied.

"Isabel Daniels." She removed her gloves, one finger at a time, just to make sure Nelvern Bembrey noticed she had the refinement to wear them. "How are you, Mrs. Bembrey?" Nell didn't say a word. Her face was pinched like she smelled something foul.

"And where are you from, Miss . . . Daniels?" He knew damn well where she was from.

"Kindred Bluff, sir," she answered.

"Passing through?" The Reverend lifted his robe on one side and slid his hand in his pants pocket.

"Ain't decided yet. But when yo' lovely wife here invited me to services, I thought I'd come to pray."

The Reverend looked at Nell incredulously. "Well, young woman," he said to Isabel, "may God bless you wherever you wind up." Then he turned to Brother Lewis, and Isabel moved on.

Viola slowly made her way to the door. She stood on the church steps, but Isabel was nowhere to be seen. In the bright sun, most of the departing congregation members held their hands to their eyes.

"Baby girl," Isabel called as she approached Viola from behind.

Viola felt everyone staring as Isabel walked up to her. She glanced toward the church entrance where the Reverend and Nell were still surrounded by congregation members.

"You sang that song," Isabel said, "thought I was about to catch the Holy Ghost my damn self!"

Sister Gladys nodded her head as she passed. Cynthie looked at Viola with a strange grin.

"Can't believe you made it to church," Viola said.

"I knew you wasn't gettin' to no Snookie Petaway's," Isabel said. Viola looked back toward the church doors. The Reverend or Nell could walk up on her at any time. "Will you relax, Viola," Isabel said. "You ain't gon' to hell jes' for standing next to me." She grabbed Viola's hand playfully but Viola pulled away. "Lord, you act like singers cain't come to church."

"I didn't say that."

"You didn't have to. And it ain't like I ain't seen none of yo' church folk up in Snookie's place."

"Like who?" Viola asked.

Isabel looked around quickly. "Well, maybe none of these folks exactly, but I seen Miss Day from Wayside Church, Otis James, Sneed Bennett and his wife, Essie, from Calvary." Viola's eyebrow raised in surprise. "It don't mean a damn thing, Viola. Folks go to church one day, have fun the next."

"I don't mean no disrespect," Viola said, "but . . . what did you come here for?"

"Come to pray. Come to see you. You was so nice and stuff . . . and Lord, but did that surprise me." Isabel laughed out loud. "With yo' daddy always trying to run us out . . ."

"Run you out?"

"You know what I'm talkin' 'bout, Viola," she insisted. "You ain't blind and you ain't stupid. Yo' daddy and them preachers been trying to shut Snookie down fo' years."

Like most of the women in New Pilgrim, Viola stayed out of these affairs. "Well, I better go in," she said, walking toward the door.

"I guess I'll be on my way too." Isabel slipped on her gloves and smoothed her dress over her thighs. "I got things to do myself, you know. In fact, I'm rehearsing a few new numbers with the band."

For a moment, Viola envied Isabel. "Sounds like something."

"Yep." Isabel was about to walk on. "Maybe we can talk another time. Wanna go to the beach?"

Viola turned with a smile. "What?"

"The beach down around Corman Island . . . up near the Bluff?"

"I've never been to that beach," Viola said.

"Shame." Isabel walked down the three church steps.

"When?" Viola asked, before she could even think about it.

"I'll come get you."

"No," Viola said quickly.

Isabel shrugged her shoulders. "Whatever you say, baby girl." She walked past a few parked cars, but then stopped just before the main road. Isabel removed her shoes, slung them over her shoulder, and walked barefoot past the remaining congregation members. Without even turning, she raised her hand and wiggled her fingertips as if she knew Viola was still watching. She started down the sloping road like a proud horse, her hips swaying, shoulders dancing, and that wild mane trailing behind her. Soon she disappeared and it seemed to Viola that she had stepped right off the earth.

CHAPTER
3

Hattie had to kneel in a chair just to reach the top of Forestine's head. She yanked and tugged as she tried to separate the tightly coiled strands of hair.

"Why I got to go through all this?" Forestine protested.

"Turn yo' head," Hattie barked.

"He ain't comin' here to see me," Forestine went on. "Why I gotta get dressed?"

"Seventeen and ain't never had her head pressed," Hattie muttered. "Damn shame." Forestine cringed when her mother drew near with the smoking comb.

"Keep your head still," Hattie snapped. She set the comb against a clump of hair. Even with the oil and heat, the comb resisted. Forestine yelped when she heard the sizzle behind her ear.

"Need to fluff yourself up some, Forestine," Lilian argued. "Wouldn't be right for my future husband to come in here and see you looking like one of them big men drilling holes in the middle of Atlantic Avenue. Besides, I can think of worse things than you looking like a decent woman for a change."

"Future husband?" Forestine asked.

Lilian sat at the kitchen table. "He said he wanted to spend time with my family, and that can only mean one thing."

"Only one thing that I can think of," Hattie smiled.

"But why *I* got to go through all this—" Forestine screamed as Hattie yanked the top of her head.

"Man don't wanna think he marryin' into an ugly family," Hattie replied. "He might fret about what his kids gon' look like."

Lucas Campbell and Lilian had been seeing each other for the past four months. They usually met in front of the library and then went to the movies or the park or wherever it was they'd planned to go. Hattie knew him from church, where he played piano at service every Sunday morning. Lucas was an educated man whose daddy owned two liquor stores. Forestine began to think that maybe Lilian was ashamed of the Bent family. Embarrassed by Willie's drinking, Hattie's mouth, and the way Forestine looked.

"I need to bend your hair under a bit," Hattie said, picking up the iron curler.

"Bend it how?" Forestine watched in horror as she set the curler on the flame.

"Jes' sit yo' ass back!" Hattie snapped.

Lilian applied makeup to Forestine's cheeks, eyes, and lips, while Hattie finished her hair. Then, Forestine put on a dress that had been laid out on her bed. Not one of the usual dresses that Hattie would buy from the old ladies' thrift sales, but a pale blue summer knit that hugged her hips and stopped just above her knees.

"Where this dress come from?" Forestine asked as Hattie zipped her up the back.

"Yo' daddy bought it for you. Bought it last year."

"Last year?" Forestine asked.

"It's been in yo' closet the whole time. You woulda never put it on, lessen I gave it to you. All I ever see you in is slacks."

The dress was clingy and girly, more like a dress that Lilian would wear. Hattie turned her toward the mirror, and Forestine couldn't believe the person who looked back at her. In this dress, she looked almost sexy. Her hips finally had some definition and her breasts, just shy of a B cup, appeared to be bigger. Her eyes, which always looked too small and far apart, were now topped with blue powder and shaped like horizontal diamonds. Her cheeks actually had angles and her chin didn't look so long and thin. But the part Forestine liked the most were her lips. They were beet red, just like the girls from *Ebony* magazine.

Even Willie, who liked her just the way she was, had to stop and take notice of how nice she looked. He let out a loud whistle, like the Brooklyn Union Gas men did when they sat on the curb eating their lunch and the young girls passed. Forestine dropped her arms to her sides and rolled her eyes up in her head.

"Stone fox," he said. "Wearin' yo' new dress and all. Fine, Forestine. Real fine."

The attention embarrassed her, but Forestine had to admit, if just to herself, that the touch of the knit swishing against the back of her legs made her feel special.

At the stroke of six, Lucas Campbell knocked on the apartment door. Lilian and Hattie fretted back and forth about who should answer, so Forestine opened the door herself. Lucas Campbell wore silver-rimmed glasses. He was tall enough to stand face-to-face with her.

"Hey there, Forestine," he said.

"Lucas," she answered, and then stepped aside and allowed him to enter. He walked into the apartment with his shoulders bent. "Lilian's in the living room," she said as she led him through the short foyer.

"Is today your birthday or something?" he asked.

"No. Why?"

"I just mean that you look different," he mumbled.

"Thanks."

Lucas wasn't bad-looking, especially when he held his head up, which was hardly ever. He would sit in church hunched over the keyboard with his glasses dangling on the tip of his nose. Last Sunday, when he played "I Stood by the Banks of Jordan," she could only see the top of his honey-colored face as the music pulsed through his body and his wavy hair whipped across his forehead.

They walked into the living room, where Hattie was sitting on the floral sofa next to Willie. Lilian posed in one of the twin armchairs across from them.

"Evening, all," Lucas said as he sat in the other armchair.

There was an uneasy chorus of hellos. Forestine settled on the armrest of the couch beside her father. She had never seen the Bents wear such plastic smiles.

"So," Hattie started, "still working in yo' daddy's package sto' on the weekends?"

"Yes, ma'am," he answered.

"That's fine," she smiled. Her voice brightened even more when she said, "And, I hear tell you instructin' music at the elementary school over in Bed-Stuy."

"That's right," he replied.

"Same school Lilian and Forestine went to when they was lil' girls," Hattie went on. "Ain't that correct, Lilian?"

Forestine had never heard her mother use the word "correct." Even Willie's head turned at the strange sound of it.

"That's correct, Mama," Lilian replied softly.

This was the first time Forestine could remember hearing her sister whisper.

"Say you attended the college in New Jersey?" Hattie asked.

"Yes, ma'am. Piscataway."

"Piscataway College?" Hattie smiled. "My, but that sound like an important place for a real college man."

"Actually, it's Rutgers University in Piscataway, New Jersey, ma'am," he said.

"Oooh, Lord, but you college men talk up a mess of words," Hattie laughed. "Ain't that right, Lilian?"

"Uh-huh," Lilian stuttered. Forestine tried to stifle her laughter.

"Mama!" Lilian pleaded.

"Shut up, Forestine," Hattie snapped.

"I can't help it, Mama," Forestine said, and laughed out loud.

"If you ever git yo'self a man, then you can open yo' damn mouth," Hattie snapped. Then she turned and smiled at Lucas with all the grace she could muster. "You got anything to ask the young man, Willie?" Hattie said.

"Nope," Willie answered.

Hattie held on to her smile. "Sho'ly you have one question," she insisted.

Willie searched the drapes with his eyes. "Yo' daddy still got that Johnnie Red on sale?"

"Damn it, Willie," Hattie hissed.

"You say ask the boy something! Well, I asked him!"

"Why don't we leave these children alone so they can talk," Hattie said, rising and pulling Willie and Forestine up. Lilian looked humiliated. She only calmed down after Lucas took her hand, led her to the couch, and sat down beside her.

In their five months of dating thereafter, Lilian thought it best they continue to meet in front of the library. When they married and Willie got so drunk at the reception that he pissed in the punch bowl, Lilian didn't fret. She was already Mrs. Lucas Campbell. So as far as she was concerned, the Bents could go on and act a fool.

Lester Ashford came in from the sidewalk, wiping the water spots from his three-piece suit. He almost ran into the bar as he tried to walk and dry at the same time. "Damn kids," he mumbled under his breath.

"What happened?" Willie asked. He was sitting at the bar beside Forestine, nursing his second Seven and Seven.

"Goddamned kids turn the fire hydrant on out front. They gushing water like it ain't nothin', but in the meantime it makes my water pressure low." He took one of the napkins from behind the bar and wiped at the spots on his wide lapels. "Hydrant been on all day and water trickle from my tap like an old man's peter. Ain't them lil' bastards supposed to be home 'sleep by now?"

Lester's Pub was one of the few legitimate clubs in the Brownsville section of Brooklyn. It maintained a real liquor license and most times even passed safety and health inspections. Lester's Pub used to be Ashford's Fish and Chips, but when Lester realized there was more profit in music and booze, he revamped. The front counter became the bar, he added ten more tables to the dozen he already had, threw on some red tablecloths and cup candles, knocked down a wall in back to make space for a small stage, and Lester's Pub was in business. He even converted the small storage area that had held the old fish bins into a dressing room that fit four people. No one seemed to mind the odor of fried porgies still entrenched in the walls.

"Who you got on tonight?" Forestine asked him.

Lester looked up, noticing her for the first time. "What the hell you doin' here, Forestine?"

"Come to sing tonight."

Lester scanned the front door, where a line of people were waiting to enter. "What's the day of the week?" he asked her.

"Saturday," she answered. Forestine had been living in her new painted face and hot-pressed hair for about five months, and she'd finally gotten the courage to come into Lester's Pub on a Saturday night. The club became a whole other place on Saturday night. The room was already packed and the liquor was flowing. On the stage, a five-piece band played Jackie Wilson tunes. Forestine looked over her shoulder at the crowds entering and the people waiting near the door. Lester's Pub was one of the few places in Brooklyn that sometimes pulled some of the talent and crowd from lower Manhattan. Still, it never got this crowded on a Wednesday.

"Damn right it's Saturday," he said. "And I ain't got to say no more." He turned to walk away.

"Aw, come on with it, Lester," Willie blustered. "Forestine pack 'em in here on Wednesday night. And man, look at her. She look good and you know it."

Lester used his tongue to roll a toothpick around in his mouth while he looked Forestine over. Having Lester's eyes on her to approve or disapprove of her appearance was humiliation, plain and simple.

"I been seeing this *new you* on Wednesdays," he said sarcastically. "It's better," he admitted. "You lookin' better." He thought for a moment. "And since I ain't got but one group on tonight, we might work something out." Then he added, "Still got a long way to pretty, though."

"We ain't ask you that," Willie said.

"See, that there is pretty." Lester's eyes followed a woman in a tight yellow dress walking into the dressing room. "That's Louise from Rosetta and the Daffodils, and she is sho' 'nuff pretty."

"What good is it if they can't sing?" Forestine asked.

"Who say Rosetta and the Daffodils cain't sing? They sing jes' fine and even if they couldn't," he said, smacking his lips, "who gives a damn?"

Forestine knew that Lester was an asshole. Nick thought so, Willie thought so, and most of the girls who came and went thought so too, but this was his place and she'd have to hold her tongue.

"I'll give you one song after Rosetta and the Daffodils," Lester offered. "And that's providin' nobody else show up."

"You mean nobody pretty," Forestine cut in.

Lester pulled the toothpick from his mouth. "One damn song, Forestine. Take it or leave it."

"She'll take it," Willie cut in.

"Why don't you go in the dressing room and put on some more of that lipstick," Lester said.

Forestine kissed Willie on the cheek and pushed past Lester toward the dressing room. She was singing on a Saturday night. The people who would come in tonight had discussed coming here since the beginning of the week. They'd counted the little extra money they may have saved just for the purpose of entertainment, got dressed, and waited on a line outside to get in. And they wouldn't accept just anything or anyone.

Forestine opened the door to the dressing room, and Rosetta and the Daffodils turned all at once to look at her. Two of the women wore tight yellow dresses. The oldest of the three, in a hot pink dress and high hair, had to be Rosetta. Forestine nodded and nervously squeezed past them to the last chair.

The small room smelled like three different perfumes, and makeup was strewn along the narrow dressing table. Each seat at the long, thin table had a light-up mirror with six bright bulbs, but on the one in front of Forestine, only two were working. At first, she sat there looking at herself in the dim mirror. She already had on her makeup, and wasn't quite sure what to do. She took a comb from her purse and smoothed her short bangs in the front. The girls went on talking as if she weren't even there.

"I quit him months ago but he still come around," the one called Louise said. She teased her hair until the top and sides were stiff and nearly transparent. "Say he wanna take me nice places. . . . I told him, I say, man, get me a gig and then maybe we can talk."

"He can't find a gig of his own," the other Daffodil added. She wore a pageboy wig and her lips were frosted pink. Rosetta remained silent.

"That's what I figured," Louise said. "But, Paula girl you know it was worth a try."

Forestine took note of the way Louise blotted the coral lipstick and applied eyeliner to make her eyes look oriental. Lilian didn't even know how to do that.

"Then he come around," she continued, "and said he was gonna take me to the Big House."

"What?!" Paula gasped. Even Rosetta turned around.

"Yes, girl. Told me to put on my stole and fix my face 'cause we partying at the Big House."

"You actually *went* to the Big House?" Rosetta turned to ask.

"Well, let me finish," she squealed. "Niggah had me put on my best shit, you understand. We get in the car, go over the Brooklyn Bridge, up to Harlem, and I'm so excited that I'm about pee. We get there . . . to the door of the Big House, mind you, and, girl, I ain't lyin' when I say the music that was coming out of there. . . ." She fanned herself from the excitement. "Them children were up in there jammin'. I even saw a Jaguar right out in front that I heard belonged to Miles."

"Davis?" Rosetta and Paula asked.

"And they say Miss Dinah Washington was up in there too."

"You saw Dinah Washington?" Rosetta asked.

"Not exactly," she said. "See, my guy knocks on the door to the Big House and this man opens the door and says 'Who you know?' Just like that, 'Who you know?' And this sorry-ass niggah that I'm with, who don't know shit from shit, just stands there and stutters to himself like he retarded."

"And?" Rosetta asked.

"And?! Girl, they closed the door on my ass so fast."

Rosetta stood up and heaved her bosoms up to the top of her bright pink dress. "Sorry," she said dryly.

"*You* sorry? I was through."

"So you never really got to the Big House?" Paula asked.

"Well, you ain't been there neither," Louise defended. "Shit, even Rosetta ain't been to the Big House, and she way older than us."

"You don't know where I been," Rosetta said, heading for the door. "Come on, ladies."

"She ain't been to no damn Big House, I know that much," Louise grunted as she got up and checked her face one last time. She turned to look at Forestine and seemed about to ask if she had ever been there, but then changed her mind.

Forestine knew what she was thinking. Even with Forestine's pressed hair and red lips, Louise still saw a hulking, plain woman who didn't belong in this room, let alone this club. Although Forestine was used to the feeling, she couldn't get past the pain.

Lester stopped the band to introduce the Daffodils as they waited at the dressing room door. When he announced their name, they made their way through the standing crowd. Forestine followed behind them amid the men's whoops and hollers. Rosetta and the Daffodils walked onto the stage like they were on a Paris runway. Forestine stood in the back and watched as they froze in a sexy tableau until the music started. Then, with perfect timing, the women spun and stopped before their mike, caressing the long neck like an anxious lover.

Most girl groups looked alike. Fancy steps, bright dresses, and lots of hair, but few had any significant talent. When the yelling in the room died down, Forestine moved to what Lester called the "talent table." It was about three rows from the stage and off to the side, right next to the kitchen. The table itself had one leg shorter than the rest and was covered with a red cloth that had been singed with lit cigarettes.

Forestine had to admit that Rosetta and the Daffodils were one of the better girl groups. Especially Rosetta. Her voice was soulful and no-nonsense. She put a particular hurtin' on a song called "Maybe," and the audience even clapped in the middle of it. After three songs, Lester set them up with champagne and a plate of ribs. They sat just a few feet from Forestine at what Willie called the "Lester tryin' to get a piece a ass table."

Forestine felt the nerves coming on her and blotted her lipstick with a bar napkin to keep her hands occupied. She had no high hair, bright dress, or sensual sway, and wondered how a Saturday night crowd might receive her. She waited for Lester to introduce her, but saw that he was busy near the entrance of the club. He embraced a tiny older woman who had just walked in. The four men with her didn't look like the typical Lester's Pub audience. One of the men, round and mustard colored, had a red beard and mustache and wore a porkpie hat. The two taller ones in sharp tailored suits looked like they were brothers, except one was clean-shaven while the other had thick sideburns. The fourth and smallest of the men wore a Stetson that made his head look too big. They all walked with confidence, nodding as the audience applauded their arrival. Forestine wasn't sure who they were, but the woman seemed to be the star.

Lester held the older woman by the hand as he led her across the club. They stopped at the Daffodils' table, and Forestine finally saw the woman's face. She was Lil' Eartha McClain. Nick loved to play her albums, and he called her the last of the old blues divas. Her birdlike features weren't exactly beautiful, but Lil' Eartha had style. She was wrapped in a white fur stole, and at sixty-some-odd years, she didn't have a single line on her deep brown face that Forestine could see.

"Who's these pretty gals, Lester?" Eartha asked.

"Rosetta and the Daffodils." He said their name like the earth should stop moving. "They just finished their song."

"Sorry we missed you," Eartha said to them.

"We can sing something else," Louise offered.

"Cool," Lester said. "Ain't got nobody else on."

"What about Forestine?" Willie cut in. He had come over from the bar to see what the buzz was about.

Lester's eyes darted quickly to the talent table. Forestine felt her body fold at the waist. Her heart was about to beat through her chest.

"Damn," he hissed. "How long can you stay, Eartha?"

"A minute or two," she said. "Jes' wanted you to wrap up some ribs, 'cause we got a show in Greensboro tomorrow. Gon' be on the road in another hour."

Lester said, "Just have to have Forestine back tomorrow."

"Hell no you won't," Willie cut in. "You promised my baby a song tonight."

"This must be the husband," Eartha smiled.

"The daddy," Willie said proudly. "Willie Bent, ma'am." He extended his hand to Lil' Eartha.

"Forestine gon' have to just wait 'til Eartha leave," Lester insisted.

"I'll tear this muthafuckin' place in two," Willie said, jumping in his face.

"It's alright, Lester," Eartha laughed. "Let the woman sing and I'll wait for the flower girls."

"Alright, goddamn it, shit, piss," Lester spat. "Tell her to get her ass on up there." Forestine didn't even wait for Willie to tell her. She rose from her seat and went right to the stage. "Eartha, baby," Lester said, "she only doin' one song. I really want you to see these gals." He motioned to the bartender to send another bottle of champagne.

"Either of you young ladies sing the blues?" Eartha asked.

"Every day," Louise replied.

"And how long y'all been together?" Eartha asked.

"Paula and me met a couple of years ago at a high school talent show," Louise answered. "And Rosetta here is my big sister and we all jes' got together."

"High school talent show, huh?" Eartha chuckled. "Lord, ha' mercy."

"We been together two whole years," Louise said. Forestine started singing "Never Let Me Go," but Louise kept talking. "We had a three-week run at Moses Edmonds' place, downtown Brooklyn."

"You don't say," the man in the Stetson said, and smiled. "When the Caravan got together, you gals prob'ly hadn't even been thought of. Ain't that right, Eartha?"

Eartha's attention had drifted to the stage. Without taking her eyes away from Forestine, she reached into her purse and slid on a pair of black-rimmed glasses. "Who the hell is that?" she asked.

"You mean *what* the hell is that," Paula giggled.

But there was no room for jokes now. Forestine had them. Even the usual chatter from the bar had been hushed by the simple beauty of her voice.

"I'll be damned," Rosetta whispered.

Forestine's hands clutched the mike so tight that she could see the beige in her dark knuckles. She never knew what to do with herself when she sang. Nick always said, "Don't do shit. Stand with your head up, and the words'll guide you." By the second verse, Forestine felt the blood flowing back into her arms. She looked quickly toward Lil' Eartha's table, and the woman was still. That was always a good sign. Forestine didn't give the audience a chance to catch their breath before she went right into Victoria Spivey's "Any Kinda Man," and that was just it for Eartha. The little woman was on her feet screaming while her band hollered. Not only did Eartha stay but she dropped her stole on the chair and walked onto the platform with her band following. The red-haired man removed his porkpie hat and dismissed the house piano player. One of the tall brothers pulled a mouthpiece from his pocket and borrowed a trumpet, while the other took the drummer's chair. Forestine was about to leave the stage, but Eartha grasped at her arm like an ant pulling at a huge hunk of black bread. Eartha was completely undone when Forestine knew the words to her song, "As Blue As It Gets."

The two women exchanged fire. It became a duel between the younger Forestine and the older Eartha as to who could sing the lowest of lowdown. Of course Eartha and all her years easily won out. The crowd loved the battle and didn't let them leave the stage until Eartha sang another song. Forestine sat on the stage beside her and watched the older woman work out. Then Eartha wrapped her arm inside of Forestine's and led her back to the table. They passed Rosetta and the Daffodils, who were on their way up to sing another song.

"You got yourself some style," Eartha said as she dabbed her forehead with a handkerchief. "But I'm sure you used to hearin' that."

"Yes, ma'am," Forestine said softly. The Daffodils were singing, but Lil' Eartha's eyes stayed at the table.

Eartha introduced her band. "This here is Creer, Beck, Ernest, and Doug."

Forestine nodded at each. For a moment she recalled the yellowing snapshots of Nick's time on the road. The way his group, the Delta Boys, along with the woman singer named Odella, would take a photo in front of a club or some fancy car. All richly dressed, everybody was pretty, even the men, and they smiled like they had such interesting things to say. That's the way Lil' Eartha and her Caravan looked. Only the small man named Ernest seemed out of place.

"How old are you, baby?" Eartha asked her.

Forestine considered lying, saying she was twenty, but thought the better of it. "I'll be eighteen in a few weeks, ma'am."

"Damn," Ernest said.

"I thought so," Eartha smiled. "You tall as a tree but got a baby face." Eartha took another sip from her glass as the waitress set down a greasy brown bag. Forestine could smell the vinegar of barbecue. "Look, sweetie," Eartha said. "I cain't offer you a spot now 'cause we promised another gal, but you can bet I won't ever forget you."

"Ma'am?" Forestine's mouth dropped open.

"I know it don't sound like nothin' now, but I'm sure we gon' see you again."

"See me . . . ?" Forestine said in shock. "Yes, ma'am."

"That all you can say, woman?" Eartha laughed along with the rest of the band.

"Yes, ma'am," Forestine said. "I mean . . . well . . . yes, ma'am."

"How long you been singin' blues?" Eartha asked her.

"Since I was little."

Eartha's eyes started at Forestine's feet and went to the top of her head. "Musta been a long time ago," she said. The band laughed again. "And where you been doin' all this singin' . . . since you was little?"

"Just here, ma'am," Forestine answered.

"Sound to me like you been round a lil' mo' than this," Eartha said. "And damn if you don't sing the blues *and* some jazz."

"I know that's right," Ernest put in.

"Old man Nick says it's just colored folks' singing," Forestine said. "He says just go with the groove."

"Old man Nick?" Beck said, rubbing his red beard.

"He's the one who taught me."

"You not talking 'bout Nick Cambridge?" Eartha asked.

Forestine was embarrassed to find that, after all these years, she didn't know Nick's whole name. "I don't know his surname."

"Nicky Cambridge? Saxophone? Bad hip?" Eartha put in.

"That's Nick," Forestine smiled.

Eartha looked at Beck as if she couldn't believe what she was hearing. "Like I say, you good. Trained by the best. I want you to git ahold of my album called *Blue Party*."

"Oh, I got it, ma'am," Forestine said. "Nick gave it to me."

"Damn, but I like this gal," Eartha said. "Next time you listen to it, pay attention to all the songs by the gal what ain't me." Lil' Eartha stood up and gathered her stole. Forestine walked alongside of her as she headed toward the door.

"Miss Eartha, this is my daddy," Forestine said, grabbing Willie by the hand.

"Oh, we already met, yo' daddy and me." She reached up and kissed Forestine on the cheek. "We'll cross paths again," she said as her band filed out, "and you keep on singin', you hear."

"Yes, ma'am."

Eartha gave Forestine another quick hug before she left. Forestine stood outside the club and watched her walk toward her bus, which was painted with a picture of a brown sheik holding a guitar. It wasn't until Eartha got on that Forestine went back in.

The Daffodils were still singing, but the attention was on Forestine as she made her way back to the table. Audience members stopped her on the way to shake hands. Forestine couldn't stop herself from smiling and she settled back, closed her eyes, and enjoyed the good feeling.

"Mind if I set down?" Eartha's piano player, Beck, was standing over her table.

"Not at all," she said.

"Thought I'd have me one last drink while they gassin' the bus." He placed his hat on the table, then motioned to Lester to send another round. For a moment Beck didn't say anything. He eyed Forestine like he was admiring a rare painting. Forestine wasn't quite sure where to look.

She figured Beck to be about Willie's age, somewhere in his early forties. His smile was warm and revealed one gold cap, but it was his flaming hair and beard that Forestine found so striking. "Wish I could do somethin' to get you in now," he said, "but Eartha got this here woman that she promised the space to, and Lil' Eartha McClain is good with her word." A waitress set down two drinks.

"You don't have to explain." Forestine leaned on the table with heavy forearms. "I can't believe she even thought about me like that."

"Oh, she doin' mo' than thinkin'. Girl, you can sing," he said, squeezing her hand. "Make a grown man wanna cry out loud. You sing blues and jazz like they were meant to be sung, like two sides of the same coin. Cook with that old blues, just like Eartha. Most girls your age don't know nuthin' 'bout that, but I guess that's Nick's style. You're gon' be joinin' us real soon," he said, shaking his head.

"What makes you so sure?"

He swirled the brown liquor across the ice cubes. "You look like a woman that don't like to be lied to."

"I am."

"That lil' weasel named Ernest..." He whispered so close that Forestine could almost taste the sting of the rum on his breath. "Eartha keep him beside her like a dog on a leash. An old dirty, flea-infested dog." Forestine couldn't help but laugh. "Well, you met him yo'self," he chuckled. "None of us can understand what she sees in him. Don't sing, don't play nothin', just hang on to her and drink up everything he can find. But for whatever reason, she loves him. And if another woman even look his way, she fall out in a jealous fit. He cain't even take a piss wit'out her permission."

"How can a man live like that?" Forestine asked.

"That's the point," Beck insisted, "he ain't no man. He a weasel and sometime he do stuff jes' to git her goat. And this new gal, Lola, well, she's a pretty little tight thang, and we all know that it's just a matter of time befo' Ernest say something to her. Then we'll be lookin' for another singer. Ernest have his eye on Lola, and Eartha have her eye on you."

"Because I'm not a pretty little tight thing, huh?" Forestine asked.

Beck looked down into his glass. "There's a whole lot of pretty gals around, Forestine, but the Lord only give yo' gift to a precious few," he said politely. "Precious, precious few." Beck finished the whiskey in one gulp. "Jes' wanna say that we all pullin' for you."

Forestine stood up with him. He picked up his hat from the table and flashed his gold smile. Forestine had to smile with him. "You are one long drink of water, ain't you, girl?" he said.

"That's what they say," she answered.

"I'm gon' see you in a minute," he said, pulling on his hat.

Beck walked off. Willie stopped him to shake his hand, then came over to her table, wearing his overcoat and carrying hers. He was quiet and mostly sober.

"We best get on, fo' yo' mama send the police," he said, helping her on with her coat.

"Don't you wanna know what happened?" she asked him.

"We'll talk about it," he said.

He walked with his head up and she didn't even have to guide him to his car. He opened the door himself and got right into the driver's seat. It was dark, but as they pulled out, the blue neon above Lester's Pub lit a tear in Willie's eye.

"You okay, Daddy?"

"Oh yeah," he said, brushing it off. "I'm fine." He drove in silence for a while.

Forestine thought about turning on the radio but somehow she knew Willie needed the quiet.

"You fin' to be something, Forestine," he said. "Sooner than I ever imagined."

"I got a long way to go."

"Naw you ain't either," he sighed. "Everything happenin' so quick. I guess all I'm tryin' to say is that I'm proud as hell and don't you ever forget that." She reached over and kissed him on the cheek. "Girl, stop that," he scolded. "Gon' make me crash up the car. Then what yo' mama gon' say?"

"I'm sorry, Daddy," she smiled.

"Oughta be sorry," he barked. "Kissin' all over me while I'm drivin' and stuff."

"I'll never do it again," she laughed.

As Willie drove, Forestine thought about the night, from start to finish. Even that damn fool Lester had nodded his approval at her. She couldn't wait to tell Nick. The old man wasn't one to do a whole lot of smiling, but he would certainly break his face when she told him about singing with Lil' Eartha McClain.

Willie parked and they entered the building arm in arm. Hattie was still awake when they walked into the apartment. Forestine thought about telling her mother about her night, but she could see by the look on her face that Hattie Bent would never understand.

She sat up on the couch and pressed her cigarette out so hard that the ashtray toppled and stopped just short of turning over. Hattie had stopped complaining about their nights out, but since Lilian had moved away, the woman seemed to be filled with more steam and piss. Forestine felt a fight coming on, and could see Willie slipping on his suit of armor.

"You go on to bed," he whispered. "I'll take care yo' mama."

"Y'all know what time it is?" Hattie said calmly.

"Yes, baby," Willie answered while Forestine went into her room.

She hated leaving her father, but Forestine knew that with pride filling his heart and the bit of vodka lightening his head, Willie Bent would endure just fine.

Nick hadn't answered his door in over two weeks. Forestine had tried to see him at least six times, and on each of those days she knew he was home because she could hear his saxophone playing the deepest, darkest blues. He had been like this in the past, not opening his door for a day or two, but never this long.

"I know you in there, old man," she yelled. "What's wrong with you?" Still she heard his long and painful riffs. "I need to talk to you," she yelled. "I got news, Nick, good news." There was no break in the music. "Alright," she called, "but this is the last time I'm coming." Forestine pushed away from his door and went to the elevator. His playing stopped, and as she was about to press the down button, the front door opened.

Nick was dressed in a suit and seated by the window, pulling bleeps and bursts of senseless notes from his sax. He stopped to light half a cigarette that he fished from the bottom of the ashtray, took two quick puffs and then crushed it out. Forestine could see that the tips of his fingers were burnt. Nick never neglected his fingers.

"What's wrong?" she asked.

"My wife passed," he said.

Forestine hadn't even known he was married. "I'm sorry."

The sound of his sax cut the air again and then suddenly, he stopped. "Cancer ate her up so bad that it's prob'ly a blessing."

Forestine nodded awkwardly. "Did she live in New York?"

"Kansas City," he answered. "And I mean Kansas City, *Kansas*, not no Kansas City, Missouri. They right 'cross the river from each other but there's a big difference." He shook his head and the tears started rolling down his face. "I met her at the Gem Theater, you know. Gem Theater, Eighteenth and Vine. Big-time blues and jazz come outta there. We talkin' cats like Jay McShann, Coleman Hawkins . . . Yardbird."

"Kansas City, Kansas?" she asked.

"Kansas City, *Kansas*. Big difference."

"How long has it been since you've seen her?"

"I don't know . . . thirty, forty years." He held his sax on his lap. "I know what you saying, Forestine . . . I know you saying, why Nick so messed up behind this? He ain't seen the woman in two of my life-times but . . . damn, I cain't tell you what a hole it leaves in me." His saxophone fell to his feet and he bawled like a baby. She wanted to tell him about Lil' Eartha, but it didn't feel like the right thing to say. Forestine sat beside him and took one of his hands.

"You ain't alone, Nick," she said. "You always got me and Willie." She really did love this old man. She wanted to give back even a little of what he had given her over the years.

"The only time I ever wanted my sight, needed my sight, was when I met my wife, you know," he said. "Only wanted my sight fo' a minute . . . a minute . . . jes' to look at her face. Damn, but I'm feeling bad, Forestine," he said, rubbing her hand.

"I'm right here," she said.

He moved her hand to his lap. "Stay wit' me."

"I will, Nick," she said, but she could feel herself begin to panic. She tried to pull away but he held her hand tight.

"Please don't leave me, Forestine," he said.

Nick had done more for her than anyone she knew. Taught her more than most seasoned singers would ever know. She was singing at Lester's Pub on Saturday nights because of him. Lil' Eartha McClain actually told her she was good because of him. Forestine looked away. Maybe if she didn't watch him put her hand on the swell in his lap, she could pretend that it wasn't happening. But no. He unzipped his pants and placed himself in her hand and then guided her to a rhythm. She could feel her eyes well with tears, and not from shame or embarrassment, but from sorrow. No one should ever be this lonely, she thought.

Her hand slapped against the side of his thigh harder and harder and then she felt his whole body shudder.

Forestine calmly got up but couldn't look back at him. She got her bearings, and then walked out. She stood trembling in the hall before taking the steps down from the fifth floor two at a time. She ran through the back of the projects, past sweating trash cans and men palming brown-papered bottles, then sat down on the bench under the streetlight outside her building. Her face was wet with tears, and Forestine never cried. She rocked herself back and forth until she was calm. In a moment she'd go in, take a bath, and think about her song for next Saturday night. There was no harm done and besides, who had to know?

"This cain't be Viola." Reverend Dr. Morgan pulled himself forward in his seat. For such a big man his voice was high, calm, and sweet. His thick neck flowed over his crisp white shirt collar. "I 'clare, gal, you lookin' jes' like your mama."

"Thank you, Reverend." Viola set out a tray of tiny yellow cookies. "More tea, sirs?"

"Yes, young lady, that would be fine," Reverend Baines answered. He smiled and his pointy white beard hit the top of his tie. Viola slowly filled his glass until the lemon slice bobbed at the rim.

Reverend Emmet Baines and Reverend Dr. Rupert Morgan were meeting at the Bembrey home to discuss a community matter. Nell had set out the good crystal glasses and ironed the white linen napkins. Reverend Baines was minister of the AME Church in Camden County, just a few miles away, and Reverend Dr. Morgan was pastor of Wayside Baptist Church, about three miles out in the woods. To Cleveland Bembrey they were what most men, given a transgression or two, aspired to be. Along with Reverend Lightfoot, minister of the Calvary Baptist Church, they had been responsible for Cleveland Bembrey's appointment to New Pilgrim. Reverend Lightfoot never attended these types of meetings. He left community affairs to the younger ministers.

"What a beautiful family you have, Cleveland," Reverend Baines said.

"Thank you, sir." This was what Cleveland Bembrey lived for. Praise. A sense of stability.

"I was tellin' my wife, Eloise, the other day," Reverend Baines went on. "Tellin' her that we need to visit with you and Nelvern mo' often. Always such a nice feeling in this house."

Reverend Dr. Morgan held out his glass, and Viola filled it. She refilled her father's, then took her seat by the door and waited. Nell used to host these meetings, but since Viola was now "of age," she had passed the duty to her daughter. Viola felt silly, almost like a life-sized doll sitting quietly in the corner in a Sunday dress, waiting until the men's glasses were half-empty again.

"The sacredness of the family," Reverend Dr. Morgan started, "that's what's important, Cleveland. Good stock."

"Yes, sir."

" 'Of old thou hast laid the foundations of the earth: And the heavens are the work of thy hands.' " Reverend Dr. Morgan nodded. "I've seen the results of a shaky foundation and it's a sad sight indeed."

"Amen," Reverend Baines said. "Pitch a tent on the devil's campsite and prepare to be hideously consumed."

"Yes, sir," Reverend Bembrey put in.

Reverend Dr. Morgan pulled out a handkerchief from his jacket pocket and wiped his hands before reaching for a wedge of cheese. "Which brings me to the point of our visit," he said. "Mr. Snookie Petaway."

Viola had hosted more than a couple of meetings of the church board, the deacons, and the church financial committee. Usually, her attention wandered, but today, she had to stop herself from looking so interested.

"The filth and degradation is spillin' out of that place and into where decent folk worship," Reverend Dr. Morgan said. There was acid in his voice, but his expression remained unruffled.

"I have to agree, sir," Reverend Bembrey put in. "It's gettin' out of hand. One of them crazy folks wandered into my service, Sunday last."

"You don't say," Reverend Baines replied.

"I believe in savin' souls just like the next man," Reverend Bembrey went on, "but that woman was insolent and mocking, during that very service. It was Etta's gal . . ."

"Lord, today," Reverend Baines said.

"Etta's chile," Reverend Morgan droned. "Ain't got to say another word, Cleveland. But that's gon' keep happenin', what with Snookie just spittin' distance of our three tabernacles. I ain't lyin' when I say that sometimes I come into church on Sunday mornin' and the sinners are jes' retirin' from the night befo'."

Snookie Petaway's was the kind of place folks whispered about behind their hand. It was way out in the sticks, so far out that some folks called it the "Jungle Hut." But the only way it could be far enough for any of the reverends' comfort was if the club was out of Jasperville altogether.

"And Wayside has the displeasure," Reverend Dr. Morgan went on, "of being the closest to those folks. See 'em out there like animals . . . wild animals."

"Reverend Dr. Morgan, sir . . . ?" Viola cut in. Her voice sounded small among the men's voices in the room. The three reverends turned to face her, now standing in the doorway.

"Viola?" Reverend Bembrey said. "Don't yo' mama got something for you to do back there?"

"It's okay, Cleveland," Reverend Dr. Morgan said. "What is it, precious?"

"Well, sir . . ." Viola began. At this moment she wished she had never started. She could see her father's apprehension as he shifted in his seat.

"Go on, baby, and speak yo' piece," Reverend Dr. Morgan insisted.

"I was just going to say that . . . well . . . sir, Snookie Petaway's is way back in the woods. What harm can that be?"

The reverends chuckled. Her father didn't find it funny at all. "I got one at home 'bout the same age, Cleveland," Reverend Dr. Morgan said. Then he turned back to Viola. "It's a little more complicated than that, dear heart," he answered. Nell appeared in the doorway. "Besides, I'm afraid you too young to understand the ramifications behind it all."

"Viola," Nell whispered.

"Sir," Viola said to Reverend Dr. Morgan. "Mr. and Mrs. Otis James . . . they're decent folk, right, sir?"

"Fine couple." He buffed his nails with the linen napkin. "Otis James is first deacon in my church."

"Well, sir, suppose you . . . found out that he was in Snookie Petaway's?"

"Viola?" Nell said, a bit more sternly.

Reverend Dr. Morgan placed the napkin in his lap. He held on to his smile. "How do you know about such things?"

"I don't know personally, sir," she defended.

"It's that gal that come into my church," Reverend Bembrey insisted. "Viola is an impressionable young woman. Filth affectin' decent folk . . ."

"But, Reverend," she said.

"That's enough, Viola," Nell said, reaching for her hand.

"And Miss Day," Viola went on. "Miss Lucy Day. She's a fine, churchgoin' woman, right, sir?"

"She is," Reverend Dr. Morgan answered.

"Suppose she was up in there too? At Snookie Petaway's, I mean."

"That's enough, Viola," Reverend Bembrey said, edging forward in his seat.

"But, sir . . ."

"I said that's enough!" he thundered.

Viola looked at her father and knew that if she stayed a second longer, he would strike her down. And Reverend Baines and Reverend Dr. Morgan would think him justified. Nell grabbed her hand and pulled her out of the room. There would be consequences, Viola knew, but right now, she didn't regret a thing.

Reverend Dr. Morgan smiled politely before he heaved his body out of the chair. "Gotta git hold of that one, Cleveland. She's like a train speedin' down a track. Bedlam is all that can result from a train outta control."

"Sometimes Viola's mouth gets the better . . ."

" 'A fool's mouth is his destruction and his lips are the snare of his soul!' You recognize that one, don't you?" Reverend Baines asked.

"Proverbs eighteen:eleven," Reverend Bembrey said.

"Proverbs eighteen:seven," he corrected. "Study yo' Bible, sir."

Reverend Dr. Morgan placed his hat on his head and followed the small brim around until he broke it comfortably over his left eye. "It's about the foundation, Cleveland. Gotta start with something strong. If not, sometimes you gotta tear down the whole damn building." They walked toward the door, where Nell waited to show them out.

Reverend Bembrey sat in his dark parlor. He ran his hands over his face. "Forsake thy wrath," he whispered to himself. He repeated the scripture again, but still his anger was so strong that it had a presence. He had done everything he could think of to quell this streak in Viola. In the last two years especially, she seemed to buck against plain decency. At least half a dozen times he had punished her for everything from mouthing off at school to staying out past curfew. This was only after cutting a switch didn't work anymore. Then there were the debates about her future and her lack of interest in the teaching college and just about everything else.

There was a soft knock on the door and the creak of hinges, then Nell slipped in and sat on the chair across from his desk. She was rarely any comfort. Subdued, always so damn quiet, the most she could do was sit and agree. In his younger years, that's what he'd wanted in a woman. Now he needed more and he couldn't ask for it. She was a creature of his own making, as fragile and scattered as a pussy willow. She cleared her throat. He hated when she cleared her throat; what would follow wouldn't be worth the dislodging of her spit.

"Donald Hinson gave me a beautiful turkey to dress for tomorrow's dinner. I'm gon' stuff it with corn bread and sage."

"Fine," he grumbled.

"I was thinking of inviting him to dinner. He would truly appreciate a home-cooked meal." She looked down at her hands folded in her lap. For a moment she was silent. "Reverend, sir," she started softly, "the scriptures say, 'But if they cannot contain, let them marry: For it is better to marry than to burn.'"

"Viola isn't studyin' on no Donald Hinson," he replied.

"She has no choice. We've worked too many years for this kind of nonsense. She'll either marry . . . or run."

Reverend Bembrey looked at his wife for the first time since she walked into the room. He really looked at her. Nell, at thirty-nine, was still a pretty woman. Lean, yellow, sharp-nosed. And now she'd given him hope. With the quoting of one small scripture, he noticed how soft her skin looked, and the roundness in her breasts. Somehow her usual scent of honeysuckle, which had often sickened him, was at once as wild and primitive as the natural scents that had flowed from her years ago. They sat across from each other; and when the house was completely dark and the tensions of the day settled, they retired to a place they hadn't visited in over a year.

The Hinson Butcher Yard had started out on two acres of land. It was purchased by Donald Hinson's great-grandfather, Jory B., a former slave, back in 1879. After three generations of Hinsons, all hog men in the proudest sense, the yard had tripled in size. Now it lay in the capable hands of great-grandson Donald, and he was as good at his job as any. In one quick stroke he could behead a hog still on its feet. Then he'd dismember and disembowel it, hooves in one pile, ears and feet in another, and innards thrown into buckets for chitlin dinners.

New Pilgrim had come to know Donald for providing sides of the pinkest pork ribs. Some of the women in the congregation considered him as good a catch as one of his prized Chester Whites. At thirty-three, he was a widower in serious need of tending. Narrow as he was tall, his face wavered on the brink of albinism. A thin black mustache set off the pink around the rims of his eyes and the tiny red spots on his forehead. His rigid exterior put off some of the younger ladies in church, but others, the ones nearing twenty-five with no prospects, swooped down on him, cooking his meals, cleaning his house, or simply watching television with him. Donald was one of the few in Jasperville who owned a floor-size model. The New Pilgrim sisters petted and pampered him, each vying for the Hinson name. Until the Saturday afternoon Reverend Bembrey invited him to come and chat.

Donald nervously removed his hat, then put it back on again before rapping with the small silver knocker. Invitations into the Bembrey home were scarce and usually reserved for other ministers and their wives. Donald kept himself active in church and had been waiting for the day when the Reverend would make him a deacon, but he never thought the honor would warrant an invitation to the Bembrey home.

It was just past two P.M., too late for lunch, too early for dinner, so Donald figured the visit would be brief. Sweet tea, maybe finger sandwiches, perhaps some cookies. He looked down at his high-glossed shoes, then straightened the lapels of his tan suit, glad that it hadn't yet wrinkled in the heat.

"Brother Hinson," Reverend Bembrey said when he opened the door.

"Reverend, sir, thank you for having me."

"Mrs. Bembrey has set up refreshments for us on the back porch. Why don't you follow me out there."

Donald caught sight of Nell snapping peas in the kitchen. "Afternoon, Mrs.," he called.

"Brother Hinson." The wind carried her voice past the mint green chiffon drapes rustling in the afternoon breeze.

The two men stepped onto the back porch, and the Reverend closed the screen door behind him. Then he motioned for Donald to sit. "I'm gon' get right to the point." Reverend Bembrey handed him a cold glass of lemonade. "Now that you've had a suitable amount of time to mourn Clarice's death...lovely woman, Clarice was...I think you should consider getting on with your young life."

Donald gulped like a man used to drinking from Mason jars. He wondered what Clarice's death had to do with being made deacon, but then, important positions in the community were always filled by men with good women. "I have been thinking 'bout askin' to set with Betty Jamison."

"Fine girl, Betty...make the best apple slaw I ever had in my life, but I have someone else in mind."

"Sir?"

"I was thinking more along the lines of Viola."

Donald's mouth fell open. "'Scuse me?"

"Me and the Lord both know that lately she's a been little... spirited, and that's why I chose to talk to you about this, because if anybody can handle my Viola, it's you."

"Me, sir?"

"You're strong, mature, and intelligent...study your Bible and don't indulge in spirits. I know that God has a definite place in your life. Am I right?"

"You are sho'ly right, but..."

"Don't you think she's pretty?"

"Oh...oh, sir...she one of the most prettiest gals I ever did see in my life! She pretty for true...but...well...Viola ain't interested in me, sir."

"I wouldn't be too sure, son. She's still bashful about a lot of things."

"Bashful?"

The Reverend spoke gently. "Like where gentlemen are concerned." Reverend Bembrey laid his hands on his thick chest. "I'm gon' tell you something, Donald, that I never told another living soul outside the family."

Donald leaned forward in his seat. "Yes, sir."

Reverend Bembrey tucked both lips into each other, an expression seen many a Sunday morning on the pulpit. "My wife and I recently had the honor of having Reverend Dr. Morgan visit...."

"That is quite an honor, sir," Donald agreed.

"Yes," Reverend Bembrey went on. "Viola took a notion that she wanted to be a part of the conversation...."

"While men was talkin', sir?"

"To be sure." Reverend Bembrey paused before he went on. "Viola...stood up befo' Reverends Morgan and Baines and actually tried to defend that barrelhouse out there in the sticks. That Snookie Petaway's..."

"Oh, Lord, no."

"Further, I'm afraid that she has taken a fancy to this Daniels woman. The one live out there in the bluff."

"Etta's chile?"

The Reverend nodded like his head hurt. "I had to run the woman off the other day. I come out late one night and they sittin' here on the porch talkin' like they best girlfriends. Etta's chile! Talkin' to my Viola like it was alright."

"Ha' mercy," Donald whispered.

"I knew you would feel that way 'cause you're a lot like me..."

"I am, sir?"

"Rule your house with an iron fist. Don't leave no room for Satan to slide in through your window."

"No, indeed not."

"After that, I knew that it was time Viola settle down. Find herself a good man. One that would protect her future, protect her soul, and set her feet back on the path." He stopped talking and looked into Donald's eyes. "What would you think of joining the family?"

Donald was astounded. "Join the family, sir?"

"Viola can be a handful," Reverend Bembrey went on, "but you have my blessing to handle her whatever way you feel fit in order to maintain the sanctity of a loving household and to keep her on that true and righteous path."

"As in marriage?" Donald asked.

"I can't think of a better man. Of course, Mrs. Bembrey... Nell and I are blessed to offer a generous dowry on her behalf."

Nell. Only a few folks called the Reverend and his wife by their first names. Folks like the mayor, Reverend Dr. Morgan, Reverend Baines, and surely Reverend Lightfoot from Calvary. Donald sat back in his chair and stroked his chin. He had always been the "hog man," and that was honorable, but now he would be much more. He had come here expecting to be made a deacon. A small task next to this one. "Well, sir, there ain't nothin' I want mo' than to be wit' a fine woman like Viola. Nothin'. I jes' hope that she likes me as much as I know I'll like her."

"Oh, she will, son." The Reverend rose and shook Donald's hand, then quickly led him to the front door. "Why don't you start your courtin'... say... next Sunday after church. Dinner with the family, okay?"

"That would be jes' fine, sir." Donald stepped out onto the front porch. "God bless you, Cleveland."

"Bless you, Deacon Hinson."

Nell had a way of beating the carpet like it was personal. She rolled it down the middle aisle of New Pilgrim and out into the sunlight. She draped it over the railing, then spanked it like a rude child, raising a cloud of dust so thick that she could barely be seen behind it.

Inside the church, Viola wiped down the pulpit. She hardly ever did this kind of work. Cleaning New Pilgrim was a job for at least four, and the sisters in the church were always willing to help. They'd happily lemon-polish the pews, dust the insides of the Bible and hymn racks, and smooth any dull blemishes from the stained glass panes. Today there was only Nell and Viola. Nell had even packed a picnic lunch for the occasion.

"Come help me turn the carpet," Nell called. Viola reluctantly walked out, squinting in the sun. She took one side of the dusty carpet, Nell took the other, and the two women flipped it quickly. "Grab that broom and help me, girl," Nell said as she stopped to adjust the scarf tied around her head. The dust mixed with her sweat and made a dark smudge across her forehead. "Last Saturday afternoon when you were at choir rehearsal," she started, "Donald Hinson stopped by."

Viola didn't respond. She slapped the broom against the side of the rug, barely shaking any dust loose.

"He's a good man," Nell went on. "Works as hard as anybody I know. He asked your Daddy's permission to sit with you."

In the two months since Viola's conversation with Reverend Dr. Morgan, there had been no repercussions. Punishment was usually swift, and she knew that after embarrassing her father—and in front of reverends, no less—it would be severe.

"I'm sure I know what the Reverend's answer was," Viola mumbled.

"What about your answer?" Nell asked.

"Does it matter?"

"Of course it matters," Nell insisted.

Viola had always been put off by Donald Hinson. He never spoke much and when he did, it was about hogs. When he waited on the departure line after Sunday services and shook her hand, his palms were damp and cold.

"I always wondered something about Donald," Viola said. She abandoned the broom and sat on the steps.

"Why don't you ask him." Nell's tone brightened. "He certainly wouldn't mind talking to you about anything."

"I wonder how a man can see one of them hogs being born, feed it every day, watch it grow, and then turn around and slit its throat like it was nothing."

"Oh please, Viola," Nell groaned. "You sound like a child. It's what the man does. It's not a testament to his character or anything." Nell swung at the carpet again.

"I think it is."

"That's his job." Nell removed the scarf from her head and wiped her face with it. She reached for her wicker basket, then sat beside Viola on the step. "Think you might be interested in sitting with him?"

"No."

"Why?"

"Because I don't know him."

Nell pulled out a jar of lemonade. Slivers of ice crackled against the sides of the glass container. "That's why a woman sits with a man, Viola. You'll know him in time."

"Like you got to know the Reverend?"

"Exactly." Nell sucked her teeth and sighed. "I left the cups."

"There's got to be some inside," Viola said, welcoming the distraction.

"No bother." Nell popped open the jar and took a long and noisy swig. Viola was stunned at her defiance of propriety. "You rounding eighteen, Viola," she said, "and you have to think about your future, and I don't mean just the teaching college. I mean settling down and keeping a house." Nell set the cold jar on her lap. "I see how you look at that gal . . . that Etta's chile . . . because she dress so bright and talk so fresh, but that's not the kind of life for a lady. All that drinking and being around folks who cuss and cut up. It's not right, Viola. Not for you."

"Most just like the music and live decent lives."

"There is nothing decent about them folks. Nor is it safe in the company of people who stay out at that hour."

"I know that ain't true," Viola said.

"Ain't?"

"Isn't."

"That's what the Reverend says, and I have no reason to doubt him." Nell took another drink from the jar. "You have to make a choice."

"Well, if one of the choices is Donald Hinson, then I'm ready to go straight to hell."

"Viola! Why don't you sit with the man. You might even grow to love him."

"I don't even *like* him."

"How do you know that?" Nell asked.

"I know!" Viola insisted.

"But how do you know for sure?"

"Do you love the Reverend?"

Nell was surprised by the question. "I certainly do."

"Are you sure?"

"Am I sure?!" Nell suddenly looked confused. "He's my husband . . . for heaven's sake, Viola."

Viola looked into her mother's eyes. Eyes that were now moist and angry. Viola wondered if Nell had *ever* felt love for the Reverend. For as long as she could remember, she had never seen a hug, a kiss, or even a heated glance between them. At first, she thought it normal. But as Viola grew older, she noticed other couples in church. Mattie and Alvin Bullock would sit in the pew, arm in arm. Jarvis Mapp would quietly lift his wife's hand and kiss it on the brown side. Even Sister Trench and her husband, Jimmy, as old as they were, would exchange a tender smile. Viola never saw this at home. The saddest part was that now her mother was asking the same thing of her.

Nell fastened the top on the jar of lemonade and placed it in the basket. She angrily wound the rag around her head and started on the carpet again. "I think you should marry Donald," she said. "He'll make you a good husband and set you up in a fine house. Many women would be honored to have him."

"Many women can go to it."

"You are stubborn, Viola," Nell argued. "Stubborn and fresh!"

"And the Lord don't like stubborn and fresh, yes, I know."

Nell gripped a handful of Viola's hair and yanked her head up. "*I* don't like stubborn and fresh," she said.

Viola sat on that top step barely moving. Nell's eyes were full of fire, and Viola had no choice but to look directly into them. They held a desperation that Viola had never seen before.

Nell opened her hand slowly and released Viola's hair. She took tiny sips of air until she calmed herself enough to speak. "If you're not gonna help me," Nell finally said, "then go on home." Viola stood up and looked over her shoulder. "Well, go on!"

Viola could still feel the sting at the top of her head. Her mother had rarely touched her to hug her or to hurt her. Viola started on her way home. She was well up the road when she turned back and saw the little figure of Nell, thrashing the carpet like a woman possessed and no more dust left to lift.

> *Separate house, separate road,*
> *Country mistress carry a separate load,*
> *Got the blues and she know how,*
> *'Cause she take the mess no wife allow . . .*

Viola woke to the sound of a gritty, whispered song she heard in the dark. She sat straight up in bed, listening for a radio somewhere in the house, but the sound came from outside. Still in the fog of sleep, she stumbled to her window and looked out. Isabel was sitting on the back porch right under her screen. She looked like a beautiful spirit as the half moon cast a silhouette of her body. Her legs were folded under her and, as usual, her hair was flying everywhere. Isabel had on that same lavender gingham dress that she'd worn to New Pilgrim. Viola lifted up the screen and looked out.

"Good day for the beach?" Isabel said without turning.

"It's four in the morning," Viola whispered.

"I finished at Snookie's and wasn't in the mood to go home. So I say I want to see my lil' girlfriend. Cain't see you in the light of day when decent folk is around, right?" Isabel pulled her hair back from her face to look at Viola. "Say I'm lyin'." Viola couldn't.

They sat almost cheek to cheek even though Isabel was on the outside. "What was that song you were singing?" Viola asked.

Isabel quietly sang again.

Country mistress don't fuss or fight,
Open the do' and say goodnight,
She lay alone, and she know why,
'Cause her life is nuthin' but a big damn lie . . .

"Sho' 'nuff the blues," Viola smiled.

"Sho' 'nuff Lil' Eartha McClain," Isabel replied with a contented smile. "Can I come in?" she asked. "I'll be quiet as a church mouse."

Viola looked over her shoulder into the room, lit only by the moon. She couldn't imagine what the Reverend would do if he found Etta's chile in his house. But it would be hours before he woke. Viola grabbed the girl's hand and helped her through the window. Isabel landed on the bedroom floor with a thump. Then she heaved herself up and tiptoed through the room, squinting as she tried to make out the detailed carvings in the baseboards and the sleek wood of the dresser.

"I want me a house like this one day. But . . . not here. Not in this town."

"Where you wanna go?" Viola asked.

Isabel sat beside Viola on the bed. Her makeup had worn off, and Viola could make out a patch of freckles on either cheek, and a forehead as round and open as a child's. "Somewhere up No'th," Isabel said. "I figure," she said, leaning back on her open palms, "I get me some mo' time at Snookie's, then I'm gon'."

"Where in the North?"

"Chicago, maybe New York City," she replied.

"You're going to New York City?" Viola asked incredulously.

"Cut my teeth on the road first," Isabel said. "You know, hook up with somebody like Victoria Spivey or Sunnyland Slim, hell maybe I git with Lil' Eartha . . ." Isabel sounded like she was forming the plans as she spoke. "Get me some shows out there first and then I be ready fo' New York." She stretched out across Viola's bed. "Feels so warm here and smells so damn good."

Viola lay beside her. "Miss Rosalee's sister lives in New York."

"Most every singer that come through Snookie's talk about Honeybee . . . since she's from here . . . you know. Hometown girl doin' good and such like that. Folks say the Big House, that's where she live, they say it ain't no joke. It's where singers go to hear singers. Musicians go to hear other musicians."

"Miss Rosalee's sister lives in a nightclub?"

Isabel sucked her teeth and turned her face toward Viola's. She touched the tip of Viola's nose like she would a baby sister's. "It's an after-hours place. Where all the big niggahs go to jam. Make you or break you 'cause ain't nobody walkin' up in the Big House that easy. No, ma'am. Anybody can sing in a club . . . and 'specially if you fuck somebody."

Viola cringed at the word but tried not to show it. The two women lay silently for a moment. Isabel was so still that Viola thought she might have fallen asleep. There were so many questions she wanted to ask her friend. Viola used to confide in Cynthie Nettles, but their friendship had been cut short. Then she started talking to Miss Rosalee, but Miss Rosalee was old, saved, and had never been with a man in her life. That usually limited the things they talked about. "How you come to sing?" Viola asked.

Isabel stretched her arms over her head with a slow yawn. "I was 'bout eight and my mama took me to this picture in Charleston. We got all dressed up and took the bus into town. I never will forget the day we rode on the bus next to folks coming from church, you know . . . *yo'* kinda folks."

"*My* folks?" Viola replied.

"You know what I mean." Isabel pushed her nose up with her finger. Viola laughed. "Me and Mama are on the bus and there y'all are whisperin' and clicking ya teeth and such . . ."

"I wasn't there, Isabel," Viola added.

"But Etta didn't give a damn," she went on. "She just crossed her legs the other way and looked out the window. When we got to the cinema, it was such a pretty place. Them heavy velvet drapes and a big ole crystal chandelier hanging from a ceiling as high as the sky. Suddenly the lights went out and I thought we had to leave. I 'member sayin', 'Mama, somebody done blowed the lights.' Etta hushed me 'cause folks around us was laughing at me in the dark. Them curtains opened and the screen lit up. There was this woman on it . . . she was pretty . . . and her hands were just a movin' when she sang. Movin' like two pretty birds. Her lips opened just wide enough for this song to slip out as easy as butter cream. Lena Horne was her name, and I knew that's what I wanted. I really didn't care if I sang the blues or that white folks' stuff she was singing. Just God make me happy like that. Folks in that movie treated her good. Men talked to her like they jes' wanted to be by her side and call her name. And women actually smiled at her." Isabel turned her head and they were nose to nose again. "That part I didn't believe," she insisted, " 'cause ain't no way in the world a woman look like that could walk down the street with other ladies *smilin'* at her."

"Ladies smile at me," Viola said.

"Church ladies though . . . that's different," Isabel said. "And plus you the Reverend's gal, so they know you ain't gon' fuck they man."

Viola reeled from Isabel's cussing—especially that word. But there was something so honest and straightforward about the girl that Viola didn't really mind. "You still live in Kindred Bluff?"

"Girl, you say Kindred Bluff like it's in the middle of hell. It ain't all folks think it is. Most of the Bluff is pretty. Po' as hell, but there's some good things there."

"I haven't heard about the good things." Viola looked hesitantly at Isabel. "Is it true," she asked. "I mean, what they said Etta had you doin' out there?"

"Suppose it is?"

"What kind of mother is that?" Viola asked.

"Ain't nobody's mama perfect. Etta just didn't know no other kinda life and neither did I."

"You mean having strange men all over you?"

Isabel pulled herself up on the bed. "Might not believe this, Miss Princess Jane," she said, "but one of these days, and even in yo' perfect little life, you might have a strange man doin' things to you too."

"What's it feel like?" Viola said, sitting up beside her.

"What?"

"Having some man . . . you know."

"You how old and ain't never had a man?"

"I'm seventeen, and no," Viola answered. She couldn't quite look at Isabel. "What's it feel like, having somebody . . . put it in?"

"Put it in where?" Isabel asked.

"Where else?"

"Girl, there's a lot a places it can go. I was with one man wanted to stick it in my ear."

Viola wondered if she really wanted to hear any more.

"I swear fo' gawd," Isabel went on. "But he was a different story. Most men want to put it in the place you think or maybe your mouth or—"

"Your mouth!" Viola gasped.

"You git used to it." She walked around Viola's room again.

"Suppose he gets too excited and . . . you know . . . what men do . . ."

"You just pray it happen quick," she said indifferently.

Viola had never met anyone like Isabel and probably never would again. She couldn't stop laughing on this early morning. Every time there was silence, Viola would giggle from the last thing Isabel had said. There had never been such down-and-out honesty in the Bembrey house.

"Come on," Isabel said, opening the screen again and putting one foot through. "Come go with me to the Bluff."

"It's almost five," Viola said. "The sun'll be up soon."

"Oh, come on, Viola, we'll be back befo' nine. Yo' daddy won't even know you been gon'."

"Are you sure?"

Isabel climbed through the window and pulled Viola's arm until she followed. They walked down the dark road hand in hand like two little girls, then climbed into Isabel's tan rusted pickup truck.

After an hour, the sun began to rise and they were in Kindred Bluff. Maybe it was due to the soft light of early morning, but the place seemed peaceful and as pretty as Isabel had said. They drove in and out of heavy patches of fog that covered trees dripping with weeping vines. Viola could smell the ocean. Isabel took her to a small inlet with fertile palms and white sand. They sat on the shoreline and watched the sunrise. The tide came in and out, making its way over their toes and up their ankles. They lay back in the wet sand as the low waves gurgled around their ears.

"I heard you been hurt by some man," Viola said. "Say he left you for dead."

"He didn't leave me fo' dead," Isabel said. "I *was* dead."

Viola nodded; she was beginning to get used to Isabel's bluntness.

"I know exactly when I slipped away," she went on. "One minute I was hurting so bad and the next I was . . . well, I couldn't even feel myself." She chuckled. "You must think I'm crazy, huh?"

"No."

"Etta told me that I had been dead. She said it made me special. Etta said that when I get to heaven, God's gonna make me an angel because I suffered so when I was a child."

"Suppose you don't wind up in heaven?" Viola asked.

Isabel pondered the question. "I never thought about that befo'," she said. "I damn sho' won't start now."

"The Reverend says that when—"

"Excuse me, Viola, but fuck Reverend Bembrey!"

Viola laughed so hard that it sounded like she was singing. Isabel laughed with her. Then they talked about Etta, Nell, heaven, Sister Rosalee, sex, hell, babies, men, and they sang the blues together until well past eight. As they started back to Jasperville, the music continued to play in Viola's head. Then they passed that spot in Kindred Bluff. Isabel stopped to show Viola the sad place in the woods, right beside a hulking angel oak, where she had lived, died, and lived again.

It was after ten P.M. when Viola made her way from the house to the edge of the road. Even the black night ahead didn't make her turn back. Slipping away was the easy part. Now there was at least a six-mile walk before she made that turn by the twin palmetto trees into the woods.

The thought of Isabel and the promise of her song kept Viola's feet walking the path. She had set out last Saturday night but turned back when it began to rain. She thought about getting there with her hair dripping wet and her new white dress plastered to her back and hanging with twigs and wet leaves. That was no way to walk into Snookie Petaway's for the first time.

As far back as Viola could remember, she had heard people talk about the place. Mostly talk about closing it down and boarding it up.

To hear the Reverend tell it, the godforsaken barrelhouse was so base, the music so loud, and the patrons so rowdy that they had been forced to move from the green thicket to the dense black bush. Whenever they managed to close Snookie Petaway's, like the spore of a noxious plant it took root and grew somewhere else.

According to Isabel, those who appreciated Petaway's knew it to be a famous stop for blues players all the way back before Prohibition. Players like Sippie Wallace, Lil' Eartha McClain, Bubber Miley, and Eva Taylor, and the Clarence Williams Blues Five as well as the local singers. On any given Saturday night, Petaway's could ignite the backwoods on raw energy alone.

About a half mile down Route 31, Viola heard a car approaching from behind and quickly stepped off the road and into the green. Certainly she didn't want to explain to anyone why the Reverend's daughter was out walking the road this time of night. The car stopped and her heart raced. It sat on the side of the road with its lights on. The car door opened, and Viola ducked behind a large oak.

"Hey," a woman's voice called. "Viola Bembrey?"

She stepped farther into the bush as a dark figure walked toward her.

"It's me," the voice whispered in the dark. "It's Cynthie."

Viola could now see Cynthie Nettles' two side buns and the frizz that sat right above her forehead. "Cynthie," she called back.

"I knew that was you. What the devil you doin' out here?"

After a long breath, Viola walked toward her. "You got to promise not to say a word to nobody."

"Alright."

"I'm not kiddin', either, Cynthie," Viola warned.

"I said alright."

Viola walked back toward the road and Cynthie followed. "I'm on my way to Snookie Petaway's."

Cynthie laughed. "Where you goin' for real, Viola?"

"I just told you," she said.

Cynthie looked Viola over in her pale pink lipstick and white cotton dress and immediately lost her smile. "Damn!" she said in disbelief.

"Can you carry me to the two palmettos?" Viola asked.

"Are you out yo' mind? I got Leah in the car and we on our way home. Max would break my ass if he found out I even went near Snookie Petaway's. And the Reverend would crucify you."

"Just tell Max you broke down," Viola pleaded.

"I cain't believe you, Viola," Cynthie said.

"Oh, come on, Cynthie . . ."

"Just 'cause you runnin' 'round lyin' to ever'body . . ."

"Oh forget it!" Viola snapped, and started on her way again.

Cynthie got in her car and slowly drove past Viola. Then she stopped and waited until Viola caught up. "Get in," she said, scooting Leah into the backseat. Viola opened the passenger door and slid in beside her. "And listen," Cynthie said soberly. "You didn't see me tonight. I didn't take you nowhere and I don't know a damn thing 'bout what you fin' to do."

"I'm hearin' you," Viola replied.

Leah was quiet, but Viola could feel the three-year-old's eyes burning into the back of her head. "Lord," Cynthie said. She glanced sideways at Viola as she drove. "You used to be 'fraid of everything, Viola Bembrey. So righteous and stuff." Viola sensed that Cynthie was getting satisfaction out of this.

"Wasn't all like that," Viola said, looking out the window.

"When I got pregnant," Cynthie went on, "you stuck up fo' me, that's fo' true. But when you first heard the news, girl, you looked at me like I was bound fo' hell." Cynthie smiled at the recollection. "Gi' me that Bembrey look."

"What?"

"You know what I mean," Cynthie said. "Yo' mama do it, yo' daddy sho' 'nuff do it."

"What are you talking about, Cynthie?"

"The one where y'all look at folks like you scrapin' somethin' nasty off the bottom of yo' shoe." Viola rolled her eyes at Cynthie. "That's the one! That's the look! And here you are on yo' way to Snookie Petaway's. God damn." Cynthie laughed. "I guess you got mo' piss than I thought you had." Cynthie drove for a while without speaking, and that was fine with Viola. After ten minutes or so, the paved road turned gravelly and the trees began to thicken. The farther

Cynthie drove, the more nervous Viola got. She began to wonder if she might see anyone there from church. Part of her wanted to ask Cynthie to turn back, but then Viola thought about Isabel. Cynthie stopped on the side of the dirt road.

"This it?" Viola asked.

"Two twin palmettos." Cynthie pointed.

Viola got out. She looked at the trees as if they were portals to heaven. "Thanks," she said, slamming the door.

"How you gon' git home?" Cynthie asked.

"I'll find a way."

"Cain't believe you, girl," Cynthie laughed. She turned the car back in the direction she came. After her taillights disappeared, there was nothing but black.

The darkness was unnerving when Viola passed between the palmettos and into the bush ahead. She plodded through woods she scarcely knew, pulling as much into focus as the mist-covered moon would allow. There was a small beam of light a ways ahead and off to her left. When she reached the clearing she saw that it was Wayside Baptist Church and knew that Snookie Petaway's couldn't be far. As she walked on, she thought about how ironic it was that the light of Reverend Dr. Morgan's church was leading her right to Snookie Petaway's. She heard a strange rumble in the distance. As she walked toward it, the rumbling seemed to get louder and stronger. It led her past thick loganberry bushes, scratching dashes on her brown ankles, leaves slapping across her face like offended palms. She heard voices and hard laughter, and soon saw a small red glow in the distance. The light turned into another clearing and the thumping grew to a strong rhythmic beat.

The music pulsed from a small lean-to overflowing with people. From where Viola stood, she could see bodies tapping and bouncing to the beat of the place. Arms and legs, elbows and knees thrashing, butts brushing and grinding. Snatches of happy and silly conversation, giggles, guffaws, and downright snorts of hilarity pervaded, but what glued her feet in place was the music. A man's coarse voice pleaded in song as folks yelled back in sympathetic laughter, and the little shack seemed to lift in its spot.

Viola stood with her hands over her mouth. Now that she was

here, she couldn't find the courage to actually go in. She moved a little closer and stood beside several parked cars. Viola recognized Isabel's old truck. She moved in close enough to touch the wood of this place and found a nook where she could watch the faces without them watching her back.

A group of five men played beside the makeshift platform. The eldest wore a red bandanna on his head and had a gap in the front of his mouth so wide that he appeared to be missing a tooth. He was banging a guitar for every one of his years as sweat coursed down his dark face. Another had a melted conk, and locks of wet hair swung in his face. He looked to be eating his mouth harp as he held it to his lips like a slice of ripe honeydew. The drummer was a young boy, no older than fifteen. His elbows were little thicker than his drumsticks and they moved so fast, they blurred in front of him. The singer, in a stained white T-shirt, strutted back and forth across the stage. Justin Moore played the piano. He worked at the filling station in town. Viola rested against a splintery plank, and let her senses absorb the heat and the smell of musty cologne and clean sweat.

"Go on in, sugar," a throaty voice said. Viola turned to see a woman standing beside Isabel's truck, smoking a cigarette.

She wore a black skirt with a large ruffle that hugged her backside. She was as old as Nelvern and brick brown. Her hair was cut above her ears and dyed strawberry blond. "Ain't much fun standing on the outside." She released the smoke. "What, you a little nervous or something?"

"No." Viola held her hands behind her so the woman couldn't see them trembling.

"I'll take you in," she said. "Jes' lemme finish my cigarette here." She leaned against the truck. "You look to be fu'ther from home than I am. Where you from?"

"I'm from here," Viola answered.

"Get on away," she laughed. "Must be *way* on the other side of town."

"Clydie!" a woman's voice called from inside. "Girl, where you go to?"

Viola recognized that voice. She felt as shy as ever, but relieved to see Isabel's pretty face.

"Viola . . . ?!" Isabel said, hugging her. She wore the green satin dress that she had bought at Miss Rosalee's place and those slinky black shoes. "Where in the world you come from?"

"Home," Viola answered.

"Reverend know you here?" Isabel asked.

"What do you think?"

"Reverend?" the woman said. "Why does that make sense?"

"Clydie, this here is Viola Bembrey, my new friend," Isabel said.

"A reverend's chile?" Clydie asked.

"And, Viola," Isabel introduced, "this is Miss Clydie Drummond. She a singer too. Come all the way from Memphis just to sing here tonight. Clydie already did her number and the woman practically to' the stage in two!"

"Girl," Clydie said modestly. She crushed out her cigarette under one red pump.

"Are you stayin' in town?" Viola asked.

"Naw, baby," Clydie answered. "Prob'ly leave tonight. But first I'm gonna hear my girl sing," she said, pushing a lock of hair from Isabel's face. "Best to get on in, 'cause you up next." Clydie walked in and Isabel followed with Viola by the hand.

The temperature was at least twenty degrees hotter at the center of the room. People sat at card tables, end tables, lawn tables. A few men perched on wooden crates with women sitting on their laps. When moved to, folks rose, grabbed hold of each other, and danced where they stood.

Isabel and Clydie had their own table just feet away from the stage. There were several full glasses lined up on top. Clydie pulled a flattened pack of Lucky Strikes from the top of her dress and set it beside one of the glasses.

"You want a drink?" Isabel asked.

"No, thanks," Viola answered.

"We got plenty, as you can see," Isabel said, referring to the glasses.

"Men jes' love givin' Isabel things," Clydie smiled. "Drinks, hams, rent . . ."

"Clydie," Isabel laughed.

"Tell me I'm a lie," Clydie insisted.

"You a lie," Isabel laughed, "but so am I."

Clydie puffed and laughed at the same time, jiggling the cigarette in her mouth.

"Viola does some singing herself," Isabel said.

"That a fact?"

"Not really," Viola said.

"Oh come on, Vi," Isabel said. No one had ever called her Vi. It was warm and friendly, and Viola loved the sound of it. "You shoulda heard her in the choir," Isabel went on. "Had her a solo and I swear, it went straight to Jesus." Isabel lit a cigarette of her own. She was beautiful, Viola thought.

Isabel and Clydie stopped talking when a man stepped up on the platform. The crowd erupted. This was Snookie Petaway himself. He wasn't handsome, but not unpleasant to look at either. In fact, other than his white suit, shirt, and tie, there was nothing really distinguishing about him at all. Yet Viola couldn't stop her cheeks burning from the excitement of being right here at his place.

"I know who y'all come to see . . ." His voice rose above the laughter. "I ain't gon' talk much fu'ther. But I wanna say Isabel—" Men hollered at the mention of her name. She rose from the table and walked toward the platform. Snookie went on, "Isabel gon' come on up—"

"Aw, jes' bring the woman up," someone yelled.

"Shut yo' ass down," Snookie laughed into the mike. Viola laughed right along with the crowd. "Ladies and gentlemen, y'all welcome Miss Isabel Daniels."

Viola could hardly catch her breath. Snookie switched off the two bare bulbs right beside the platform, and the dark room blended with the pitch black of the woods. All that could be seen were the red tips of lit cigarettes. The music started, and when the light came back on, Isabel was standing there. She turned around, and with her backside to the audience, lifted that green satin dress to her thighs, leaned over, and picked up a white feather that rested on the floor right beside one po' de soir shoe. She rose with a slow and sensuous shimmy that made Snookie Petaway's roar at the sight of her.

Treat me right, Daddy, I'll treat you right too,
If you treat me right, Daddy, I'll treat you right too,
I'm the kinda woman, make you feel what a smilin' man do . . .

Sitting on Viola's back porch or singing together on the beach at Kindred Bluff, Isabel had sounded different. Then, her voice was higher and younger. Here at Snookie Petaway's with the band behind her, she sounded more gutsy than sweet.

> *I like to set my man down and rub his tired feet,*
> *Say, I like to set my man down and rub his tired feet,*
> *But if you do me wrong, Papa, I'll find someone else to*
>   *take yo' seat . . .*

This couldn't be real. Viola couldn't actually be sitting here in Snookie Petaway's, listening to Isabel sing the blues onstage. She grabbed her mouth to stop herself from yelling out with the rest of the audience.

"Ain't she the slickest thing you ever did see?" Clydie asked.

"She's so good," Viola answered.

> *Sometimes a woman take all the mess she could,*

"Slow it down, baby," a man yelled.

> *Say, sometime a woman take all the mess she could,*
> *And if that woman stay, it's 'cause the lovin' is so*
>   *damn good . . .*

The band took over. Isabel stepped down from the stage and grabbed the hand of a tall man in a rumpled gray suit. She pulled him onto the platform, threw her arms around his neck and danced close to him.

"Hey, Edgar," a baldheaded man yelled out. "You's a lucky son of a bitch!"

"Just don't fo'git where you got him from, baby," a woman yelled to Isabel.

Viola saw nothing less than happy faces and good times. People dancing, talking close, bodies swaying. A handsome man in alligator shoes and a wide brim hat had pulled up a chair beside Clydie and was whispering in her ear. Clyde threw back her head and laughed.

Viola liked it here. She liked the energy, the people, but more than anything, she loved the music.

Isabel stepped up to the mike again, and the man was now dancing onstage all by himself.

> *Treat me right, baby, I'll treat you right too,*
> *If you treat me right, baby, I'll treat you right too,*
> *I'm the kinda woman, make you feel what a smilin' man do . . .*

Viola could hardly keep herself still, and swayed with the rest of the room. She eased one of the sweaty glasses toward her and sipped it slowly. At first it tasted watery from the melted ice, and then the heat stung the inside of her cheeks. The man beside Clydie stood up and offered his hand to Viola.

"Go'n and have some fun, baby," Clydie said, pushing her shoulder.

The stranger pulled Viola up and led her just a few inches away from the table. He wrapped one arm around her waist, and they moved slowly to Isabel's song. Most everyone was dancing now. Edgar was still onstage behind Isabel, but his wife had joined him.

> *I set my man down, rub his shoulders side to side,*
> *I set my man down and rub his shoulders side to side,*
> *But if you do me wrong, Daddy, it'll be time for you to*
>   *take a ride . . .*

"Dance, girl," Viola heard Isabel call from the stage.

Viola moved easily to the music. Each sip of the strong, clear liquid made the next dance smoother, and the voices around her friendlier. At first Viola feared she'd see someone she knew here. It didn't matter now. She couldn't care less about Kindred Bluff, the Reverend, or New Pilgrim. Isabel was her friend. One who helped her into the truck right before the sun came up, drove her home, and poured her through her own bedroom window.

The screen in her bedroom was still ajar. Her white dress, slung over the foot of the bed, was tinged with the ripe and smoky air of

Snookie Petaway's. Viola stretched the sleep from her body. Last night's blues still hummed inside of her. She thought about the words of Isabel's song, and shuddered at the desperation behind them.

"Viola," Nell called from the hall. "The Reverend wants you outside."

The music in her head stopped. Saturday morning chores, she thought. Viola pulled herself from bed and into a pair of jeans and a cool cotton top. She wished she could stay with the music, with Isabel, Clydie, and Snookie Petaway, if only in her head, just a little longer. Viola opened the bedroom door. As she walked the cool, buffed halls of the Bembrey house, it seemed strangely quiet this morning. She heard no water running or hedge clippers chopping, nor did she hear the whir of the lawn mower outside. Just the sound of her feet on the shiny wood floor and the constant ticking of the hall clock.

Viola turned into the kitchen and saw Nell sitting at the table with a coffee cup in front of her.

"What's going on?" Viola asked.

"Good morning to you too," Nell said without looking up.

"Excuse me. Good morning." Viola looked out and saw the Reverend standing in the front yard talking to Deacon Best. "Why is Deacon Best here so early?" Viola asked.

"I'm not exactly sure. He came to get your daddy a couple of hours ago. They went out and just got back. The Reverend didn't say where they went or anything, he only told me that he wanted you outside."

"But why!?"

"Don't ask no more questions, Viola," Nell snapped, "just go on."

Viola walked out onto the porch to find the Reverend standing in the driveway in front of the deacon's car. Deacon Best nodded at her politely.

"I'll see you over at the church, Reverend," he said. Then he got into his car and drove away.

Reverend Bembrey opened the passenger side of his own car for Viola.

"Something wrong, sir?" she asked.

"Get in," he said flatly. He walked around the car and got into the driver's seat. It wasn't until he pulled onto the main road that he turned to look at her. "A woman was found in the woods this morning," he said. "Beaten so badly that no one even knows who she is."

"In the woods?" Viola asked.

"Deacon says she must be a transient, not from around here, because no one recognizes her."

"It's a terrible thing," she said sadly. "But, Reverend, sir . . ." Viola treaded lightly. "What's this got to do with me?"

"Look like one of them party people. Seeing as yo' *friend* Isabel is one of them kinda folks, I thought maybe she can help us identify this woman."

"Isabel lives way out in the Bluff."

"One of the deacons went to fetch her," he said.

They pulled up to the church, where a few sisters were milling outside. Viola warily followed the Reverend down the aisle of New Pilgrim. Mr. Bainbridge, the undertaker, was standing by the altar in front of something draped in a white sheet stained with drops of blood and oil.

"Find out who it is, sir?" Bainbridge asked.

"Not yet." Reverend Bembrey stood with his hands dangling in front of him and his fingers woven together. The sheet over this woman outlined a forehead, breasts, and the tips of feet.

"Need to take the body to the morgue," Mr. Bainbridge said.

"Give us a few minutes," the Reverend said to him.

"I'm just sayin', Reverend, that this ain't the kinda sight for a young woman. Body need to be at the morgue."

"Please, let us alone, Mr. Bainbridge," the Reverend said.

Viola shifted from one foot to the other. She understood the Reverend's plan. He had brought her here to see something that was supposed to scare her into submission. Fine, she thought. There'd be a speech about hell and what was going to happen if she didn't straighten up, and on and on and on. She had heard it all before. Then he'd raise the sheet on some woman pickled from liquor, some poor woman who would never wake up and whose tortured soul was now searching for somewhere, anywhere that was cool and familiar. Lord, help her, whoever she was.

There were no speeches. The Reverend unlaced his fingers and flipped back the sheet. Viola couldn't gasp because her breath fell back inside and almost choked her. She backed away from the naked woman, whose mouth was twisted into her neck. Her eyes were closed and her nose was nearly not there, but the thing that caused Viola to lose her water and weep like a baby was one bloodied foot still wedged in a po' de soir shoe.

Forestine lined up her peas alongside her mashed potatoes like the spokes of a wheel, while Lilian talked on. She and Lucas came to dinner the first Sunday of every month. The conversation was usually about things like hemming drapes or cleaning turnip greens. Tonight Lilian chattered about needlepoint pillows and crocheted blankets. When she stopped talking to get her husband's opinion, Lucas looked up from his plate just long enough to say, "Yes, Lil."

"At first I thought they were just a bunch of old ladies," Lilian prattled, "but Miss West can make just about anything with a pair of knitting needles."

Hattie pushed a chunk of meat loaf into her mouth. "I ain't got the patience to set with them biddies and they colored threads and them damn thimbles."

"Them *biddies* know what they doing, Mama," Lilian said. "Mrs. Simon sold one of her quilts, the one with the American flag in the center . . . sold it for fifty whole dollars."

Forestine looked over at Willie. His eyes had glazed over. Lucas held his head down and, like always, she could only see his forehead and the bridge of his nose. Then he glanced up and caught Forestine's eye. Lucas flashed a tiny smile, then lowered his head again.

"Miss West promised she'd help me crochet a blanket," Lilian went on. "She got this pattern from the Simplicity...."

"Didn't know Simplicity did crocheted stuff," Hattie said.

"Oh, yeah, Mama," Lilian replied, "but when she asked me what color yarn I wanted, I told her that I wasn't sure if the baby would be a boy or girl...."

Willie looked up from his plate. "What you say?!" he mumbled.

"You heard me, Daddy," Lilian smiled.

Hattie stopped chewing. Out of her open mouth came a squeal that caused Forestine to put her hands over her ears. Then Hattie jumped up from the table. She hopped up and down in place like she had the Holy Ghost. "I knew it," she yelled. "I just knew it! Knew it 'cause I felt it right here," she said, pounding her chest. "Dreamt of fish last week and everything, remember, Willie? Told you the next morning I dreamt of fish. Tell 'em, Willie."

"Did say something 'bout some mackerel," Willie confirmed.

"Hallelujah, hallelujah!" Hattie yelled.

"Congratulations," Willie said, reaching across the table to shake Lucas's hand.

"Now hold on, Mama," Lilian said.

"Hold on what, baby?" Hattie cried.

"It's not official yet."

"You miss yo' visitor this month?" Hattie asked.

"Well, yes, but..."

"Then it's official," Hattie yelled. "And it's gon' be a pretty baby too," Hattie insisted. "She'll have that good hair like Lucas and them pretty brown cheeks, jes' like my baby."

Forestine was happy for her sister. She got up from the table to hug Lilian, and when Lucas stood, she hugged him too. Since they'd been girls, Lilian had always talked about having children. She'd spend hours combing her dolls' hair and arranging their clothes. Then she'd take them all, including Holly Hobby, Sassy Sue, and all her friends, and tuck them into her bed. She'd insist that everyone in the apartment speak in a whisper until nap time was over. Forestine never got into that doll-baby stage. Until she discovered music, she mostly read. She once found a book about Josephine Baker and read it so many times that the back cover began to flake away.

"Even though it isn't *official*," Lilian smiled, "I have been thinking about some names."

"Do tell," Hattie said.

The conversation began to bore Forestine again and her thoughts started to drift. Her mind was like a hi-fi; she could drop on an album and just sit and listen. Lately it had been songs by Lil' Eartha. Since she hadn't been able to rehearse the tunes with Nick, they sometimes skipped in places or the voice slowed and then stopped altogether.

"How about Patricia for a girl or Brent for a boy?"

"Brent?!" Willie put in. "What kinda name is that fo' a colored chile. Sound like a butler."

"Shut up, Willie," Hattie snapped.

"What about jes' plain ole Lucas," Willie suggested. "Or better yet, how 'bout Willie?"

"One Willie in the family is enough," Lilian giggled.

"What you got to say, Forestine?" Willie asked.

"I say yes," she answered absently.

"Yes?" Willie replied. "That's a funny name fo' a chile."

While the conversation swirled around her, Forestine thought about Nick. Whenever he came to mind, she forced herself to think of the good times. She hadn't gone to see him in over three weeks. Not seeing Nick was such a change in her life that Forestine began to feel displaced. She wasn't quite sure where to go now or what to do with herself. She missed him, but more than that, she desperately missed his music.

"I think I still might have a couple of my old maternity dresses," Hattie said, "back from when I was pregnant with Forestine. Lord, but I musta gained close to sixty pounds then . . ."

"I wanna buy new dresses, Mama," Lilian said.

Forestine excused herself from the table and went outside to sit on the bench. It was quiet tonight, no conga drums or cow bells. She tapped lightly on the tar with her heel, trying to duplicate the blues in her head, then hummed a song from Eartha's album called "Sittin' Pretty." The song would be perfect for Lester's Pub, but Forestine couldn't quite get it down. Though she had taken to closing the door to her room and going over some songs alone, it wasn't the same. After just minutes with Nick, she'd have had that song down pat.

Forestine looked up to find Lucas Campbell standing on the steps of the building, lighting a cigarette. She didn't even know he smoked. He looked at her and smiled, then approached the bench.

"Evenin'," he said awkwardly.

"Hey," she answered.

"Pretty night."

"Yep."

This was about as much as she had ever said to Lucas. Without Lilian by his side, he looked taller and friendlier.

He rested one hand against the side of the bench. "I saw you over at Lester's Pub last night."

"You were at Lester's?"

"I go by every now and then to hear the music. Actually, I saw you a few weeks back too," he went on. "That's why I went back last night."

"Why didn't you say hey or something?" she asked, surprised.

"So many people were around you, shaking your hand and everything. I figured I'd see you today at Sunday dinner." Lucas sat down beside her. His manner was surprisingly pleasant. "You know, Lilian told me that you sang some but, whew . . ." he said, smiling. "I can't recall hearing anyone sing like that."

Except for Willie and Nick, Forestine had rarely heard a man say good things about her.

"I was thinkin'," he said, "if you ever want . . . I'm sure I can't . . ." He took a breath to get his words just right. "I mean to say that, if you ever want me to play the piano for you, I'd be honored."

"Play for me?" she asked.

"I know I'm not the best piano player but—"

"I didn't mean it like that," she said. "I just mean that . . . I never even thought about that before." She looked down at her hands resting in her lap. "You know any blues songs?" she asked.

"Oh, hell, yeah," he smiled.

Forestine hadn't realized that Lucas had such a charming smile. Perhaps because he hardly ever used it.

"No lie?" she asked.

"No lie," he answered.

"Any Lil' Eartha?"

" 'Make Me Say Yes,' " he started, " 'Oh Me,' 'Country Mistress,' 'As Blue as It Gets' . . ."

She turned to look at him. "I cannot believe you know all of that Lil' Eartha stuff." She smiled. "Why didn't you tell me?"

"I guess the subject never came up," he said.

"Every Sunday," she smiled, "we sit across from each other at the table like zombies." They both laughed.

"So what do you think?" he asked.

"I think . . . sure," she laughed. "But I wouldn't want to come around disturbing Lilian, especially if she's in a family way."

"I got the keys to the school," he said. "We could go over there any time."

"You know 'Sittin' Pretty'?" she asked.

"I listen to that one, but I haven't played it. I'm sure I can figure it out, though."

"I been trying to work that song for weeks now," she said. "Just can't get that middle part . . ."

"Something like, '*Only when you lonely and can't find the light,*' he said.

" '*And you pray, but you stay in the same ole way,*' " she sang.

"Damn you," he laughed.

"You know the song, alright," she smiled.

They sat quietly for a moment. Lucas looked over his shoulder toward the third-floor window and then back at Forestine. "I bet Lilian is going to be busy for hours talking about babies and everything . . ."

"Yeah."

"Probably wouldn't even notice if I left for a while . . ."

She was amused by the thought. "What you saying?"

He shrugged his large shoulders. Lucas stood up from the bench and nervously jingled the change in his pants pocket.

"You mean, go over to the school now?" she asked.

"Why not?"

"Right now, you say?"

"I mean, just for a few minutes. Probably only take a minute to work the song out."

"Just a minute or two," she said, rising.

"I'm parked right out there on Atlantic Avenue." His walk was leisurely at first, but when he spotted his car, he seemed to gallop, and Forestine skipped to keep up. Lucas opened the passenger door and waited until she got in, then crossed to the driver's side. Before he pulled out, he clicked on the radio and "Please, Please, Please" by James Brown charged into the car.

"James Brown," she said, closing her eyes.

"Some spiffy cat, huh?" Lucas smiled.

Forestine could see that her time at Lester's was turning her into quite a sophisticate. At the club, they might say James Brown was righteous, outta sight, or just plain dangerous. But spiffy?

"That cat James Brown came on the scene," Lucas went on, "set it clean on fire."

If Forestine hadn't known better, she would have sworn that Lucas Campbell was trying to impress her by talking like a fool. But why? The only man who had ever wanted her was as blind as a bat. Lucas actually seemed excited by her presence. Like what she said, and how she felt, mattered to him.

Five minutes later they stood at the entrance of P.S. 287. Lucas unlocked the front door with a heavy set of keys and snapped on the lights. Though it was a weekend, the halls still smelled like a cafeteria: the odor of tomato sauce and Spam. Forestine hadn't set foot in this school in over six years. The cream plastered walls and rusted lockers extended as far as the eye could see. Each room they passed looked the same as it had years ago. The desks now seemed minuscule but even then, Forestine had had to turn her legs sideways and sit with her feet in the aisle. Of course the kids laughed. They always laughed. Forestine had tried to convince herself that the remarks made by her classmates about how big and ugly she was didn't hurt. Now, walking these halls provoked a surge of emotion she hadn't expected.

Lucas unlocked the music room door and clicked on the lights. A piano sat in the far corner. The desks were pushed back against the walls, and several chairs and black metal music stands stood in the middle of the floor. The words for "Down by the Riverside" were written in three neat verses on a green chalkboard that extended across the whole front of the room. A light layer of chalk dust fell from its ledge and powdered most of the floor underneath. Lucas began to take the sheet music from a couple of the stands and push some of the chairs back toward the desks.

"My domain," he said nervously.

"I see." Forestine stood in the center of the room with her arms folded across her body. "Mrs. Dexter," she recalled. "That was the name of my music teacher."

"She retired about five years before I got here," Lucas said.

"Good. If I'da listened to that woman, I wouldn't be singing today."

"Why?"

"She told me I had a 'lovely voice,'" Forestine mocked, "but said I didn't have the 'essential tools.'"

"And that means what?" Lucas asked as he sat down on the piano bench.

"You're very kind," she said as she sat beside him.

Forestine could feel his anticipation as Lucas lightly touched the keys with one hand. He nervously glanced at her. Then he placed both hands on the keyboard and his fingers skidded across, all the way to the end, where the notes were so high that she could hear the hollow sound of his finger striking the ivory. This was a familiar sight. Lucas Campbell sitting at the piano . . . just like in church, only the music was different. It wasn't gospel. It wasn't even the blues. It was jazz. Soon, his whole body relaxed into it.

"I don't know this song," she said over the music.

"That's because I'm making it up," he said. "It's called improvisation."

Forestine wasn't used to words like that. Educated men's words. Nick's way of teaching was as old and primitive as he was. Now Lucas riffed in a bluesy style. His hands, big as plates, maintained a light touch against the piano keys. "This is what they call barrelhouse." He switched again and the music was tinkly and playful, like the background of a silent movie. "This is called rag," he explained. "Ever hear of Cripple Clarence Lofton?" Forestine hadn't. "This is how he plays."

She could hardly believe that he could make all these types of music come alive. Every other Sunday she sat across the table from this man without even knowing. "I woulda never thought." Forestine smiled.

"Thought what?"

"That you had talent like this. You're always so quiet."

"Well, so are you. I mean, you're quiet until it comes time to sing, and then look out world!" Lucas's fingers glided playfully across the keys while Forestine laughed out loud. And not that dainty titter that Hattie told her was polite for a woman, but the guttural kind that started way down at the bottom of her body and rose to the top of her hot-pressed head.

"There's something else too," he said. He stopped playing and removed his glasses. "When I saw you singing, you made me seriously think about what I really wanna do with my life. But . . . I don't have the nerve. You are some brave woman."

"I'm brave?!" she laughed.

"Oh yes. If I could do what I really wanted, it would be exactly what you're trying to do. I would play jazz and travel and . . . whew, you are brave, Forestine Bent."

"You mean to tell me that all this time that you were sitting in church playing 'The Old Rugged Cross' you been wanting to play Cripple Clarence Lofton?"

"At least," he laughed.

Lucas seemed an entirely different man, no longer just an extension of Lilian. His body was solid and strong. His lips were full and his eyes deep, with an intense curiosity in the hazel flecks. His large shoulders danced, almost comically, but with a pure joy in the awkward groove. This was a side of Lucas Campbell that Lilian would never, ever know.

Lucas looked down at his hands now resting quietly on the keys. "I don't know when I'm going to get to talk to you again like this, Forestine," he said. "So I'm going to tell you what else I think too." He paused to summon his courage. "Lilian is a fine woman. She's been a good wife in many ways. I only hope that this time she *is* pregnant so I can give her the children she wants so bad, but . . ." He shook his head. "Since that first time I saw you at Lester's Pub, you've been on my mind. I know what people call you," he said, turning toward her. "They say you a big girl. Say you plain and all, but . . . I always thought you were different from all the rest and when I heard you sing . . ." His smile lit up his whole face. "I'm not gonna do wrong by Lilian. Like I said, she's a good woman." He finally looked straight at her. "But I just wanted to be close to you, Forestine. To let you know."

Forestine was dumbstruck. Sitting beside him felt good, for reasons beyond the music. She liked the way he spoke, the strength of his hands, and the way his shoulders touched her own. She liked the sound of his voice when he told her pretty things about herself, and the way their laughter mixed. But more than anything, she loved that feeling that shot straight through her when his calf brushed against hers.

"I think we better get on home," she said.

Lucas stood up. He looked everywhere but at her, and she knew that he felt like a fool for opening himself up like he did. He pulled the noisy key chain from his pocket and opened the door that led back to the hall. He was about to snap off the light when Forestine stepped in front of him. She wanted to see his face, and not just from the side as she had at the piano or the dinner table. When she looked him in the eyes, Forestine recognized some of the same insecurities she felt every day of her life. Not measuring up, having the talent but, in his case, not the courage. Forestine put her arms around Lucas and he drew her in so close that she could lay her head on his chest. It felt good to lay her head against someone's chest. Then he gently tugged her downward. Forestine's hesitation made him stop, but just for a moment. He pulled her onto the chalky floor, surrounded by all the tiny wooden desks and ugly memories of taunting children. When he kissed her, the voices quieted. When he made love to her, they disappeared.

Lucas pulled his pants up around his waist. The music room's acoustics made the chiming of his belt reverberate like a xylophone. Forestine had heard that sound before, the chiming of a man's belt. It meant that Willie was home and changing out of his uniform. But this ring was a little different. It was her sister's husband closing his pants.

Forestine lay on the cold linoleum, looking up at the ceiling. The bottom half of her body felt different now. Open. Overwhelmed. At once, she felt desired and pretty, like she was part of some kind of girls' club that she had never gained entrance to before now. But the top half, the part that held her heart and her guilt, felt she had violated some sacred code. Lilian might not be her friend, but she was still her sister.

Forestine pulled herself up and rested her back against one of the school chairs. Lucas lay on his side now, with his back to her. After her encounter with Nick, Forestine had felt mostly sad. Now she felt ashamed. Not only had she foreseen what would happen, she had initiated it. She could hear Willie saying, "You jes' want what you want, Forestine, and you don't think about the consequences." She didn't even want to consider what would come out of Hattie's mouth.

Then there was Lilian. Though she and her sister didn't get along, Forestine wouldn't have dreamed of hurting Lilian in this way.

Lucas sat up. He pulled both knees into his chest. "Isn't anybody's fault," he said, "not yours, not mine."

At that moment Forestine didn't want to hear a sound. No voices. Even music would be intrusive.

Lucas lifted himself from the floor. He offered his two hands and pulled Forestine to standing. "There's a little mirror on the wall there past my desk," he said, pointing.

Forestine walked over, but couldn't look at herself. She stood on the opposite side of the room from Lucas as they pulled themselves together. When she finished, he was waiting at the door. He had one hand on the knob and the other in his pocket.

"Probably need to get going," he said.

"Yep."

"I'm sure Lilian's pitching a fit," he said.

Her sister's name made Forestine flinch.

He opened the door but stopped Forestine before she stepped out. "We won't mention this to . . . anyone, will we?"

"No."

Lucas lifted her chin and looked into her eyes. "Don't feel bad, Forestine. I loved spending this time with you."

Forestine wished she could say the same. This was her second encounter with a man, and again, she felt only sadness and guilt. That's not the way it was supposed to be.

"We didn't get to practice your song," he said, smiling.

"No."

"You really are something, Forestine. And don't take this the wrong way," he went on, "but I want to get together with you again." She turned away. "To *rehearse*," he said. "This was something that happened. Something wonderful, but I'd be just fine if we got together to practice only."

"I don't know."

Lucas took his glasses from the top of the piano and placed them on his nose. Just that quickly, he became the Lucas she was used to seeing with Lilian. An hour ago, his body had radiated heat and his voice had been full and deep in his chest. Now he was the same man who sat hunkered over his plate every other Sunday evening. Somehow the sight comforted Forestine. This was a different Lucas. One she probably wouldn't have noticed in a lifetime.

"Sorry I can't sit for dinner, Mama," Forestine called into the kitchen. "I told Mrs. Moore I'd help her clean that lot on Dean Street." Forestine walked quickly toward the door and Hattie followed. She reached up, grabbed Forestine by the earlobe and led her back into the living room past Lucas, Lilian, and Willie. Hattie only released her when Forestine lowered herself into one of the armchairs.

"You can clean all the lots you want *after* dinner," Hattie snapped. Then she went back into the kitchen.

Lucas and Lilian sat on the sofa and Willie in the other armchair, watching the baseball game. Forestine hadn't seen Lucas or Lilian in two weeks. Now she sat face-to-face with them both. Forestine tried to watch the game. The players just seemed to stand on their bases and wait. She could feel Lucas's eyes on her, but felt if she returned his glance, even for a moment, their secret would be known. Lilian was surprisingly quiet tonight. She sat beside her husband, twirling her hair around her little finger and staring absently at the TV.

"Help me bring some of these bowls to the table," Hattie called to Forestine. Without being asked twice, Forestine went into the kitchen. It seemed strange to be in a quiet room when Lilian was around. Forestine began to think that maybe she had an idea about what happened. She looked at her sister across the room twirling and releasing the lock of black oily hair.

"Willie," Hattie called. "Come bless the table."

"Inning almost over," he mumbled.

"Inning *is* over," Hattie said, clicking off the TV. Without batting an eye, Willie rose and sat down at the head of the dinner table. Lucas and Lilian took their usual seats, and Forestine sat across from Lucas.

After grace, Forestine looked up to find Lucas's eyes on her. They begged her, with that soft glare, not to turn away. Lilian passed him a bowl of macaroni salad, and his attention was taken.

"Why you so still, Lilian?" Hattie asked.

"Yeah," Willie put in. "Ain't seen you this quiet in . . . shit, forever."

"Please, Daddy," Lilian whispered.

Forestine felt Hattie's suspicion hovering above the table like a thick cloud. "What's wrong, baby?" Hattie asked.

Lilian looked at Lucas, then back at her mother. "I know I shoulda told you this sooner, Mama," Lilian started, "but I got my period a few days ago."

Forestine let out a quiet sigh of relief.

"Oh, honey," Hattie consoled. She pushed away from the table and hugged Lilian from behind. "Baby doll, I'm so sorry."

"Damn shame," Willie put in.

"Why didn't you call and tell me?" Hattie asked.

"Just didn't want to talk to nobody." Lilian used a paper napkin to dab the corners of her eyes.

"I understand," Hattie said. "But you a young woman. And lil' babies," she said, "they have a way of coming when they s'posed to. It'll happen befo' you even know it. Right, Willie?"

"And even if it don't," he added, "y'all have yo'selves a time trying."

"Shut up, fool," Hattie snapped.

"Maybe Daddy's right for a change," Lilian said. She reached for Lucas's hand across the table.

"There's my girl," Hattie cooed.

"There is one good thing though," Lilian said.

"What's that?" Hattie asked.

"I saw the Avon lady today."

Lucas looked down into his plate. Lilian went on about moisturizers. Life, as Forestine had known it, continued. She didn't rehearse with Lucas again, and only saw him at those awkward dinners with the Campbells every other Sunday. The high point of Forestine's week was singing at Lester's on Saturday nights. It was the *only* point in her life. She didn't see Nick anymore, and even the Puerto Ricans hadn't been around lately. The Kings County projects were getting smaller and smaller. The Brooklyn summer heat seemed to be choking her. So when Lil' Eartha McClain pulled up in her bus two months later, Forestine didn't hesitate for a second. She didn't even ask which way they were headed. When Eartha opened the door to the Caravan, Forestine jumped aboard.

CHAPTER 6

Women in Jasperville raided their gardens. Flower shops in Bell-wood, Hooley, and Camden Counties delivered crates of yellow and white roses, amaryllis, and lilies to the New Pilgrim Baptist Church. Orchids and gardenias arrived from Columbia and Charleston. New Pilgrim blossomed with nearly every yellow and white fresh flower in the state of South Carolina. Yellow and white flowers only. Nelvern Bembrey insisted on it. Viola's bridal gown was flown in from New York, as were the lemon satin bridesmaids' dresses. Miss Rosalee spent nearly a month altering the gowns so that each fit just right.

Canopied tents of billowing white chiffon shaded the manicured back lawn of the Bembrey house. For the reception here, Nell had laid out a dozen rows of tables covered with white tableclothes and topped with glass bowls of floating gardenias. Between each bowl a tapered white candle sat in a silver holder. Ivory linen napkins, bone china, and crystal stemware framed every place setting. Yellow and white fresh flowers strayed through the alleys between the tables and spilled over the rims of huge golden vases marking the entrances and exits of the tent. Nell hired a catering company from Spartanburg that had handled the governor's daughter's wedding. They designed a cake with ascending amber rosettes that started at the bottom of three tiers and wound upward toward a porcelain bride and groom standing in soft white butter cream. The only exception to Nell's color scheme was her own garden of red roses and the backdrop of Hopper Hill. But, red and green aside, all in Jasperville would agree that the wedding of Viola and Donald Hinson was the grandest since Nell had married Cleveland Bembrey some twenty years ago.

The bride herself looked as picture-perfect as the reception. Viola felt like a doll in an elaborate doll's house. Her two bridesmaids, Mabel, Reverend Dr. Morgan's niece, and Effie-Lynn, a deacon's granddaughter, she had met only once or twice in her life. Viola would've preferred Miss Rosalee and Cynthie Nettles be her bridal attendants, but the Reverend insisted that Miss Rosalee was too old and the likes of Cynthie Nettles was unacceptable. So Viola stood with two women who she could've passed on Main Street with no more than a polite hello.

Viola looked across the table to where the Reverend was chatting with Congressman McNair and Nelvern was talking to Mrs. Reverend Baines. Everyone here was a friend or colleague of the Reverend. With the exception of Reverend Lightfoot from Calvary and Mayor Everson, the whole town seemed to be present. Reverend Lightfoot was said to be out of the country and Mayor Everson sent his deputy along with a lovely silver tea service.

Viola had felt numb since the moment she woke up. Nell guided her through every step and stood back only when Viola walked down the aisle of the New Pilgrim Church. The pews, the altar, and even the Reverend's dais, all dotted with white lilies and baby's breath, appeared odd and plastic. But the strangest sight of all was Donald Hinson standing at the altar, smiling like they were so in love and eager for a long, full life together.

She wearily looked around from her bride's throne. Viola felt her smile beginning to melt. In quiet moments she saw Isabel's face. After seven months, the thought of the woman still reduced her to tears. Only after seeing Isabel, battered and broken, did Viola realize how right Nelvern was. Isabel's life, although exciting at times, had brought her nothing but pain. Because of it, she died an even worse death than her mother Etta.

Donald reached for his wife's hand across the table. She jumped at his touch. "You okay there, Mrs. Hinson?" he asked with a smile. Viola nodded. He pulled her from her seat and led her to the thirty-square-foot wooden floor set up for dancing. He drew her in close, put his lips to her ear, and whispered, "I've never seen a mo' beautiful woman." Viola knew that he liked the picture they made. He liked to appear to have a secret only a new husband could whisper. As far as she could tell, he complimented her beauty because he didn't have much of anything else to say. The only other things he ever spoke of were scriptures and swine. His favorite verses were from the book of John. More than a few times, Viola held the Bible to test his memory while he recited and, of course, she'd pretend to be impressed by his skill.

Viola spoke mostly about her days at the teaching college, about the curriculum or her new students at the lower school. Sometimes she and Donald would walk the half mile to Glover's Creek, where they'd sit on the bank and throw stones in the water. Donald wasn't fond of spending money. The most expensive thing they did was go into town for some ice cream. Viola liked rum raisin, strawberry, or rocky road, but for Donald, it was always the same vanilla.

Donald held her so close while they danced that she could feel the stubble on his cheek. Through layers of lace and crinoline, Viola felt him stiffen against her thigh, and her pulse quickened. She had come to accept the idea of the marriage, heaven, and the community's good wishes, but the thought of the wedding night made her heart race. He pecked her lightly on the lips and then escorted her back to her seat. After a quick caress, he crossed the room to talk with a group of reverends.

For a moment, Viola was actually able to sit alone. Most people were dancing or moving about the yard. She kicked off one ivory satin shoe and separated her toes from what felt like a permanent point. The silver teeth in the tiara above her veil burrowed into her scalp, and her birthday pearls hung heavy around her neck.

Suddenly she felt hands on her shoulders. Viola wanted to scream for whoever it was to go away. But the hands softly kneaded the kinks from her neck. They were good hands, understanding hands.

"Just a lil' while longer, baby," Miss Rosalee whispered. "Hold on jes' a lil' longer." She sat down and pulled Viola's uneaten piece of cake in front of her. Miss Rosalee scooped up a dot of white frosting on her finger and held it out for Viola to taste.

"No thanks," Viola said wearily.

"Ain't even had a piece of yo' own wedding cake," she said. Behind her cat-eye glasses, she had on blue eye shadow to match her chiffon dress. Miss Rosalee rarely wore makeup, and when she did, it always seemed heavy and out of place. "Nelvern say y'all waitin' awhile befo' you take yo' honeymoon."

"This is Donald's busy time at the yard," Viola answered. "He promised we'll go to New Orleans in a couple of months."

"Kinda hot in New Orleans this time of year anyway." Miss Rosalee took a forkful of cake. "I do declare," she said after swallowing, "you, Viola Hinson, are actually a married woman now." Miss Rosalee wore a big smile. "And having a husband . . . well, that there is a big responsibility. I ain't never had one myself," she allowed, "but I think I'm old enough to say that it ain't no easy thing."

Viola realized Miss Rosalee was trying to have a womanly talk. Nell's own version had come before the ceremony, when she lifted Viola's long veil and said, "You listen to what Donald says, you hear." That was as much advice as Nell could offer, and Miss Rosalee knew it. Isabel had given Viola some idea of what men were like. She once spoke of getting a "creamy feeling" at the touch of a man that you desired. She said it was like "wanting to be so close that a man had no choice but to be inside." In eighteen years Viola was embarrassed to admit, even to herself, that she had no idea what "creamy" could possibly be.

"It ain't no secret," Miss Rosalee whispered into Viola's cheek, "that you gon' need to . . . get used to each other. And maybe, maybe without the benefit of—" she chose her words carefully, "without the benefit of some heat. You know what I mean?" That someone actually spoke her fear out loud made Viola feel a little more at ease. "Ain't the first time a marriage started out like this and it won't be the last. This don't mean"—Miss Rose smiled—"that the two of you won't grow to something real good. It could happen, Viola. It could happen if you jes' keep yo' heart open." Viola felt tears coming for the first time since the day had started. "Girl, don't you get my water to flowin',"

Miss Rosalee scolded. "I'm just tryin' to say that you're gon' be alright. You have a knack fo' drawin' angels."

"Drawin' angels?" Viola asked.

"Mama always told me and my sister Honeybee that some folks are just blessed like that. She say they're protected. You come out with such love and curiosity from a place that's closed and doubtful at best." Miss Rosalee sat back like maybe she had said too much. "You gon' be just fine. Too fine. Okay?"

"Yes, ma'am."

She kissed Viola on the cheek. "Now I'm fixin' to get me mo' of that cake. Yo' mama Nelvern do know somethin' 'bout some cake."

"Miss Rose," Viola said, stopping her. "What if I don't want to . . . you know? What if I just don't want to?"

She sat down again. "Wish I had an answer for that, baby," she said. "Donald Hinson look to be an understanding man. Seem like he'd know if a woman is ready or not. But Viola," she said with a soft voice, "you're married now and . . . there are jes' some things that go along with that. You know?" Before Miss Rosalee left the table she brushed a curl from Viola's cheek and said, "You gon' be fine."

The closer they were to the end of the day, the more nervous Viola became. The busier she stayed, the less she thought about her wedding night. From that point on, her day was certainly occupied. Dancing with her husband. Dancing with her father. Sitting for her wedding pictures, posing for the Jasperville *Bugle* with Donald and the more important guests. For at least half an hour after the flashing of camera bulbs, Viola held their half moon in her eyes.

The sun was setting behind Hopper Hill. Light gusts of wind began to lift the white chiffon against the orange skyline. The lighting of Nell's white candles on each table signaled the end of the reception. There was no alcohol, so there were no toasts, but each Reverend— and there were seven of them—offered long and individual prayers for the new couple. Then Nell gleefully led Viola to a gathering of about fifty women who stood clapping just below the small balcony in front of the house. These were the unmarried women. Her mother led her through the house and upstairs to the top of that balcony and handed her the bouquet of white roses, lilies, and stephanotis. The two young bridesmaids stood beside Miss Rosalee, giggling and clapping. Viola couldn't help but smile as the women stood poised and waiting. As if the snaring of a bunch of flowers offered a promise of happiness.

When Viola tossed the bouquet, she aimed it right for Miss Rosalee, but it bounced against her head and landed on top of Mrs. Reverend Morgan's hat, who stood with the married women at least ten feet away. Miss Rosalee reached into Mrs. Reverend Morgan's hat to snag the bouquet, and the hat tilted and fell off, along with her wig. Viola giggled behind her hand. Even Nell had to stifle a laugh. The younger women were less tactful and laughed out loud. For a moment, Viola forgot her fears. She forgot the setting sun, the forthcoming wedding night, and the fact that she had no idea who Donald Hinson was.

Five miles from Jasperville, in a town called Ranton, just ten minutes shy of the slaughterhouse, stood the tiny Hinson home. It was a sturdy framed house made of logs, each sanded smooth to the touch. The front porch was bare, but there were hinges on the ceiling where a swing might have hung. In their months of courting, Viola had never been inside. Donald didn't think it decent for a young woman to be in his house with him alone.

Donald stepped up the three porch stairs and Viola followed. The screen door squeaked open. Then, suddenly, he lifted Viola over the threshold and carried her inside. After wobbling and weaving, he finally set her on the overstuffed sofa. He was silent as he clicked on the lamp and sat down in an old rocking chair across from her.

She folded her hands in her lap and looked around like a guest. The house was immaculate, which didn't surprise her, because there was something oddly neat about Donald. The furniture was old and worn, which also didn't surprise her, because there was something oddly cheap about Donald. There were no pictures on the wall, no plants or pillows. The only thing in the room of any expense was the floor-model TV that rested right across from Donald's rocking chair.

Viola shifted nervously on the sofa. The crinoline in her dress made her thighs itch. She carefully removed her wedding veil and lay it beside her. She had the feeling of being in someone else's body.

Everything was even more frightening sitting here in Donald's house, with his bedroom surely just up the stairs.

"May I have some ice water, please." Her voice sounded strange in this house. In Donald's house.

"Kitchen right that way," he said, pointing behind her. "Git me some when you go."

Viola's dress swooshed against the checkered sofa as she got up and made her way into the dark kitchen. She searched for the light and clicked it on. Everything was in its place. Folded white napkins fanned across an old green and yellow Formica tabletop. Silverware in different patterns rested on top of the napkins. Through the glass cabinet doors, Viola could see empty jelly and pickle jars placed open side down. A clean but stained dish towel hung from a hook over the kitchen sink. A stove heated by wood logs looked as if it hadn't been fired up in as many years as it was old. Viola smelled a slight odor of sulfur mingled with boiled potatoes. Carefully she removed two jars from the pantry and filled them with cold water from the near-empty icebox. She walked back into the living room to find her new husband with a transistor radio to his ear. He clicked it off when she sat down. Then he took several gulps from the glass. Donald didn't attempt to make conversation.

"Beautiful ceremony," she said. Viola had never expected to be sitting across from her own husband, making small talk on her wedding night.

"Miz Nelvern did a good job," he said, placing the radio on the seat beside him.

"Yes . . ." Viola answered. "Can you turn the TV on?"

"Most of the stations done signed off," he mumbled.

"Oh."

Donald leaned forward, and when he removed his tuxedo jacket she felt her heart pound. He folded it and placed it across his lap and sat back again. "Maybe we shoulda gone to the Howard Johnson's," he said. "I mean, this bein' our weddin' night."

"You have to be at the yard first thing in the morning," she said sensibly.

"That is the truth."

His eyes grazed the neckline of her dress. Viola got up and walked through the room, looking for something to take his attention away from her. She stopped and lifted a tiny porcelain angel that sat on top of the TV set. The paint on one of its blue eyes had chipped away.

"You take care with that," Donald said. "Used to belong to Clarice."

"Clarice?" Viola hadn't thought much about Donald's first wife. He never spoke of the woman. As a young teenager, Viola remembered seeing Clarice Hinson in church a few times but mostly her name had come up in prayers for the sick and shut-in. "I bet you miss her bad," she said.

"Used to. She's dead now."

Viola set the angel back in its place. "I always meant to ask you . . ." she said, brightening her voice. "Meant to ask you how long you been in this house?"

"Fifteen years or so."

"That's a piece of time in one house," she said.

"Yes, indeedy," he answered. "I built it with these two hands."

"Get on away from here," she said. Donald had nice hands. Strong hands. That he did. And he wasn't too bad-looking. In fact, at least two young women at New Pilgrim thought he was kind of fine.

"My daddy and me worked on this house fo' four years."

"Seems like a mighty strong house," she said. Pride. Nothing wrong with that. Maybe with some work and sacrifice she might learn to be happy with this man. Maybe.

"We chopped the trees for wood and everything," he went on. "Daddy would be proud of what I made of it. Put the back porch in since he died and then Clarice nagged me fo' years 'til I added on a pantry fo' preserves. . . ." Suddenly a distant, high-pitched squeal echoed outside.

"What the heck was that!"

"You watch yo' mouth!" he thundered. "I don't abide that kinda talk." Donald's eyes were hard and unflinching.

"Excuse me," she whispered.

After a moment Donald settled back in his chair. "Butcher house is right up the road," he explained. " 'Bout this time a night we takes the pigs out to slaughter."

"Every night?"

"Might as well git used to it."

Donald Hinson rose from his chair. When he stretched his arms his suspenders fell from his shoulders. "Long day," he said.

"Yes, sir," Viola whispered.

Without looking at her, he walked toward the steps and climbed the narrow staircase. "Rinse the glasses," he said, "then come on up."

Viola could hardly move. During their courtship, Donald had treated her respectfully. He hadn't tried to kiss her too passionately, nor had he made a discourteous move. Donald Hinson was a God-fearing gentleman and there was no reason to believe that would change.

"Viola," he called.

She jumped at his voice. After gathering the glasses and rinsing them in the kitchen, Viola stood looking up the dark staircase. She recalled Miss Rosalee's words. "Seem like Donald would know if a woman is ready or not. Maybe he'd wait and be understanding about it." Perhaps they *could* grow to something special, just like Miss Rosalee had said.

Viola raised the hem of her skirts and walked up the steps. The heels of her shoes clopped against the stairs where the carpeting was old and thin.

Inside of Donald's room, she saw her little green suitcase with the black handle sitting beside the bureau. It seemed foreign there. Nelvern must have packed it and brought it by. Viola looked over at the bed where Donald lay on top of the covers, wearing only his shorts.

"Come on in here," he said.

She stepped in cautiously and stood just inside the door. A small black-and-white TV sat on a stand by the foot of the bed. There was no sound, and the picture skipped in horizontal lines. A bent clothes hanger served as the aerial.

"I don't know many folks with two TVs," she said nervously.

"You gon' jes' stand there like a statue?" he asked.

Viola took a quick glance around. "Is that the commode?" she asked.

"Yes. You hurry along in there."

Viola walked in with her suitcase and quickly shut the door behind her. She lowered the top on the toilet seat and sat to calm herself. The bathroom was the same as every other room in the house, stale and filled with the bare necessities. The yellowing mirror above the sink had a crack right down the center. On the washstand, a toothbrush rested its frizzy head against a covered straight razor. A scent she knew so well, the odor of Magic Shave, seemed entrenched in these four walls. Every Sunday morning, that same smell drifted into the kitchen from the bathroom where the Reverend prepared for church.

Viola removed her satin shoes. The tiles felt cool under her stockings. She caught sight of her two selves in the cracked mirror. In one side, it was her hair, yes, piled high on her head in a mass of coils and spirals that had taken Miss Ida three hours to do. And yes, there was her deep brown face and large dark eyes. But the other self, Donald's wife, eluded and frightened her. It looked like Nelvern.

Viola removed her pearls—the birthday pearls her mother had placed around her neck before giving her a gentle shove down the aisle. She pulled the long zipper in back of the wedding dress, then fumbled to undo the tiny hooks and eyes at the nape of her neck. When she finally stepped out of the gown, it lay on the floor like a mound of melted ice cream. She picked it up and placed it on a wire hanger that Donald had on the bathroom door.

"Hey there," he called again.

"Be right out." She could feel the quiver in her voice.

Viola quickly removed her stockings, then opened the little green suitcase. A white silk nightgown was draped neatly on top of her clothes. She lifted the nightgown over her head and it slid down her body like cool water. Five white velvet ribbons laced under her cleavage. For the first time, she wished it buttoned up to her neck like everything else she ever wore.

Viola felt herself begin to panic. She couldn't start to cry now. She sat on the toilet seat again and tried to think of anything that would take the fear away. She thought about Miss Rosalee, the schoolhouse . . . she even tried to pray. Then Isabel flashed in her mind. This time it was the pretty and whole Isabel, the Isabel of the satin dresses. Viola welcomed her spirit. Lord, what would Isabel say if she saw Viola hiding in the bathroom on her own wedding night? Then again, Isabel would understand better than anyone. She would understand having to be with a man she didn't desire. For Isabel, it was work.

Viola slipped into the soft pink bed jacket, opened the door, and walked into the room. Donald lay in the same position as when she'd left, but now his shorts were bunched and high in the crotch. He had turned the TV off.

Viola sat on the edge of the bed.

"Is it too cool in here?" he asked.

"No. No, sir, it is not."

"I can surely close that window."

"I'm very well, thank you." Viola could feel his breath on her shoulder.

He turned her to him. "Come on now," he said. When Donald kissed her, his skin felt cool and glassy. She would get used to it, she kept repeating to herself. There was no heat yet, like Miss Rosalee said, but that would come. He kissed her again and this time he forced her mouth open with his tongue. Donald Hinson had never done that before. She could taste his saliva, thick and bitter.

"It's my time," she whispered.

"Time for what?"

"My monthly time."

That was a lie. Nell had carefully planned the wedding between her periods to avoid any possibility of soiling the white dress. Donald stopped, and Viola's chest caved in relief. He reached into the night table beside the bed, pulled out a towel, spread it underneath her, and started to kiss her again.

"How could you want to . . . be with a woman that's on her monthlies?" she asked.

He kept on as if in a trance. Donald pulled off her bed jacket and flung it away. It landed on the small bedside lamp, casting a pink glow across the room. Then he yanked open each velvet tie of her gown. Hands that she thought a short time ago were so nice, now fumbled at her breasts.

"The Reverend says that laying with a woman during her monthlies is a sin, did you know that?"

"Reverend ain't in this room." Donald's voice was heavy. He pulled her gown up from the bottom and lifted it over her head. Donald plucked the two pins that gathered her hair in an elegant knot, and it tumbled down around her shoulders. Tears welled in her eyes as she sat on the side of the bed holding her bare chest. This wasn't the way it was supposed to be. No heat. No cream. Donald removed his shorts. Viola tried desperately not to look at the small yellow worm between his legs surrounded by a clump of matted black hair.

He cupped both breasts in his hands, then pulled her until she lay like dead weight across the bed. She tried rolling away but he dragged her back, yanking at her panties. The only sound in the room was Donald's heavy breath. Again, Viola rolled away and suddenly felt herself slipping off the side of the bed. Just as she was about to fall off, she gripped the inside of his thigh. Donald bucked and let out a wail as if the Holy Spirit took him. Then he lay there so still, she thought he might be dying. His eyes were closed and his body trembled.

She sat up and looked at him curiously. "Donald," she whispered without getting too close. "Donald Hinson?"

"Girl—w-where you learn to do that?"

"Learn to do what?"

"Yo' daddy say you was a virgin."

"I didn't do anything but stop myself from falling off the bed. Just happened to grab your . . . you know."

He lay in the same spot, a strange smile on his face, his body shivering and leaking. Viola pulled on her gown and turned onto her side. She wasn't sure what had happened, but she knew it was over when she heard him begin to snore softly. Was this what she'd have to go through every night? Was this what her mother had to endure? Would she become Nelvern, living without ever having known love and holding on to nothing but a good name?

When Donald's snores deepened, her body slowly relaxed. The day had been endless. Then there was tomorrow, her first Sunday as Mrs. Donald Hinson. She almost wished for a honeymoon just to avoid the eyes of the congregation the day after her wedding night.

As she was about to fall asleep, Donald pressed against her again, kissing the back of her neck. This time he quickly removed her panties. Instinctively, she reached down and touched him on the inside of his thigh. Maybe he'd jump around like before and go to sleep for the night. But it didn't happen. Her husband pulled himself on top and jammed into her. Viola tried to shove him off, but still he pushed against what felt like a burning wall. She couldn't avoid it, so

Viola lay back. In a moment, the wall of fire broke, and then it was over. She lay there silently crying.

Perhaps Viola would reach that middle ground. She couldn't imagine pleasure, but like Nelvern, she'd find acceptance someday. At the very least, she prayed that a time would come when she didn't feel that nauseating catch in the top of her throat every time the sun went down.

CHAPTER

7

Lil' Eartha McClain and the Blues Caravan took second billing at
the Gator Aisle in New Orleans. Preston "The Pickleman" Monroe
and his Jazz Quintet headlined, and a local R&B group called the
Coronets were third on the marqee. Eartha had a small space inside
the Gator Aisle dressing room, but Forestine and the band were rele-
gated to changing on the bus.

The men in the Caravan respectfully gave Forestine her privacy
and her time. Doug and Creer went to the club early for a drink. Beck
sat in the driver's seat and waited. He had fastened a makeshift curtain in back by hanging up several garment bags. When Forestine had
dressed, she came to the front of the bus and plopped down in one of
the seats with her cosmetic bag in her lap. The French Quarter was lit
up with neon, but the dim light on the bus made it hard for her to ap-
ply her makeup. She tried three times to put on mascara, only to
smudge the black liquid on the top of her cheek.

"Damn," she said.

Without asking, Beck sat down across from her, took off her shoe,
and gently massaged her stockinged foot.

"My mama had feet like yours." He spoke easily, a cigarette dangling from his bottom lip. "Big-ass feet. This is what I used to do for her after a hard day's work."

"What kinda work she do?" Forestine asked.

"Cleaned the courthouse. Main courthouse in Lexington, Kentucky. But I don't think even Mama looked as tired as you do right now."

"Never worked this hard in my life." Forestine sighed.

"Ain't easy being out here," he said, gently pressing his thumbs into the ball of her foot. "A girl like you probably figured this to be some kind of good life. Truth is, it'll bust yo' ass if you let it."

"I won't say these months have been easy," she smiled, "but I have learned a lot from you and Eartha." She took her makeup brush and whisked it across his face. When he smiled she caught the glint of his gold tooth. "I wouldn't trade it for anything in this world."

"You ain't a-scared a much are you, Forestine?" he asked.

"What do you mean?" she replied.

"Young gal like you out here on the road like this. Takes a lot of courage."

"Why are people always telling me that I'm so brave and stuff?" Forestine asked. "Don't y'all know I'm afraid of everything and everybody."

"Jes' 'cause you 'fraid don't mean you ain't brave." Beck sucked in hard, then exhaled a thick puff of smoke, all the time massaging her tired muscles. "You the kind of woman that step in with yo' dukes up. Jes' like Joe Louis."

"Lord, if you only know how hard it is to even get into the ring."

"That might be true," he said, "but at least you don't show it. That first night you got up there with the Caravan—most girls yo' age woulda pissed in their pants, but you hung in there like you been singin' with the likes of Lil' Eartha McClain fo' years. Brave, I tell you."

"Man, please." She smiled.

In the three months Forestine had been out with the Caravan, she always seemed to turn to Beck for conversation and advice. His easy nature reminded her of sitting and talking to Willie. Beck took everything in stride. After being on the road for over twenty-five years, he had seen and heard just about everything. But it was more than that. He also had a kind ear and a soft heart.

"You a team player, Forestine," Beck went on.

"If you trying to get on my good side, Beck Pinkney, you did that months ago."

"I'm serious. Some of these lil' gals Eartha hired to sing pitched a fit when they had to change on the bus, let alone sleep on it. You a team player. Don't complain when it gets tough. Just like now," he said, switching to her other foot, "you walking 'round here pretending that you ain't as pregnant as a partridge."

She pulled her foot away and sat straight up. "What?"

"Come on, Forestine," he smiled.

"What are you talking about, pregnant?"

He stroked his red beard and looked at her with a suspicious grin. "I'm the oldest of eleven kids. A young fella git to know the feeling of a pregnant foot," he said, pulling hers back into his hands.

Forestine sat back in her seat. Her mind had been focused on re-hearsals and clothes and club dates. She'd felt fatigued lately but thought it was the grueling schedule. Then a week ago Forestine real-ized she hadn't had a period in two months. "You probably figured it out before I did," she said with a confounded gaze. He shrugged his pudgy shoulders modestly. "I've never met anybody like you, Beck Pinkney," she smiled.

"It's a good thing too," he said.

"But can you imagine," she said with a laugh. "Forestine Bent— somebody's mama?"

"I can think of worse," he said. Beck paused to knock a line of ashes from the tip of his cigarette. "So . . . ?" he said.

"So?"

"What's yo' plans?"

"Haven't thought a whole lot about it," she confessed. "I guess I'm still trying to get used to the idea. And just when things are starting to cook for me."

"There ain't never a right time fo' a singin' woman to have a baby," he said.

"I don't know," she said vaguely. "Guess I'll sing as long as I can and then have a baby."

"Just like that, huh?"

"Yes."

"The road ain't no place for a pregnant woman," he said. "It's hard for anyone to be out here, even in the best of health."

"The best of health?" she laughed. "Man, you make it sound like the twenties, when a pregnant woman had to stay inside. In the bed. With her feet up!"

"Well, forgive this old man, Forestine, but I ain't come to your way of thinking yet." He crushed out his cigarette under a shiny wing-tipped shoe and went back to kneading her ankles. She could tell Beck wanted to ask about the father of the baby, but he wouldn't. "So what you gon' do *after* the baby's born?"

"Probably stay home until he's old enough to travel a little," she answered.

"Then you gonna take a chile with you on the road?"

"I—guess," she stuttered.

"And where exactly *is* home?" he asked.

"What?"

"I said where is home?"

"What are you asking? In Brooklyn . . ."

"With yo' mama and daddy?"

"Yes. I mean . . . look, I don't know," she snapped. "I'll figure it all out."

"There ain't no rule," Forestine," he started. "Ain't no rule that says you gotta have this chile."

"Rule?" Forestine placed both feet on the floor. She tossed her makeup bag on the seat beside her. "What do you mean, rule?" Thinking about everything at once made Forestine feel trapped and flustered.

"Just settle down," he said.

"There *is* a rule, Beck." Her voice was angry. "It's called God's rule."

Forestine wasn't a religious person, but still, there was something about destroying a child that felt wrong.

Beck slipped Forestine's shoes back on her feet. He took his jacket from the seat behind him and threw it over her shoulders. She hadn't mentioned that she was chilly, but Beck seemed to know exactly how she was feeling without being told. "Take a swig," he said, handing her his flask filled with gin. "This'll warm you."

She took a little sip and held on to the flask. She would have to answer for certain things, sooner or later, Beck was right about that. Forestine did wonder how Lucas would feel if he knew. She imagined he would probably be thrilled. Even though Lilian was the one trying so hard to get pregnant, a baby was something Lucas wanted too. He might even leave Lilian if he found out. Forestine pictured a life in Brooklyn with a new baby and Lucas Campbell. It was an interesting reflection . . . for a moment. Then she thought about Hattie. Even worse, Forestine considered a life without music, or at least without the music she had come to know. She could never be content like Lucas, singing with the kids and playing "The Old Rugged Cross" in church.

"Think you'll be okay tonight, Forestine?" Beck stood in the aisle looking out the window. Blinking neon lit the whole Quarter. A large crowd stood waiting to get into Gator Aisle.

"I'll be fine. I'm a little tired, is all."

"You ain't the only one this road is punishing," he said, taking the flask from her. When Beck sipped from the silver bottle, his pinky finger jutted out. Forestine thought it looked classy. "Eartha been out here over fifty years," he went on, "and that woman is tired. T-I-R-E-D, tired." He smiled. "Her daddy, name was Judd McClain, played guitar, banjo . . . anything wit' strings. Played wit' folks like Robert Johnson and Ma Rainey . . . Eartha started travelin' with him when she was just knee-high. Royalty! That's what she is." Forestine sat back and listened. His voice was soothing. "People are losing respect for the bluesman, though. Take them folks there," he said, pointing out the window with his chin. "They ain't here to see no Eartha McClain— not most of 'em anyway." He put the flask in his bag, pulled out a wrinkled tie, and slung it around his neck. "They here for the Pickleman or that R&B group . . . them there Coronets. That's what folks wanna hear now. But you ain't got to worry 'bout nothing," he said. "You sing blues, jazz . . . that rock and roll they doing now. Hell, you can sing *Madame Butterfly* if you wanted."

"You give me too much credit."

"Cain't take a compliment to save yo' life, can you?" he smiled. "Got some jazzmen out there, Forestine, that'll lay a piano up under a voice like yours and folks'll swear they died and went on to heaven. And them horns . . . shit," he hissed, "folks like Bud Powell, Bird, and that there boy Eddie Bishop. Make you sound like an angel singin' from a cloud." Forestine loved hearing Beck talk about jazz. All she knew was the little that Nick had taught her. She loved the feel of jazz. The sophistication. "We need to start workin' some jazz songs," he said. "Standards, you know, Mercer, Ellington, folks like that."

"I once did this song with Nick," she mused, "Called 'Stolen Heart.' One of the most beautiful songs I ever heard in my life. Different attitude than the blues. I would sure like to do that one day."

Beck stopped fiddling with his tie and worked the notes in the air, trying to remember the melody. Then he started to sing, out of tune, *"And were you once an angel, sent down to be my guide? My special, private angel, always by my side . . ."*

"And were you disappointed," Forestine sang simply, *"when you were earthward bound . . ."* Beck stood in the aisle of the bus with a smile on his face. *"Far from the angel choir, to light upon the ground."*

"Fuckin' *Madame Butterfly*, if you so desire," he said, tucking the bottom of the tie into his pants.

"I was about fifteen when Nick played an album by Basil James," she said. "I heard him sing that song and I was hooked. There wasn't nothing else in this world for me to do but sing."

"We gon' start working some jazz, R&B, hell we'll even add a couple of Elvis tunes to your repertoire."

"Eartha won't let me do songs that aren't in the show."

"You ain't all the time gon' be with Eartha," he snapped. "We done talked about this befo', Forestine. A woman like you wasn't made to sing second to nobody, not fo' a long stretch anyway. I think you'd be good to jazz. Couldn't get it myself," he confessed, "but I tried." He chuckled at the thought. "I 'member, years ago, Don Byas and those was doing a set at the Big House and I tried to sit in . . ."

Forestine had heard about this Big House from the Daffodils and other musicians who had come through Lester's. They all spoke as if it were the singer's promised land. "What is this Big House?" Forestine asked.

"What *ain't* the Big House." He smiled. Beck seemed to have to reach for the right words. "A musician's haven," he said. "An oasis . . . hell, I once heard Muddy Waters say that the Big House was like a big ole pan of hot water with some Epsom salts." Beck laughed so hard that he cackled. "It's a place to jam, talk . . . a few folks is lucky enough to even live there awhile . . . and Lord, but can they cook up some ox tails."

Forestine could feel her stomach turn at the thought of food.

"So anyway, I'm up there at the Big House," Beck continued, "I'm on the platform tryin' to work out with Don Byas, no less . . . they knew I was a bluesman but they let me hang with them a minute. We were playing this song called 'Cherokee.' Erroll Garner actually got up to let me sit down at the piano." Forestine only recognized some of the names. "After just a few bars," Beck went on, "the fellas started looking at each other. Then they looked at me." Beck laughed. "See, I wasn't ready fo' no jazz, 'specially no Don Byas, so I bowed out. I'm a bluesman, plain and simple. Some cats try to push it. They sit and sit 'til somebody embarrass 'em, and tell 'em that their shit ain't ready. I surely wasn't waitin' that long, though. That look was enough fo' me. But the Big House is like that. You can try stuff. Folks is honest and the air is laid-back."

"You really think I can sing jazz?" Forestine asked.

"You can sing anything," he replied. "Fo' fact I think you mo' of a jazz singer than anything. Got that smooth attitude to your music. Like I said befo', blues and jazz are two sides of the same coin."

Forestine loved the sound of Beck Pinkney. He seemed to say things in just the right way.

"I also wanna hear you do some big band," he went on. Beck sucked in like the word tasted good. "Now, there's some music," he said, shaking his head. "Big band is a goddamn plate of ribs, Forestine. Strings blow through you like the Holy Spirit. You'll see what I mean." He held on to her hand like it relaxed him. "Cain't say I'm the best at big band or jazz, but you need to get as much practice as you can." Beck got up and sat in the driver's seat, released the clutch, and pushed open the heavy door. "Come on in and we'll get you some tea."

"I don't need no tea, Beck."

"You need some tea, Forestine."

He pulled her from the seat and helped her down the steps of the bus. Then he led her through the crowd past the stage door. In the small noisy kitchen, Beck poured some hot water into a cup and begged a tea bag from a dishwasher. They went down the hall again and into the crowded dressing room, where he carved out a little space in the corner for Forestine to sit.

Snatches of jazz and R&B came from different parts of the room. Eartha idled on the couch with Ernest, and Beck squeezed in beside them. The Pickleman was already onstage warming up while the four men in his ensemble got ready here in the dressing room. They were simply dressed, two in dark slacks and shirts, one in an African-print top, like the Puerto Ricans from her neighborhood wore, and the fourth in a white tunic with what looked like pajama bottoms. Forestine felt overdressed in her beige sweater with its rhinestone collar.

She looked past the Pickleman's ensemble and was surprised to see a white girl at the dressing table keying a flute. She appeared to be in her twenties. The woman had on faded jeans and a pair of pointy-toed boots. Her skin looked almost iridescent pink next to her red hair and big green eyes. She reminded Forestine of a thin Raggedy Ann doll. Across from her, three of the men from the Coronets sang softly together. The fourth combed his conk in the mirror, singing along. This was one of the better dressing rooms, Forestine thought. Once in Mississippi, a stranger lay out drunk on the floor. In some other places, a tiff or full-fledged fight would break out between members of a group.

Pickle's ensemble began to file out to take their places onstage. Eartha tried to stand up from the couch but the cushion was sunk so low that Beck had to pull the woman up. "We gon' take a seat outside, Forestine," Eartha said. She was about to leave the room when she turned back. "You lookin' a little peaked, sugar," she said. "Please tell me you ain't comin' down wit' nothin'."

"I'm fine, ma'am," Forestine answered.

"Good," she said. "We damn sho' need you."

Eartha walked out with Ernest and Beck following. Before Beck closed the door, he whispered, "You stay put and finish that tea."

The Coronets' harmony relaxed her after the frenzy of moments ago. The white girl still sat at the dressing table. She leaned on her elbows and stared at her own reflection. Her flute rested on the table in front of her next to half a glass of whiskey.

"Now, there's something I don't see too often," she said to Forestine through the mirror.

Forestine started at the woman's voice. The timbre, inflections, and the silk of it sounded like a colored woman's. A heavy, husky, colored woman. "Excuse me?" Forestine asked her.

"I never see nobody at Gator Aisle drinking a cup of tea . . . lessen it got a shot of something in it."

"What makes you think it don't?" Forestine smiled.

"Touché, *mon cher*," she said, smiling.

The girl stood up in front of the mirror. There was hardly anything feminine about her. Her denim shirt with patches on the elbows was as faded as her jeans. She wore a red bandanna around her neck, and her face was free of makeup.

"You work here?" Forestine asked her.

"I'm fixin' to sit in with the Pickleman," she answered.

"You a singer?"

"Musician," the white girl answered. The Pickleman's ensemble started playing outside. She picked up her flute.

"Musician?" Forestine asked. "You a *jazz* musician?"

"I know," she said with resignation in her voice. "White gals ain't s'posed to know nothin' 'bout no jazz. That right, *cher*?"

"I didn't mean to say . . ."

"It's alright." The girl smiled and emptied the whiskey glass in one swallow. She walked toward the door and smiled again. "You know what I like to say 'bout that? I say, *laissez les bon temps rouler*, baby. Let the good times roll." Then she turned and left the room.

On top of the dull throb in her stomach, Forestine felt a twinge of embarrassment. She was doing the same thing that had been done to her. Forestine Bent was judging someone on the way they looked. She wanted to apologize to the woman, because Forestine understood that feeling. She had neither the right nor the desire to ever inflict it on anyone else. Forestine set her cup on the dressing table and went out into the club. The white girl was sitting at a table just under the stage. Her eyes were closed, and she sat, trancelike, listening to the Pickleman's ensemble. Forestine took a seat with Eartha, Beck, and Ernest at a table in the back of the house.

"Beck say you had a bit of that stomach flu," Ernest said to Forestine.

"A bit," she answered. Most times it was bad luck talking to Ernest about anything.

"That ain't no joke," he went on. "Had that once my damn self. I was a hockin' and spittin' and carryin' on. 'Member, Eartha?"

"Yes, honey," Eartha answered.

"But my baby nurse me," he said. "Right, Eartha?"

"Yes, honey."

The Pickleman stepped up to the mike while his ensemble started "Fine and Mellow." "Ladies and gentlemen," he announced, "Miss Bethanne Dieudonne." The white girl picked up her flute and rose from her table. She walked onto the stage with as much confidence as any of the men and took a seat on a stool beside the Pickleman. The audience applauded politely. Even the white people looked skeptically at this little girl. Her music was small at first, and the conversation in the room went on. Then she started her solo. Forestine had to adjust her ear from the weight of the Pickleman's sax to the light sound of the flute. Then it happened. Forestine recognized it instantly. That moment when the audience turns from their drinks and their indifference. The moment when, slowly, their attention turns to consideration, consideration becomes respect, and respect changes to awe. The white girl played for ten minutes while the entire club sat transfixed.

"White gal got some magic," Beck said.

"Sho' 'nuff," Eartha said, holding her glasses up to her eyes.

"*Laissez les bon temps rouler,*" Forestine whispered to herself.

"What you say, Forestine?" Ernest asked.

"Nothing," she answered. Forestine no longer wanted to apologize to Bethanne for judging her. Now she wanted to sit the girl down and talk music like she would with any other jazz queen.

"Bethanne Dieudonne," the Pickleman called into the mike.

"Sound like a Cajun," Eartha put in.

"Cute lil' gal," Ernest said, and then he caught sight of Eartha's glare. "Mean to say, if you go in for that type. Me myself I prefer—"

"Hush up," Eartha snapped.

Beck moved in close to Forestine. "You sure you gon' be okay?" he asked.

"I'll be fine," she whispered. Though in truth, Forestine could feel the sweat beading on her forehead. Her stomach griped and she felt exhausted. When the Pickleman finished his set, Forestine literally pulled herself up and went onto the stage. Her head throbbed under the bright lights but still she strutted and belted out her three songs like she had every night. Beck watched. Like always, he would be there just in case she fell and needed someone to catch her.

The Caravan mostly stayed at rooming houses and ate from tiny hole-in-the-wall kitchens on the circuit. But every once in a while Lil' Eartha liked to stretch out and stun the ensemble with one of her home-cooked meals. In a little town called Puckataw, right outside of Sarasota, Eartha found a rooming house with a kitchen big enough to cook in. The band sat around the dinner table as she brought in platters of pigs' feet in tomatoes and vinegar, and glazed yams with chunks of pineapples. Greens swam in pot liquor, and potato salad piled in a mound with sliced olives staring out like bright eyes. Everyone oohed and ahhed, as was customary and polite. Eartha sat down at one end of the table and Ernest at the other.

As tired as Eartha was after this last stretch, she had still managed to create a masterpiece. Although she liked the sound of forks clinking almost as much as the applause of a crowd high on the blues, her primary motivation for preparing such a meal was Ernest. Lil' Eartha was sixty-three, and her days on these back roads were numbered. She was looking to settle down.

"You put your foot in these sweet potatoes, Eartha." Forestine had scooped the last one from the bowl onto her plate and was spooning the thick glaze on top.

"And woman, these feet," Beck said, biting into a pig's foot.

"I second that," Doug said with a mouthful.

Praise was the reason Eartha could cook for hours. Her face opened into a childlike smile. Then she turned to Ernest. He'd been drinking all day and was now staring into his plate. "Oh yeah . . . yeah, baby," he said. "Everythang good."

"Thank you, pumpkin pie," she said.

"But, hold on—" He waved his fork in the air. "I ain't tasted none of them yams." He spotted one on Forestine's plate. There was a little piece of it on her fork and he bent over and eased it off with his teeth. Forestine recoiled in shock when Ernest then lifted her hand and licked the sweet glaze from her little finger.

"Shit," Doug mumbled.

For a moment it seemed the air had been sucked from the room. Forestine could see her career coming to an end just that quickly. But when she looked over at Eartha, the woman was sitting there grinning. Forestine looked at Beck. Creer looked at Doug. Everyone looked at Eartha.

"You jes' a silly lil' ole rabbit," she said playfully.

"Yeah, baby," Ernest said, still in a stupor.

This wasn't like Lil' Eartha. They had seen her get in scuffles across the country with women who simply nodded at Ernest. Once she pulled a woman's wig off after Ernest lit her cigarette. Eartha had been jealous of everyone, including an eighty-year-old crippled woman in Detroit. She moved to Ernest's lap, cooing like a teenage girl. Forestine was baffled. Watching the woman act so disgustingly sweet toward Ernest almost made Forestine long for the time when Eartha used to go upside his head.

After everyone excused themselves from the table, Forestine went to Beck's room. His door was ajar and she found him settled on his bed having a drink.

"You damn sure know what's on my mind," she said as she sat down in the chair across from him.

"You mean, why didn't Eartha try to cut yo' throat?"

"This was grounds for an axing." Forestine laughed.

"There's a reason," he said.

"No kidding?"

"I told Eartha that you was my girl."

"What?"

"I figure she'd know you wadn't interested in no damn Ernest."

Forestine laughed out loud. She leaned back in the chair and crossed her long brown legs. "Well, it surely worked."

"I knew it would," he said. Beck leafed through some sheet music on the bed in front of him. "I was thinkin'," he said without looking up. "I was thinkin' that . . . maybe we can make that lie a truth." He paused for her response, and when there wasn't one, he went on. "I know we ain't known each other but fo' a few months, but I ain't a bad guy, Forestine."

"You a good guy, Beck," she said bashfully.

"I know I drink some but I'm a helluva piano player. I ain't got no lot of money but if there's anything you ever want I'll put fire to the devil to get it. I know I got, what . . . twenty-some-odd years on you but I'm responsible and I'll never cheat . . ." He looked around as if he was trying to think of more good things to say about himself. He stopped talking and looked up at her. "Say you'll be my wife."

"Your wife?!!" she said. "Man . . . shoot, I thought you were asking me to be your steady girl. Your wife?" Seemed like since she laid eyes on Beck, they could talk about anything. He protected her, nursed her from bad health, and she felt good with him. Moreover, he made her laugh like no one before. "Is this because of the baby?" she asked.

He raised his hand for emphasis. "It's about you and me, Forestine. 'Bout how I feel for you."

"I never even told you about the baby's daddy," she said.

"You ain't got to tell me a damn thing."

"Yes I do," she insisted. For a moment all that could be heard were the raindrops beginning to patter just outside the window.

"You wanna marry this fella or something?" Beck asked.

She looked down into her lap. "He's already married."

"Oh?"

"To my sister Lilian."

"Oh." He paused for a moment, but just a moment. "Girl, I got me some things I ain't so proud of," he chuckled. "Fo' fact, some things they might put me under the jail fo'."

"You are too much . . ."

"I figure that's all the mo' reason fo' you to marry me," he said. "You need someone to take care of you . . . and that chile."

"You crazy or what?"

"Don't matter none, Forestine. Anything inside of you is a part of me." His eyes were as gentle as any she had ever seen.

"I'm a hard colored woman to get along with. Sometimes impossible. I don't trust many people . . . but when I do, I know it right away. I can tell by the way they smile, the look in their eye."

He blew a light puff of air through his lips. "So what you sayin' 'bout me?"

"I trusted you right away. I knew we were gonna be friends a long time but..." She cocked her head. "Well...I never did think I was gonna say yes to your marriage proposal."

"You mean—you sayin' yes, woman?"

"Guess I am."

Beck jumped up from the bed like he had just hit the number. "I guess now I'm supposed to hug you, kiss you and stuff, right?"

"Man, I don't know," she laughed. "I've never accepted a marriage proposal before. But that sounds like a good idea to me."

He leaned over her from behind and very gently, almost too gently, he wrapped his arms around her shoulders and held her. There was nothing like being held by this man, she thought. Beck made her feel safe.

"Tell me something," he said, with his arms still around her shoulders. "You say you know when to trust somebody?"

"Yes."

"Do it usually work?"

"Always."

"What about Hattie?" he asked.

"Not as far as I can spit the woman. I looked right at her from my crib and said, now there's a woman I'll never trust."

"You crazy, Forestine," Beck laughed. "What about old man Nick? Did you trust him right away?"

She paused. "Yeah, I did."

"So I guess it don't work all the time."

"I would still trust him."

He sat on the bed. "How you trust a man do what he did to you?"

"I don't know why," she said. "I swear I don't, but somehow I didn't feel violated. I didn't feel betrayed either. I was embarrassed as hell, but more than that, I just felt sorry for him. It's like if you came to me and said, Forestine, I'm hungry and I need some food. Well damn, I couldn't let you starve. Or you come to me and say, baby, I'm cold and I need some heat, well, I'd have to put my arms around you. Nick was a lonely old man who needed some company."

"He was a horny-ass old man, that's what he was. You too good,

Forestine. Shoulda called the damn police." He kissed her on the cheek and then pulled her toward the bed. "Forestine, I'm cold and I need me some heat," he laughed.

"You crazy." She lay down beside him.

"Baby, I'm hungry and I need me some neck," he said, nibbling around her ear.

"A stone-cold fool!" she laughed.

He lay back with his arms wrapped around her and was quiet for a moment. "I got a house in Kentucky," he said. "Lexington."

"I never knew you had a house," she said.

"All that traveling I been doin' over the years . . . You know how lonely it is, not having a place to lay yo' bags? I was born and raised in Lexington and I decided that I was gon' get me a lil' piece of land and build something or other. It ain't much, but it's home. We'll leave fo' Lexington tomorrow and you can stay there 'til the baby comes. . . ."

"I won't stop singing, Beck," she said. "Not no time soon."

"Girl, you talkin' foolishness. The road ain't no place fo' a delicate woman."

"Do I look any kinda delicate to you?"

"Yes, baby, you do," he answered.

"Aside from being a little tired sometimes, I feel as strong as ever," she said.

"You gotta think of what's important, Forestine, and the baby's health is important."

Everyone seemed to come back to this same tired point. Priorities. Hattie talked about it, Nick, Willie, and now Beck. Forestine's priority was the music—the only constant from day one.

"You don't have to tell me what's important," she said.

"You think Eartha gon' let you stay out here like this?"

Forestine stood up over the bed, glaring down at him. "You can do what you want about the damn marriage," she hissed, "but don't make me regret telling you this. I say I trusted you, man, and that's why I told you my business. I couldn't imagine if you went behind my back—"

"You know damn well I won't tell Eartha or any other living soul if you don't want me to. Settle down, baby. I want you to be my wife 'cause I love you. If you want to stay out here, well, I think you acting crazy but I'll respect yo' wishes and do what I can to help."

She let Beck hold her and soothe her into once again accepting his proposal. Finally she relaxed and fell into a safe sleep. He was the best friend she ever had.

At four months' pregnant, Forestine married Beck Pinkney. By then, she had been getting her own stunning reviews, and in some towns people came only for her. Forestine was so successful at hiding her pregnancy that, just five weeks later, she got an offer from a promoter in Mobile named Justin Laws. At six months' pregnant and with Beck by her side, Forestine headed her own show, the *Bent Down Blues Revue*. Three and a half months later in Chicago, Illinois, Benjamin Campbell Pinkney was born. As she held the tiny baby in her arms, Forestine realized she loved him more than she had thought possible. Benny was the most beautiful part of her. For the first time in her life, Forestine Bent had someone to sing for.

CHAPTER 8

Viola jumped up from the kitchen chair to turn off the flame under the burning pot. It was too late. Half the grits had already stuck to the bottom. Still drowsy, she took a round of sharp cheddar from the icebox, shaved a few pieces, and stirred them into the pot to cover the burn. Viola pressed out most of the lumps and spooned the grits on the plate beside the bacon and eggs. Then she set a pot cover over it and waited for her husband to take his place at the table.

After three years of marriage, she still wasn't used to rising at 4:30 A.M. Especially since she usually stayed up until after midnight grading test papers or homework. But at 4:30, she made herself rise in the pitch black to cook a breakfast for Donald. It was always the same: two eggs over easy, three strips of slab bacon, fresh-squeezed grapefruit juice, toast and grits. Scorched grits.

She heard the shower turn off upstairs. Viola knew it would be just a few minutes before Donald came out for breakfast. Her husband was a stickler about cleanliness and time. Most everything was on a schedule. Breakfast had to be set on the table no later than 4:50 A.M., he was in his car and gone by 5:20 and arrived at the slaughterhouse before 5:30. Dinner was as exact, as were prayer, TV, and sex.

Viola walked to the back door and looked through the screen. Moonlight glistened against the thin ice coating the grass. Frost covered even the bare gated spot in the yard that Donald used for smoking fowl. The strong nip in the air helped to rouse her. Lately, she couldn't seem to get enough sleep. During the quiet moments at school, Viola would feel herself nodding off. One of her students actually had to shake her awake once after the class finished a reading assignment. She had awakened at her desk to find the eyes of fourteen curious eight-year-olds staring her down. Her lack of energy was worse at home. Viola wondered how she'd get through the holidays.

On the calendar hanging from the pantry door, an orange and brown paper turkey marked today's date. Nell had attached it to what she called the two-week warning. This meant that Viola had to start planning for Thanksgiving. She hadn't given the festivities any thought until now, and the day was right on her heels.

The idea of hosting again made her ill. Time was, Nell had Thanksgiving dinner at the Bembrey house, but this year, just like last year, Viola would carry the ball. She wasn't good at social affairs, especially when she had to plan them. If Nell hadn't told her exactly what to do last year, the dinner would've been a disaster.

The guest list read the same: Deacons Best and Temple and their families. Miss Rosalee and Sister Harper, because they either had no family in town or no family to speak of at all. Reverends Morgan and Baines and their wives. This year Donald invited Mack and Amos from the slaughterhouse. Viola hoped that one or the other might be a match for Miss Rosalee or Sister Harper.

She heard the bathroom door open upstairs. The odor of Magic Shave made its way down to the kitchen. Minutes later, Donald came rushing to the table as if he were actually late.

"Coffee," he called. She filled his cup. "Where the cream, Viola?" She took the black and white ceramic cow from the refrigerator and poured some into his coffee and then her own. "Cain't use my fingers to cut my eggs, now can I?" he asked. She got up again, opened the silverware drawer, and took out a knife, spoon, and fork. Then like every morning, Donald poured some of his coffee into his saucer. He waited until the steam subsided and then sipped it from a teaspoon. He ate with his head down, glancing over his shoulder every once in a while toward the front door, like he was expecting someone. "Ain't you eatin'?" he asked.

"I'm not hungry."

He looked up quickly.

"I'm not with child, Donald," she said, "I'm just not hungry, is all." Whenever their daily routine varied in the slightest, he would ask. Years ago, there had been rumors in New Pilgrim that Clarice was too sick to have children, but Viola was beginning to think that maybe Donald was the one. She prayed Donald was the one.

"Yo' daddy call this mo'nin?" he asked.

"The Reverend would never call anyone this early," she answered.

"Not usually," he said. "But he's meetin' me at the slaughterhouse today. Say he'd call if he couldn't come."

"Why is my daddy going to the slaughterhouse?"

"Business," he mumbled.

"What kinda business? He never mentioned anything to me."

Donald gave her a look that said her tone was too brusque. "Men's affairs, Viola," he said. He eyed the door again at the distant sound of a car.

"I thought you said he was meeting you at the yard."

"That's what I said." Donald wiped his mouth with a paper napkin. "My truck ain't working good so Amos is gon' gi' me a lift."

"What happened to your truck?" she asked.

"Nothing to concern yo'self with," he answered. "Just set another plate."

Whenever Amos stopped by, he ate. He'd pop in for dinner once in a while on a weeknight and always on Sunday. Viola didn't mind, though. Aside from Nelvern and sometimes Miss Rosalee, the Hinsons didn't have many visitors. Even though Amos spoke mostly of hogs, at least he talked to her. She spooned some grits on a plate and put a slice of toast and the last two strips of bacon beside it. Just as she filled a third cup with coffee, Amos rapped on the front screen door and came right in.

"Mornin', Donald, Mrs. Donald," he yelled. Amos always talked loud. He handed Viola his usual bag of pecans and small bouquet of wildflowers.

"Thank you, Amos," she said, tucking the flowers in a drinking glass on the counter.

"Pleasure, Mrs. Donald."

At first the name "Mrs. Donald" had bothered her, but Viola realized that Amos Flowers wouldn't offend anyone. He was genuine. Even this early in the morning, his smile spread so wide that it bunched his cheeks and made two slits of his eyes.

"Good-lookin' breakfast you got there," he said, standing over the table.

"Sit down, Amos." Viola set his plate before him.

He yanked at the thigh of his overalls and threw his thick leg over the chair. "You sho' know something 'bout some breakfast, Mrs. Donald," he said with a mouthful. "Dinner too." Amos looked up at her with a playful grin. "And girl, when you stop burnin' up the grits, you'll be in business."

"Amos Flowers," she scolded. Viola stood with her hands on her hips.

"She think I don't notice that she scorch the grits," Donald said. "Think 'cause she put cheese in 'em, I won't know."

"Still taste good, though," Amos said. "Got a smoky flavor to 'em." He slurped his coffee and set the cup in the saucer with a loud clink. Amos had very few social graces. But then, working around hogs all day, he didn't really need any. "So you-all having Thanksgivin' this year?" he asked.

"Looks like it," Donald answered.

"Good," Amos said.

"Sister Harper will be dining with us again," Viola said casually. "I thought maybe you'd like to talk to her, Amos." Donald rolled his eyes up in his head.

"That Sister Harper is a teacher, ain't she?" Amos asked.

"She's the headmistress at the lower school where I work," Viola answered.

"All respect, Mrs. Donald," he said, dunking a piece of toast into his coffee, "but I ain't interested in no teachers. They scare the bejesus outta me. Always correctin' me, tellin' me how to talk and stuff."

"Viola is a teacher," Donald said. "She don't do you like that."

"It be different when you courtin' 'em, though. If I set with this lady, she'll start that stuff, alright. Might even hit me wit' a ruler."

"You are a mess," Viola laughed.

"And plus," Amos went on, "I ain't interested in no church ladies."

Amos Flowers was about the only one of Donald's friends who didn't attend New Pilgrim or any other church. Amos had come to work at the slaughterhouse about three years ago. No one really knew where he was from; he just appeared one day. And since he was a tireless worker and pleasant to be around, no one bothered to ask. Even Reverend Bembrey liked him. They had met when Donald invited his friend to a New Pilgrim picnic. Although Amos could care less about Sunday service, a picnic—even a church picnic—was fine with him. Reverend Bembrey wound up laughing the whole time they talked, and getting Cleveland Bembrey to laugh was no easy task.

"With all respect, Reverend," Amos had said, "I ain't got to come to church to converse with the Lord. Got my own places where we set and discuss things."

"Oh?" Reverend Bembrey replied.

"Oh, yes, sir. I go down by the creek. To the top of Hopper Hill . . . heck, Lord prob'ly hear me better up there," Amos chuckled. "I figures a church ain't the onliest place the Lord listen. Am I right or wrong?"

"You do speak the truth," Reverend Bembrey said. "But the church is the Lord's house. Every once in a while, it'd be nice to come and set in his living room."

"Think he turn the ball game on, sir?"

"You are a caution," the Reverend laughed.

"Well, they say I'm a quick wit," Amos said, "or maybe they say I'm a nitwit. Cain't recall which."

Reverend Bembrey had nearly reached the point of cackling.

"Miss Rosalee's going to be here for Thanksgiving too," Viola said.

"Miss Rose old 'nough to be Amos mama," Donald cut in.

"She's not that old," Viola defended. "Besides, she got a young heart."

"Miss Rose is fine," Amos said. "Fine, fine, fine, but she ain't no mo' interested in me than I am in her."

Viola knew Amos was probably right about that. "Well, have you *ever* had a woman friend?" she asked.

"Sho' he has," Donald jumped in. "Remember I told you he used to go with a girl named Alfreda that worked at the slaughterhouse."

"Yeah, Alfreda," Amos said. "She was real nice."

"She come to me one day," Donald said, "and she say, Mr. Donald, I'm afraid I'm gon' have to quit the slaughterhouse. She say she need to git wit' a different line of work."

"Couldn't stand being around all that killing?" Viola asked.

"That's right," Amos said. "So she moved to Summerville and now she work up at the poultry ranch."

"I see," Viola said.

"Hey, boy," Donald said, standing up. "Need to git on our way."

Amos quickly scraped the last of the grits onto a piece of toast. He stuffed it in his mouth as he walked toward the front door. "I thank you fo' the breakfast, Mrs. Donald. 'Spect I'll see you fo' dinner come Sunday."

"Oh, I 'spect," Viola replied. She walked behind them.

"Maybe one day I'll cook a dinner fo' you and Mr. Donald at my house."

"You ain't gotta do that, Amos," Donald said. "In fact, please don't," he joked.

"You be surprised what I can cook," Amos said.

Viola knew that Donald would never go to Amos's house for dinner. He lived way out in a town named Caldwell and it took him close to forty-five minutes each day to reach the slaughterhouse. But more, Donald Hinson couldn't imagine a man cooking dinner. That was just unheard-of.

The two men's workboots hit the wooden porch like claps of thunder. Viola stood on the steps and watched them drive away.

The laughter left with Amos Flowers. The life and the laughter. That's why Viola didn't mind having him for dinner. Aside from Sunday, she rarely knew when Amos would show up, but when he did, he'd arrive right before she set the food on the table. He'd have a small bouquet of wilting wildflowers and a bag of dusty pecans, both of which he'd picked from his own yard. Amos even had his own chair in their living room and a seat at the dinner table. What an odd little man he was, she thought. Such a dry sense of humor. Dry but funny.

He didn't go to church, but Amos still possessed a certain spirituality. Everyone seemed to like having Amos Flowers around. Miss Rosalee joked that he reminded her of one of Santa's little colored elves.

The sun was beginning to rise. Viola only had a couple of hours before school and she still had papers to mark. Sometimes at night she sat in front of the heap of childish third-grade scrawl and wanted to cry. Most of the teachers at the school loved what they did. They enjoyed being with the kids, planning, disciplining, and rewarding. Viola just seemed to squeak by. She hadn't even planned her lesson for today. She walked back into the kitchen, gathered the dirty dishes, and stacked them in the sink. For a moment she stood and looked at them. Bacon grease swirled in the heavy black skillet. Grits clung to the bottom of the steel pot in a dark brown knot. How long would she have to scrub to loosen the hard, dry flecks? It had taken her nearly twenty minutes the last time. Twenty minutes out of her life to loosen some damn grits, she thought. Viola grabbed the pot and chipped away at it, trying to remind herself how blessed she was. At least, that's what everyone in New Pilgrim told her. Good husband, nice house. She was blessed. Viola's breath started coming in shallow pants. She felt a nausea rising in her stomach and a lightness in her head. Then came the tears. She dropped the pot in the sink. How could something like scorched grits set her off? She stood there trembling in the middle of the kitchen, trying to calm herself. In her first year of marriage the attacks happened rarely, and in the second, they came once or twice a week. Now they happened almost every day. Viola left the pot, the uncorrected homework, the lesson plan, the paper turkey on the calendar, and crawled back under the covers.

Nell sat in the Hinson living room with her hands folded in her lap, her neck straight and her lips tight. It was three days until Thanksgiving. When Nell's eyes scanned the room, her disgust was as clear as her disappointment. "What exactly have you been doing for the last month, Viola?"

"Working," she answered.

"Today is Monday. Thanksgiving is Thursday. When I hosted this dinner, I would have had my fall drapes up by now and the cranberry wreaths on the door. You've done nothing." Nell enunciated each word, as if she spoke to a three-year-old.

"Yes, I know," Viola whispered.

Nell lifted a cardboard box from the floor and set it on the coffee table. "You've watched me plan a dinner every year since you were old enough to walk. You hosted last year—sort of. You know how things are done."

"Why don't we go down right now, and we'll pick out the wreaths and whatever else—"

"I am not thinking about going to town now. It's after five and I need to get home for dinner. Besides, you and Donald should've done this weeks ago."

"He's been busy at the yard," Viola said. In truth, she rarely saw him lately, except for meals and bed.

"That doesn't sound like Donald," Nell said. "He's always so . . . precise. I've never known him to neglect his responsibilities at home."

"He's been busy with the Reverend . . . I mean with their business project and all. . . ."

"Business project?" Nell asked.

Viola looked into her mother's eyes. Nelvern was just as clueless as she. "I just mean that Donald's been real busy," Viola said.

"You need to keep up with your husband, Viola, busy or no." Nell pulled a set of silver candlesticks and several orange and green cloth napkins from the cardboard box and set them on the coffee table. "You do have the tablecloth, yes?" she asked.

"Yes," Viola answered.

"And you had it dry-cleaned?" Nell asked.

"Dry-cleaned?"

"Oh, Vi-ola," Nell groaned. "Give it here," she ordered.

"It's somewhere in the hall closet. I can't put my hand on it right now."

"Well, you best to put your hand on it," Nell said, going to the closet. Viola watched as she pulled out boxes and bags, talking the whole time.

Viola knew that her mother would surely take over the dinner preparations, so as not to embarrass herself before the Reverends and their families. And she'd gladly let Nelvern have her way. Viola settled back on the couch and closed her eyes as Nell continued clattering in the hall closet. Lately when Viola shut her eyes like this, Isabel's face appeared. Not the grotesque memory, but the pretty Isabel singing at Snookie Petaway's. *If you treat me right, daddy, I'll treat you right too. I'm the kinda woman make you feel what a smilin' man do.* Isabel was gone. Snookie Petaway's was gone. The juke joint was now a heap of planks and nails in a spot deep in the woods.

"Do you ever clean this closet, Viola?" Nell called. There was rattling for a while longer and her mother walked into the living room with the brown cloth draped over her forearm. "I need to get to Mr. Canyon before he closes the cleaning shop," she said. "I'll pick up the wreaths while I'm in town. And Viola—" Nell stopped and stood over her daughter. "*I'll* plan the menu. I'm sure you haven't done that either?"

"No."

"Lord, have mercy," Nell gasped. "What is wrong with you? Even now, you're sitting here like you don't know which end is up. What is the problem, girl?"

"I'm . . . just a little down. . . ."

"Down?" Nell replied. "You don't have the right to be down. You have a good husband, a good job for a woman, and a beautiful home. You come to church every Sunday, you in the Lord's good graces, and your daddy is as proud as he's ever been. So what is it, Viola?"

"You've never . . . felt like you had the blues?"

Nell seemed about to object to such a common expression, but then her face softened. She sat across from Viola again. "There were times when I have been . . . hushed," she said. "Times when I had to think on things. Even a time or two when I didn't feel I could go on."

Viola sat up. "Like when?"

"That's not important. But your father and I have had some . . . trying moments."

"And what did you do?"

"My mother reminded me of my blessings, just as I'm reminding you of yours. Then I picked myself up, went to church, and I was fine." Impatience inched its way back into Nell's voice. These rare human glimpses of her mother often ended quickly. "You're talking about being down," she said, grabbing the tablecloth and her purse. "There is too much work to do and you need to get yourself *up*. I'm not always going to be here to come to your rescue. Now get to it," Nell said, pulling Viola onto her feet. "Need to get yourself moving." Then Nell left, slamming the front screen door behind her.

Viola sank back onto the couch. She pulled her feet up and lay back. She was about to close her eyes again when she heard a car out front. At first she thought it was Nell driving away. Moments later, she heard what sounded like tiny pebbles hitting the porch. When Viola opened the door, Amos was leaning over and stuffing spilled rock candy into a brown paper bag.

"What in the world are you doing," she asked.

"Thought I'd stop by to bring you this here candy today, Mrs. Donald," he said, handing her the bag.

"But you just dropped it on the floor," she replied.

"Be good as new when you kiss it up to God."

"Lord, Amos Flowers," she said, taking the bag. "I'm afraid Donald isn't here yet."

"Oh, I left him at the yard," Amos said. "The man was in his office, workin' like a demon possessed. Say he'll be along directly."

"Dinner isn't ready yet." Viola wasn't quite in the mood for Amos or anyone else today. Then she looked at his wide smile and the candy in the wrinkled brown bag. "Come on in," she said.

He paused outside the door. "I got a lil' somethin' else fo' you too," he said. Before she could respond, Amos bounded off the porch to his truck. He went around to the back and after a bit of tussle, lifted a huge live turkey. He clamped both arms around the bird, and it screeched in fear.

"Gracious a lie," she laughed.

"Mr. Donald say you ain't pick out yo' dinner bird yet. I figured I'd go to the poultry ranch and at the same time, I git to see Alfreda. You know, kill two birds wit' one stone." He began laughing at his own joke, but just then, the turkey bolted from his arms and ran down the steps. "Hey, there, fella," he yelled, and went running down the drive behind the terrified bird. Amos tried unsuccessfully to recapture the turkey, so Viola joined him, and together they cornered the poor creature. Amos grabbed the bird and carried it around back, where he penned it behind the gate. Viola watched out the back screen as Amos emptied his pockets of dried corn.

"Pretty thing, ain't it," he said, walking up the back steps.

"And big," Viola added.

"Chester twenty-five, if he a pound," Amos said, coming into the kitchen.

"Chester?" Viola asked.

"I name ever'thing," he said, taking his seat at the table. "Even the hogs at the yard."

"Doesn't that make it difficult when you have to say good-bye?" Viola asked.

"Sometimes," he admitted. "But least they got a name to say good-bye to."

Viola looked up at the wall clock in the kitchen. It was past the time that Donald usually came home for dinner. He was rarely late, but right before the holidays was a busy time at the yard. "I never had to live with a bird before I had to cook it," she said. "My daddy brought the turkey to the house every Thanksgiving eve, dead, plucked, and ready to roast. You're gonna have to take care of the ... you know."

"Hell, no, not me," he said.

"That's what you do every day—at least to hogs."

"I don't kill no nothin'," he insisted.

She pulled her head back in surprise. "Then what do you do?"

"I tends to the hogs," he said. "I feeds 'em, clean the pens, inventories 'em, make sho' the yard is runnin' right, but damn if I kill anything. Might say I make their last days comfortable. Now, yo' husband, he the one. And he good at it too."

"How can anyone be good at killing?" Viola asked.

"'Cause he merciful. Hit that hog, whop! Right upside the head. Knock 'em right out. Then he ... well, git to doin' what he do, you know?"

Viola never really knew about the particulars of the job and never wanted to know. She placed a stack of three plates at the table, along with the silverware. Amos began to set them.

"You don't have to do that, Amos."

"Be my pleasure, Mrs. Donald," he said, getting the napkins from the counter.

"So did you get to see Alfreda at the poultry ranch?" she asked.

"Naw," he said. "Say she done moved to Gaffney."

"I'm sorry."

Amos shrugged. "I waited too long, I guess," he said. "Shoulda got my butt there months ago."

"Maybe she'll be back," Viola said. "And if not, Gaffney's just a few hours away."

"Well, they say she met a fella. That's who she went with," he confessed.

"I'm real sorry, Amos." She looked up at the clock again and then took the roast from the oven. "Isn't like Donald to be this late," Viola said. "Maybe we should start to eat."

"Ain't no sense fo' ever'body to eat dry roast," Amos said. "I'll do the slicin', okay?"

Viola was used to doing all the setting, serving, and slicing. Donald just sat and received. Her enjoyment deepened when Amos clicked on the radio that was sitting on the counter. He fiddled with the knob until he found the blues station. Viola loved the sultry sounds filling her own kitchen. Sometimes when she came in from school and knew Donald wasn't due in for hours, she would turn it on herself. There she'd sit at the table, listening and singing, while keeping an eye on the door. How splendid it was, having someone to enjoy the music with her.

"That's Victoria Spivey, you know?" Amos said.

"I've heard of her." Viola removed the salad from the refrigerator.

"I've seen her sing in person."

Viola stood in the open refrigerator door. "In person?" she asked. "Like at Snookie Petaway's?"

"Naw," he answered. "I was traveling through Memphis and she was at one of them clubs on Beale. That woman is somethin' else, I'll tell ya." Amos looked at her curiously. "What the hell *you* know 'bout Snookie Petaway's?"

"I know a few things," she answered.

"You mean what them church folks say?"

"Not exactly. I went there once."

"Git on away from here," he laughed. "Cain't believe that. Oh, wait a minute, I know," he said, like he finally understood. "You went there when yo' daddy and them other folks stomped it out, right?"

"I went there when it was running," she said plainly. "I went there and saw the show." She couldn't believe she was actually telling this to Amos Flowers.

"Whewww!" he said. "Did you like it?"

"I *loved* it," she smiled. "I never had such a good time in my whole entire life. All the stuff I'd been hearing about how bad it was and everything . . ." She blew a puff of air. "Well, it was nothing like that. It was the happiest group of people." Amos kept on slicing as Viola talked. "I went to see my friend Isabel sing, you see. She died before you even came to town. But she was my best friend, Amos. My very best friend."

"Sorry she gone."

"Everything's gone," Viola said quietly. "Isabel, Snookie Pet-away's . . ."

Amos dropped a piece of roast beef in his mouth. "Snookie Pet-away's ain't gone," he said. "He got a club over in Camden County now."

"What?" Viola exclaimed.

Then Amos said quickly, "Don't you tell yo' daddy nothin' 'bout what I said."

"I won't." Viola smiled at the thought of the blues still living not too far away.

"Talkin' 'bout Snookie's place and listening to this here music seem to be something you fancy," Amos said. "You walkin' 'round now like old Chester out there. Got yo' tail feathers all up in the air, got some orange in them pretty brown cheeks."

"It was fun," Viola admitted. "Lots of fun but, that was a time ago."

"Any Kinda Man" continued to play in the background. The room suddenly felt filled with fresh air. Even when the conversation drifted off, the glorious energy remained. Just as Viola was about to take the bread from the oven, Amos swept her in to dance. He hummed the song, badly, while he guided her in small circles.

"I got to get the bread from the oven, Amos," she laughed. "We don't want the bread to brown too bad."

"I wouldn't recognize yo' food if it wasn't burned up," he said.

She punched him playfully. Amos's chest was as hard and thick as a wall. He turned her and dipped her, all the time singing. Then the front door slammed shut, and Amos spun her away from him. Donald charged into the room and stood there with a smile on his face.

"You will never believe this, boy," he said to Amos. "You ain't hardly gon' believe it!" He didn't notice dinner on the table or Chester clucking right outside the back window. He didn't even hear the blues playing. Viola clicked it off.

"What is it, boy?" Amos asked.

"Reverend Bembrey come to the yard about a half hour ago."

"So?" Amos asked.

Donald paced the room with energy to burn. "He ain't jes' talkin' 'bout giving me the money to expand the yard," he said.

"Expand?" Viola asked. Amos dashed her a look, surprised she hadn't heard.

"Now he got Morgan, Baines, and maybe even Reverend Lightfoot in on the deal." Donald fell into one of the kitchen chairs with his skinny knees wide open and his arms stretched up in the air. "Thank you, Lord," he yelled. "Thank you, Lord Jesus."

"Go on, man!" Amos said, slapping him on the shoulder. Viola wondered what this all meant and how it would affect her.

"But wait a minute," Donald said. "That ain't even the best of it. Since we got the other reverends involved, they talkin' 'bout opening a second yard over in Dresden. Even found a site out there by the cotton plant. You are good to me," he yelled to the ceiling. Then he shot forward in his seat. "Amos, boy, we got some work on us fo' the next few weeks."

"Sounds like it," Amos said.

"They sending folks to the yard to check things out, you know. Make sho' stuff is running alright. Got to tighten everything up over there." Donald stood up. "Yep, we got some work on us," he said, walking into the living room deep in thought. "Viola," he yelled. "Get dinner on the table."

"It's already there," she said, more to herself.

"Maybe I better git on," Amos said to her. "Let you talk to yo' husband 'bout this."

"Please stay," she said. "Please . . ."

The look Amos wore was kind. One of a man who recognized something rare and beautiful and couldn't understand why the whole world didn't see it. He sat down at the table. Moments later, she called Donald in and, like always, the three sat and ate, while the men talked.

Chester was still eating seed and walking the earth at eight P.M. on Thanksgiving eve. He should've been seasoned, stuffed, and sitting on the bottom rack of a high oven by now. Last night Donald had promised to "set Chester down fo' a talk," but he came in past midnight, ate, showered, and dropped straight off to sleep. Then he said he'd tend to Chester this afternoon. But it was past the afternoon, past the evening, and well into the night.

Most of the side dishes were made, as were the roast beef and cloved ham. Miss Rosalee had come by this morning and dropped off her famous coconut cake with pineapple slices between the layers. Nell was making the ambrosia and would bring it when she arrived tomorrow. The thought of her mother made Viola take a nervous breath. Nelvern would have a stroke if she knew that the turkey wasn't in the oven by now. Viola had to ban her from coming to the house because her nerves couldn't take it. But every hour Nell called.

"Is everything okay?" she asked on the phone. "Are the greens on?"

"Yes, Mother."

"I decided not to put banana in the ambrosia this year," Nell said. "It's not as pretty with the banana."

"Whatever you think," Viola said.

"Keep the turkey on low for the next few hours, Viola. That'll keep the juices in."

"Yes, I will."

"And Viola . . . don't forget to baste."

"I won't. . . ."

Viola hadn't even started her cleaning yet. Nell would have already had her table set. In fact, her guests could show up any Thanksgiving eve and Nell could just about set them down for the full meal. Viola began to pace the living room. The nausea started in the pit of her stomach again. How could Donald leave her with all this work?

She could feel herself starting to cry and she clapped her hands loud and hard to stop the tears. Sometimes clapping halted the anxiety. It didn't work today. Panic hit Viola with the force of a windstorm.

She sat down and took a few breaths. Yes, Chester is a creature of God, she thought, but for Thanksgiving he's supposed to be dinner. She got the short ax and went out to the back gated area. When she saw Chester proudly strutting the pen, pecking at the dry dirt, Viola had to wonder how folks did this kind of work. The bird was so unsuspecting. Maybe if she inched up slowly, tiptoed behind him, she could hit him with the back of the ax and knock him out first. But as Viola tipped, Chester tipped. She swung and the bird jumped out of the way, then he turned to her as if he finally understood what she was doing. He stared at Viola as if he felt betrayed. She quickly grabbed Chester to turn his eyes away, but when Viola gathered him to her chest, she could feel his heart beating. Beating like a tiny person who knew his fate.

She set him down and then set the ax down. Viola hated Donald Hinson. She hated that she slept with a man who could do this every day. She hated how he smelled, spoke, ate, touched her. She hated him for leaving her alone tonight. And Viola hated that she would have to march down to that slaughterhouse and haul him home to kill this bird.

She got into her car. Viola had been to the yard only about a dozen times over the last few years. Usually she pulled up at the door, delivered a message to a worker, and waited for Donald to come out from the office. There were no workers around this late on Thanksgiving eve, so Viola parked and went in.

She detested the feel of the place. The mud that clung to her shoes and the hog pens she had to pass. It was like watching innocent men gathered on death row. Tonight the yard was calm and dark. Viola walked past several pens and glanced at the pigs rolling in stiff mud mixed with carrot tops and corn cobs. She felt tears coming to her eyes. Lately just about everything brought her to tears.

"Donald," she called out as she walked toward the small office. She pushed open the door, and Amos was sitting at his desk, going through a pile of papers.

"Mrs. Donald?!" he said when she walked in.

"Where is my husband?"

"Yo' daddy just come by wit' a bunch of folks. Reverend Baines, Deacon Best, and Deacon Dawson…the lot of 'em went over to Dresden. Reverend Morgan was s'posed to go along," Amos rambled, "but I guess he couldn't make it." Amos rose when he saw how distraught she looked. "You okay, Mrs. Donald?"

Viola stood in the middle of the floor with her face in both hands. She felt like she couldn't breathe at all. "When will he return?" she asked.

"Hard to say," Amos answered. "I s'pose 'bout an hour."

She cried out and her whole body shook. Her wails were so loud that even her two hands couldn't mute them. Viola couldn't clap hard enough to control herself, and she fell to her knees.

"Hold on a minute there," Amos said, coming to her. "Now, you jes' stop that." He looked at her, kneeling on the dirt floor, bawling and clapping. He helped her up and led her to the old ottoman across from the desk. "Mr. Donald be back in an hour," he said, trying to calm her. "He be back."

"He didn't kill the turkey, Amos," she cried. "He didn't kill the turkey."

"That's a shame," Amos said, not quite getting the full picture.

"It's supposed to be in the oven. And I tried. I really tried."

"You?"

"I chased him with the ax but I couldn't."

"Of course you couldn't," he said sympathetically. "And see, that's yo' problem right there, Mrs. Donald. I ain't one fo' killin' nothin', you know that, but I believe you s'posed to wring the bird's neck."

"My Lord," she cried out.

"See, that bird be too fast to knock him out. That bird be like Joe Louis, duckin' and weavin' and carryin' on."

Viola looked at Amos through her tears. "Wring his neck?"

"That's what they do," Amos said.

Still in a daze, she got up from the chair. "I need to go," she said. "I need to go—right now. An hour, you say? Donald will be back in an hour?"

" 'Round 'bouts," he assured her. "You gon' be alright, Mrs. Donald? You don't look too good."

"What?"

"You look—" he reached for the right word. "You lookin' troubled."

"Troubled?"

"Fo' fact," he went on gently, "I don't mean to scare you none, but you got that same look as my crazy sister Caroline." Viola chuckled. "See there," he said, pointing at her, "that's exactly what Caroline does, a laughin' and a cryin' at the same time."

Viola sat down again on the ottoman with Amos beside her. She tried to pull herself together. She used Amos's handkerchief to dry her face. Then Amos began to softly hum. At first he hummed "America the Beautiful," and it was soothing. Then he stopped in the middle and started to hum "Any Kinda Man," the song they had danced to on the radio. Viola actually smiled.

"I knew that'd do the trick," he said.

"I guess you know how to even me out," she said.

"Well, that's my name," he said, patting her hand. "Old Even Amos." The contact felt good, but he pulled away and went back to humming. "You feelin' better now, Mrs. Donald?"

"I think so."

"Be good to see you like you was the other evening," he said. "Fo' fact, I never seen you that excited." He took her hand again and this time held on to it. "Talkin' 'bout music and yo' gal friend, that Isadora..."

"Isabel," she corrected.

"Yeah," he said, pressing her palm between the two of his.

"Well, I better get on," she said, standing up. Amos stood as well, but he still held on to Viola. Then he gave her a look she had rarely seen in any man: warm and loving but filled with longing. The strangest part was that Viola felt the exact same way. "I have a lot to do at home," she said.

"I was thinkin'," Amos started. "Maybe we can go on over to the poultry ranch. They most prob'ly got some turkeys already dead."

"It'll take close to an hour to get there," she said. "Donald's coming back in an hour..."

"I s'pose," he said. She could see Amos thinking. Thinking of a way that he could hold on to her hand awhile longer. "Maybe I'll come on over and help you with Chester there..."

"The blind leading the blind." She smiled.

"Most prob'ly." Amos slowly lifted her hand and kissed it on the inside. Viola never imagined that her palm could seem so raw and sensitive. It stunned her when he pulled her in close. Even through her coat, she could feel the tips of her breasts against his chest. His face was so close to hers that she felt his warm breath on the tip of her nose. Then Amos kissed her. Other than Donald, she had never been kissed by any man before. The feeling nearly lifted her off her feet. Amos's kiss was gentle, and when she returned it, it became deeper and more desperate. Then he eased away from her.

"Maybe I shouldn'ta done that," he said.

"I better go."

"Viola," he said. "All you needed is somebody to talk pretty to you. Speak to you like you matter. Touch you wit' some . . . nice skin, you know?"

She nodded.

"Ain't a damn thing wrong with that," he insisted. "Ever'body need that. Hell, I ain't heard no pretty words since Alfreda left two years ago."

"Thank you," she said.

He ran one hand slowly down the length of her arm. A chill shot through her body, then it warmed.

"I ain't foolin' myself," he said. "I'm only gittin' this close because I think you need me as much as I need you. You a special woman. One that deserve much mo' than any farmer, and a pig farmer at that."

"You're a good man, Amos," she said. "And much more than just a pig farmer."

"I ain't talkin' 'bout me," he said.

Amos lifted her hand and lightly kissed each finger. He moved closer still and brushed his knuckles against her cheek and then down her neck to the top of her chest. Then came that feeling. That "creamy" feeling Isabel had spoken of. Viola couldn't describe it as anything else when Amos undid the first few buttons of her blouse and kissed the top of her breast. This little man was the first one she had ever desired. He led her to the ottoman, one that Donald proba- bly sat in every day, and he kissed her, caressed her, and wound his body around hers. Then he lifted her skirt. Amos Flowers ran his fingers along the inside of her thigh, the side that felt as soft as butter. And he didn't stop. He used the tips of his fingers to explore and browse. It felt good to return his every touch and to hear his reaction. So neither heard the footsteps before a pair of perfectly buffed shoes stopped in their tracks. Neither saw the figure of a man staring from the door. Neither heard a sound until he cleared his throat. Viola jumped. Amos turned slowly, his hands still tucked in her private places. It wasn't Donald Hinson. It wasn't even Reverend Bembrey. It was Reverend Dr. Morgan. And all he said before he hurried away was "Pardon me."

Thanksgiving came and went without a single yam, biscuit, or cranberry wreath. Chester was probably still clucking around in her backyard. Viola wasn't quite sure because she hadn't been home in two days. She knew she was supposed to be upset. She knew she was supposed to be asking a lot of folks for a lot of forgiveness, but sitting here on Miss Rosalee's porch swing in the twilight of the day, Viola felt mostly relief.

She found out this morning that Reverend Dr. Morgan hadn't been alone when he discovered her and Amos. Mack from the slaughterhouse and Deacon Smalls from Wayside Baptist Church had stood in the doorway right behind him. Viola knew she was supposed to feel guilty and humiliated, but for the first time in years, there were no tears, no shortness of breath, no blues.

The door squeaked open and Miss Rosalee stepped out softly. "Can I get you some mo' lemonade?" she asked.

"No, thank you."

"If my baby need anything . . . jes' open yo' mouth, okay?"

Miss Rosalee called every child under the age of thirty her baby, and the words felt comforting. She seemed to understand people and that sometimes they did contrary things. Even when Isabel had walked the aisle of New Pilgrim, noxious whispers following on her heels, it was Miss Rosalee who had moved over and cleared a seat for her to rest herself. Miss Rosalee was a good Christian woman, but when Amos had called her to pick up Viola from the slaughterhouse, even she had been at a loss for words. Then she came right over. The ride back to her house was the quietest time Viola had ever spent with Miss Rose. Her silence wasn't judgmental, nor was it angry. It was more like that of a woman who had just seen the aftermath of a storm she'd predicted long before it hit.

Miss Rose took the other seat in the swing, alighting as gently as one would on the edge of a hospital bed.

"I'm gonna leave a clean dress for you to wear to church tomorrow," she said.

"Church?" Viola smiled cynically.

"You've always gone to church, Viola. My Lord has forgiven a lot worse."

"My daddy hasn't."

"I guess you know him better'n anybody do . . . and Donald too. But there are other churches beside New Pilgrim."

"Maybe I'll go to Reverend Baines' church," she said. "Or better yet, how about Reverend Dr. Morgan's."

"A fresh mouth don't suit you, Viola Bembrey!"

Viola sighed. Amos had comforted her. He soothed her, and yes, things had become more intimate than they should have, but Viola hadn't ever experienced such warmth. She wondered if Amos felt as innocent as she did and if he could recall her touch as vividly as she could recall his. More than that, she wondered why he hadn't phoned or come by. Before Viola had left the slaughterhouse with Miss Rose, he had kissed her right in the palm and said, "I'll see you in a minute. Don't you worry none." But every time Miss Rose's phone rang, it was someone calling to find out if what they'd heard was true. Out of respect for Viola and the Bembreys, Miss Rose never confirmed or denied.

"You gon' have to decide what you wanna do," Miss Rosalee said.

"About what?"

Miss Rosalee stopped the glide of the swing abruptly with the ball of her foot. "You a smart gal," she started, "so don't you sit up here talkin' to me like ain't nothin' happened. What you did was a sin befo' God."

"We didn't have sex, Miss Rose."

"When a man puts his hands on you, Viola . . . when he touch you in private places . . . that there is sex too, make no mistake. I think you know that. You also know it was dead wrong."

Viola had been lying with Donald, her husband, for nearly four years, and from day one she had detested every moment. Amos Flowers had laid his hands on her for ten minutes and made her feel more desired and loved then she had felt in her entire twenty-one years. Maybe it was wrong, Viola thought, but it didn't feel wrong to her body or her heart.

"You need to start thinkin' 'bout yo' next step," Miss Rosalee said. "You need to start thinkin' about sittin' down and talkin' to yo' husband."

"I need to talk to Amos first."

"Girl, are you hearin' me?!" Miss Rosalee exclaimed. "This ain't got ne're a thing to do wit' no Amos Flowers. This got to do with you and yo' husband. You and yo' family. Later fo' some Amos Flowers."

"He promised me he'd call," Viola insisted.

"Lord, ha' mercy," Miss Rosalee cried. "You don't know if you comin' or goin', do you, girl?" Miss Rose threw up her hands. "Just like my sister. You and my sister, Honeybee . . . I tell you, y'all are like two peas in a pod. Both spirited, impulsive, willful. She took up with this boy when she wasn't supposed to." Then Miss Rosalee added, "But she weren't married like you. I guess that there is a little different." Miss Rose stood up from the swing. "I'm gon' give you Honeybee's address in New York. You oughta write her and maybe she'll talk some sense into you. Lord, but she got some tales to tell. Prob'ly set you right straight." Miss Rose opened the screen door. "And I'm still gon' leave a dress for you in the spare room, in case you change your mind."

"I won't," Viola insisted. Miss Rosalee went in and the screen door slapped shut behind her.

The cool Jasperville evening was quiet. Viola hummed "Any Kinda Man." The chords wouldn't leave her, nor would the taste of Amos's lips or the feeling of his arms around her.

"Miss Rose," Viola called into the house. "I need to take a walk."

"Girl, it's getting dark," Miss Rosalee said, coming to the door again.

"I'll be back soon."

Miss Rosalee stood on the porch with folded arms as Viola started down the walkway. "I don't think this is a good idea, Viola," she called. With a disapproving sigh, Miss Rosalee reached behind the screen door and took her car keys from the peg. She threw them down the walk toward Viola. "Take the shortcut down Tucker Road, left past the fork," she yelled. Viola turned back and picked up the keys from the ground. She knew Miss Rosalee didn't approve, but somehow, the woman did understand. "About twenty miles past Graham Breen and you'll be there. You'll be in Caldwell." Miss Rosalee stood on her porch as Viola headed for the house where Amos lived.

Caldwell seemed a long way into the sticks, past the point where brick and timber became twigs tied together to make a wall or a roof. Green fields with tobacco and peaches spread seemingly for miles. An occasional dwelling popped up here and there, often with a well and an outhouse. Viola knew Amos's home was out this way, because he had mentioned the onion fields just a ways up the road. He said that the only time he ever cried was in the hot summer months when the west wind blew.

The first house she passed after the onion field couldn't have been Amos's. There were children's toys in the yard and frilly yellow curtains on the windows. Viola drove a couple of miles farther to the next house just beyond the thick weeping vines of a family of willows. In the darkening yard was the large pecan tree Viola had heard so much about. Amos often joked that when he left for work on a windy day, he had to raise an umbrella to avoid the storm of nuts. On one side of the house was a field of purple wildflowers growing like they had been encouraged. Viola thought them as beautiful as Nell's rose garden.

A small light shone through the paper window shades. She walked onto the porch. Viola knew that her life would change when Amos opened that door. It had already changed. They'd make love. She'd have to leave Donald, but at least she'd be happy. Viola took a small breath, then knocked. She waited, but no Amos. Viola knocked again, then walked into a bare living room. Not a stick of furniture remained. Toward the back of the house, she heard music playing.

"Amos?" she called out.

The kitchen had no table or chairs, not a spoon or a fork. Even the wallpaper had been pulled off, and splotches of copper-colored glue stained the walls. Viola went into a smaller back room that she assumed was the bedroom, and it was likewise empty. Only the pecan tree, purple wildflowers, and the blues hinted that Amos had once lived here.

Viola sat on the floor against the wall in the bare bedroom. She'd never imagined that he would leave. The Amos she thought she knew would've stood up for himself and her too. Viola lowered her head to her knees at the thought of staying in Jasperville without him. The pretty fog was lifting, and the realization of what she'd done broke through, harsh as a searchlight.

Viola pulled herself up from the floor, her legs trembling. She'd have to go back to that house, sit at that table, and eat breakfast and dinner with Donald Hinson, without even the Sunday light of Amos Flowers. Where else could she go? She didn't try to stop her tears this time, or the cries to God. Viola could almost hear the voices of the congregation urging her to fall down on her knees and give thanks for a husband like Donald. Give thanks for the life she had. Was it such a bad life? Maybe she hadn't really given herself a chance to be happy in it. Maybe she hadn't really given Donald a chance. *A good husband, a good job for a woman, and a beautiful home.*

Miss Rosalee was right when she said that the Lord would forgive a pure heart. Perhaps, eventually, the Reverend and Donald would too. Viola started on her way out. She *would* put on the dress that Miss Rosalee had set out and go to church tomorrow. It would be hard and humiliating at first, then after a while she could resume this life everyone insisted was so good. It *was* good, she thought. It would be even better when she really gave it a chance. Donald would distance himself from her, but eventually things would come back to normal. At least now she had a plan. She would support her husband and his expanding yard, even if it meant getting out there in the mud. They'd work on that child he wanted. Yes, she would go back and, sooner or later, there would be forgiveness. That was what the church was for. Forgiveness and divine grace.

Viola walked into New Pilgrim with Miss Rosalee by her side. Eyes that usually met hers with warmth now filled with judgment and pity. Everyone knew what she'd done, there was no mistake about

that. Senior Brother Clark nodded to Miss Rosalee but glanced away
when he saw Viola. In the choir box, Cynthie Nettles' expression held
no sympathy at all. Mrs. Baker didn't bother to wave Viola up to sit
with the choir. Miss Rosalee thought it wise that they sit in the back
of the church, anyway. At least until things got back to normal.

Donald was on the amen bench, just left of the pulpit, staring
straight ahead. Viola could only see Nell from the back. Her mother
looked down into her lap, a navy hat deliberately tilted over her face.
Viola didn't see the Reverend at all, but knew it would just be a moment before he stepped onto the pulpit.

Viola bit her thumbnail. Surely her father would lash out at her in
front of the entire congregation. She would accept it. She knew she
deserved it. After talking and praying with Miss Rosalee half the
night, Viola understood that her actions were wrong, even if she did
need Amos's touch. Her stomach tightened. Only Miss Rosalee's firm
grip on her hand stopped the full-fledged panic. Viola could hear
whispering around her but she had expected that. There'd be talk,
isolation, and lots of lectures. Donald would be cold, and Nell simply
wouldn't speak to her at all. Eventually, though, her life would come
back.

Miss Rosalee squeezed her hand when Reverend Bembrey entered
the church from the small back room. The congregation quieted as he
calmly took his place on the pulpit. Viola braced herself to receive her
father's wrath.

"Cherished friends..." The Reverend's deep voice resonated
through the church. "I say to you all, that Satan can corrupt even the
most devout households." He leaned on the side of the dais. "The
weakest link in the chain," he continued. "We have to try to
strengthen that link, make it equal with the rest, let it pull its own
weight. However, if we can't make it strong, I say ... cast it out," he
said calmly. "Cast it out!! Lest we all get pulled down into that big ole
black hole. Cast out the scorner and contention shall go out, yea,
strife and reproach shall cease."

The congregation was silent this morning. Viola noticed Sister
Harper crying into her handkerchief.

"Forgiveness," he began again. Miss Rosalee offered Viola an encouraging smile. "How much can one really forgive, and where do you draw the line, dear Lord." His voice rose slightly. "We'd all like to believe that we can forgive just about anything."

"Amen," Brother Clark called.

Sister Harper glanced in Viola's direction and winked.

"But comes a time, when in order to save a crate of fresh apples from being infected with rot and decay, we must cast out the one bad apple. 'And the great dragon was cast out, that old serpent, called the Devil, and Satan, which deceiveth the whole world: he was cast out into the earth.' " Reverend Bembrey paused as if in pain. "And now," he said, "I humbly hold myself up as a testament. Sacrificing, to the evils of the world, my own flesh and blood." He pushed his salt-and-pepper brows almost to the point of his hairline. "Viola . . ." His voice cracked. "Come to your father."

The church shifted as she rose to her feet. Viola had no idea what would happen next, perhaps some cleansing, like a Baptism. Miss Rosalee's hand held hers tight and didn't loosen until Viola started down the aisle. "It's gonna be alright, Miss Rose," Viola whispered. She gently pulled away and walked toward the altar. She glanced at her mother, who further lowered her head, and then at Donald, whose stare remained emotionless. Viola finally reached the dais, where she met her father's outstretched hand.

"This is my daughter," he said to the congregation, "flesh of my flesh. I love her more than anything in this world." Tears rolled down his face. "But the daughter of any priest, if she profane herself by playing the whore, she profaneth her father: she shall be burnt with fire." Donald stood up from the amen bench and handed the Reverend her small green suitcase and a Bible, which he in turn gave to Viola. She took the suitcase and looked around in confusion. Then Reverend Bembrey caressed her face and kissed her cheek. "Viola, baby . . . please, go with God."

Viola stood paralyzed, unsure of what she should do. The congregation seemed just as baffled. Then Reverend Bembrey motioned for two young ushers to open the double doors in the back of the church. Sunlight burst through. People in the back pews lifted fans to foreheads, like visors. Two deacons came down the aisle, and Viola could hear their heavy shined boots touch down on the worn carpeting. This was her excommunication. The Reverend was now sitting beside Donald, both watching as if she were a stranger. A numbness spread through Viola's body. Through her tears, she saw Nell, head down, her arms wrapped around herself. One of the deacons came up behind Voila and took her by the elbow. He escorted her down the long aisle and through the front door.

It was November 1961, when she started to walk the road. Viola held on to the handle of her suitcase and followed the rail tracks. Jasperville got smaller and smaller until it was out of sight.

CHAPTER 9

Forestine waited in the backseat of the car for Beck to come out of a Michigan blues club called the Cross Roads. He had put on his manager's cap to go in and ask for pay in advance of their performance tonight. Forestine shifted a sleeping Benny from one knee to the other. She didn't even know what city they were in.

The car engine chugged and chortled. Though the sound was annoying, at least the car was warm. Forestine more than expected the old station wagon to completely conk out, but somehow Beck kept it running. She pulled the blanket up past Benny's ears. His cough had gotten worse since winter had come. Even though the child was wrapped in heavy wool, Forestine could feel the cold rattling in his chest. He was bundled so snug that she could see only his large brown eyes.

A pink neon sign flashed on in front of the club. In just moments the block would fill with multicolor lights. Down the block a sign blinked on in front of the Sparrow. Forestine realized now she was in Detroit. Coleman Hawkins was on the marquee, and she smiled to herself at the thought of his music. She wanted to pull the old station wagon up to that door and get out. She'd even heard that Eddie Bishop and his Quintet had played there just a few weeks ago. She sighed at the thought of all this jazz going on. Going on without her. Soon that would change.

Under Benny's breath she heard a small wheeze—not strong enough to take him to the hospital but present enough to make her worry. Benny had come into the world jaundiced and asthmatic, and though he always bounced back, he was rarely without a cold or infection. From the time he was a tiny baby, Forestine hardly ever left his side. She had rehearsed while Benny lay in a bassinet on top of Beck's piano. She had spent her meals cooing and playing, while he pulled milk from a reservoir at the very bottom of her soul. And still, the only time she left her son was when she stepped onstage to perform.

Now three years old, Benny insisted on calling Forestine by her first name. She tried to get the child to call her Mommy or Mama, but Benny was growing up around adults, and adults called each other by their first names. Beck hated that Forestine allowed the child to get away with it. He was known to Benny as Daddy Beck.

"For'stine," Benny said through a clogged nose.

"Yes, baby?"

"Can I go in tonight?"

"I don't know, sweetheart," she replied. "This might be one of them clubs," she explained, "that don't allow children. We'll see what Daddy Beck says when he comes out."

"I'll be quiet," he said.

"I know you will, sugar," she said. "But some grown people don't think it's right for a child to be in a nightclub. You get what Mama's saying?"

He nodded, but Forestine didn't think he quite understood. The boy asked to be with her always, and Forestine obliged him. He remained as close to her as one of her own limbs. Aside from the music, he was the only thing in her life that was pure joy. Whenever she could slip him into the club dressing room before her shows, she did. She wanted him to hear her.

The heat from the engine felt good, but sooner or later Beck would have to turn it off and the Michigan wind would whip through the car as sharply as a straight razor. Forestine yearned for that old Caravan bus right about now. When Lil' Eartha had gone on her way, everyone had been left to their own lodging, heat, and transportation. In Forestine and Beck's case, they were sometimes one and the same. It had been almost four years since she'd seen Eartha. The woman had finally married Ernest, and the happy couple went to live in Alabama. Forestine had been thrilled when Creer and Doug decided to join her Bent Down Blues Revue. Beck lined up some of the same houses where they'd performed with the Caravan. Or at least the ones that were still open. But the Bent Down Blues Revue had gone about as far it could. With the exception of the big players like Muddy Waters and B. B. King, blues shows were thinning out. Most clubs preferred to book R&B or jazz. That's why, over the past couple of years, Beck had slowly steered Forestine toward a less bluesy repertoire.

Jazz was what she longed for. Straight-up jazz. After sitting in with players across the country, she felt confident enough to really sing it. Players like Stan Baylor at a club in Tulsa and Seymour Huggley's Quintet in Oakland. Forestine loved the feel of a song like "You Go to My Head." She liked the sophistication of it, the way it made her stand tall. Beck was right. Her voice was good to jazz, lending it a smoothness that was rare for a singer so new to the style. As much as she had come to love Creer and Doug, they played only the blues, and so soon they'd have to part ways. Beck, of course, would always be by her side and would act as her manager.

Beck emerged from the club and Benny yanked his arms from the snug blanket and pounded on the window. Beck hurried across the cold street, pulling his overcoat around his pudgy body. He slid into the driver's seat and turned to face Forestine. "He give us half," he said. She shrugged. He looked down at Benny, listening to the faint whistle under the child's breath. "The baby don't sound too good."

"Better than it was."

Beck removed his coat and nestled the two of them in it. "After the gig tomorrow I want you to take Benny and go on back to Kentucky fo' a while," he told her.

"And what are we supposed to live on?" Forestine sounded exasperated.

"Ain't like we gon' starve," Beck told her. "But I'll tell you, if we stay out here, Benny will surely not make it. That child is sick all the time."

Right after Benny was born, Forestine had stayed in Kentucky for three months. Since then, they'd gone back for a week or two at a time when Benny was at his sickest. Even a few days spent away from the business made Forestine feel she had to work that much harder to get back into the light. It was a fine house in Kentucky, but Forestine Bent wasn't used to the South. The quiet paralyzed her, and she knew the world and her career were moving past her. Lexington, Kentucky, was the last place she wanted to be. Besides, most of the doctors agreed that Benny might soon outgrow the asthma and the sicknesses.

"We got the gig in North Carolina tomorrow," she said, "and then at the Paradise in Knoxville... and that's a top house. After that, I'll take Benny and go to Kentucky for a while."

Beck looked at her suspiciously. "After Knoxville?"

"Yes, honey."

"Don't shit me, Forestine," he warned.

"I told you what I told you," she spat.

"Alright," he conceded. "We can most prob'ly bring him into the Cross Roads tonight," Beck said, thinking out loud. "And I'm sure the folks at the Blues Shack in North Carolina won't mind. We just gotta find someone to take care of him during that Knoxville show."

"I surely remember how Tiny carried on when we brought him into the Paradise the last time."

"I don't blame her, Forestine. A nightclub ain't no place for a three-year-old child, and the boy did raise a whole lotta Cain."

"Well, he wasn't feeling good," she said defensively.

"The boy ain't never feeling good," Beck retorted. "And if the gig wasn't so much money, I'd say to hell with it." Beck reached into the backseat with a tissue, lifted Benny's head, and wiped his nose. He opened the window and tossed the tissue out, then quickly closed it again. "What about that lady that own the boardinghouse in Knoxville?" Beck asked. "Miss Edmonds... she took care of Benny before. Maybe she take him for the night."

"Don't trust her," Forestine said.

Three years with Forestine Bent had just about worn Beck out. She had a way of looking at things that didn't allow for anyone else's opinion. Her stubbornness made it possible for Forestine to overcome adversity in the business, but it also pushed people away. She could've been singing with a jazz drummer named Major Carlyle over a year ago, but Benny got sick. Instead of letting Beck take the child home to Kentucky, she had insisted on keeping Benny by her side. The boy got even sicker and had to be hospitalized. Forestine was forced to go to Kentucky for a while, and Major Carlyle hired another singer.

At the beginning of their marriage, Forestine and Beck had squabbled about smaller things like vocal arrangements or costumes. Now, just about everything was open for a fight. A year ago, Beck nearly got on a train and rode away, but two things had stopped him. Her voice kept him with her no matter how stubborn the woman was. But more, Beck had become Benny's father. Forestine loved the child, but she was hurting him by insisting on keeping him so close. Benny wasn't built for the road. Although Beck would never say it out loud, he was beginning to feel that maybe Forestine loved her music even more than her child.

"It's gon' have to be Miss Edmonds at the boardinghouse," Beck said. "Plus, she likes Benny."

"But Benny don't like her," she said. "Ain't that right, baby?"

"Nope," Benny answered.

"I hate it when you do that, Forestine," Beck shook his head. "I don't like it when you bring a child in on grown folks' discussions."

"Benny can make up his own mind about some things and so can I. I don't care for Miss Edmonds. Don't like her eyes or her smile. Plus the woman smoke like a chimney and Benny is all stuffed up as it is."

"You think the club is any less smoky?"

"Man, if you lookin' for a fight, you gonna have to slug it out by yourself tonight," she argued.

"What about leaving him in New York with yo' mama?"

Forestine shot Beck a look meant to pierce his heart. Her family didn't know that Benny existed and she wanted to keep it that way. "I'll find someone my damn self," she said. "Someone *I* trust."

Forestine was running out of options. She'd keep singing, no matter that she told Beck she wouldn't. He was right about Benny, though. The child couldn't take life on the road. But Forestine refused to leave him behind. She felt her son's forehead, then pulled the blanket up past his neck again. He'd sweat the fever out and then rally back. Forestine held him and lay her head on top of his. Miss Edmonds, she thought to herself. Miss Edmonds wasn't the one for her son. Forestine would think of someone . . . something. She always did.

He was a veterinarian trained to treat horses, deliver breech birth cows, and cure chicken diseases. In an emergency Dr. Kintz looked in on people. It was usually a woman in labor, a severed limb, or heatstroke. He patched, sewed, rehydrated, and went on home. But when he arrived at the rooming house in Sobel, Georgia, and saw the child with a fever just over 103 degrees, bordering on delirium, he instantly bundled Benny up and took him to the hospital in Atlanta. Forestine was hysterical and Beck was furious. She had promised to take Benny to Kentucky after Knoxville. That was a month ago. Then came an offer for the Blues Revue to do five weeks opening for jazz singer Trent Addison. Beck didn't object to her going as long as she took Benny to her mother's in New York. Again, the mule in Forestine kicked and she refused. Now the boy was in the hospital, again, hooked up to a tube with bags of fluid suspended above his head.

"They said he'd be fine," Forestine whispered. "They gave him some antibodies—"

"Antibiotics," Beck hissed. "Should know that word in yo' sleep by now." They sat on the cushioned bench outside of Benny's room. "I spoke to a woman," he said, "name is Birdie and she got a house about thirty miles from here in Decatur. Said when Benny get out we can bring him there until he strong enough to travel."

"I ever meet this woman?"

"Don't you ask me no mo' questions, woman!" he yelled. "I don't wanna hear shit about nobody's face." A nurse dashed Beck a look, reminding him that he was in a hospital. He settled back, the fire still in his eyes. "If you wanna talk about somebody's face, you go on in there and look at that child's face."

"You saying this is all my fault?" she asked.

"Yes, I am," he spat. "I can't get through to you, Forestine, and you ain't a stupid woman!"

"You saying I'm a bad mother?"

"I'm sayin' that you just don't think." He paused to collect himself.

"I know you love Benny, and he worships the ground you walk on, but all you think about is the music. I'm a musician too, so damn it, I know. But I don't put it in front of the folks I love."

"I'm singing for Benny. I want him to be proud of his mother."

"He's already proud of you, Forestine. The boy could care less if you were a singer or a meter maid. What he needs is for you to take him home and make him chicken stew. You gotta either take him back to Kentucky or to yo' mama in New York. Those are the choices. The chile needs to be home, Forestine. *He needs to be home!*"

"Then I'll take him home!" she yelled back. Forestine's back lengthened against the cushion. "If that's what you feel I should do, I'll take Benny home."

"If that's what *I* feel you should do?" Beck was at a loss for words. "I've never met anybody like you, Forestine. Are the police gonna have to come and lock yo' ass up fo' you to understand? Is that what you want?"

"Oh, man, please," she said. "Benny is sick. If we were home in Kentucky, he'd still be sick. So just . . . please."

Beck stood up. A look of complete helplessness washed over his face. "Do you really believe that?"

"Yes, I do," she answered.

"Then God help you, Forestine." He turned, walked into the stairwell across the hall and lit a cigarette.

Through a glass pane in the door, Forestine looked in at Benny sleeping comfortably. On the tray beside his bed, a small baked chicken thigh hadn't been touched, nor had the green beans or shredded carrots. Even the chocolate pudding remained uneaten. She entered the room, sat in a chair beside his bed, and gently rubbed his legs and arms. She knew that her son needed to be somewhere warm and permanent, but if she went home now, she'd have nothing and Benny would have even less. Forestine could have both Benny and her career. Many women did it. She clutched her hands in her lap. Her head throbbed at the thought of taking him to Hattie Bent. The idea of Lucas and Lilian was enough to give her palpitations. If Forestine took Benny back to Brooklyn, could her family somehow find out that Lucas was the father? That was something even Willie might not forgive.

She sat with her son awhile longer before she came out and stood over Beck.

"I'll go to Kentucky," she said. "I'll take my son home."

"I'm supposed to believe that?" he asked.

"Believe what you want. I'm taking Benny home."

"Alright, Forestine," he said. "The nurse say Benny might still have a bad night, and she set up a bed for us beside him."

"Good." She put on her coat and lifted her bag on her shoulder. "I'll be back in a few hours."

"A few hours? She say we can stay here, Forestine. Where in the world are you going?"

"I promised to sit in with the Gus Hannen Trio tonight."

"What?"

"It's no big deal. I'll call you from the club."

In just days, Benny's cold sores were scabs and his runny nose crusted above his top lip. He dashed through the rooming house in Decatur as if he'd never had a sick day in his life. As usual, Forestine started making excuses about why it wouldn't be a good time for her to go to Lexington right now. She'd been offered an eight-week gig with the Gus Hannen Trio. Smaller houses but bigger cities. The Trio wasn't well known, nor were the musicians first rate, but it was a chance for her to sing jazz. Beck didn't think them worthy of her talent. He felt she should accept no less than an offer from a king. A king like Cannonball Adderly, Eddie Bishop, or Miles Davis. But more important, Beck didn't think Benny should be traveling. Forestine's ambition, once again, clouded her good reason.

"Gus wants to add 'Stella by Starlight.'" Forestine excitedly flipped through the sheet music. "The Trio used to do it and he thinks the song would suit me. . . ."

Benny played with his wooden blocks in the middle of the floor while Beck packed the suitcases. He didn't seem angry, but he wore a look that Forestine recognized. It was the same expression she herself had worn when listening to Hattie talk, when she heard the voice, but not the words.

"I wanted him to add 'Midnight Sun,'" she went on, "but not only would I have to learn it, the band would have to learn it too. Gus didn't want to have to do a full rehearsal for one song."

Beck sat at the edge of the bed with his bags at his feet. Without bothering to pour his Jack Daniel's into a glass, he turned the pint up to his mouth and emptied a quarter of it in one swallow.

"I haven't seen you drink like this in a while," she said.

"One of us had to keep a clear head, Forestine." There was no bitterness in his voice. Just resignation. But Benny noticed something had changed. The boy went over and jumped onto Beck's lap.

"Why you crying, Daddy Beck?" Benny asked him.

"Daddy isn't crying," Forestine corrected. "Daddy is just drinking," she teased. "He gets a little weepy when he drinks, baby."

"Daddy Beck is cryin'," Benny insisted.

"Yes, he is," Beck said. Forestine looked up from her sheet music. "Daddy Beck got to go away fo' a while," he said.

"You got a gig?" Benny asked.

"Yeah, Daddy, you got a gig?" Forestine asked playfully.

He didn't answer. She could see that he had finally crossed some sort of line. She saw in him the fatigue that comes from being put upon, time and time again. Over the years it seemed the light had gone out of his eyes. His pain hit her all at once. She couldn't dare apologize now, because she didn't have the courage to say she would try to change. Nor did she really want to.

"I got a couple of gigs," Beck said.

"Wit' For'stine?" Benny asked.

"Not this time. Daddy Beck need to run solo fo' a while." He hugged Benny tight. "You gon' make sho' yo' mama give you yo' medicine, right?"

Benny seemed perplexed. "Yes, sir."

"She forgets. I need you to stay healthy, okay?"

"Yes, sir. Can I go with you, Daddy Beck?"

"Not this time," Beck said, holding out his open palm. "My man," he said, and Benny popped him a quick five. Beck lifted the child off of his lap. He stood up, pulled some keys from his pocket, and handed them to Forestine. She could barely look at him. "These are fo' the station wagon. Figure you gon' need it mo' than me."

"How are you going to get around?"

Beck slapped the side of his leg. "Mo' reliable than the Greyhound."
He handed her an envelope. "Been savin' a bit," he said. "This is fo' you
and Benny. Get you through for a few months, even if you ain't
workin'." Beck wore a bit of smile, but his eyes were glassy. "Which
brings me to the last lil' trinket," he said, pulling out another set of
keys. "These are to the house in Kentucky. I cain't tell you what to do,
Forestine, but I pray that's where you'll go. Even fo' just a time." He
slipped on his suit jacket and picked up his bag. "Hey, man," he called
to Benny. "I'ma see ya in a minute, you hear?"

"Yes, sir."

"I love ya," Beck said to him. "You know that, don't you?"

"Yes, sir. But why can't I go with you?"

"Not this time, partner. You take care yo' mama."

Forestine could've stopped him. Calling his name, telling him that
she loved him, would have made Beck Pinkney turn and come back.
It would've made him stop and try again. But she couldn't. Forestine
didn't say a word as he left the room, nor did she shed a tear when she
looked out the window and saw him get into a waiting car and drive
away. She couldn't allow herself to be that vulnerable.

Forestine was beginning to think that Benny had finally outgrown
the asthma. Three months later, he'd had a few small colds and low-
grade fevers, but nothing serious. His energy was boundless. Bookings
were picking up for the Gus Hannen Trio. They had started to get into
bigger houses because of Forestine. They were not great, Beck was
right about that, but *her* reviews were always outstanding.

On a pretty June day she checked into the Briarwood Motel in
Norfolk, Virginia. This week, they were performing in a new club
called Jazz Haven. Benny had a tiny wheeze, but Forestine didn't
think it was cause for concern. While she dressed to go to the club, the
wheeze turned into a gasp and his fever shot up.

She hadn't refilled his prescription in weeks. Beck had always
taken care of that. Whenever they pulled into a new city, the first
thing he did was find out where the nearest hospital was. He always
got Benny's medicine, stocked juice, and took the child's temperature,
even if Benny didn't feel warm. Forestine desperately scraped the last

of the fever medication from an old bottle. She tried three inhalers before she found one that worked. Then she sat on the bed, holding Benny in her lap and crying.

"Got the car running," Gus called from outside. "Need to be at the club in twenty minutes. We'll be downstairs waiting."

"I can't go," she called back.

Gus opened the door and stood there. "What do you mean?"

"Benny's sick." Forestine knew that if she raised her head to look at Gus, she would fall apart completely.

"What's wrong with him now?"

"I just gave him some medicine . . . the orange one, but I need to take him to the hospital."

"Where the hell is the hospital?" he asked.

"I don't know," she cried. "I just don't know."

"Did you call the front desk?" he asked. "They'll know at the front desk."

"I will," she said. "And Gus . . . maybe I just better meet you in Philly."

"That's five damn days from now. We still got five days here."

Forestine lay Benny on the bed and covered him with a blanket. "Sorry," she said.

Gus looked at the child and then at Forestine. He wasn't unfeeling. He had a show to do and she understood that. But Gus Hannen's Trio hadn't known success until he met Forestine.

"We'll be down in the car waiting," he said. "I'll ask the desk clerk where to drop you and the boy off."

"Thank you," she said.

"Got you enough money and everything?" he asked.

"I think so. Really, Gus," she said. "Thank you." He closed the door as he left. Forestine pulled off Benny's damp shirt and put on a clean one. He seemed dizzy and lethargic.

"I wanna go out," he said to Forestine.

"We are going out, sugar. We going to the hospital."

"I wanna go to the house," he said.

"What house?" she said, stuffing the damp shirt into a plastic bag.

"With Daddy Beck. I wanna go to the house in Kentucky," he said.

Forestine froze. She could feel herself starting to crumble. Benny had always fought to be with her, even if it meant he had to stay at the hotel with a stranger while she sang. Never before had he wanted to be away from her side. She looked into his watery eyes, and she could see that Benny was tired.

"Daddy's not in Kentucky right now."

"I wanna see Daddy Beck," Benny insisted.

Forestine bit the inside of her lip. "How about if I take you to your aunt Lilian?"

"Who?"

"She's my sister."

"You have a little sister or a big sister?" he asked.

She laughed. "She's big but she's littler than me. And you know what?"

"What?"

"There's nothing that she would like more than to have you stay with her for a while. I just know it."

"I'm gonna stay there?"

"For a little while. You're gonna like it because she got a backyard and everything." She put on Benny's jacket and then her own.

"With swings?" he asked.

"I'm not sure about that, but if I know my sister Lilian, she'd probably put some there just for you."

"For real?"

"For really real," Forestine answered.

"How long I gotta stay?" he asked.

"Just for a while. Until Mommy can . . . well, get her singing goin' a little better. Then maybe we can get ourselves a house."

"But we got a house in Kentucky," he said.

"Well, we'll have two," she said. "But before we go to your aunt, we need to get you to a doctor, okay?"

When they got into Gus's car, Forestine touched the child's head lightly with her lips, hoping the medicine had cooled his fever. His wheezing was heavier now. Gus pulled outside of the emergency room ten minutes later, and they admitted Benny right away. Once again, the child lay in a room with a machine to help him breathe and a bag suspended above his head. Benny stayed there for two days, and Forestine never left his side.

On the third day, she found a phone and dialed her sister's number in Brooklyn. When she heard Lucas's voice, she almost hung up. For Benny's sake, she said, "Hello."

"Forestine?!" he yelled into the phone. "Where you at, girl?"

"I'm in Virginia," she answered.

"Got you a gig in Virginia?"

"I need to talk to you, Lucas."

She could hear his smile fade. "What's wrong?"

"Is Lilian there?"

"Her and your mother went to one of them Tupperware parties there in the projects. . . ."

"Good," she said. "Why don't you sit down. This might take a minute."

The cab stopped in front of a small house on Nostrand Avenue. Forestine had to dodge the children darting by her on the sidewalk. One thing she had missed about Brooklyn was the families. She could see Benny curiously watching little girls skip double Dutch on the sidewalk and boys playing Skelly just off the curb. A pretty tan Buick sat in the open garage beside Lilian's house. It looked like the Campbells had moved along in their lives.

Forestine straightened Benny's collar. She knocked on the front door and could feel her knees shaking as she waited.

"Is this where Miss Lilian lives?" Benny asked.

"*Aunt* Lilian," she corrected. A pang of guilt shot through Forestine. Benny was so unused to having family, he didn't even know what to call them. After a moment she heard heavy feet approaching from inside. Lucas opened the door, his shoulders filling the entire frame.

Forestine had thought about this moment so many times, colored it every shade of blue in each of her songs. Not just standing across from Lucas with their son, but actually seeing him again after four years.

He looked at her and then down at Benny. Forestine could see him searching the boy for pieces of himself. A tiny grin passed over his face when he found one. Lucas stood there without speaking, then he shook his head. He looked over his shoulder into the house and stepped outside on the porch, closing the door behind him.

"Did you talk to her?" Forestine asked.

"Oh, yes," Lucas said. He watched as Benny hopped up and down the three porch steps. "In fact, she's still in the back getting the room ready for Benny."

"What did she say, Lucas?"

"She said that she'd love to have Benny stay with us, as long as he needs to—"

"You didn't say anything else," Forestine cut in.

"No," he replied. "I agree with you, Forestine. All that other stuff isn't necessary."

She was relieved. If Lucas *had* said something, the whole Bent family would be lying in wait. Lilian was family, and Forestine's son was simply staying with family. "But what if she finds out and I'm not around?"

"She won't find out," he insisted. "And even if she does"—Lucas moved closer to Forestine—"I'll be here to protect him because he's my son." He looked at Benny like he couldn't believe these words. "Besides, Lilian would never take her anger out on a child."

"I guess that's true."

"Go on in and talk to her for a while," Lucas suggested. "I know that there isn't any love lost but, for Benny's sake, you need to sit down like sisters."

Forestine hadn't seen Lilian in four years. She hesitated awhile in the foyer and then walked toward the bedrooms in the back. The house was frighteningly similar to her mother's apartment; its colors and textures the same, its pictures and crucifixes big and gaudy. Only the upright piano in the living room spoke of Lucas's presence. Lilian stepped out of a room just as Forestine was about to look in. She started as if she had seen a ghost standing in her hallway.

"Forestine—?"

For a moment Forestine observed the picture of her sister. The sassy twitch that once had made her wide hips sashay in lively arrogance had been sedated by the deafening quiet of a childless home. Her lips, once pouty and full, now looked flesh-colored and pedestrian. Her eyebrows were thick, her voice seemed to have lowered an octave, and the look of youthful caprice and just plain old haughtiness had been replaced with barren indifference. Lilian was a settled, married woman.

"I didn't know you'd be here this early," she said.

"I took a different train."

"I suppose there were no telephones in that train station?" Lilian asked.

"I should've called," Forestine admitted.

Lilian walked down the hall toward the living room. Forestine assumed this meant she should follow.

"So where's the baby?" Lilian asked.

"He's not exactly a baby," Forestine said. "Benny will be four next month."

"Four is still a baby, Forestine." Lilian looked from the living room window at Benny on the steps outside. "What a precious child."

"Yes." Forestine sat down on the peach-colored sofa. Lilian sat across from her.

"Who would've thought you'd be the first," Lilian said. "To have a child, I mean."

"Certainly not me," Forestine replied.

"Nor me," Lilian said, sounding almost defeated. "I suppose Lucas is giving us a chance to talk. He's nice like that."

"Yes, he is." Lilian's civility surprised Forestine. "How's Mama?" Forestine asked, though she really didn't care.

"You know Hattie," Lilian answered.

"And Willie?"

"He says that you write or call him ever' so often. You probably know better than me how Daddy is doing."

Forestine could feel Lilian's growing impatience, but her sister was being polite. "You have a lovely home, Lilian. So roomy . . . so . . . quiet."

"I've worked hard on it. We had hoped to fill it with children, but I guess it wasn't meant to be. The Lord didn't see fit to bless Lucas that way."

"Lucas!!?" Here was the Lilian she remembered.

"I know you didn't come here to talk about me and Lucas's reproductive abilities," Lilian said smugly.

Just then Benny burst in, with Lucas following. "For'stine," Benny shouted, "there's a big old dog next door—"

"A dog," Forestine said, pulling Benny toward her.

"His name is Terry and I pet his head," he said with excitement.

"Isn't that fine," Forestine said. She turned Benny toward her sister. "This is your aunt Lilian," she said.

Lilian knelt in front of the boy. She offered her hand to Benny with a gentleness Forestine hadn't thought her capable of. "How are you, precious?" Lilian asked.

"Say hey to your Aunt Lilian," Forestine said.

"Hey," Benny replied.

"What a beautiful baby, Forestine," Lilian said.

"Thank you."

"May I?" she asked, approaching Benny again.

"Sure."

"You are so very handsome," Lilian whispered to him. She picked him up and held Benny in her arms. "And tall just like your mother, aren't you?"

"Yes, ma'am," Benny answered.

"Ma'am?" Lilian was impressed by his manners. "Isn't he lovely?" she asked, looking up at Lucas.

"Good-looking boy," Lucas smiled.

"Do you have swings?" Benny asked.

"Well, no, we don't," Lilian answered. She held him as if he were a piece of glass. Her voice was soft. "But we have us a big old yard out there in the back. And you know," she said, leading Benny to the couch and gently setting him in her lap, "I do recall seeing a swing set on sale at the Times Square Store. It had swings and a slide. Ain't that right, Lucas?"

"Long slide," Lucas added.

It happened quickly. Lilian looked at Benny, then at her husband, and at Benny again. Her expression changed like the colors in a prism, moving from disbelief to doubt and then stark realization. She slid Benny off of her lap and stepped away from the child. Lilian didn't raise her voice but she turned to Forestine. "You evil," she said. "Evil as Satan himself."

"Hey, buddy," Lucas said. "How 'bout we get us some cookies in the kitchen." Benny nodded. "See that door over there. That's the kitchen and I'll be right behind you." Benny ran through like the house was one big playland. "Let's just calm down, here," Lucas said to his wife.

"Mama told me something was going on years ago, and I said not my husband," she went on. "Not my Lucas." Her voice went up at least an octave. "You evil, Forestine. Mean and evil . . . Lord, what a waste of a soul," she screamed.

"I can't leave my child with this woman," Forestine said.

Lilian was quickly losing control. "You lay wit' my husband and then want me to care for your bastard child. You somethin' else!" She began to pace the room uncontrollably. "How could you?" she screamed at Lucas. "How could you give this woman a child. She a lie, she blaspheme . . . wicked adulteress . . . you always had blessings you never deserved, Forestine. Why am I even botherin' to talk to this . . . jes' git the hell out my house!" Lilian ran toward the back rooms screaming.

"Now, *that's* my sister," Forestine said.

"What did you expect?" Lucas defended. "I've always been behind you, Forestine. Always wanting you to do well, and I swear, swear to God, that I would do anything to help you. Then you walk in here after four years with *my* child, whom I knew nothing about, and when your sister figures this all out, she's supposed to just understand? Aw, hell, no," he said, and went into the kitchen.

Forestine sat on the sofa, amazed at how wrong things were going these days. Beck, Lucas, and Lilian—all seemed to point the finger at her. But everything she did, right or wrong, was out of love for Benny. Lucas walked from the kitchen with his son by the hand. Benny was smiling, his lips dark with chocolate. He had two cookies pressed into his tiny hand, and he gave one to Forestine.

"Thank you, sweetie," she said wearily.

"I wanna give this one to Aunt Lilian," he said.

"I think she'd like that a lot," Lucas told him. "We can go to her room and see her, okay?"

"Lucas?!" Forestine said.

"It'll be fine," he assured her. "Your aunt Lilian, she got a little angry at your mother. Sometimes people do that, but it doesn't mean they don't love each other."

"Daddy Beck was always mad at Forestine," Benny said.

"I'm sure he was," Lucas said. "Come, let's go see her." He took Benny by the hand, and they walked to the bedroom.

"Are you sure . . . ?" Forestine called.

"It'll be fine," he said.

Forestine knew in her heart that Lilian was a decent person and wouldn't take her troubles out on a child, but she had to see it with her own eyes. Lucas had left the bedroom door ajar, and Forestine looked in from the hallway.

Lilian lay on the bed wrapped in a blanket, rocking back and forth. Lucas sat down beside her with Benny in his lap. He rocked with her and seemed to soothe her. She stared at Benny for a while. Forestine could see, even from the hallway, that Lilian was trying to hold on to the anger, but couldn't. She turned on her side and cried some more.

When Benny offered her the cookie, Lilian pulled herself up. She accepted the cookie and then gathered the boy to her chest. The look in her eyes clearly revealed the pain she felt every time she held a child, any child. She was like a tree that desperately wanted but could not bear fruit.

Forestine felt the thread between her and Benny start to break. But it was a natural break, like when a child goes to kindergarten for the first time.

"I don't forgive you, Lucas," Lilian said.

"I know."

"This does not mean I forgive you."

"Yes, honey."

Lilian pulled Benny's sweater off and tossed it on the bed. "This child is burnin' up and you are just wrong, man."

"Yes, Lilian, I know."

She grabbed a tissue from the box beside her bed and wiped Benny's nose and the chocolate around his mouth. Forestine knew that Benny would be just fine. When Lucas got up, Forestine hurried back into the living room.

"We'll keep the boy here," he said. "We'll give him a home for as long as it takes, as long as you need, but you have to do something for us too."

"Yes?"

"Lilian wants you to stay away for a while," he said.

"What's a while?" she asked.

"I don't know. A year?"

"Hell, no!" Forestine began to pace the room, her arms folded across her chest.

"He needs a chance to settle in. He needs some stability. And it gives me and Lilian time to build some kind of relationship with him. We can't have you running in and out of the boy's life."

"But a whole year?"

"Well, you tell me," he said. "How long is it going to take you to put your career in order?" She didn't have an answer. "Benny will always know who his mama is," he said. "Always."

Forestine wasn't the best mother in the world, but no one could say for a second that she didn't love Benny with everything she had. She just didn't have a lot right now. A voice. Energy. Was it a crime that she wanted Benny to stay with her? Some children could take that kind of lifestyle.

Lucas brought Benny out and placed the boy in Forestine's arms. His forehead was warm, and he was so congested that he had to breathe from his mouth. She was doing the right thing.

Forestine had cut her heart out and given it to Lilian. But she would create something special with her music. She would hit the jazz clubs in Manhattan. Fifty-second Street, the Village, uptown in Harlem—maybe she would even find this place called the Big House. The thought of a whole year without her son was unbearable, but just like the pain of growing up, of taunting children and her own mother's slurs, she would put the anguish into the music. Soon it would be time to come back and get him.

From the window of the Eastern Penn Express, Viola watched images of the South flicker by like a moving picture show. Five days ago she had witnessed her own excommunication. Now she sat on a train heading for New York City. She held tight a scrap of paper Miss Rosalee had given her. It said, "*Honeybee McColor, West 139th Street, Harlem, New York.*"

"Honeybee'll understand," she had said to Viola. "If nobody else, my sister Honeybee will know."

Viola had carelessly stuffed the paper into her skirt pocket, deeming it as useful as a thick winter coat. Now she needed both. She would have never imagined that one day she'd find herself on a train bound for New York City, exiled from her home, her church, and her family. Jasperville was already miles away. New Pilgrim was long gone. But Viola could still see the back of her mother's perfectly tailored navy blue suit and the brim of the large dark hat that dipped to touch the tip of her shoulder. Nelvern Bembrey hadn't budged from the pew when they handed Viola her bag, nor made eye contact as they led her away.

Viola carefully placed the address in her pocketbook. The white envelope that sat beside it looked crisp and official. It was the papers Donald had signed, signifying the end of their union. Reverend Bembrey called separations "an atrocity in the eyes of the Lord," but in this case, he had used his own influence to help Donald get the papers drawn up in under a week.

Viola leaned back in the cushioned seat, massaging the dull throb in her temples. She didn't know what she'd actually do in this new city. Isabel once spoke so excitedly about New York. Viola had lain beside her on the beach at Kindred Bluff, chatting in the dark morning while the salt water thinned their hair and carried it as far as their shoulders.

"Folks in the city," she had said, "they don't look at you like you crazy. You can do anything you want. You can praise the Lord, you can sing the blues . . . hell, you can sell turnip greens. Don't much matter there."

Viola suddenly felt an excitement she couldn't quite understand. While she knew she'd be terrified to step foot off the train, she also couldn't wait to get there. Viola recognized similar feelings in some of the faces around her. Expressions both thrilled and anxious. There were women with children, men in army uniforms, and families talking in respectful whispers as they passed foil-wrapped food to one another. The older man sitting beside Viola had his hat tilted over his eyes and his hands folded across his chest. He was so slight in stature that his shoulders were even with Viola's. The sound of his snoring seemed to blend with the steady clacking of the train.

The car lurched suddenly and the man's head leaned against her. Viola jumped at his touch. She nudged him a little. His hat had fallen to his chest, and Viola could now see the whole of his sandy-toned face frozen in slumber. His open mouth looked like a small, dark cave between a bushy gray mustache and beard. She edged closer to the window, and leaned forward to pull a small cardboard box from under her seat. Miss Rose had packed this box with hard-boiled eggs, sharp orange cheese, purple plums, and fried chicken. When Viola opened it, the man beside her woke up.

"How do," he grunted.

Viola nodded.

He dented the crown of his hat and placed it squarely on top of his head. "Look like you come prepared fo' a trip or two," he said, referring to the box of food in her lap.

"Yes, sir." Viola was content to just stare out of the window, but it would be rude to ignore the man. "Can I offer you something, sir?" she asked.

"Aw, no," he said with a smile. He took out an oily bag from inside his suit jacket. "Ever have home-fried pork rinds?" he asked.

"No, sir, thank you kindly," Viola replied.

"Missin' out." He munched loudly, and crumbs fell on the peppery part of his beard.

Viola turned toward the window. The sun was beginning to set on a large field of grazing cows.

"Where you headin'?" he asked.

"North."

He laughed with a closed mouth full of pork rinds. "There's a whole lotta north, daughter," he said after he swallowed. "What you runnin' 'way from?"

"Beg pardon, sir?"

"Ev'rybody on this train runnin' 'way from somethin'." His voice was deep and slow. "Headin' to someplace mo' pros'prous, mo' quiet, mo' loud. Runnin' away from someone, runnin' to someone . . . or both. Which one are you?"

"Which one are you?" she shot back.

The man seemed surprised by her candor. "You just violated rule number one of the game," he said, "and that is, never answer a question with a question."

Viola looked at the stranger suspiciously. "Whose rules and what game?" she asked.

"See—there you go breaking rule number two," he said, pointing into his palm as if they were written there. "Rule number two says that the person answering the questions cain't be no smarter than the one doin' the askin'. Didn't catch yo' name," he said.

"Viola Bembrey, sir."

"Bembrey," he said. "I recall knowing a few Bembreys in my life. One woman . . . name was Merlene Bembrey . . . lived down in the low country and sold straw hats on one of them roadside stands." He glanced at Viola, and when she didn't react, he went on talking. "Nice lady, that Merlene Bembrey . . . nice. Had a pretty round face just like yours. Also knew a fella name Bembrey . . . cain't recall his first name but . . . naw," he said, tossing his hand, "you cain't be no kin to him."

Viola lifted a chunk of cheddar on a toothpick and took a small bite.

"I know you ain't his kin," the stranger went on, " 'cause he a self-righteous jackass!"

"What did you say?" Viola asked.

"That ain't even the worst of it," he went on. "This fella named Bembrey . . . well, folks respect him. Got a high position in the community," he declared, "and sometimes this fella lay down judgment like the man on the top flo' himself."

Viola took a good look at the man, but couldn't recall ever seeing him before. Apart from Isabel, she had never heard anyone speak of Reverend Bembrey so disapprovingly.

"And when a fella of that nature," he went on, "get one of them respectful kinda positions, well . . . that's 'bout the worse place he can be. The worse place, 'cause ain't a one of us perfect." He munched on a pork rind and went on speaking. "One man might take a drink, a woman might not rise to cook and clean on a particular day." He wiped the oil from his mouth with a hankie from his jacket pocket. "One man might notice the round hips of his neighbor's wife, another woman might lay with a man befo' she's married . . . hell, *while* she's married." He shook his head. "Sad indeed. But these are the frailties that make us human. Don't mean we any less to the man upstairs, and it damn sho' don't mean that this Bembrey fella got all the answers."

Viola kept her eyes in her lap. This man was speaking her life, and she wasn't sure if she wanted him to go on talking or just leave her alone.

"So, what is it that you plan on doin' in the North?" he asked. "Got you a fella up there or somethin?" Viola's fears began to heighten. The stranger gently said, "Not quite sure, huh? Well, you're young and there's a lot to do up there if you're willin' to work hard." A smile opened his face. "Fo' fact, you such a pretty gal . . . look like one of them actresses, dancers, or some such."

"I do . . . sing some," she said shyly.

"Shut yo' mouth, woman," he declared. "I knew you looked like one of them kinda folks. I'm sure yo' family is plenty proud of that."

"Hell is full of murderers and them kind of folks, sir," Viola said. "My family thinks there's a thin line between the two."

"Is that right?"

Viola began to feel that she knew this man, or maybe he knew her. "Mister, you never did tell me your name," she said, extending her hand. He turned it over and kissed the back of it.

"Reuben Lightfoot," he said.

Viola snatched her hand back. "Reuben Lightfoot? From the Calvary Baptist Church in Charleston?" Viola had heard of Reverend Lightfoot many times when she was growing up but had never actually laid eyes on the man. His name was always uttered with the same reverence as those who mentioned Christ's name. She knew members who had left New Pilgrim altogether and traveled the two hours into Charleston every Sunday just to attend Calvary.

"Durham!" the conductor shouted. "All those for Durham, No'th Ca'lina."

"Are you *Reverend* Lightfoot?" she asked.

"Yes, ma'am."

"As in Reverend Baines, Morgan, and Lightfoot?"

"Well, they ain't exactly the two I would pick to be in a trinity with but, well, yes, ma'am." He smiled. "Guess they most prob'ly mentioned me along the way."

She stared at him half in awe, half in embarrassment. "You know who I am, then?" she asked softly.

"I know exactly who you are." Reverend Lightfoot rose and buttoned his suit jacket as the train slowly pulled to a halt. A few passengers pushed past him, and he leaned his body toward her. "I know who you are, alright. You, Viola Bembrey Hinson, are a beautiful, intelligent, God-fearing woman . . . and don't you let a soul tell you no different." Then he kissed Viola on the forehead, placed the oily bag of pork rinds on her lap, and walked down the aisle. Through the window she watched him cross the platform and board a train waiting on the opposite track.

She stopped the ticket taker as he walked down the aisle, and she pointed to the train on the other side. "Where's that train headed, sir?"

"Going back to Charleston." The ticket taker stood over the empty seat beside Viola. "Seemed like that fella bought a ticket jes' to sit on this here train."

Through the steam between the tracks, Viola could see a hazy picture of Reverend Lightfoot as he took a seat by the window directly across from her own. The train whistle blew and there was a long hiss. Then, like any proper gentleman, he lifted his hat and smiled as his train pulled away.

Viola had to wonder if, after all that happened, the Lord actually could forgive her. Seemed Reverend Lightfoot came all this way just to tell her so. If he did, she loved him for it, appreciated the effort, but the fact was, Viola had been "put out."

Night lay a soft gray blanket across the sky as the last of North Carolina sped by. The air changed as the train traveled farther north. The sweet smell of country woods and the pungency of fall pine slowly faded. The red-brown that used to be the Carolinas became the white winter of the Northeast. She had been traveling close to six hours and still had more than eight hours to go. Viola felt as if two silver dollars rested on her eyelids. Soon she'd be in Harlem. At 1:02 A.M. this train would pull into New York City.

At 1:10, Viola stood near the information window, right under the sign that said Pennsylvania Station. This was where Honeybee McColor had told her to stand. Strangers here seemed to walk too close to each other. The area was big, with booths for at least ten people to direct you. In Jasperville, there was just one man named Clark, who not only told you where you were going and dispensed your ticket, but also sold Nehi pop from a picnic cooler.

Another brown-skinned girl waited right under the station sign. Her arms were wrapped around her plump chest, and her large doleful eyes looked as baffled as Viola's. She seemed startled by the echoing loud speaker noises, the gritty smells, and the fast pace. Viola caught her eye, and the girl smiled but then looked away. Viola recognized that look. She had seen it when Cynthie Nettles knew that she was pregnant for the first time. Although Viola had never had that kind of trouble, she understood the look because it was as full of shame as her own.

"Which one a you gals waitin' on Honey McColor?" a man, just a few feet away, yelled over the noise of the station. He wore an old green military-style overcoat with a lone medal unceremoniously stuck into the lapel. The gold buttons strained to close around his pudgy body. His brow knit above a dark, oily face that resembled a bulldog. Viola could see the relief in the other girl's eyes that this man wasn't her ride.

"Who are you, sir?" Viola asked.

"Name is Fred Nastor," he shouted. "Honey sent me to carry you to the house. My car's outside." Fred scooped up Viola's bag like it weighed nothing and turned on his heels.

"Excuse me, sir," Viola said, running behind him. "Excuse me, please! You *are* talkin' about the Big House, right . . . sir?"

"Gon' to gather!" he said. "Gon' to gather with Honeybee Mc-Color!"

Viola had no idea what he was talking about, but she was sure that there could only be one somebody in the world named Honeybee McColor.

"Jes' a little ways fu'ther to the outside curb," he yelled behind him.

"Curb, sir?" she asked, trotting to keep up.

"Yeah, curb," he said. "What, you ain't got no curbs where you come from?"

"Not that I know of," Viola replied.

"Curb is the gutter," he shouted. "Where you park the damn car!"

"Why are you hollerin' at me?" she shouted back.

He stopped and turned. "Sorry."

Viola had the feeling that Fred Nastor had heard this question before. She also began to think that maybe he was a little slow in the head.

He pushed open the station door with one hand and waited. "Well, go'n through," he said.

Viola stepped out of the station and onto a cold city street lit up with colored lights. Christmas was just a few weeks away, but these weren't holiday lights. Pink, purple, and blue flashed for blocks and blocks ahead. Somehow Viola couldn't quite get her bearings as she tried to take this city in. She could hardly catch her breath as it rose above her head in frosted puffs. Even the simple things, like fire hydrants and mailboxes, looked different. She had to wonder what this Big House would be like. At least she'd be with Miss Rosalee's sister. Since the two women shared the same looks, there would surely be warmth in those eyes and that gentle smile.

"See, that there is a curb." Fred Nastor kicked the sidewalk. "See that? Curb!" He threw her bag into the trunk of a sleek black Chevrolet with white leather seats. "Honey say you had some trouble back home," he said.

"Some." Viola stood outside the door to the front seat, but Fred opened the back door for her to get in. It was like on her wedding day, when Nelvern had hired the limo driver to take her and Donald from the church back to the house for the reception. She wondered if Honeybee McColor traveled like this all the time.

"Honey say you a friend of Rosalee's," he said as they pulled off.

Viola tried making polite conversation but her mind was clicking like a camera, quickly snapping the concrete streets of New York City. Between some of the buildings, a light on a pole would illuminate the whole block. The only lights on the roads in Jasperville were the moon, the twinkle of stars, or the flicker of click beetles. Here Viola could make out florists, bakeries, milliners, picture houses, bookstores, schools, and big office buildings, lots of them. And there were still people on the street, even after 1:00 A.M.

"So you gon' to gather?" he asked.

Viola's attention quickly turned from the city streets to the tight hairs on the back of Fred's neck.

"I say, you gon' to gather?" he repeated.

"Gon' to gather," she said. "I don't know what that means." She could feel the tension in her body start to grow. This man seemed to be speaking a whole other language.

"Y'all don't ha' no gathers where you come from neither?" he asked.

"What is a gather, sir?"

Through the rearview mirror Viola could see the surprise on his face.

"A jam," he said. "An affair!" Then Fred Nastor waved his hand and said, "You'll see in a minute."

The office buildings began to thin out, and there were more liquor stores, hat shops, and meat markets. Seemed like every few doors on this main street called Lenox Avenue, Viola saw a church. Sometimes houses, where folks actually lived, were squeezed right beside a funeral parlor or what looked like a tiny food market. Viola couldn't imagine living next door to a funeral parlor or even a church, for that matter.

Fred Nastor turned off of Lenox Avenue and traveled along a row of stone houses. Strong and dignified, they stood like tall brown men with their arms linked together. A low, black, wrought-iron fence surrounded each home, and two silver tin cans sat in most of the gates. The houses were neat and uniform, every one with a long ribbon of steps that led to the front door, but each seemed to have a personality all its own.

Fred slowed toward the end of the block and stopped where cars were parked two deep. He got out, opened the door for Viola, and she stepped onto the sidewalk. Fred set her bag in front of a brownstone. Like the others, it had large picture windows covered by wooden shutters. But this house, the Big House, had a silver knocker and two thin panels of ruby stained glass. Viola could see silhouettes moving behind them. She had never seen a house like this, even in a magazine. The Bembrey home, one of the stateliest in Jasperville, didn't have half the character of this one. Viola followed Fred through the gate. From the bottom of the steps she could smell a tinge of barbecue and hear the muted music that pushed at the house's very seams. Then, like the top of a pressure cooker, the front door swung open and jazz poured out onto the top step.

A woman the same size as Miss Rosalee stood illuminated in the doorway. A floor-length silver dress clung to her body. Her feet were poised like a tiny ballerina's.

"Come here, sugar dumplin'," she called with her arms open. Already Viola could sense Miss Rosalee's same warmth. By the time she reached the top step, all Viola wanted to do was lay her head on this little woman's shoulder. But she couldn't take her eyes off of Honeybee McColor. Her face was as different from Miss Rosalee's as it was the same. Her nose was pugged and small like Miss Rosalee's, and her skin was the same soft ginger. Her eyes were wide and gentle like Miss Rose's, but long lashes hung over them like languid palms. Her lips were full like Miss Rosalee's, but they were bright red. Viola bent down to receive her embrace and could smell sweet oil and the slight scent of burnt hair under her neatly pressed curls.

"What a pretty young woman you are," she said to Viola. "The men gon' be lined up at my door to get a look at you. Fred!" she called out. "Take Viola's bag up to the third room."

"One what got all that damned pink inside, Honey?" Fred yelled.

"That's the one, sugar. Then I need you back on the door." Miss Honeybee took Viola's hand and led her into the vestibule. "We gon' wait here a second 'til Fred come back down, okay, baby?"

"Yes, ma'am." The music and laughter grew even louder as Viola stood waiting in the foyer. She could feel her hand trembling inside of Honeybee McColor's. She glanced down the hall at people talking and laughing with paper cups in hand. Most were dressed as elegantly as Miss Honeybee. Viola looked at her own baggy knit dress, beneath a short blue trench coat meant for the spring, and she felt even more out of place.

She could see at least two rooms off of the hall, and Viola figured that the first one was where the music came from. Just above her head, carpeted stairs led to another floor. She watched as Fred Nastor took her suitcase up.

"You happen to land here right in the middle of one of my gathers," Miss Honeybee explained. She patted the top of Viola's hand. "I'll explain it all later, but needless to say, baby, there's a party goin' on."

Viola looked down the hall nervously.

"Oh, sweetie, you ain't got to fret none of these folks," Miss Honeybee assured her. "They probably look a little different from those in Jasperville, but I promise that they some of the nicest people you ever will meet. And speakin' of looks," she chuckled, "Lord, but do you look jes' like yo' mama. Nelvern is pee color, I know, but y'all both got that same lovely face."

"Thank you, Miss Honeybee."

"Honeybee!" she laughed. "Lord, Jesus, I ain't been called no Honeybee in fifty-leven years. Girl, you sound like Rosalee. She the onliest one still call me Honeybee. Jes' call me Honey, okay?"

"Yes, ma'am."

"Fo' fact, I just hung up with Rose," she went on. "She called to see if you made it in alright."

"Say, Honey." A large yellow man stepped into the hall from the first room. He wore a three-piece suit, and his hair was slicked from his face. He had the fingers of one hand woven between the keys of a cornet and he had a drink in the other. "Niggah talkin' shit again, Honey," he laughed.

"This here is Sinclair," Miss Honeybee said to Viola. "Sinclair that need to watch his mouth."

"Oh . . . excuse me, young lady," he said to Viola. "Ain't nothin' but some stuff," he went on. "But you need to come on in here, Honey. Need to settle something once and fo' all."

"I'll be in directly," she called back.

The laughter that erupted from these rooms was as unrestrained as the sounds that had echoed through the backwoods behind Snooky Petaway's.

There was another knock at the front door. "Hell done froze," Miss Honeybee shouted as she flung open the door. "I *know* hell done froze." She embraced a tall man in a calf-length mink coat. Viola had never seen a man in fur, but it suited him perfectly. He had an instrument case flung over his shoulder. "I ain't seen you in a hundred years," she said, hitting him on the arm. "Boy, I nearly wrote you out."

"Why you wanna do me like that, Honey?" he said. His voice was deep and playful.

"I know when you playin' in town," she said. "And you don't even stop by to say boo or nothin'," Miss Honeybee scolded.

"You wasn't gon' let me in," he replied. Everyone in the hall laughed because they understood. "Lessen it's a gather, you might as well take yo' black ass right back home," he joked.

"You need to stop," Miss Honeybee laughed.

"Am I lying, y'all?!" he yelled.

"You know the boy ain't lyin'," Sinclair called back.

"You just a rascal is all," Miss Honeybee squealed.

Viola was squeezed into a corner of the vestibule. She could feel the cold rising from the man's fur. It was all too intoxicating, she thought: the smell of cooked pork, sweet perfume, and the musty leather cases that were the beginnings of all that wonderful music coming from somewhere inside.

"Where you been, Eddie?" Miss Honeybee asked him.

"You know me," he said, patting the instrument case. "Just trying to get paid."

"That's an understatement," Miss Honeybee said. "What brings you my way tonight?"

"Ain't seen my baby in too long," he said, kissing Miss Honeybee on the cheek.

"Come on, now," Miss Honeybee leered.

"And plus . . ."

"Here come the real reason," Miss Honeybee laughed.

"Wanted to meet this bad bitch they call Forestine. They say she stayin' here."

"She is, but she out singin' with the Coy Williams Quintet."

"Coy and his no-playin' ass?" he said, lowering his case off of his shoulder.

"This is a lil' girl from my home," Miss Honeybee said. "Name is Viola." Eddie turned to face her. "Viola, this is Eddie Bishop."

"How you doin', baby," Eddie said.

Viola felt herself shrinking farther into the corner. It was hard to look directly at this man with his penetrating eyes. His face was smooth, dark, and clean-shaven, and his lips were full. His half smile seemed to brighten the dim vestibule. He had one slightly chipped tooth in the front that made his grin seem boyish.

Eddie looked back at Miss Honeybee. "She don't know who the fuck I am, do she?" he laughed.

"You ain't nothin' but a mess, Eddie," Miss Honeybee laughed. "Go on in and make yo'self at home. Willa got some ribs and pig feet in there."

"Sound like something I wanna do," he declared.

"You know you playin' fo' yo' supper," Miss Honeybee yelled after him. There was a roar from the crowd inside when Eddie entered the room. "We need to get you a plate too," Miss Honeybee said, turning back to Viola. "After that train ride I know you must be hungry."

"I'm here," Fred said, hurrying into the vestibule.

Miss Honeybee quickly peeked at herself in the vestibule mirror and then clutched Viola's hand. As they entered the parlor, Viola took a breath. She felt like she was about to dive into deep water. The room was huge and crammed with people, talking, drinking, and dancing. An adjoining room ahead seemed to be as crowded as this one. "Everybody—" Miss Honeybee yelled over the music," this here is Viola from Jasperville. Treat her good. She family."

There was a chorus of, "Hey, baby," and, "Welcome, lil' girl."

"Folks'll introduce themselves by and by," Miss Honeybee said into her ear. She hooked her arm through Viola's as they made their way toward the loud brass and the gamy smell of pigs' feet. They stepped around a red floral sofa and three or four plush armchairs where men and women lounged, drank, and chatted. Folding chairs lined up against the windows were filled with women talking knee to knee. People sat on the floor or the arms of furniture, or stood pressed together in groups, holding drinks and lit cigarettes above their heads. Some were dressed in suits and ties or bold African print shirts, while others wore blue jeans or threadbare suits.

"Jes' hold on to me, dahlin'," Miss Honeybee laughed. "We'll git where we going."

A tall grandfather clock stood beside a mantel covered with rows of framed pictures. Above the mantel was a painting of a toy piano played by a man with a small head and gigantic hands. Viola lifted herself on her toes as she walked, trying to look over heads, especially when she heard a man's voice begin to sing.

"Miss Honeybee—" Viola leaned down to speak into her ear. "Where is the band?"

"The platform's in the living room," she answered. "We gittin' there, sugar." But every few steps someone stopped Miss Honeybee to whisper in her ear or peck her on the cheek.

They finally reached the archway of the adjoining room. A bar covered the entire side wall with a dozen high stools topped in red suede. Just like in the parlor, all of the seats were taken, mostly by musicians waiting, instruments in hand. On the platform were a piano player, two saxophones, drums, and a bass. The man singing had to be close to seventy. Viola didn't recognize the song, but the man's smooth, cool voice repeated the phrase, *you'd be so nice to come home to.*

Although his eyes were gray and his skin almost as white as his hair, his features were as colored as Viola's. He held the mike with a jeweled hand, and every once in a while he reached behind him and took a sip from his glass. Viola wanted to stay right there and listen to the music and watch these magnificent people, but she realized there was more of this house, the Big House, and she wanted to see every inch of it. Miss Honeybee tugged her arm to move her along.

Suddenly they made a sharp turn into the kitchen. There seemed to be no end to this house. The first thing Viola noticed was the black-and-white tiled floor. The countertop had smaller tiles in the same bold pattern.

"Buster," Miss Honeybee shouted to a big yellow cat who sat beside the door, "move your tail out the way, baby, fo' somebody mash it." Even the cat looked like a strange new thing. "That's Buster Brown," she said. "He and Fred help me keep an eye on things."

There were only a few people in the kitchen. A window was open beside the stove, and the air was cooler here. A woman in a tight red dress sat on the sill next to a man tapping the edge of the pane with drum sticks. Her breasts jiggled as she hummed in time to his beat. Beside them were two paper plates with rib bones and salt pork left from half-eaten greens. When the woman burst out laughing, the man kissed her right above one quivering breast. Two ladies in aprons were busy preparing the meal. They both looked to be in their fifties, just like Miss Honeybee. One, in a flowing white caftan, was as tall as she was heavy. Straight black hair was feathered around her large, light face, and she wore rhinestoned glasses. She stood over the stove and removed her glasses before lifting the lid from the steaming pot. The other at the counter, just as brown as Viola, wore a simple black dress with sequins around the collar. She moved quickly as she sliced three sweet potato pies into thin wedges.

At the dining table, two men were talking so close that the tops of their heads nearly touched. One was Eddie Bishop. He did most of the talking, in between sips from a shot glass. The other, with a black goatee and mustache, sucked the last bit of meat from a bone. He deposited it on top of a plate piled high with more bones. Before he could look up, the big woman in the white caftan pulled the plate away and left another, loaded with steaming pigs' feet. He didn't miss a beat as he plunged into the food again.

"Say hey to Viola, ever'body," Miss Honeybee called.

"Hey, Viola," they all repeated, and then went back to their conversations.

"Go on over and Willa'll fix you something to eat," Miss Honeybee said. "I got to make my rounds but if you need me," she hollered over her shoulder, "just shout out and somebody'll find me, okay?"

"Thank you, ma'am." Viola stood in the doorway. She felt as small and insignificant as Buster Brown, who lay right beside her feet.

"Lord, but these folks can eat," the big woman said, scraping the bones into a can behind her. "Got to run just to keep up." She turned to Viola and extended her hand. "You must be Honey's lil' friend from the South. I'm Vernon."

Viola started. She was a he. His large hand wore two diamond rings. A bit of chest hair peeked from behind the long string of pearls that hung from his neck. Viola slowly looked from his hand to his face. Behind the rhinestoned glasses were friendly, welcoming eyes.

"How was your trip, sweetie?" he asked.

"Fine . . . sir."

"Well, you just relax yourself," he said. "I'll have you a plate in no time." He was comforting to her, this big man in women's clothes.

"I'm Willa," the one in the black dress said. "I know you must be tired, so don't you feel obliged to stay down here with all these folks. We got your room ready and you can go up anytime you want." Viola couldn't imagine leaving this music and these people to sleep or to do anything else.

"Trotters or listeners, baby?" Vernon asked as he lifted the top off of a large pot again, allowing an oily puff of steam to filter out of the open window.

"Feet, please," she answered. The food wasn't so different from home, but after all, Honeybee McColor was straight from Jasperville.

Vernon set her plate at the table and gestured for Viola to sit. She nervously walked over to sit across from Eddie Bishop and the bearded man. When she pulled out the chair, the two men looked up briefly. The bearded man nodded.

"You straight off the boat, ain't you, sugar?" Eddie asked Viola.

She swallowed and wiped her hands on a paper napkin. "Took the rail, sir," she answered.

"God bless a country gal," he laughed.

"Now, Eddie, I know you ain't causing trouble already," Vernon scolded.

"Leave that chile alone," the woman in the red dress yelled from across the room.

"Where exactly are you from, sugar?" Eddie asked.

"Jasperville," she answered.

"Same like where Honey is from," Willa called.

"And you got one of them sweet names," Eddie said. "What is it . . . Rose or Lily . . ."

"It's Viola, sir."

"That's right," he said. "Sweet like a flower."

"Vio*let* is the flower," Vernon said.

"So is Viola," Eddie argued. "Viola is a flower too . . . and I know that 'cause my aunt Cora used to grow black-eye violas. Don't tell me what I know." He took a sip from his glass and his voice softened again. "You a sweet lil' thing," he said.

"Now, Eddie," Willa called.

"I can jes' eat you up," he purred.

"Mind yo'self, Eddie," Willa said.

"This here is Curtis Atwater," Eddie said, referring to the thin man with the beard and mustache. "You know Curtis Atwater, right?"

When Viola hesitated, the thin one looked at Eddie and shrugged his shoulders.

"Curtis Atwater . . . ?" Eddie asked in disbelief. "Acoustic bass . . . played with Yardbird and Dizzy?" Viola's face remained a blank. Eddie shook his head. "Look a here, Att," he said to Curtis, "she just a country gal. She don't know shit."

"You need to stop, Eddie," the woman in the red dress yelled.

"And you need to mind yo' damn business, Shirley," Eddie yelled back.

"Don't pay this man no mind, miss." Curtis Atwater's voice was calm and easy. He looked as young as Eddie—neither could've been more than thirty-five. "I been away from the scene for the last few years, so most people wouldn't know me."

"You don't play anymore?" Viola asked.

"Every once in a while I might do a set."

"Att got his own club," Eddie said. "But he need to take his colored ass back out there 'cause he a bad muthafuckah. Play a mean bass." Eddie jumped up suddenly, which caused Viola to jump too. When she looked under the table, Buster Brown was weaving slowly around Eddie's feet. "Damned cat," he said, lifting his foot.

"Kick my cat and I'll kick yo' ass," Miss Honeybee called as she walked in again.

"I wasn't gonna kick him, Honey, I swear," Eddie assured her. "I was just gonna move the little fella on his way."

"What you bring for the pot, Eddie?" she asked.

Eddie Bishop reached inside his suit jacket. He removed a black leather wallet, peeled off two fifty-dollar bills, and set them on the table. He placed the salt shaker on top.

"That'll do jes' fine," Miss Honeybee said.

"Mo' than fine," Willa added.

"And you, Curtis?" Miss Honeybee asked.

"Carton of Beefeaters," he answered.

"Lovely," Vernon said.

"Nice," Miss Honeybee agreed. "Appreciate it to the high."

"Anytime, Honey," Curtis said, standing up. "Next time you ladies come over to the Parrot, bring this pretty flower here...drinks on me." Curtis kissed Miss Honeybee on the cheek and he left the room, with Eddie Bishop following.

"Lord, that Curtis Atwater," Willa started. "If I was a few years younger..."

"...you'd still be too old," Miss Honeybee said. Then she winked at Viola.

"I ain't studyin' you, Honey," Willa puffed.

Miss Honeybee sat at the table beside Viola. She crossed her legs and kicked off one silvery pump. Then she removed a wad of bills from the top of her dress, folded Eddie's onto the bottom, and started to count.

"What's the pot?" Viola asked.

"When you show up here at the Big House," Vernon explained, "you leave something for the next gathering, 'cause that's how we keep on going."

"Everybody that come here have always understood and honored it," Miss Honeybee said, separating the bills.

"We get envelopes with money," Vernon went on, "mostly folks bring liquor, but sometimes they bring meat, sweet potatoes . . . stuff like that. That's what we call, somethin' for the pot."

"We store all the things people bring in the basement," Willa said. "On any given night you likely to see just about anything down there."

"Like a collection plate?" Viola asked.

The three looked at Viola like a trio of mothers. "Ain't she the sweetest thing?" Miss Honeybee smiled.

"Precious as a stone," Vernon said.

"It's gon' be nice havin' another gal around the house." Miss Honeybee touched the point of Viola's chin with her finger. "There's a young woman that's been staying here. Name is Forestine and she's . . . maybe a year older than you."

"I'd say about that much," Vernon put in. "She came here about three months ago, but she's been out fo' the last few weeks singing with Coy Williams."

"She's a singer?" Viola asked.

"Extraordinaire," Vernon said.

Miss Honeybee stopped counting and looked at Viola. "That's right," she said. "Rose did mention somethin' 'bout you singin' in church."

"Yes, ma'am."

"Singing in the choir," Willa said. "Just as sweet as she can be."

"You'll get to meet Forestine in a couple of weeks," Miss Honeybee said.

Viola looked toward the room where the music was coming from. "Can anybody just get up there and sing?" she asked.

"Anybody that take a notion," Miss Honeybee answered. "But most of these people are professionals. They sing or play every day of their lives." Miss Honeybee slipped back into her shoe. Before she rose to make her rounds again, she tilted her head and studied Viola like an old friend. "I do declare, this is Nelvern Bembrey sitting right here in my kitchen," she smiled. "A sleepy Nelvern."

"Girl, you look like you ready to git *under* the bed," Willa quipped.

"Baby, we do this every other Friday of the month, rain or shine," Miss Honeybee said, reading her face. "First and third Friday of *every* month, so there'll be plenty of time for socializing and such."

"I just want to stay for a while," Viola said.

The three looked at her like they understood. Before Miss Honeybee left, she said, "Your room is the third door upstairs on the left, whenever you're ready."

Willa and Vernon went back to the counter, and Miss Honeybee started her rounds again. Viola wanted to go into the room with all the music but couldn't find the nerve. Everyone there seemed so interesting and comfortable. She pictured Isabel standing somewhere in that room, a drink in one of her pretty hands.

At first, she lingered in the hall and listened. The horns seemed to make the room swell. Then the woman in the tight red dress eased past her and into the crowd. Viola followed her. Bodies slid tightly against each other, and Viola squeezed into a corner and stood against the wall. She could barely see the stage, but gladly, no one paid her any mind. Right now she was almost invisible, but ironically, it gave her a freedom to move among them. She slowly walked through the room looking for a place to sit, and stopped at the end of the bar when she couldn't find one. Then she spotted Curtis Atwater sitting in one of the chairs near the platform with his bass beside him. The instrument's wood looked as smooth as his face as he held it gently around the neck. He crooked his finger when he saw Viola and patted the thick armrest beside him. He instantly gave her the chair and squatted beside her on the floor.

"I thought you didn't play anymore," she said.

"Cats here make me feel like a real musician again." He whispered close to her. He placed his ear against the neck of his bass and plucked each string. "You a singer?"

"No," she responded. Viola couldn't believe that anyone would think of her as one of these glamorous people. "I mean, I sang some back home but not like here."

"Sang some what?" he asked.

"Mostly hymns . . . gospel," she answered.

Curtis smiled. "It's all connected. Gospel, blues, jazz . . ." Suddenly the room began to holler. The woman from the kitchen in the tight red dress had walked onto the platform.

"Shirley DeGrace," he said, answering the question in Viola's eyes. Again Curtis spoke close to her ear. His thick beard smelled like fresh-cut wood. "She's from a group called the Sweet Potato Girls. A little before your time, though." He smiled. "Hell, before my time too." The crowd was laughing and yelling, even though Shirley DeGrace hadn't yet sung a note. Viola was lost to the joke until the woman started to move. Slowly at first. Then everything on Shirley that *could* bump and shake, *did* bump and shake. As she leaned over on the platform, her breasts practically jumped from the top of her dress. Viola watched, shocked, as the room went crazy. Then the woman sang:

> *My mama said,*
> *Shirley, take it slow,*
> *But it sho' won't hurt her,*
> *What Mama don't know*
>
> *That man just oozed me,*
> *Made me tingle and sigh,*
> *Just tho' back my head and scream,*
> *My, my, my . . .*

"Shirley DeGrace?" Viola laughed.

"None but," Curtis replied. "And this is tame compared to her younger years."

Viola sat with her hands covering her mouth as she listened to Shirley DeGrace sing:

> *He say you taste so good,*
> *And you know what I mean,*
> *Come sit in my pot, girl,*
> *And season my greens . . .*

"Nasty and can't help herself," Curtis said, shaking his head. "Nasty, nasty," he said with a smile. "But the salt of the earth."

"You've played with her?"

"We played on the same bill," he replied. "Never got deep into the blues . . . not performing it, anyway." He laughed. "But I've played with just about every one of the jazz folk you'll meet here," he said. "Betty Rawlins," he said, pointing to an older woman at the bar, "Sarah Vaughan, Dinah Washington, Abel Drake—and I haven't even started to name the musicians."

"You musta been something else," she said to him.

Curtis looked at Viola and chuckled. Everything that came out of her mouth seemed to make him smile. He brushed her cheek with his knuckles, hoisted his bass, and made his way through the crowd to the platform. There he waited by the edge with his eyes closed while Shirley DeGrace wrapped up her song. Then he and a few other musicians took their places on the platform. The mood in the room took a turn from the raunchy blues to a serene jazz.

Moments after he started to play, Curtis's dark face misted with sweat. His shoulders turned down toward the strings, and his eyes stayed closed as his lips silently sang each note. Curtis pulled back to take a swallow of water, and it felt as if the heartbeat had fallen from the song.

Eddie Bishop walked onto the stage carrying his trumpet, and the room broke out in heavy applause. The look of arrogance that he had worn throughout the evening was replaced with an intense gaze. Eddie sat on the stool in the middle of the platform and lifted his trumpet. He eased into the song, then played a solo for over fifteen minutes. After he finished, Viola realized she had been so enthralled that she had barely taken a breath. After much applause and in the middle of the song, Eddie Bishop walked off the platform. Viola followed him with her eyes as he headed toward the hall. After a while, Fred hustled through, carrying the fur coat like it was still living. Then Eddie Bishop was gone.

Viola sat back in the plush red armchair. Her nerves had all but disappeared, and she let the music fill her. For the first time in her life, she didn't feel like she was being watched or picked apart. Sure, she was a child to most of these folks, but the world looked a little different right now. Still strange, a bit scary, except now there was freedom and hope. She also knew that with the beginnings of all this freedom came even more confusion. What was she supposed to do in this town, and especially in this house? The thought of being a singer had seemed like a great idea when she sat on the train, but she could never match the level of music and glamour that she saw here. Viola would let her doubts go no further. Not tonight. She sat back, pushed the thoughts from her mind, and let the music fill her.

The cab driver set Forestine's luggage on the sidewalk outside the Big House. He opened the car door and offered his hand, and Forestine unfolded herself from the backseat. New York City cabs weren't made for tall people anymore. The large checkered ones could fit three Forestine Bents, but the newer ones made her tuck her legs beneath her like a lame horse.

The flight back from Chicago had taken three hours. Standing in the cold night air, she realized how tired she was, but the music coming from the Big House energized her. From the sidewalk she heard the Pickleman's horn, Atwater's strings, and Myer Louis on piano. "Gathering good," she whispered to herself. Most times the old players like Shirley DeGrace, Ben James, and Abel Drake took the stage. Other times, like the natural alignment of the stars, a handful of prevailing kings and queens might be in town at the same time and stop by the Big House for a taste. She could tell from the sidewalk that this was a good gather.

Forestine had made it a point to get home in time. That meant she had to take a late-night flight after her last set in Chicago. She had been singing with the Coy Williams Quintet for the past four weeks.

Not quite a king, Coy opened for some of the larger names, and the exposure and experience were good for Forestine. She got to sit in with folks like Art Blakey and Sonny Rollins. The topper was a gig at Jimmy Mack's in St. Louis. Miles Davis was in the audience. He had sat in the back of the small club, perfectly still, yet totally conspicuous in dark glasses, his shoulders so high that he looked like a prince . . . or a pimp, one. After the set he came into the dressing room. In a gravelly voice, he said, "You got something beautiful. Trust it." And then he was gone.

"Forestine." Fred started down the front steps.

"Hey, sweetie."

He met her in the middle and took both suitcases. "You took so long to come home, Forestine," he said.

"Been working." She pecked him on the cheek and straightened the silver medallion he had clipped to his tie.

"And why you take the taxi car, huh?" He banged one bag against the inside door. "Coulda called me. Coulda called me to get you."

"You got enough to do on a gather night."

When she walked in, the parlor was jumping. Forestine waved to a few folks in the hall and slipped upstairs to throw some water on her face. She stood in her bedroom doorway for a moment and inhaled the fragrance of lilac. Forestine had gotten so spoiled by the scent that she took some on the road to place on the night table in her hotel room. She also brought some to the clubs to sprinkle in the stale dressing areas alongside her framed pictures of Benny.

Lying on the bed, she could feel Atwater's bass vibrating into the small of her back. Don't close your eyes, she thought to herself. It felt so good in this room. She had been at the Big House for only two months before she went out with Coy Williams, but it had become home. Forestine knew, from the moment she left Benny at her sister's, there was no other place for her to be.

It was a Wednesday when she first had arrived at the Big House. Anybody who knew anything about Honey McColor knew that to darken her door at a time when there wasn't a gather was something you just didn't do. But Forestine had a plan and a purpose. She took the number two subway train from Brooklyn, got off at 135th Street in Harlem, and Wednesday or no, she walked right up to the Big House and rang the bell. The door opened a crack, and through it she saw a man's dark face.

"Honey McColor, please," she said.

"What fo'?"

"Is she home?"

"I say, what fo'?" he barked.

"I'm looking for a room."

"Ain't got no room." He was about to close the door, but Forestine stuck her hand in.

"You crazy?" the man yelled. "This do'll chop yo' hand half in two."

"I'd like to see Honey McColor, please," she insisted.

"Honey don't see nobody today," he hollered. "She don't see nobody." He tried again to push the door closed, but Forestine had her hand and foot against it. "Woman, I'll call the goddamned police on yo' ass."

"Look," Forestine said calmly, "I'm a singer . . ."

"So!"

"Will you ask her if she'd at least see me?" Forestine asked.

He finally opened the door and his stout body filled the whole frame. "She ain't gon' see you. She don't see nobody today!"

"Just tell her that I'm a singer—"

"Everybody sing," he yelled. "My mama sing!"

A small woman placed her hand on the man's shoulder from behind. Forestine could see only the top of her finger-waved head and lavender-dusted eyelids. "What's going on, Fred?" she asked.

"You go on back in, Honey," he yelled.

"Fred?" Miss Honeybee said.

"You ain't got to worry 'bout a damned thing," he spat.

Miss Honeybee rubbed one of his shoulders to settle him down. "Lord, I don't know what I'd do without you," she said to him, "but I'll take it from here. Go on, baby," she gently ordered.

"I can take care of this," he pressed.

"I know you can," she said. "Oh, I know you can! But I don't want you to hurt nobody. Now go'n." Before Fred walked away, he looked at Forestine like she had taken something away from him. He walked back into the house, muttering.

"What can I do for you, sugar?"

Beck had told her what a grand woman Honey McColor was. Forestine expected the beauty, the grace, and the voice touched by a Southern bend as sweet as pecan pie, but somehow the strength of this small woman was immediately startling. Her words were accommodating, but her tone was sharp.

"I'm a singer, ma'am," Forestine started, "and I'm looking for a room. Most everybody says this is a good place—"

"Most everybody's right," Miss Honeybee cut in. "I'm kinda in the middle of something right now, sugar, and I really ain't lookin' fo' no boarders."

"I just need a place for a few months, ma'am," Forestine said. "My husband, Beck, told me that your place is the only place."

"Your husband?" Miss Honeybee asked.

"Yes."

"Beck Pinkney?"

"Yes, ma'am."

"You *married* to Beck Pinkney?"

"Yes, ma'am."

Miss Honeybee stepped out onto the stoop, her thin heels clicking against the hard brown stone. She raised a pair of gold-rimmed glasses hanging around her neck on a pretty chain and looked up at Forestine like the side of a mountain. "Beck Pinkney is yo' *husband*?" she asked. Forestine nodded. "Pink got to be a hundred years older than you."

"Ninety-seven, ma'am," Forestine replied. A tiny grin turned the sides of Miss Honeybee's mouth. "We both worked with Lil' Eartha," Forestine explained.

"Eartha McClain," Miss Honeybee said, shaking her head. "Lord, ha' mercy, is that woman still alive?"

"Living down in Alabama with her man."

"Not that ole drunken dawg . . . what's his name?"

"Ernest," Forestine replied. For once she was actually pleased to say the man's name.

Miss Honeybee stepped back into the doorway and folded her arms around herself to ward off the chilly air. "You know, *your* husband used to play wit' *my* husband."

"He did mention that, ma'am."

"Pink stopped by this house many times. That was back when we only had a few folks comin' 'round. One of the finest men I've ever met, Pink was. My Clay always said that he know more 'bout this business than anyone."

"Yes, ma'am," Forestine answered.

"Well, where is he?" she asked.

Forestine kept her head up. "He's . . . not with me, ma'am," she said. "He's not with me at all."

"I see." Miss Honeybee took a breath. "Lord knows I don't need no boarders . . ."

"Yes, ma'am."

". . . sometimes we got all we can handle just doin' the gathers . . ."

"I understand, ma'am." Forestine's heart beat a little faster.

". . . but I s'pose we can try it. Cain't promise you no months or nothin', but we'll try it fo' a while." She took a step back and opened the heavy door. "Well, come on in."

Forestine never forgot the excitement of walking into the Big House for the first time. There was no music playing, but she could still hear it. She heard it in the tiny lace curtain on the inside door and in the carpet that lined the halls. The scent of clipped flowers—roses, gardenias, and lilies—all blended together like the blush in Miss Honeybee's face.

A burst of laughter brought Forestine back. She sat up on the bed, feeling the tautness in her neck and legs. She blotted her lipstick, then pulled a few defiant strands of hair into a feathered clip. She certainly didn't want to miss a gather. It had a different energy than doing a set in a club. You could *choose* to sit in, sit out, drink, eat, dance . . . or jam. Of course, you didn't get paid, but the love of family and close friends made up for it. Fred surely hadn't told Honey that Forestine was home because, gather or no, the three—Honey, Willa, and Vernon—would be sitting at the foot of Forestine's bed demanding to know everything about the tour.

"Skylark" was playing as Forestine started down the steps. She stopped and sat in the middle of the stairway when Curtis began his solo. His playing demanded stillness, and she settled there with her eyes closed. Curtis Atwater was a different breed of musician. Although he was *of* the business, he was able to stand miles away from it. Curtis Atwater had been a king, until he decided that he no longer needed the title. Forestine liked the way he lived, but more than that, she admired the man he was.

No one noticed her slip in, but that was typical when Curtis played. She stole a corner in the parlor just beyond the arch. Forestine still found it hard to walk into the center of the room. She felt remnants of the insecurity she'd get at old church dances, when Lilian would wind up cutting a rug all evening while Forestine sat on the side watching. It wasn't until Willie insisted that they boogaloo together that Forestine would get to dance. Even now, when she entered a gather, she usually stayed on the fringes. But Forestine never sat for too long because, just like Willie Bent had, someone would always grab her hand and take her to where the action was lively and thick.

Forestine looked around at the faces in the room. There were some new ones at this gather. There always were. A few younger musicians stood below the platform, instruments in hand, waiting. Curtis controlled the stage tonight, and it was up to him who came up. Curtis was good like that. He always broke off some time for the new players. A pretty brown-skinned woman, her thick hair swept back from her face, was talking to Willa. Surely she was a singer. Shirley DeGrace sat on the lap of a man Forestine had never seen before. His skin was as red-orange as his hair. He wore a multicolored African print outfit from head to toe. Aside from Curtis, there was at least one other king present tonight, Forestine thought, as she noticed pianist Bobby Timmons and his wife, Stella. They sat beside Miss Honeybee just under the platform. Forestine had heard Bobby play in Ohio a few weeks ago. She'd wanted to speak to him after the gig, but he had to get on the road for another club date.

Forestine's attention shifted back to the platform when Curtis called her name into the mike. Like always, they had found her. She smiled modestly as the room applauded.

"You trying to hide from us, girl?" he asked.

The love in this house always made her feel like a star. Forestine made her way through the crowd and onto the platform.

"Hear you been smokin' 'em out there," Curtis said as she stepped onto the stage.

"I do what I can," Forestine answered.

Curtis hugged her and whispered, " 'The Man I Once Knew.' " And just like that, Forestine was gathering.

"Hi, Honey," she whispered into the mike.

"How was yo' trip, sweetie?" Miss Honeybee called to her.

"Just fine," she said as the group played her introduction.

"How's Coy?" Miss Honeybee asked.

"Honey?" Forestine said.

"Yes, dahlin'."

"Can we talk about this later?" The audience laughed.

Forestine pulled the mike from the stand and settled back on a stool beside Curtis. By the time she opened her mouth, the room had hushed. It was so quiet that Forestine could hear only the sound of her own voice.

> *I wish I could say why I'm feeling so blue,*
> *It must have something to do with you . . .*

She opened her eyes but quickly shut them again. Then she let loose a phrase that caused one man to yell out loud.

> *No heart, no soul, no love, no me,*
> *No laughter, no sharing, no joy, no we,*
> *No sign of the man I once knew . . .*

Forestine rarely felt as comfortable as she did on this stage. To her left was Preston "The Pickleman" Monroe, underlining each phrase with a perfect saxophone riff. And to her right was Myer Lewis on the piano, every strike of his finger tickling the nape of her neck. Then there was Curtis Atwater stealing a heartbeat with each plunk of his strings. Gathering good.

> *I wish I could say why good times are so few,*
> *It must have something to do with you,*

Drinks are abundant, and I still dress the part,
Waiting for the moment to retrieve my heart,
No sign of the man I once knew . . .

The Pickleman stepped up to the mike and lifted his horn. The notes slipped easily from the gleaming brass. She liked to see his face, so serious, when he played. Forestine turned her back to the audience to watch him. This was one of the beautiful things about jamming at the Big House. Conventional rules, like having your back to the house, could be broken. As long as a player had respect, you could do whatever you wanted. More than a few times during a solo, drinks were handed up onto the platform, and once or twice, a musician stepped down during another's solo to take a pee. A body had that freedom here, and the paycheck was Honeybee McColor's hospitality and one of Willa and Vernon's meals.

Curtis Atwater played again. He wore a sleeveless T-shirt, even in the dead of winter, because he liked to watch the muscles in his arms work. But as hard as he seemed to play, he never forced the sound.

Miles between us, yet a heartbeat away,
I live to miss you another day,
But still, no sign of the man I once knew.

When a record played on the hi-fi during a gather, it was a final cue that the night was winding down. Bessie Smith's voice now filled the empty parlor of the Big House. Miss Honeybee stood on the top step outside as she said good-bye to her guests. Most had already left, but Bobby Timmons and his wife, Stella, had paused in the hallway to talk to Willa. Forestine hesitated to interrupt. Bobby must have felt her presence because, after excusing himself to Willa, *he* walked over to *her.*

At first Bobby just stood in front of her, eye to eye. A neatly trimmed goatee made his long face look even thinner. An almost devilish expression lurked in his eyes. "So when?" he asked.

Forestine lowered her head bashfully. "You tell me."

He seemed as much in awe of Forestine as she was of him. "Amazing," he said.

"As are you," Forestine returned.

"All this love going around," Stella said as she joined them. Her almond eyes made her face even more bright and welcoming. "Love, love, love," she laughed.

"I'll tell you what," Bobby said to Forestine. "Let me look at a few things and we'll talk. We'll definitely talk."

"You know where I live," Forestine smiled.

"Stell," he said. "You got my ribs?" She patted the brown bag in her arms. "Soon, come," he said, pecking Forestine on the cheek.

Stella reached up and gave Forestine a hug. She whispered, "He'll see you in a minute, and so will I."

There had been many promises by many musicians, including kings like Bobby Timmons, so Forestine knew not to get excited about a "might be" offer. They all had good intentions, but she would only take it seriously when the phone rang and the gig was set.

Forestine passed through the music room, littered with paper cups and full ashtrays, and saw Curtis reclining in one of the chairs. He usually left the gather early to get back to his club. If he was still here, the music must have felt especially good. She sat down in the chair beside him. Curtis lifted Forestine's hand from the armrest and laced his fingers into her own.

"What did I miss in the last few weeks?" she asked him.

"Last gather," he started, "Willa made one of the best sweet potato pies on this earth. . . ."

"*Music*, Curtis," she emphasized.

Curtis tugged the pointy end of his beard. "Never underestimate a good potato pie," he said.

"So?" she asked again.

"Now, don't get mad," he started.

"Don't tell me Miles or Dizzy was here," Forestine said. " 'Cause if you tell me I missed either one . . ."

"Diz is in Europe," Curtis said. "Miles is in Japan. But you in the right stratosphere."

"Who?" she asked.

"Eddie Bishop."

"*Eddie Bishop* was here?"

"Yep."

"Did he play?" Forestine asked.

"One song," Curtis answered. "Smoked it."

"Damn!"

"He'll be at Crawford's in a few weeks, though," Curtis said.

Eddie Bishop was one of the few horn players who Beck had actually listened to for the sake of relaxation.

"What you got lined up?" Curtis asked.

"Not a damn thing," Forestine replied.

"Dexter is at Birdland," Curtis said. "Prez is down at the Blue Note...." Curtis faced her with an expression that Forestine knew well. "I won't say it again." And he smiled.

"I know."

"You always got a spot at the Parrot. It ain't the big time, but it's somewhere to play the game for a minute."

"I appreciate it. Probably take you up on it too."

Curtis sat up when he saw the pretty brown-skinned girl in the adjoining room. She was emptying ashtrays into a paper bag. Guests occasionally stayed behind to help Miss Honeybee straighten up after a gather, but the pretty girls never bothered with such things. Even more interesting was the way Curtis watched her. He tried to appear calm, but his eyes told Forestine a different tale. They looked at the girl the way Beck had always looked at her.

"Have you met Viola?" he asked.

"No," she answered. "But obviously you have."

"Viola is ... different," he said, standing. "Alice in Wonderland kinda different, you know?"

"No," Forestine replied.

"I just mean she's nice," he said. "Simple girl." Forestine was used to Curtis downplaying his feelings. His eyes lingered on Viola awhile longer and then they respectfully came back to Forestine. "The Pickleman's coming to the Parrot tomorrow," he said. "Should I warm up the mike for you?"

"Maybe," she said. "I'll call you."

Curtis gave Forestine a strong hug. One that made him groan like a bear. "Good to have you home, woman," he said. "But don't you stay around here too long."

"Not if I can help it," she said. Curtis kissed her on the cheek, then he left.

Forestine sat for a while and took in the calmness of the parlor. She always liked the look of the room, the drama of the black velvet drapes, the whimsical painting and the framed pictures on the mantel. The room was Honeybee McColor herself: fun, classy, and deep into family traditions. Forestine felt a rumble in her stomach and suddenly realized she hadn't eaten since early afternoon. She walked past Viola and out into the hall toward the kitchen, where Fred was sitting at the table. The last of the barbecue and three deviled eggs were on a plate in front of him. The meat was covered in an oily, congealed sauce, and the mayonnaised yolks were edged in a deeper shape of yellow. The sink was piled high with empty pots and bowls. Without a word, Fred pulled out a chair for Forestine. He slid half of his food onto another paper plate for her, and the two sat eating in an exhausted silence.

The Big House rarely saw an early Saturday morning after a gather. It didn't exist. But when thoughts of Benny roused her, Forestine woke a couple of hours after she went to sleep. She sat up against the headboard, listening to the quiet house. Such a difference from a few hours ago.

She thought about what Benny would be doing right now. Lilian usually woke early and would probably be making his morning oatmeal. Oatmeal with honey, warm milk, and just a pat of butter.

"No milk," Forestine whispered. She had remembered that milk gave Benny the phlegm something awful. Lilian would know about things like that, though. Since they were children, her sister seemed to have a natural knack for mothering. Benny could probably only have jelly beans once a week and a small slice of apple pie, and only after eating everything on his plate. Lilian surely set a pot of steaming water on the radiator in his room and rubbed his thin chest with Vicks when he couldn't breathe. If Forestine knew her sister, Benny was safe and in fine health.

A rush of emotion made Forestine sit up. Guilt cut through her stomach like a straight razor. She swung her legs to the side of the bed and tried to catch her breath. Sometimes walking the floor helped, so she threw on a terry robe and went downstairs. The parlor and music rooms were cool and dark as she passed through. Having a cup of Willa's coffee would focus her mind, she thought as she walked toward the kitchen. After a gather, the three didn't wake until close to noon, but Forestine thought she smelled coffee. It was so quiet downstairs that she knew it was most likely wishful thinking. Forestine could make a pot herself, but the only thing worse than a Forestine Bent meal was a Forestine Bent cup of coffee.

The kitchen was dim, except for the light on the oven range. Then she noticed a pot over a lit flame on the stovetop. Forestine was startled to find Viola sitting at the table. They both jumped at the sudden sight of each other.

"I didn't expect to find anyone down here," Forestine said.

"Neither did I," Viola replied.

Forestine stood over the table, holding her robe closed. "I didn't know you were staying here. Curtis never mentioned it . . . not that it's any of my business who Honey has staying here . . ." Forestine said.

Viola simply nodded.

"You must be a singer," Forestine said.

"No," Viola replied.

"Then a dancer or something?"

"No, ma'am," Viola smiled.

Forestine nodded. "What do you do?" she asked.

"Not much of anything right now."

Forestine heard Honey's same Southern flavor in Viola's voice. She began to understand what Curtis meant about that "Alice in Wonderland" thing.

"Looks like Willa was up early," Forestine said, referring to the pot of coffee that was just beginning to perk on the stove.

"I made it," Viola said.

"You make coffee?"

"Yes, ma'am."

"Just call me Forestine. Lord, please, call me Forestine."

"Sorry."

Forestine realized that her girl-talk skills were rusty. She had never really had a chance to use them. "So . . . you from Honey's hometown?"

"Yes."

"A friend of the family?" Forestine asked.

"Yes."

"You just get here?"

"Two weeks ago."

"Long visit," Forestine said.

Viola smiled timidly. "I'm staying," she said.

Forestine's eyebrows raised involuntarily. "Staying?"

"Yes."

Forestine turned back to the stove, trying to think of something else to talk about. "Coffee smells good."

"A Jasperville tradition," Viola said. "If nothin' else, we women know how to make a pot of coffee."

"Jasperville tradition," Forestine said. "I'm afraid nobody told Honey." Viola laughed. Maybe a little too hard. "So . . . how do you like it here . . . at the Big House, I mean?"

"Everybody's been so nice to me," Viola said. "In fact, Miss Honeybee's taking me to get my hair done today."

"Isn't that . . . good," Forestine said. She looked toward the stove again, willing the pot to finish perking.

Fred Nastor slammed the basement door shut, breaking the tension. He lumbered down the hall and stopped in the kitchen door.

"Y'all up too early," he said.

"Couldn't sleep," Forestine said. "Where you off to this time of the morning?"

"Got to git the trash to the dump," he answered. "Otherwise it set 'round 'til Monday. Them damn stray dogs," he said, putting on his coat, "they be out there all day tryin' to get at them rib bones." Fred's voice trailed off until the front door closed.

"Does he always wear that pin in his coat?" Viola asked.

"I've never seen him without it," Forestine replied. "Fred is a little . . . special. He moves a little slower because he got a steel plate in his head."

"From the war?" Viola asked.

"Honey said he was in the service," Forestine explained, "stationed down there at Fort Benning in the mess hall. The officer's mess hall."

"That doesn't sound dangerous," Viola said.

"She said that a sergeant or general—one of them high-ups—was choking and Fred saved him. That's when they give him that medal. They say he made it through the service just fine," Forestine went on. "But a few months after he came home, he drove into a telephone pole 'cause a wasp flew into his car. When he got out of the hospital, the poor thing was practically livin' on the streets until Honey gave him a room here at the house. She told him he could help out in exchange for his board. That was sixteen years ago, and he's been helping out ever since. One of the few things he remembers is that he got that medal for savin' someone. And just like these musicians, we celebrate him."

Forestine took two floral-rimmed cups and saucers from the pantry. They rang like chimes as she set them on the counter. Miss Honeybee appreciated delicate china, but Forestine often worried that if she bit too hard, she'd eat clean through the glass. She filled them with the hot coffee, placed one in front of Viola, and sat down across the table. "Must be hard leaving home."

Viola's smile was tentative.

"Coming from a small town like that," Forestine went on.

"I guess," Viola said.

"Having to leave your people and all . . ."

"Wasn't too hard," Viola said. "Especially when they *ask* you to leave."

Forestine looked directly at Viola. "You got put out?" she asked. Forestine realized she was prying into the woman's business. "I forgot the cream," she said, getting back up.

"*I'll* get it," Viola offered.

Forestine watched as Viola removed a creamer from the icebox. Even in this early morning, the girl's face, free of any makeup, was just as pretty as it had been at last night's gather. Forestine rarely saw such a natural beauty. A year ago, a woman like Viola might've unnerved her, made her insecure, but Forestine was finally developing a sense of her own virtues. That had a lot to do with the long, hard roads and the love and patience of Beck Pinkney.

Viola set the tiny china creamer on the table. "Never heard it said out loud like that before . . . but, that's the God's honest truth."

"What does a girl like you do to get—"

"Put out?" Viola laughed. "I was married. And . . . with a man that wasn't my husband."

"You got *caught*?" Forestine asked.

"Yes."

"By your *husband*?"

"By one of reverends in the community," Viola said boldly.

"Daaamn!"

"The man had his hand where it wasn't supposed to be," Viola said. "*Way* up where it wasn't supposed to be."

"Thank goodness they don't put people outta New York City for something like that," Forestine said. "There wouldn't be a soul left—including me."

"What you saying?" Viola asked.

"I'm talking loud enough." Forestine couldn't believe what she was admitting to. "And the man I was with was married to my sister."

"Lordy, lordy," Viola said, shaking her head. "They wouldn't've just put you outta Jasperville. Girl, they'd've locked you up."

Forestine was shaking with laughter. Aside from Beck, she hadn't ever spoken these thoughts out loud, and she got the feeling that Viola hadn't, either. They sat laughing and talking about things that, just weeks ago, had been raw and painful. For at least a couple of hours, the only thing that could be heard in the Big House was an occasional giggle and the clink of fine bone china.

CHAPTER
12

Viola turned onto her stomach to look at the wind-up clock on the night table. After talking this morning, she and Forestine had retired to their rooms to sleep awhile longer. Now the smell of grits, sausage, and overly brown toast was drifting from the kitchen. This meant that the three were up and Willa was preparing her after-gather brunch.

Viola pulled herself out of bed. She parted the pink chiffon curtains to look down on 139th Street. A New York City bus hissed as it made its way up to Lenox Avenue. Two weeks ago, the roar of the bus had scared her, but she had since grown used to the sounds of a Harlem morning. Even though the block was still calm and only a few people passed, she could feel the excitement and energy on the street. Or maybe the excitement came from Viola herself.

There was a knock on her bedroom door. When she opened it, Fred Nastor was standing in the hall looking down at her feet.

"Honey say to wake you if you still asleep. You ain't, so I'm s'posed to say she got lunch downstairs." Fred was about to walk off. "Oh, and she say be ready to go to Pet's Place right after."

"Pet's Place?" Viola asked.

"That the hair lady," he replied.

"Thank you, sir," Viola said.

He turned back with an embarrassed smile. "I'm just Fred. Done tole you that befo'. I'm Fred." He continued on his way down the hall, and soon she could see only his head as it bobbed down the carpeted steps.

Viola removed her nightgown and slipped into a pair of gray wool slacks and one of her better white blouses, the one with the pearlized buttons and frilly lace collar. In the haze of sleep, she had forgotten that Miss Honeybee was taking her to get her hair done today. The three often mused at the lack of glamour in Viola's thick ponytail. For the gathers, Vernon swept her hair up and back, dropped frizzy curls around her face, and pinned it with rhinestone clips. But the three came to the conclusion that Viola needed a professional. Miss Honeybee insisted that a woman's true beauty always started with a good perm.

Her soft yellow nightgown lay at the foot of her bed. Viola hung it in the first of two closets in her room, where she kept her own few dresses. It was the second closet that Viola loved to explore. The scent of mothballs rushed out, and she was faced with a wall full of long, shiny, feathery, and sparkly frocks. Dresses, sweaters, and stoles that Miss Honeybee had saved from years ago. The entire closet reminded Viola of the fancy section in Miss Rosalee's dress shop. She delighted in trying them on, and though Miss Honeybee insisted that Viola was welcome to wear whatever fit, she hadn't yet felt comfortable in anything this decadent and glamorous.

Viola quickly made her bed, then tossed on the two pink throw pillows. She could see why Miss Honeybee referred to this as the "pink room." The satin quilt was a blush color, and the floor was covered with thick mauve carpeting. A fringed lamp with a rose-colored shade sat on the night table alongside a tiny crystal bowl filled with fresh flower petals, every shade of pink. The bureau was lined with a white lace doily. Nelvern Bembrey would think it "overdone" or "heavy-handed." Viola thought it was beautiful.

Viola sat at the foot of her bed. This was the first time Nelvern had crossed her mind in days. What with the gathers and the Big House itself, South Carolina had been far from her thoughts. Compared to this city, Jasperville was so simple. Even Nelvern and the Reverend weren't hard to figure once you knew them. Everything there was black or white, but here at the Big House, Viola had seen an array of colors she couldn't have imagined. There wasn't a Vernon in Jasperville, or a Fred Nastor—and certainly not an Eddie Bishop. There wasn't a Honeybee McColor either . . . but then again, maybe Miss Rosalee would be like her sister if she lived here in Harlem. Folks like Isabel and Amos Flowers would fit in just fine at a house like this. Perhaps that had been the reason Viola was so attracted to them in the first place.

Thinking about home suddenly made her stomach quiver. She pictured Donald Hinson with Nell and the Reverend, all commiserating over morning coffee. Viola would still be the topic of conversation, not only at the Bembreys' but in all of Jasperville, for months, maybe years to come. Just the idea that she couldn't go back without shame made the acid in her gut begin to churn.

Viola left her room and could hear the faint sound of music. Downstairs, the parlor was flooded with sunlight and the aroma of fresh coffee. Willa tended to the plants by the windowsill while Vernon buffed silverware at a small table beside the couch. They both looked comfortable in their Saturday afternoon clothes. Willa, in a blue house dress, had her hair in pin curls that looked like tiny windmills. Vernon wore quilted black pants and a tunic. His face looked even larger without the benefit of hand-drawn brows. Miss Honeybee lounged on the sofa in a pleated pink skirt. Her makeup was subdued in pretty corals and her hair was swept back. She had a bundle of mail in her lap. Buster Brown lay beside her as she sliced into one of the envelopes with a letter opener resembling a small medieval sword. She raised her gold-rimmed glasses to look at one of the letters, but vanity wouldn't allow her to place them on her nose. When she saw Viola standing in the doorway, she placed them on the end table and slipped the letter opener back into its shield.

"Here she is," Miss Honeybee sang. Her voice was as bright as the room. Willa and Vernon looked up at the same time.

"Good morning," Viola whispered.

"How'd you sleep, baby?" Vernon asked.

"Very well, thank you."

"I always heard the Southern air makes people sleep," Willa said. She hovered over an elephant-leaf plant, gently lifting a branch as if it were a sore limb. "But, I ain't slept 'til I come here."

"Ready fo' yo' new do, my dahlin'?" Miss Honeybee asked.

"Honey, let the woman have herself some food," Vernon scolded. "You know she's used to having breakfast *and* lunch by now."

"Excuse my manners," Miss Honeybee apologized. "Go'n in the kitchen and get yourself some grits and eggs."

"I'm fine," Viola said, sitting beside her.

"How 'bout some juice or coffee?" Miss Honeybee asked. "Willa just made a fresh pot."

"Nothing, ma'am . . . except, maybe some warm ginger ale, if you have."

The three glanced at each other knowingly. Miss Honeybee went to retrieve a bottle from behind the bar in the adjoining room.

"Thinkin' 'bout home again?" Willa asked. "Tie yo' stomach all up. Oh, chile, I know. I know how that feel."

"Honey, put a teaspoon of baking soda in that ginger ale," Vernon called. "That'll calm her stomach good!"

"Put a hole in her damn stomach, you mean." Miss Honeybee walked back in, handed Viola the glass, and sat on the couch. "It's only been a couple of weeks. That'll go away in time."

Viola knew that sooner or later they'd want to discuss what happened in Jasperville.

"I know how you been feeling," Miss Honeybee went on. "Like you been locked in a cage. Jasperville'll make you feel like that, sho' 'nuff." Miss Honeybee set a cigarette in a black holder and lit it.

"Befo' you know it, folks is gon' forgit all 'bout what happened down there," Willa said.

"You a healthy, pretty young woman, so don't you be feeling bad 'bout nuthin'." Miss Honeybee pulled at the very end of the holder with her coral lips, and it was as elegant as anything Viola had ever seen. "That daddy of yours—and, sugar, I say this wit' all the respect intended, but I wonder if he even know what heat feels like. Prob'ly ain't never even seen yo' mama naked."

"I know that type of man," Willa chuckled.

"Me too," Vernon put in.

Aside from Isabel, Viola had never heard anyone speak so directly about sexual things, and *never* about the Reverend and Nelvern. She was fascinated by their openness.

"And from what I hear 'bout the husband—that Donald, whatever it is," Miss Honeybee continued, "girl, they'da found my ass wit' another man too."

"Honey, you a mess," Vernon said.

"You walkin' around with no feet . . . you and Forestine both," Miss Honeybee went on. "But you'll find yo' way soon enough. I promised Rosalee I would look out for you 'cause I know jes' what you feeling. Twenty-three years ago, I was sitting right there in yo' place," she confessed. "I come up here and after I settled in, girl, I never looked back." Miss Honeybee's eyes softened even more. "But I had my Clayton with me. I guess it's a little different coming to this city by yo'self. That's why we'll be with you every step of the way."

"Settle in for a while," Willa said. "Get yo' bearings and we'll figure out something for you to do, okay, sweetie?"

Viola's shoulders began to relax. She felt more at ease knowing that the women truly understood what she felt inside. Soon, though, decisions about her future would have to be made. "How did you all start havin' these gathers?" Viola asked.

Miss Honeybee sighed. "My Clay . . ."

"A musician like none other," Willa insisted. "Talented, handsome, *and* generous."

"A better man you will not find," Vernon put in.

"When we moved into this house," Miss Honeybee continued, "Clay opened it up fo' all his friends 'cause he say a musician need a place to hang loose and be with his own. And back then, girl, we used to gather every night of the week. That's how I met these two rogues," she joked. "Willa here was married to Byron McGhee, a saxophone player in Clay's quartet. Willa played piano for 'em . . ."

"You play the piano?" Viola asked.

"I do indeed," she answered.

"And Vernon here was with Cutler Simms," Miss Honeybee went on.

Most folk in Jasperville would whisper something like that, two men together, if they spoke it at all. Viola thought about Reverends

Bembrey, Morgan, and Baines listening in on a conversation like this. For a moment, it tickled her.

"Cutler Simms was a drummer and a half..." Miss Honeybee went on.

"Don't get me to cryin'," Vernon said.

"What about Clay?"

"My Clay was a crooner," Miss Honeybee answered.

"And we ain't talkin' 'bout no ordinary singer," Willa put in. "To this day, I still say that Billy Eckstine took his style from Clay Mc-Color. Stole it like he was supposed to."

"Girl, don't let Billy hear you say that," Miss Honeybee squealed. "Mr. B would not like that. He used to come up here to the house every once in a while, especially when Clay was alive. Everybody been to this house over the years. Moms Mabley, Ella, Sassy still come by...Monk, Bird. Dizzy and Lorraine's place is right around the corner on Seventh...Billie Holiday, Betty Carter, that cute lil' gal, Abbey...what is it?"

"Abbey Lincoln," Vernon said.

"Yep, her." Miss Honeybee smiled as she spoke. "Back in the days, after a session at one of the clubs, we'd all gather here. Willa and me would make a big ole platter of whiting and waffles and the men would play from can to can't."

"Honey couldn't fry no fish," Willa's husky voice bellowed. "Even Clay, who thought that Honey could do no wrong...I mean that man eat all Honey's stuff—" They broke out in squeals.

"Shut up, Willamae," Miss Honeybee laughed.

"You too fresh," Vernon said.

"But he would not eat Honey's fish," she went on. "He eat mine in a minute, though."

"Oooh, Willa," Vernon howled.

"Made Honey jealous," she went on. "He say—" she tiptoed across the room with a watering bottle in her hand and a lascivious grin on her face, "he say, 'Don't tell Honey I told you this, but woman, you got the best-tasting fish I ever laid 'cross my lips.'" The three exploded in laughter again. The conversation went flying over Viola's head.

"Ain't that right, Honey?" Willa laughed.

"Girl, don't you get me to lyin'!" she screamed. "But, believe me when I tell you, mine is the only *real* fish that man ate 'til the day he died, rest his soul."

"Amen, amen," Willa yelled.

"As you can prob'ly tell," Miss Honeybee said, still laughing, "we used to cut up just as much back then."

"Worse," Willa insisted. "Lord, you can hear the fun in the music we played, see it in all them pictures we took," she said, referring to the photos on the mantel. "Honey, how come we don't take pictures no mo'?"

Viola held her glass of ginger ale and walked to the mantel. After two gathers she could recognize some of the faces. Her eyes darted across the dozens of photos of smiling, jamming, and dancing people. Between the music on the hi-fi and Miss Honeybee's stories, the pictures seemed to come alive.

"The business was different then," Miss Honeybee said. "Plenty of gigs, plenty of clubs. The players come up here from places like the Down Beat on Fifty-second Street. . . ."

"Three Deuces . . ." Vernon said

". . . the Audubon, Lickety Split Lounge, or Minton's up here in Harlem," Willa put in.

Viola paused in front of a picture of a young Miss Honeybee, cheek to cheek with a man twice her size. "That's me and my Clay," Miss Honeybee said, taking it from Viola. The frame was clustered with silver leaves. Miss Honeybee held the photo gently, as if to shake it would disturb the memories. Then she set it down and quickly pattered back across the room to a small cabinet beside the hi-fi. She opened the drawer and pulled out something wrapped in yellow satin. She slipped an album out and ran her fingertips lightly over the grooves. Viola could see that the feel of the thick black vinyl was enough to take her to another point in time. Miss Honeybee set the album on the spindle, clicked the release, and lightly placed the needle on the record. At first there was nothing but static, then came the soulful tinkle of piano keys and a man's deep and liquid voice. This had to be Clay McColor. Miss Honeybee moved toward the center of the room. When she spun to the music, her skirt opened at the bottom like pink flower petals. She glided as if unseen arms held her in a private dance, turned her, and caressed her lovingly.

Vernon and Willa simply went on with their chores. But Miss Honeybee was somewhere else. She was dancing with Clay McColor.

There were many pictures of Clay, some with other musicians and some in lovely moments with his wife. Viola thought him a handsome man. In most of the pictures he wore a suit and tie. He had a neat, thin mustache and smiling eyes. His hair was cut close to his scalp, and the yellow tint to the photographs made his skin appear olive green. As Viola looked at pictures of Clay McColor and then at a dancing Miss Honeybee, she couldn't imagine what it must have felt like for her to lose him.

On the other side of the mantel were photos of a younger Shirley DeGrace, doing her bump and grind, and a few of Vernon and Willa alone or with other musicians. Then Viola caught sight of Eddie Bishop. She raised the framed photo to get a closer look.

"Fine, ain't he?" Willa asked.

Viola nodded. Miss Honeybee went on dancing.

"One of the best trumpet players in this lifetime," Vernon put in.

"I thought he'd be at last night's gather," Viola said with a hint of disappointment.

"I heard you ask Curtis if Eddie was coming," Willa said, pulling a yellowing leaf from a large ficus.

Miss Honeybee settled on the sofa, slightly winded. "Eddie only come around once in a while," she said. "The man is always working."

"Always," Vernon added.

"Talented, good-looking, and large as life," Miss Honeybee went on. "Ain't too many women can come 'cross a man like Eddie Bishop and not have their breath taken away . . . but he is a rascal, pure and simple."

"Chile," Willa said.

Miss Honeybee fanned herself with her hand. "We love his music, we know he's special, but we've learned to leave Eddie Bishop to the Lord."

"But why?" Viola asked.

Miss Honeybee simply replied, "Girl, Eddie Bishop is a topic for another time."

Viola went on looking at the photos on the mantel, resisting her urge to dig further. There was one of Miss Honeybee standing in a garden, knee deep in sunflowers. There was another of two young girls with the same face. Rosalee and Honeybee were both missing a tooth in front. As children, the twins looked identical. But as they grew, the faces in the photos were made distinct by their expressions. On the far left of the mantel, Viola caught sight of an old amber photo of a woman with a face that resembled both Honeybee and Rosalee. Viola figured it to be their mother.

At the back of the mantel was a picture of a woman she thought she recognized. Viola stared at the photo in disbelief. Here was a woman she had seen nearly every day of her life. Never had she seen Nelvern Bembrey look quite like this. Her face had an open expression and her mouth was wide with laughter. Her eyes crinkled in the corners from laughing so hard. Her hair was loose and the wind blew it above her shoulders like a shiny black ribbon.

"Is this Nelvern?" Viola asked as she lifted the picture from the mantel.

"Yo' mama was one of the most beautiful women I ever knew," Miss Honeybee said. "I 'spect she still is . . . but, then again, a foot in the gut tends to age a woman."

"I know that's right," Willa said.

"This is *my* mother?" Viola asked.

"She was about yo' age then," Miss Honeybee said.

"I have *never* seen Nelvern look this way," Viola said.

"She was in love," Miss Honeybee said.

"She never smiled like this around the Reverend," Viola said.

"I ain't talkin' 'bout the Reverend."

Viola was dumbstruck. "Then who?"

Miss Honeybee sat back on the couch, and her feet barely touched the floor. "A man named Ralph Mitchell," she answered. "Funny thing, but I remember tellin' Nelvern the same thing 'bout Ralph Mitchell that I just tole you 'bout Eddie Bishop. I 'clare, I used the same words and everything. I say, 'Nelvern, you need to leave Ralph Mitchell to the Lord.' That's jes' what I tole her."

"But why?" Viola asked.

" 'Cause like Eddie Bishop, I knew he was a rascal. And worse, yo' mama was already married to the Reverend when Ralph come along."

"*My* mother!" Viola asked. She could imagine just about every woman from Cynthie Nettles to Isabel, but not Nelvern.

"You have to understand," Miss Honeybee said, "Nelvern hardly knew the Reverend, and this was a man she was supposed to spend the rest of her life with. You know as good as me, Viola, there's only so close anybody could get to that man. It wasn't 'til they stood at the altar that she even kissed him for the first time. Nelvern hardly saw him in the beginning of their marriage, because he was in Virginia in that preacher college."

"Theological school," Vernon corrected.

"Thank you, baby," Miss Honeybee said. "And while the Reverend was away, Nelvern spent most of her time with me."

"With you?" Viola said.

"Doesn't surprise me that you don't know," Miss Honeybee said wistfully. "Before I left Jasperville, Nelvern and me . . . we were pretty tight. At first, Lord, but did she have her ass way up on her shoulders—or so I thought. Her father was pastor and all, just like yours, and she was so dainty and ladylike. Had that buttery kinda skin . . . you know, like she just gon' melt if you touch her. Every gal in Jasperville wanted to look like Nelvern, wanted to dress like Nelvern, talk proper like Nelvern. Never said no cuss words or nothin'. Rose and me used to see her in church every Sunday when we was teenagers, but it wasn't 'til we was in our twenties that I first really started talkin' to her. She was already married to yo' daddy, but since he was away, she come to church and sat alone. Everybody figured that she kept to herself 'cause she thought she was too damn good. Turned out she was jes' lonely as hell. One Sunday, Rose and me made the mistake of sitting in Nelvern's seat. Center first pew. Looked like yo' mama wanted to run the other way, but instead, she sat there by Rose. In fact, she sat right on Rose's skirt. Rose whisper to me, '*Honeybee, she setting on my skirt.*' I say, '*Well, tell her to move her ass.*'

"Yo' mama heard me and started laughing. She laughed so hard that Reverend Foster looked over his glasses from the pulpit. And she wasn't the least bit stuck-up like I thought she was. After that, we started talkin' and doin' things together. We'd go to the creek or into town to a picture show. We saw *Mrs. Miniver* three times. Nell and me liked them romantic kinda movies. The Reverend came home every other Saturday to visit fo' a few hours. Lord, but did she dread those hours."

"So who was Ralph Mitchell?" Viola asked.

"There was this woman in New Pilgrim named Leda." Miss Honeybee laughed. "Ole fat-ass Leda Mitchell with her big mouth. Woman was always bragging on something like somebody's actually studyin' 'bout her. Brag 'bout how she cook . . . brag that she got a telephone. Now, Leda had been braggin' for over a year 'bout this nephew of hers and how he was this flyer boy in the service and how he was so pretty, and how his mama, Leda's big-ass sister, and his daddy, who was some white man, came this close"—she held two tiny fingers up—"came this close, I tell you, to gittin' married. She say the onliest thing that stopped 'em was that he was a Catholic and she was a Baptist."

"Shut up, Honey," Willa laughed.

"I say, '*Rose*'," Miss Honeybee went on, " '*I'm beginning to believe she ain't even got a nephew.*'

" '*Honey, you just a stitch,*' Rose say. She always called me that when I was talkin' fresh. Rose called me a stitch every day. Well, that next Sunday, Leda Mitchell come to church." Miss Honeybee had to take a breath before she went on. "And, chile, on her arm was the most beautiful man I ever laid my eyes on. And fat-ass Leda, who never come to church late in her life, strolled down the aisle in the middle of first prayer, and you could just hear the women swooning."

"Swooning and praying," Vernon laughed.

"He had on this uniform," Miss Honeybee said. "His hair was laid back all wavy and he had this smooth, pretty face. Every woman in that church had their eye on him. And he wasn't one bit shy. He met everyone's gaze with a smile, never lowering his eyes at anyone, including the church elders. Obviously he wasn't from 'round Jasperville, 'cause after service when folks gathered in the basement for dinner and dessert, he spotted yo' mama and that's exactly where he took his fine self. I was standing beside her the whole time. Me and Rose, both.

" '*What's your name?*' he asked Nelvern.

"Now, anyone from within fifty miles of Jasperville knew that a perfect stranger should never approach a young woman with so fo'ward an opening. You had to go through channels to get a proper introduction. Everyone knew that this was the Southern way. Everyone except Ralph Mitchell.

" '*Are you talkin' to me?*' Nelvern asked him.

" '*That's right.*' He held a cup of red punch in one hand and his military hat under his armpit. '*Name is Ralph. Sure would like to know who you are.*'

"Nelvern turned away from him, but, chile, she was better than me. I stood there gawking at him. Even Rosalee had to stare. His face, red-bone and smooth, had just the hint of a midmorning shadow and a hollow in his cheeks big enough for a baby's fist."

"Lord, Honey, tell me 'bout it," Willa swooned.

"He sucked a shred of chicken from his back teeth. '*I'll be around for about five days,*' he said. '*You gon' let me take you out or what? Be your steady man for a minute?*'

"Nell laughed at him. No one had ever talked to her this way. Most times folks didn't talk to her at all. They left her on a crystal pedestal and talked 'round her, through her, and about her. 'Specially men, and in particular, her own husband.

" '*I'm married,*' she told him.

" '*Oh? Which one is your husband?*'

" '*He's not here.*'

" '*Took sick, did he?*'

" '*What?*'

" '*Well, that's the only reason I can think for a man to be away from a good-lookin' woman like you,*' he said."

Willa and Vernon howled. Viola lowered her head and smiled at the thought of Ralph Mitchell.

"But yo' mama wasn't so impressed... or should I say, she didn't make out to be. She shook her head at his downright arrogance.

" '*My husband's away in school,*' she said.

" '*Why don't you let me keep you company 'til he come home?*'

" '*I don't want your company,*' she said. '*Will you excuse me, I need to talk to my daddy.*'

"When she walked away, I could see one knee knock against the other. That's exactly when I told yo' mama, '*Nelvern, you best get away from this man. You need to leave Ralph Mitchell to the Lord.*'

"She didn't listen. And of course, Ralph Mitchell kept at her, just like men that need to be left to the Lord usually do. The next day yo' mama packed a picnic lunch and insisted that I go with her and Ralph to the top of Hopper Hill. That's where we used to go in them days to jes' sit and talk. That day, her and Ralph did all the talking. It was like I wasn't even there. Every other sentence that come from the man's mouth made yo' mama giggle."

"I've never heard Nelvern giggle a day in my life," Viola insisted.

"Streams and streams of giggles," Miss Honeybee said, "and sometimes she laughed out like a sailor. That's when I snapped that picture there. Couldn't figure what else to do with myself because I was the worst third wheel. It was proper in them days to have a chaperone, 'specially when the woman was married like that. And that's when they started carryin' on."

"What?!" Viola said.

"I'm the onliest one knew it," Miss Honeybee said. "I don't think I've ever seen a woman as happy as yo' mama was. For four days they met at the top of that hill and tumbled in the green until each day was over. Nelvern had never been one to leave her chores undone, but that week, she could think of nothing else except leavin' the house and getting to the top of that hill. Barely close the door, take a leap, and let the wind carry her through the trees."

"Only four days?" Viola asked.

"On the fifth day Ralph Mitchell didn't show up. Nell waited on that hill from can't see in the morning to can't see at night. It wasn't until after ten P.M. that she started on her way home, feeling she had no right to be hurt or angry. He was gone, and she was married. She come to my house the next day and begged me to go to Leda's place to find him. I went, but he had already left town. Left as suddenly as he came. No apologies, promises, explanations, or messages. Just gone. And it made things worse that, around the same time, Cleveland Bembrey came home for good. That's when everything changed for Nelvern. She stopped meeting me on the hill and wasn't even allowed to set with me in church no mo'. In fact, Cleveland Bembrey, now *Reverend* Bembrey, decided that I wasn't the kind of woman that Nelvern should associate with. Said I was wild, had me a fresh mouth, and hung out at Snookie Petaway's."

"The devil himself," Viola put in.

"I know that's right," Miss Honeybee said.

"Why didn't she go after him, Honey?" Viola asked. "Why didn't she at least try and find him."

Miss Honeybee smiled gently. "Most times when a man leave like that, mean he don't wanna be found. A few weeks after the Reverend come home, yo' mama realized she was pregnant. For nine months, Nelvern Bembrey—the Reverend's wife, the Reverend's daughter, Miss Beyond Reproach—actually held her breath waitin' to find out who you were gonna look like. She folded her hands under that big belly, lowered her eyes to the world, and became the woman that you know. When you were born, it was clear to us both that you were the Reverend's chile."

Viola thought back to all Nell's self-righteous glances. The pompous turn of her smile when she looked at someone like Isabel or Cynthie Nettles. Or when she didn't look at Viola at all as they led her away. The bitterness in Viola's stomach began to dissipate. Knowing about Ralph Mitchell seemed to level the field a bit. She wished she'd known it sooner. Perhaps this was one of the reasons that Miss Rosalee had sent her here.

"I saw a broken heart the moment I saw Ralph Mitchell," Miss Honeybee said.

"Honey's always been good like that," Vernon put in.

"And believe me," she warned, "I see it in Eddie Bishop." Miss Honeybee stood up from the couch and placed the mail on one of the end tables. "I'm sure Fred's already waitin' in the car," she said. "We need to get on to Pet's Place. She gets busy on a Saturday afternoon. And it's liable to take her a while with all that hair you got."

Fred parked the car on the corner of Edgecomb Avenue and West 153rd Street. He lumbered around to the passenger side, opened the back door, and helped Miss Honeybee out, then Vernon. Viola got out on her own and stood on the sidewalk. She had never been to a real live beauty salon before. Even for her own wedding, Miss Ida came to the Bembrey house with a hooded dryer and what she called her "beautifying bag": a hand-sewn red sack stuffed with curlers, pins, end papers and, of course, her much-needed hot comb.

Viola followed Vernon and Miss Honeybee toward 153rd Street. There was no sign of a beauty shop or any type of business. "Is the salon far from here?" Viola asked.

Miss Honeybee chuckled. "Pet don't have no salon. She work from home. I've tried beauty parlors uptown and down, but Pet is the oniliest one who can do my hair like I like."

Pet's brownstone seemed to be the size of the Big House, but there were no stained glass panes or silver knocker. The stone was chipped in places and the gate was so offline that Vernon had to lift it before they could walk through. The front door was ajar. A handwritten sign on the glass said, "Come On In."

The door whined like an injured cat when they pushed it open. "Pet?" Miss Honeybee called. There was no answer.

"She's probably in the kitchen," Vernon said, unwrapping his shawl.

The house was laid out the same as the Big House, but Viola could hear her feet touch down on the uneven wood floors as they crossed through the barren vestibule. The hissing of a radiator echoed through the hall. Instead of clipped flowers, the air was filled with the oily scent of warm pomade.

"That you, Honey?" a high voice called from the back.

"Hey there, Pet," Miss Honeybee called back.

"I'm working with lye, sweetheart," she said.

"Take yo' time," Vernon called.

"That my baby, Vernon?" Pet asked. There was the sudden sound of running water under her voice. "That my baby?" she called even louder.

"It's me, my Pet," he said.

They walked into a large, almost empty room in about the same place as Miss Honeybee's parlor. The floor was covered in white linoleum with tiny red scrolls. The walls were painted a dull sand, and there were folding chairs, snack trays with stacks of out-of-date magazines, and a black-and-white TV on top of an old hi-fi.

"Y'all turn on some music, if you want," Pet called.

"Don't worry 'bout us," Miss Honeybee said. "Go'n and do what you got to do." Miss Honeybee undid her wrap and laid it across one of the chairs. Vernon sat in another, draping his shawl on its back. Viola stood with her coat still on.

"I know it don't look like much," Miss Honeybee whispered, "but Pet know what she's doing and she'll make you right comfortable."

Viola pulled a chair close to Miss Honeybee and Vernon. She removed her coat and carefully rested it on her lap so that it didn't touch the scuffed floor. Miss Honeybee had generously given her this black-and-white houndstooth. The double-breasted car coat stopped right above her knee and made her calves look like two brown teardrops.

Miss Honeybee took her cigarettes from her purse. The sight of her jeweled hand holding the silver case seemed so strange in this room. Vernon immediately retrieved an ashtray from one of the small tables. The two seemed oddly at home in this unglamorous house, even with their manicured nails and wraps dripping from the backs of rusted aluminum chairs. Viola began to see that, no matter where they went, they brought along their own sense of enchantment.

"Have you given any thought to what you might wanna do here?" Vernon asked Viola.

Viola's eyes went from a dusty World's Fair globe on the mantel to Vernon's inquiring smile. She had actually given it a lot of thought but, up until now, hadn't made mention of it. More than ever, Viola wanted to sing. Weeks ago, the thought of being a singer was distant and unattainable, but after a couple of gathers, the possibility seemed more real. The platform was real. The singers were real. She could reach out and touch them.

"This morning," Viola started, "when Willa mentioned that she played the piano...I was thinking that maybe she could help me with a couple of songs."

Miss Honeybee looked at Vernon. "I have no doubt that you are sho'ly a talented woman," she said. "But this ain't no easy life you talkin' 'bout. And you know *I* know."

"Yes, ma'am."

"I'm sure Willa would love to help you out...."

"She lives for things like that," Vernon added.

"But you got to understand what you gettin' into. You really got to *want* this to survive, Viola. I'm not jokin' here. And you have to practice to be good."

"Then practice to get better," Vernon said, "then practice to *stay* good."

"I would," Viola said.

"And if Willa starts with you," Miss Honeybee went on, "you got to be *where* she tells you, *when* she tells you. Willa is a sweet woman day to day, but when she sets down at the piano, she don't play."

Viola could feel her heartbeat quicken.

"Lord ha' mercy," Miss Honeybee said, blowing a stream of smoke, "could you imagine the Reverend's face if he saw you up there on the platform?"

Viola laughed at the thought. That in itself made her more excited about the prospect.

Pet suddenly rushed into the room with all the force of a tornado. She was a heavyset, light-colored woman, and her bare feet slapped against the linoleum. Most of her hair was pushed off of her face and flying behind her, every which way. She had on a black smock studded with hair clips and bobby pins. Although it was the middle of the winter, she wore checkered shorts that rose up her thighs in the middle.

"Would you look at this chile's hair," she said, tossing Viola's thick braid in the back. "Gon' take me all afternoon to get through this."

"Don't she got some hair, Pet?" Vernon said.

"Mercy," Pet said, undoing Viola's clip. She shook Viola's hair loose and let it tumble down her back.

Miss Honeybee introduced her. "Viola, this here is Miss Eunice Pettiford."

"Pet," the woman corrected. "Like you pet a dawg."

"Nice to meet you," Viola said.

"When's your last perm, babydoll?" Pet asked.

"Never," Viola answered.

"Got ourselves a virgin," Pet said with a smile. Her teeth, white and straight, seemed out of place with the rest of her disheveled appearance.

"I think we better come back for Viola," Vernon said.

"Say 'bout an hour or two?" Miss Honeybee asked.

"Best make it three," Pet said, walking off. She stopped and turned back. "Well, come on, sugar," she said to Viola. "I ain't gon' eat you up or nuthin'."

Viola nervously followed Pet down the hall. The sputtering and clanging of the radiator was so loud that she barely heard Miss Honeybee and Vernon call good-bye.

Pet's kitchen was a bit smaller than the one at the Big House. Or perhaps it was the clutter. Along the side of the room, steel milk bins with jars of Dixie Peach, various shampoos, and hair spray were stacked almost three feet high. Three hooded dryers were lined up against the wall. In front of them were snack trays strewn with magazines of smiling brown girls, their hair in simple bobs or piled high on top of their heads like fancy chocolate cakes. Rhythm and blues played lightly on a radio. So light that it was practically inaudible above the hum of the dryer and the cackle of two older women sitting by the sink, one with wet hair and the other with a thick white paste on her roots. A younger woman sat under the dryer.

"Have a seat over there, babydoll." Pet pointed to a chair beside one of the hooded dryers. "I need to rinse Miss Emily, then I'll start on you. Take a look at some of them magazines," she said over her shoulder. "Find yo'self a nice style."

Pet suddenly looked graceful. With one long flourish, she wheeled the woman with the pasty hair toward the sink. Pet spun her, then reclined the chair so that her head rested under the faucet.

Viola gathered magazines from a few of the tables. She took one from in front of the young woman who sat under the dryer.

"I need that one," the woman said, opening her eyes.

Viola handed it to her. The woman closed her eyes again, and Viola skimmed through one of the magazines.

"Boring," the girl said, opening her eyes again.

Viola turned to her. With the round pod set atop her head she looked like she was from outer space.

"That one's boring," the woman said, referring to the picture that Viola had on her lap. She lit a cigarette and talked over the sound of the dryer. "Everyone wears a flip these days. Also page boys."

Viola wasn't quite sure what to say. "I think it's nice."

"It's okay," the girl conceded, "but not exciting."

About the same age as Viola, the woman was as pretty as Isabel, but far more sophisticated. Her simple maroon dress had a neckline that stopped at her collarbone. It was classy and yet still made her look like a pinup girl the way her cone-shaped breasts pointed at the tips.

"Priscilla," Pet yelled from the sink. "Start taking them curlers out, sweetie." The woman lifted the dryer from her head. Neat rows of tiny pink rollers covered her head.

Priscilla took another short puff before she set her cigarette in a full ashtray on a snack table. Just like with Miss Honeybee, the smoke looked refined and seductive. "You can do so much with your hair," she said.

Priscilla spoke like a city girl. Each of her verbs ended with a "g" that clinked like fine crystal. She quickly flipped through the magazine in her lap and stopped on a particular page. She handed it to Viola and then began to unpin her rollers. The style she had chosen was a wispy, pixielike cut.

"For me?" Viola asked.

"It's beautiful," Priscilla assured her. "Like Carmen Jones. And besides, you got that good hair that grows right back when you cut it."

"It's awfully short," Viola said shyly. "You really think this would look good on me?"

"I really do."

Viola stared at the picture and considered how different she'd look. How different she'd feel. Viola from Jasperville might not wear a style like this, but perhaps the Viola that lived in the Big House would.

"You have to consider the shape of your face," Priscilla explained. "Yours is beautifully round, just like Dorothy Dandridge. . . ."

Viola couldn't help but smile at the comparison.

"I think you'd look spectacular," Priscilla went on.

Viola thought about walking into a gather with this hair, maybe even wearing one of those fine dresses from Miss Honeybee's closet. She looked at the picture again and then at herself in the mirror. When she sat in Pet's chair, Viola pointed to the picture.

"Aw, hell no," Pet argued. "Honey ain't killin' me fo' choppin' off all that hair. No she ain't."

"She's a grown woman, Pet," Priscilla said. "How can you tell a grown woman what she wants?"

What started as a whim had turned into something Viola had to have. Up until now, she had let other folks dictate her choices. Nelvern, Donald, and the Reverend. Now Viola had made a decision.

Pet cringed when she lifted the heavy steel scissors. The two old ladies howled when she cut the first chunk of hair. Viola tried not to flinch as it fell into her lap. She tried to stay calm when she felt the air on the back of her bare neck. Then, after the locks hit the floor, Priscilla left. She didn't even stay to see the results.

Pet curled and shaped her new do, but Viola could get no clear reaction from the faces of the old ladies. They seemed stunned. Then Pet handed Viola the large oval mirror. This was as exciting as sneaking out with Isabel. It was a choice. Her own choice.

Viola lifted the mirror. The woman who looked back wasn't anyone she had ever seen before. This woman was eager and daring. This woman was sophisticated. She loved this Viola and all that life was about to bring to her.

When Miss Honeybee and Vernon returned, Pet immediately stepped into her defense mode. "I tried to tell the girl, Honey," Pet said. "Wasn't my fault, so don't look at me . . ."

Miss Honeybee couldn't close her mouth. Vernon wept at the thick, dark locks that lay under Pet's chair. But after a cigarette and a shot of Pet's Jamaican rum, Miss Honeybee decided that the new Viola was "cute." She still didn't stop the lectures about jealous women in beauty parlors, gullibility, and the fact that no colored gal *ever* cut her hair.

CHAPTER 13

The Eddie Bishop Jazz Quintet was opening at Crawford's in the Village. Forestine had been waiting almost two months for this gig after missing Eddie at the Big House. Eddie had always been one of Beck's favorite musicians. She could still see Beck, sitting in a motel room in his cotton pajama bottoms, the lights dimmed and Eddie's three albums stacked on his portable turntable. He would barely move during a song except to pull a puff of smoke from his cigarette, sip from his one and only brandy snifter, or flip the albums to the other side. Then he'd lift himself from the floor, winded by the music, and say, "Profound, Forestine. This young cat is truly profound."

Forestine put on her favorite purple knit dress and pointy-toed black pumps, borrowed Miss Honeybee's car, and grabbed Viola by the arm. The line at Crawford's ran halfway down Seventh Avenue South. Inside, nearly every seat was full and some folks were standing. Forestine was usually humble about the little celebrity she had managed to attain so far, but for the opportunity to see Eddie Bishop, she walked up to the box office and leaned her six-foot-two-inch frame in. She threw out names to the woman behind the counter like Coy Williams, Curtis Atwater, Honeybee McColor, Beck, Lil' Eartha,

Buster the Cat—*anyone* who came to mind, until she managed to snag a table all the way in the back.

The room hummed with excitement as the crowd waited for Eddie to arrive. He was already half an hour late, but the opening trio wasn't bad, so the room wasn't yet restless. Forestine sipped a straight dark rum and Viola sat smoking a cigarette. She had just recently taken up smoking and the girl's body language seemed different, more confident, when she held a cigarette.

"This is Eddie's trademark," Forestine said. "Honey says that it isn't a true Eddie Bishop gig if he doesn't get to the club late." Forestine tried to wave down the waitress for another round of drinks, but the girl breezed past. She was moving so fast that her blond hair trailed behind her and the red candle on the table flickered in her wake. "I remember Beck saying that when he saw Eddie Bishop in Philly—"

"Do you know how many times you call that man's name?" Viola cut in.

"Eddie Bishop?"

"Beck," Viola said.

"I don't talk about Beck that much."

"Almost as much as you talk about Benny."

"Come on, Vi," Forestine said.

"Beck smokes Pall Malls, right?" Viola asked.

Forestine turned her eyes away.

"He drinks dark rum just like you," Viola went on.

"Alright, Viola, I get the point."

"You ever hear from him?" Viola asked.

Forestine took another sip from her glass. "I hurt him so bad that I really don't expect to."

"You miss him?"

"Every day," Forestine confessed. "Beck Pinkney kept me together for the longest time. After he left, I thought I'd fall completely apart."

"But you didn't," Viola said.

"Not so far."

"Think you'll ever get back together?" Viola asked.

Forestine looked down into her glass. "Much too much water," she said. "The man is long gone and I don't blame him one single bit." Forestine looked up at Viola with a sly smile on her face. "How about we talk about you, Viola," she said. "Let's run your ass over the coals for a while."

"There's nothin' to say," Viola insisted.

"Oh?" Forestine smirked playfully. "How about this new hair?"

"You don't like it?" Viola had attended one gather with the new do. Most loved it, saying that she looked pretty, but a few of the women, like Shirley DeGrace, wrote her out for the drastic cut.

"It's adorable," Forestine insisted.

"Good, 'cause I think it's me," Viola said, doubtfully, running a hand over her bare neck. "So, is this the extent of your running my ass over the coals?" she said, laughing.

"I'm afraid not." Forestine smiled. "How about the way you were gonna have a kitten when you heard that Eddie Bishop was here at Crawford's."

"I have a little crush," Viola admitted. "So does every woman in this room."

"What about Curtis?"

"What *about* Curtis?" Viola asked.

"You know how he feels about you?"

"Curtis is a good man."

"Yes," Forestine said.

"I like him a lot. . . ."

"But . . . ?" Forestine said.

Viola paused to find just the right words. "I guess the earth don't exactly move."

"The earth is always moving, Viola. You just don't feel it most of the time."

The club erupted into applause. Eddie Bishop's Quintet hustled out of the dressing room and took their places onstage. Eddie was the last to walk out, and the audience stood up as he passed. He waved to the crowd with his horn, and as he stepped onto the platform, he did a silly two-step. Eddie looked younger than Forestine had imagined. And every bit as good-looking as Viola had said. He was as tall as he was handsome and seemed as self-assured as he was talented.

The waitress finally stopped and set down another round of drinks. She placed both hands flat on the table and took a well-earned breath before she said to Forestine, "They're from the lady." She pointed at a petite white woman who was making her way toward them. Her flaming red hair, elegantly bobbed, fell into eyes that looked like two large emeralds. She carried a flute and wore a minidress and black, high-heeled boots. It wasn't until the woman stood over the table that Forestine recognized her.

"That can't be New Orleans?" Forestine said, standing up. "Bethanne?!"

"I know, I know," Bethanne said. "I look good, right?" Her voice was as heavy as Forestine remembered and as raw as a shot of straight bourbon.

"You look fantastic," Forestine said.

"Girl, I look so good, I'm ready to date myself," Bethanne screamed.

"You playing with Eddie Bishop now?" Forestine asked her.

"It's been just as sweet as a vacation. He saw me playing in the Quarter . . . you know, at Gator Aisle, and he said, woman, we need to get together. I been with the Quintet ever since."

"This is Viola Bembrey," Forestine said. Bethanne offered her hand. "Viola, Bethanne Dieudonne. A kick-ass musician. Bethanne and I met up at a gig in New Orleans," Forestine explained.

"Then at another'n Memphis," Bethanne added.

"Then again in Chicago," Forestine said.

"Lordy, girl, we got some miles on us."

Forestine could see the surprise on Viola's face. It wasn't that Bethanne was a white jazz musician—there were more than a few who stopped by the Big House and completely worked out. It wasn't even that she was a woman. It was that she was so tiny, onstage it seemed the men might simply blow her away.

"Girl, what is Eddie Bishop like?" Forestine asked. The Quintet started to play.

"Flirty, fickle, and quite mad," she answered.

"A player," Forestine said.

"Oh, yeah," Bethanne said. Eddie looked out into the house. "I got to work, *cher*," she said, "but after the set, come on into the dressing room and we can talk some mo'. And move on up to my table," she insisted. Forestine and Viola picked up their drinks and followed as she led them to an empty table right under the stage. She pecked

Forestine on the forehead, made her way onto the stage, and immediately lifted her flute to play.

"This is one of Eddie's original tunes," Forestine whispered to Viola. "From an album called *Breakin' It Down*. The LP has a lot of that freedom-style jazz. Girl, it sound like noise to me, screaming trumpet and all . . . but I have to admit that Eddie takes some chances. Just glad when he came back to bebop."

"You gon' let me hear the man play or what?" Viola whispered back.

From one song to the next, no one quite knew what to expect from Eddie Bishop. He was often playful onstage. After "Our Love Is Here to Stay," he was having such a great time that he turned and shook his butt at the audience. But in a ballad he was as somber as Trane, as prolific as Miles. During, "When I Fall in Love," Bethanne was cooking so strong that he lowered himself to her boot and kissed it. This wasn't just a jazz set, Forestine thought. It was sheer entertainment fueled by the magnetism of this man.

"Everybody," Eddie said into the mike. "This is our last song for the night."

"Awwww!"

"Stay for the next set, then," he said with a laugh. "Shit, ain't nothin' but a party. But y'all got to come up wit' some more cash, is all." Laughter. "But looka h'yere . . ." he said, walking to the edge of the stage. "One Forestine Bent is in the house." There was light applause as a small few recognized her name. Forestine's mouth dropped open. "I'm gonna try"—he whispered in the mike like he was telling the audience a secret—"I'm gonna try to get the woman to come up here and sing. And if she don't, I'm gonna cry, which is perfect 'cause we doin' 'Willow Weep for Me.' " Eddie Bishop crooked his finger at Forestine. "Come on, now," he said.

"Forestine," Bethanne yelled. "We need you, girl!"

Forestine could feel her knees buckle when she got up in the applauding house and walked to the stage. She held her head high. In her favorite purple dress, she was royalty. The Quintet had already started the introduction when she stepped onto the platform. Eddie pushed a stool toward her, then handed her the mike. Forestine's hand trembled a bit, but after the first few notes, she had control of not only her nerves, but the entire house.

Eddie sat with his eyes closed and his trumpet balanced on the tip of his knee as he listened to Forestine sing. Then he rose from the stool as if a spirit had moved him. Eddie raised his trumpet, then eased himself into a solo that lasted for fifteen minutes. The club was silent, except for the sound of ice clinking against bar glasses. Forestine listened, mesmerized. When he lowered his horn, she stood to wrap up the song, regretting it had passed so quickly. She gave Eddie Bishop a hug to say thank you, bowed to the cheering house, and left the stage. As she walked back to the table, her feet never touched the ground.

Forestine sipped one of the many drinks that now lined the table. Eddie and his Quintet had already returned to their dressing room. A tape of Charlie Parker's *My Favorite Things* played as the house filed out. Viola must have sensed the beautiful fog Forestine was in and left her to her thoughts. This was the high that Forestine lived for. It didn't happen after every gig, or even after most gigs, but some sets fell together with a touch of magic that she couldn't describe.

"Beck once told me," Forestine said to Viola, "about a time when he got to do a song with T-Bone Walker. He remembered what T-Bone wore that night, what they were drinking, everything T-Bone laughed at, and every single note they played. *Every* note, Viola," she repeated. "I didn't understand it at the time . . . I mean, I couldn't see how he could recall those tiny, tiny things . . . but now I know."

Forestine could tell that Viola had sensed the magic.

The waitress approached the table. She set down a couple more drinks, then leaned into Forestine. "Don't ask who they're from," she said. "Seems like everyone wants to buy you a round." She removed a fresh rum from her tray for Forestine, then a daiquiri for Viola, and said before she walked away. "Eddie wants to see you in the dressing room."

"Can I come?" Viola pleaded.

"Girl, my legs are shaking so bad, you're gonna have to," Forestine said nervously.

More than a few times she had sung for kings. Miles told her she had something special. Bobby Timmons was still trying to arrange a tour with her. Though flattering, not much had come from either encounter. Now Forestine felt that her career was about to change.

"You walkin' to the dressin' room, *cher*," Bethanne asked as she made her way over to their table, "or do Eddie got to send his limo to carry you?"

"We were just on our way," Forestine said nervously.

"I need to fix my makeup first," Viola said, looking for the rest room.

"Viola—" Forestine said.

"Just one second, Forestine," she said as she hurried toward the front of the club. "One second, is all."

"Women always seem to do that befo' they see Eddie Bishop." Bethanne laughed.

"What?" Forestine asked nervously.

"Fluff themselves up." Bethanne sat at the table. "But you look beautiful . . . and you ain't never sounded better."

Forestine finished her drink in one gulp.

"I know you ain't nervous," Bethanne said. Forestine looked at her doubtfully. "Aw, *cher*," Bethanne moaned, "the hard part is over. Ain't nuthin' left but the details. What you think you fin' to talk to the man about? You already know how good you are."

"You still the same," Forestine said with a laugh.

Bethanne leaned in closer. "While we got this minute, lemme gi' you the heads-up about a thing or two." Bethanne sipped from one of the full glasses on the table. "You'll sing the best music of yo' life, that is the truth. You'll have the best of everything, 'cause that's how Eddie go. Sometimes he spend money that he don't even have. And whatever you've heard about the man is prob'ly true."

"The only thing I want from Eddie Bishop," Forestine said, "is some music."

Bethanne smiled. "I could tell you were strong like that when I met you years ago. You a lot like me. Bring it to me in a song, goddamn it!"

Forestine laughed out. "You so crazy," she said.

"Am I lyin', though?"

"No."

"Shit." Bethanne laughed. "I can damn sho' sleep wit' a song."

"I'm hearing you," Forestine said.

"I jes' want you to be alright," Bethanne said. "See, Eddie like them nice gals. And you nice, Forestine. Got you a good heart. But he gobble them sweet gals like jellied toast." Forestine laughed. "I seen it with my own eyes," Bethanne insisted. "And when they ain't sweet no mo', they gone. Like this gal he took a likin' to when we were in Italy a couple of years ago. Beautiful Italian gal . . . big brown eyes . . . stone Catholic. Eddie couldn't speak no Italian and this gal couldn't speak nothin' further than jazz, you know." Forestine nodded. "We were in Italy about three weeks and when we come home, Eddie brought this lil' girl with him . . . name was Teresa. Put her on a pedestal. Give her everything . . . including a child."

"Eddie is a father?" Forestine asked.

"Beautiful lil' baby girl. But as soon as Teresa started pickin' up some of his ways—and jes' to please him, mind you—she had to go. Outta his life! Never forget the day when Teresa turned to that man and said, 'Fuck you, Eddie!' Italian accent and all." Forestine couldn't stop laughing. "Well, that should never come out the mouth of a woman he's with."

"Bethy," one of the guys from the Quintet called from the dressing room.

"We got to git in there, *cher*," Bethanne said.

Just as they rose to go in, Viola joined them. The three women entered the smoky dressing room. Though not much nicer, the space inside was bigger than at most clubs. Forestine had expected the room to be packed with people but she saw only the Quintet. Bethanne sat in a wooden chair with her back to the mirrored dressing table. Three men in the ensemble stood over Eddie, who lay sprawled on a tattered beige sofa.

"Forestine fuckin' Bent," he said, pulling himself up.

"That's a title, *cher*," Bethanne cut in. "You know, like Queen fuckin' Elizabeth."

Forestine took a seat in a chair across from him. Viola sat beside her.

"Gifts were handed down here," he said, drawing on a cigarette. "I knew that when I first saw you sing."

"First?" she asked.

"A club in Mobile," he said. "You were with Eartha McClain." She covered her face with her hand. "No, no," he said. "You kicked the blues' ass. Then I saw you with Gus Hannen about a year ago. I say damn . . . the woman is singing jazz too. Gus wadn't playing shit, but you were workin' out." Forestine couldn't control her smile. "So you gonna do the rest of my engagement with me?" he asked. Just like that. "Got another week here at Crawford's and then two weeks at the Vanguard," he said. "You can think about it. . . ."

"I don't have to think about it," she said quickly. "The answer is hell, yes."

Forestine's legs trembled. But now it was more out of excitement.

"Solid on the wallid, then," he said. One of the men in the group handed him a lit reefer. Eddie pulled on it, held the smoke for a beat, and then released it. "Who the hell are you?" he asked Viola.

Disappointment flashed across Viola's face. "You met Viola at the Big House," Forestine said.

"I did?" he chuckled. He looked at Viola again. "Honey be introducing me to all kinds of folks. Violet, you say?"

"Viola," she answered.

Eddie pulled on the reefer again and handed it to Forestine. She took a puff and then handed it to Bethanne. "Singer?" he asked.

"No."

"She's a wonderful singer," Forestine said, grabbing Viola's hand. "She's been working with Willa at the house. And soon enough, she'll be singing over at the Green Parrot."

"Forestine . . . ?" Viola whispered.

"Wish I had friends like you, Forestine," Bethanne said.

"Hell, yeah," Eddie said. "Another singer'll cut yo' damn throat. But Forestine is secure in her own shit." He turned to Viola again. "So, Viola"—he pronounced her name "Vee-ola"—"you been hanging wit' my main man. Curtis Atwater is a bad mu'fuckah." He took another puff of the reefer and this time offered it to Viola. She shook her head no. "Sweetest gig I ever played was with Att . . . that's what we called him back then. Called him Att. Anyway, this gig was . . . shit . . ." he said, thinking out loud, ". . . about eight years ago at the Café Bohemia. Talk about a group of the baddest mu'fuckahs you ever heard. It was Lockjaw's gig and he had Red Garland on piano, Philly Joe on drums, I was on trumpet, and Att was on bass."

"Ha' mercy," Forestine whispered.

Eddie handed the reefer to Bethanne and then rolled a second one. He smoked it as easily as his cigarette. "That show I did wit' Att,"

Eddie said, "was the show that changed my life. Them mu'fuckahs was playing some music! And Att . . . Att was a fill-in that night. They were supposed to have Ron Carter but Ronnie couldn't make it and folks were talkin' 'bout this cat named Atwater. Well, Att stepped up and claimed the night! Said, this my mu'fuckin night, y'all. Blew everybody away!" Eddie said, shaking his head. "Now he don't want no part of the life and hey . . . I can dig it."

"But Curtis loves playing," Viola said.

"Ain't no mystery," Eddie replied. "Att was shootin' big-time drugs." Viola's eyes widened. "We had to pull that niggah out a Dumpster in Chicago one morning," Eddie laughed. "All the way fucked up! Twelve degrees outside and they thought they'd have to amputate the mu'fuckah's leg. Ain't hard to understand at all. He needed to save his life and for Att, givin' up the smack meant givin' up the business, and I admire the shit out of 'im. Gave up the music *and* the drugs." He chuckled to himself. "Kill me to let go either one." He offered the reefer to Viola again. Forestine was a little surprised when Viola took it this time. She broke down coughing as soon as the smoke left her body. Eddie seemed to think it was cute.

"So . . . you and Att . . ." Eddie said to Viola. "Y'all his'n and her'n, or what?"

Viola caught her breath and answered, "Curtis is a good friend."

"Friends, huh?" Eddie said.

"Man, hush yo'self," Bethanne snapped.

Eddie let his eyes linger on Viola. "I'm recalling your face now," he said. "In the kitchen wit' Att. But you look different."

"Her hair is different," Forestine said. "She cut all that pretty hair off."

"Yeah," Eddie said. "Still fine, though. Damn fine." For a moment he lost the arrogant smile. Then he turned to focus on Forestine. "We doin' a rehearsal tomorrow at Nola," he said, standing up. "Bethy'll show you the book, but I want you to do 'Willow'. . . ." He smiled. "You blew that mu'fuckah away, tonight."

"Thank you," Forestine said.

"Don't mean to rush you, ladies," Eddie said, "but we got the next set startin' soon and I need me some food." He slipped on a black leather jacket and a pair of shades and walked with Forestine and Viola to the door of the dressing room. "Tomorrow," he said to Forestine. "And hey, Vee-o-la. You tell Att . . . tell him I'm comin' up to see his ass 'fore I get outta here."

"I will."

He led them into the empty club, kissed Forestine on the cheek, and quickly walked toward the back door that opened out onto the street. "Bethyyyy!" he hollered before he stepped out. "I'll be back in a minute. Tell that waitress to bring me something to eat."

Forestine could smell spring when the sun poured through the screen in her open bedroom window. Outside, Miss Honeybee was pruning a thin garden trail by the front gate. The three fake petunias on her straw hat swayed as she struggled to loosen the tight soil. When the chunks of earth finally softened, she threw in a handful of mulch from a white plastic bag by her side. She did this for the length of the small garden, which ran along the wrought-iron fence and stopped at the downstairs entrance to the Big House.

The faint sound of the piano came from the music room. Forestine knew it must be after noon, because the Big House remained respectfully quiet in the morning.

Her gigs at the Vanguard with Eddie Bishop ended as late as three A.M. Last night was the end of their two-week run, but she would start another with Bobby Timmons at a club in Brooklyn called Tony's in just four days.

Forestine opened her bedroom door and could hear Viola singing "What a Little Moonlight Can Do" above Willa's playing.

She was surprised at how good Viola sounded. Forestine knew the girl had promise, but when she'd told Eddie what a wonderful singer Viola was, she had mostly been offering her encouragement. Viola's voice had weight, and each note was playful, clear, and confident. Willa repeated the same phrase over and over. Forestine could only smile at the memory of Nick. He'd repeat the same phrase as many as twenty times in a row, before she couldn't quite hear herself anymore. Willa was just as tough.

Forestine closed her door and lay across her unmade bed. Benny would be in school now. She wondered if he thought of her as often as she thought about him. Forestine tried calling him every so often, but Lilian always said that Benny was either out playing, sleeping, or doing his homework or chores. Forestine really didn't expect any less from her sister. So she started calling Willie to find out about Benny. After a litany of stories about how unthinking and selfish she was, he was able to talk like a proud grandpa.

Viola knocked on the bedroom door, then peeked in.

"Short lesson," Forestine said.

"Willa had to go out." She stood in the hall.

"Get in here," Forestine said. The two hadn't talked much since she'd started singing at the Vanguard.

Viola bounced in with that same energy Forestine remembered having after a good rehearsal with Nick. She lay next to Forestine on the bed, and they both stared at the ceiling.

"Sounding good," Forestine said.

"For real?"

"Yes."

"I wasn't gonna tell you this," Viola said without taking her eyes off the ceiling. "But I'm going to be doing a song at the Parrot tonight."

"Shut up!"

"Can you believe it?" Viola said reluctantly. "Curtis and Willa think I'm ready."

"You *are* ready," Forestine insisted. "And why weren't you gonna tell me?"

" 'Cause I know you finished your gig at the Vanguard with Eddie last night . . ." Viola pressed her lips together.

"And?" Forestine asked.

"And I didn't want you to come," Viola said. "I'll get too nervous."

"I hear you sing all the time, Viola," Forestine said, waving the notion away. "Besides, the only thing you need to worry about when you step up there is your song. Not me or anything else."

"That's what Willa says."

"Willa knows what she's talkin' about. And I'm gonna be there, so get past it."

"Guess I'll have to," Viola said. "Do you realize, Forestine, that we *both* got a gig. You and me?"

"That's the way it should be," Forestine said simply. She stared up at the ceiling again, but this time her mind began to wander.

"He in school now?" Viola asked.

Forestine took a breath and let it out slowly. "Probably still sitting at his little desk. Lilian picks him up at three."

"Your sister doesn't work?"

"Are you kiddin'?" Forestine replied. "Lilian hasn't worked a day in her life. Since the school is close to the house and the weather is getting warm, I'm sure they walk home. Then Lilian probably sets him down to the table and gives him a snack."

"Doesn't sound like a bad life for a kid," Viola said.

"Me and Lilian haven't always seen eye to eye," Forestine said, "but I know she takes good care of my son. It's just hard not being able to hug him."

"You mean your sister won't let you see your own son?" Viola asked.

"At first I thought it was crazy too, but not now. Lilian is right," Forestine admitted.

"How can you say that?" Viola asked.

"If I visit Benny," she explained, "if I look into them big eyes, hold his hand, I know I'd never be able to leave him again. It's easier not visiting until I'm ready to bring him home for good."

"So what would be wrong with just seeing him?" Viola asked.

"I told you, Viola." Forestine got up and walked to the window.

"No, I mean, just *seeing* him. And him not seeing you."

"What are you talking about?" Forestine watched a garbage truck slowly make its way down the block.

"Honey's car is out there," Viola said.

"So?"

"You said Benny gets outta school in about an hour," Viola said.

Forestine raised an eyebrow.

"How long does it take to get to Brooklyn?" Viola asked.

"What?"

"You can at least *see* him, Forestine."

"Are you out of your mind?"

"We can park outside the house and wait for them to pass."

"That's crazy," Forestine insisted. "That's what crazy people do, Viola."

Forestine sat on the edge of the bed and rested her forearms on her lap. She hadn't seen her son in six months. "It wouldn't be like I was disrupting his life or anything . . . right?" she asked.

"Nope," Viola replied.

"He wouldn't even know I was there. Neither would Lilian."

"That's what I mean, Forestine."

"He's probably grown so much," Forestine said, mostly to herself.

"Tall like his mama," Viola said.

Forestine looked at the clock on her nightstand and then at the picture of Benny beside it. It was two o'clock. She could feel her heart beginning to pump at the thought of seeing him. "It takes about forty minutes to get to Brooklyn this time of the day," she said.

Viola didn't wait for Forestine to say another word. She left the room and returned moments later, jiggling the second set of Honeybee McColor's car keys.

As a child, Forestine had always thought that Atlantic Avenue was exciting with all its shops, stores, and take-out food places. Now it looked dull in the afternoon sun, as did the cluster of neglected buildings called the Kings County projects.

The grounds outside of the projects seemed bare. Most of the children hadn't yet gotten out of school. She could only see the custodians in their drab green uniforms, sweeping the sidewalks, and a few older ladies trudging toward Atlantic Avenue with their shopping carts.

"The old neighborhood," she said, pointing to the projects.

"You gon' stop and see your mama?" Viola asked.

"Hell, no," she answered. "I mean, we only have time enough to see Benny."

They continued past the projects and turned on Albany Avenue. Forestine hadn't expected this feeling of nostalgia. It was strange seeing the old haunts. Especially now that her life was so far away.

"That's Lester's place," she said with a small grin. "I used to sing there on the weekends. Don't look like much, do it?"

"Kinda like this little place at home," Viola smiled. "Nothing but a shack."

Forestine turned on Bedford Avenue. She drove down a couple of blocks and then began to slow.

"Is this the street?" Viola asked.

Forestine nodded as she found a spot to park. It was early enough that the block was still empty of cars.

"Which one your boy live in?"

"The one with the swings in the back." Forestine stared at the house, nibbling on the fleshy side of her thumb. "I don't know if this was a good idea."

"We'll wait a little while," Viola said, "and if we don't see him, we'll go on back home. No harm done."

Forestine pressed her body against the car seat and continued to look toward the house. Worse than *not* seeing Benny might be actually seeing him, she thought. Even from far away.

"Thank God, I never had any kids," Viola said.

"They're a blessing. Haven't you heard?"

"Woulda been a disaster for me and Donald," Viola insisted. "They would've come up like I did—with two parents who hate the sight of each other."

Forestine moved closer to the window. Her face glazed over when she saw Lilian, holding Benny by the hand. Lilian lifted a book bag that he had dragging on the ground and placed the strap on his shoulder. Then she opened the front gate and Benny ran up the porch steps.

"Sweet Lord," Forestine whispered. "Will you just look at him."

"Good-lookin' boy."

It didn't seem real, seeing Benny like this. It was like a movie where he was close but she couldn't touch him. "I can't believe how big he is," she whispered. "He's gonna be as tall as Lucas." Forestine hardly blinked. "He looks like he was never sick a day in his life."

"That's what this was all about, Forestine," Viola said. "Making sure Benny got well."

Forestine suddenly raised the latch on the car door. Viola grabbed her arm as she was about to get out.

"Unless you're ready to take that boy with you right here and now, you need to leave him be."

"I am ready," Forestine insisted.

"Look at him," Viola said. Benny hopped off of the two bottom steps as Lilian searched her bag for her house keys. "You just told me how good he looks," Viola went on. "How healthy he looks."

"He does."

"Things are happening for you, Forestine. You know that. And if Benny is healthy and your career is going good . . . well, isn't that the point of him stayin' with your sister in the first place?"

Benny stood on the top step and hopped to the ground. Lilian yelled out as he landed on the sidewalk. Forestine lowered the window a crack and heard her sister fussing. Still Benny didn't respond. It was as if Lilian were talking to herself. Forestine had to smile. At age four Benny had already learned to ignore her sister's chatter. Then Lilian turned his head to look directly at her. She knelt in front of Benny and quickly moved her hands as if they were two puppets. Then Benny answered her with his own. They seemed to be having a conversation, yet not a single word had been spoken. Then Lilian opened the front door of the house and they went in.

"What the hell was that?" Forestine asked.

Viola looked just as confused. At first Forestine sat there, trying to make sense of what she'd seen. She unlatched the car door again, and Viola didn't try to stop her. She followed Forestine across the street and stood beside her as she knocked on her sister's door. It took Lilian just a moment to answer.

"Forestine . . . ?!"

"What's wrong with him, Lilian?" Forestine asked.

"How dare you come here like this, Forestine," Lilian snapped. "What the hell you doin' here?"

"What's wrong with my son?" Forestine pressed.

Lilian looked over her shoulder. "Wait here," she said, stepping back into the house and closing the door.

Through the tiny glass pane, Forestine could see her sister shuttle Benny upstairs. Moments later, Lilian came back down, stepped out onto the porch, and closed the door behind her.

"Me and Lucas wanted to talk to you," Lilian said.

"What the hell is going on?" Forestine cried.

"Just calm down," Viola whispered.

"I wasn't being mean when I wouldn't put Benny on the phone every time you called," Lilian explained.

"Oh, you weren't," Forestine argued.

"Why don't you listen to what the hell I got to say," Lilian snapped. " 'Cause if anybody was being mean, it was you, Forestine."

"What are you talking about?" Forestine implored.

"When you left Benny with us," Lilian explained, "that cold he had got worse. We took him to the doctor... there wasn't anything me and Lucas could've done," she defended. "We took him to another doctor... that makes two doctors," Lilian said. "Wasn't nothin' nobody could do."

"What's wrong with my son?"

"The boy can't hear, Forestine," Lilian said plainly. "He's deaf, and he's been that way since you left him six months ago."

Forestine felt as if she'd been chopped off at the knees, and she might have fallen had Viola not been there to steady her. She didn't remember getting in the car, the drive back to Harlem, or anything Viola said. Forestine couldn't recall seeing Miss Honeybee or Willa and Vernon as she walked past the parlor. She only remembered her bedroom door shutting behind her. And the darkness. For the first time, there was no music. None playing in the Big House. None in her head.

CHAPTER

14

Viola hurried along 125th Street to a brown wooden door where the words "Green Parrot" slowly blinked. In the store window across the street, she could see the reflection of the big neon bird under a white moon.

Curtis was prompt about opening the club at eight sharp. Although he never complained, she hated arriving late for work. After living at the Big House for four months, she had finally taken him up on his of-fer to waitress at the Parrot. It felt good giving Miss Honeybee some-thing for room and board, though it was just a pittance.

Viola opened the door to the club and was immediately hit by the scent of stale smoke and dried alcohol. She could almost taste the salt in the air. There was no one onstage yet, but a Sonny Rollins tune, "Tenor Madness," played in the background.

Only four tables were full. On a Wednesday night, the audience usually consisted of men from the construction site near the state of-fice building, some of the folks from Florsheim Shoes, and the ladies who worked at the check cashing place near Fifth Avenue. The Wednesday crowd was small, but because it was a payday, the audi-ences were consistent.

"Sorry I'm late," Viola said, slipping behind the bar.

"It's eleven minutes after eight," Curtis smiled. "You're not *officially* late until quarter past."

Viola pulled a white apron over her head and quickly tied it around her waist. She enjoyed working here, because the atmosphere was so relaxed. Most days, she spent her time behind the bar talking to Curtis. She waited tables, cleaned the spots from the newly washed glasses, folded clean cloth napkins, and refilled bowls with red-skinned peanuts. On slow nights like tonight, she occasionally got to sing.

One of the construction workers threw his hand up to get her attention. "Double shot of Wild Turkey," she said to Curtis without going over to the table. Curtis filled a glass, set it on Viola's green felt tray, and sent her on her way.

Viola had gotten to know the regulars and their drinks. She knew who liked to talk and who to leave alone. Who was harmless and who she shouldn't turn her backside to. She also quickly learned the layout of the small club. It was just bigger than Miss Honeybee's parlor and music rooms put together. Twenty or so green-clothed tables with a couple of chairs under each comfortably fit the room. There was a kitchen to the left of the bar and a platform in front that was even smaller than the one at the Big House.

Dolly poked her head out of the kitchen door. She stood with her hands on her hips. "Sweetie Lamb," she shouted. Dolly called everyone under the age of forty Sugar Dumplin', Sweet Potato, or something along those lines. She looked right at Curtis. "Them men at the poultry house ain't sent nuthin' but thighs," she said. "What I'm s'posed to do wit' all these thighs."

Curtis filled a glass with Johnnie Walker Red. He placed it on Viola's tray beside a another shot of something clear. "Just thighs?" he asked Dolly.

"Not wing the first," she called back.

Curtis pulled at the pointy part of his beard. He didn't get rattled about much. "Just season 'em up, Doll," he said. "We don't have time to send them back. We'll call it Chef's Choice."

"Chef's Choice, huh?" she mumbled. "I'm the damn chef. T'ain't my choice." She went back into the kitchen.

"You singing tonight?" he asked Viola as she placed the empty tray back on the bar.

"If you play," she said.

"Why you worry about things like that, Vi?" he said. "You got to get used to different players . . . even bad ones."

"Forestine always says that. . . ."

"What she look like today?"

Viola sat on a bar stool. "She still won't see anyone. Not me or Honey. Even canceled her gig with Bobby. The girl won't come out of her room."

"Damn," Curtis said. "Nothin' but guilt."

Dolly appeared in the kitchen door again. "Punkin' Pie," she called toward Curtis. The phone behind the bar rang, but Viola waved him on and answered it herself. She placed one hand over her ear and held the receiver close. She could barely hear the voice over the music, and there seemed to be music playing on the other end too.

"Vee-ola?" the voice said.

"Yes," she shouted.

"Bishop."

"Who?"

"I said this is Bishop," he yelled.

Viola gripped the receiver. "Eddie Bishop?"

"Yeah," he said. "Look a h'yere . . . I need to get with you. We got to talk."

"This is Viola," she said. "Not Forestine."

"I know who the hell it is," he said. "Listen, I'm at the studio . . . just recorded a nasty tune with Jimmy Smith . . . organ take you back to church . . . the cat is lethal . . ."

Viola felt like she was listening to someone else's conversation.

"I want you to meet me here," he went on.

"Are you sure you want to talk to *me*?" Viola asked.

"I'll send my car to get you in an hour, okay?"

"I . . . guess," she said.

"What the fuck you mean, you guess?"

"I mean—yes, of course."

"Solid, then."

"But . . . can you send the car to the Big House?" she asked. "I'll be at the Big House."

"Cool," he said. Then he hung up.

Viola stood behind the bar waiting for her hands to stop shaking. She rarely drank at the Parrot and only occasionally at the Big House, but she poured herself a shot of rum and drank it in one swallow. She couldn't imagine what Eddie Bishop wanted with her. Her hands were still trembling when she grabbed her coat and her purse.

"Where you running?" Curtis said, coming from the kitchen.

"I got a call," she said, still dazed.

"Everything alright?"

"It was Eddie Bishop."

"Eddie?" He smiled. "What in the world Eddie have to say?"

"He said he wanted to talk to me."

Curtis's eyes filled with understanding. "The cat is still on his game," he chuckled.

"What's that supposed to mean?"

Curtis slipped behind the bar. "So what does Eddie Bishop have to talk about?"

"I don't know."

"And you want to go?"

"Of course," she said. "You don't mind if I take off?"

Curtis's expression implied that he had a lot to say on the subject, but he simply replied, "The cat is outrageous."

"And . . . ?" she said, coming from behind the bar.

Curtis kept smiling, but it looked forced. "No ands or buts, baby," he said. "Eddie is big fun." A group of about eight walked in and stood at the door waiting for a table. Before Curtis turned away he kissed her on the forehead. "Tell that madman I said hey."

The three were in the parlor playing bid whist with Shirley DeGrace. Viola managed to slip into the house and up to her room without being seen. Miss Honeybee's card parties usually ended about eleven-thirty, so Viola had less than thirty minutes to get changed and slip out.

She quickly applied her makeup and put on her favorite black dress, the one with the thick scalloped straps that gave her a little cleavage. She tried combing her hair, but just got frustrated. It was beginning to grow out and was now too long for some styles and too short for others. Most times she turned to Vernon, who could whip it into something nice, but tonight Viola had neither the time nor patience.

She stopped fussing with her hair long enough to calm herself. She'd only be talking to Eddie, but the thought of sitting across from him got her pulse to racing. Viola tiptoed down the stairs and peeked out one of the tinted panes. Eddie's car hadn't arrived yet. The night was warm, but she knew that if she waited on the stoop outside, Miss Honeybee might see her through the window. The three were comfortable with the thought of her and Curtis. They assumed a relationship had blossomed and Viola never disputed it. Though they'd be low-key about their disapproval of Eddie, they would surely make their feelings known. So Viola stood quietly in the vestibule.

"I thought I smelled Youth Dew," Willa said from the doorway. "My, my," she said, pulling Viola into the parlor. "Would y'all look at this gal."

"Get back, Gladys!" Vernon said.

Miss Honeybee looked up from the card table where she sat with Shirley DeGrace. Alongside them were several lighters and ashtrays, and two decks of cards. This was the first time Viola had seen Shirley outside of a gather. Her makeup was just as heavy and her breasts still jutted from the top of her glittery sweater like the heads of two bashful children. "Girl, you better gimme that figure," she laughed.

"Everything jes' raise up north, don't it?" Willa said.

Vernon stood by the small food table with a paper plate in his hand. The platters held what Viola had come to know as the "colored woman's hors d'oeuvres": chunks of sharp cheddar with toothpicks in the center, pigs in the blanket, fried chicken wings, deviled eggs, and Ritz crackers. "You want me to make you a plate, babydoll?" he asked.

"Thank you, no." She took a seat by the window and looked through one of the drapes.

"Must be a special occasion for you and Curtis?" Miss Honeybee said as she shuffled one of the decks of cards.

"The man is so thoughtful," Vernon said.

"So tell us where y'all going," Willa insisted. "What lovely thing does Curtis have planned?"

"I'm not waiting for Curtis," Viola said. For a moment, all she heard was the shuffling of the cards.

"Oh?" Miss Honeybee said.

"I have a meeting with Eddie Bishop."

"A meeting?" Vernon asked.

"He's sending a car to bring me to the studio," Viola answered.

"I see," Miss Honeybee sniffed. "That why you all dressed up?"

"This *is* Eddie Bishop," Viola replied.

"Yes," Willa said, "and over at the Green Parrot is Curtis Atwater."

"Eddie Bishop can blow a horn, that's a fact," Miss Honeybee said. Her tiny hands moved quickly as she dealt a card to each of the four corners of the table. "But a man like that can turn you inside out. Eddie is the kinda fella—"

"That need to be left to the Lord," Viola put in. "Yes, I remember."

Miss Honeybee looked down at her cards. "You a grown woman," she said. "Ain't 'bout to tell you what to do, but...we know Eddie. The boy come up hard...."

"Eddie come up at night," Willa put in. "Raised right here in Harlem. Thirteen-twelve Seventh Avenue."

"The jazz building?" Shirley asked.

"Yes," Miss Honeybee said. "They call it that 'cause the apartments were filled with musicians. There were more than a couple of gathers where baby Eddie come toddling through here in the wee hours of the morning with an empty bottle and a loaded diaper. Cutest lil' thing you ever saw, but ain't no baby supposed to be at an affair like that."

"You know BoBo carry that chile anywhere," Willa said.

"His daddy was a trumpet player too," Miss Honeybee said to Viola. "BoBo Bishop. Played with Stuff Smith and those, but he never reached the heights that Eddie has."

"BoBo wasn't nearly as talented," Willa said.

"The man was too selfish to be talented," Miss Honeybee insisted. "Anyway, Clay tells BoBo that ain't no child s'posed to be where folks is drinkin' and such. And this was one of the better places he bring that baby to. Clubs, parties, women's houses..."

"Where was Eddie's mother?" Viola asked.

"I never knew her," Miss Honeybee said. "I hear she died when Eddie was being born."

Vernon joined the ladies at the card table with his plate. "I always found it quite odd," he said, "that something as ugly as an oyster can produce something as lovely and sought-after as a pearl. That was BoBo Bishop."

"That's nature," Willa put in.

"He was a sad, sad man," Vernon said, looking at Viola. "BoBo knocked on my door one night—mine and Cutler's. Eddie was with him, and the chile was about ten years old at the time. I suppose BoBo just come from playing somewhere, 'cause it was about three A.M. Po' lil' Eddie was standing on his two legs sleeping and BoBo was as high as a kite. He said he needed someone to keep an eye on the child until the next morning. We say fine, 'cause this ain't the first time we've watched the boy. I fix a place on the couch for Eddie. BoBo staggers on his way. I had to get up early the next morning because I was workin' at the time, remember Honey, I was fittin' them Cotton Club gals..."

"Oh, I remember very well," she said.

"I went off to work that next day, and when I come back, Eddie and Cutler is jammin'. Jammin' for their lives." Vernon smiled. "My Cutler is on the drums and Eddie is alternating, playing both trumpet and piano... havin' a grand time. Cutler told me even then what a gifted boy he was. A day passes and no BoBo. Two days, four days, six days. Cutler and me are mad as sin because BoBo is so wrong for not calling or nothin'. We can see that Eddie is worried about his daddy. Well, after ten days, we call the police 'cause Cutler and I are thinking that something might've happened to the man. None of the players has heard hide nor hair of him and we're thinking the worse. Then here comes BoBo. Almost two weeks later, he staggers up as wasted as he was when he dropped the boy off. He takes Eddie home, and the next day the police come to our door." Vernon placed an open napkin in his lap before he went on. "They put the handcuffs on Cutler. They sayin' that Cutler, *my* Cutler was touchin' the boy. I can't believe my ears..."

"I couldn't either," Willa said.

"I look at BoBo," Vernon went on, "that cheesy skin, all pocked in the pores from alcohol... them bulbous brown fingertips, so fat from liquor that he can't even play the trumpet no more, and I can't believe my ears."

"Nobody paid that talk no mind," Miss Honeybee said to Vernon. "Everybody knew old BoBo talked that mess just to take the heat off 'cause he stayed away so long. You good, Vernon," she said, " 'cause not only would I have pressed charges, but they'da threw his ass *under* the jail."

"Maybe," Vernon said, "but then the chile wouldn't have had a daddy. Not a single soul in the world." Vernon patted tiny beads of sweat from his forehead. "The saddest part is, that after all my Cutler gave to the business . . . and, Honey, you know that his peers were folks like Jo Jones and Zutty Singleton . . ."

"I know that, sugar . . ."

"Art Blakey still give the man his props . . ." Vernon said, "but after the career that man had, it's still that incident folks whisper about when they talk of Cutler Sims."

Viola heard the blare of a horn outside. "I'm sorry for what happened," she said, "really sorry . . . but it's not Eddie's fault."

"Believe me, I don't blame Eddie, because he was a chile," Vernon said. "A child with a sick daddy. But I look at Eddie the *man* now, and as special as he is—and Lord knows he's special—I gotta scratch my head because, dear heart," he said directly to Viola, "them same old demons that had BoBo all locked up is now a-visiting with Eddie."

"Everybody has demons," Viola insisted. "And anybody can change."

"Aw, hell," Shirley muttered.

"Cain't change a grown man, Viola," Miss Honeybee cautioned. "I cain't tell you what to do in yo' life, but . . . we want you to be careful. Be your own woman."

"I'm going to meet with the man." Viola pulled her wrap over her shoulders. "Maybe hear some music. That's all, Honey." She walked toward the door.

"You can hear some music with Curtis," Willa called. "Curtis take you to hear all the music you want."

"I'll be fine," Viola said. She stopped and looked at herself in the vestibule mirror again. As she applied more lipstick she heard the women continue to talk.

"Lord, I wouldn't want to be that age again fo' all the tea in China," Willa said.

"It ain't just age," Miss Honeybee replied. "If it were, I wouldn't be so worried. Her and Forestine is about the same age, but Forestine got a good head. That gal, though . . . maybe Curtis ain't shiny enough."

Eddie's driver honked again. Before Viola left, she heard Miss Honeybee say, "Damn shame though. Damn shame she won't believe fat meat is greasy."

The limo driver actually stopped on the shoulder of the West Side Highway to open a bottle of champagne for her. He placed his handkerchief over the top, popped the cork, and poured into her waiting glass.

"Thank you kindly," she said.

He started on his way again. "There's a icebox back there with cheese and things," he said.

"Thank you, sir," she said.

He glanced at her through the rearview mirror. She could see only his mature dark eyes, deep set in a face as worn as brown leather. His gray hair was slicked under his cap. "Prob'ly saw all them ladies' magazines in the left-hand rack," he said.

Viola was too nervous to look at magazines, but since the driver was being so thoughtful, she felt obliged. She picked up a copy of *Down Beat* magazine. On a dog-eared page inside was a picture of Eddie, standing in front of a window, a setting sun just beyond and his trumpet pressed to his lips. He wore a billowing white shirt tucked into black pants that rested lazily on his hips.

"Where you from?" the driver asked.

"South Carolina, sir."

"Where 'bouts?"

"Jasperville."

"I'm from Canaan Creek," he said.

Viola looked at his eyes in the mirror again. "We're neighbors."

"Ain't that the truth."

As she lounged in this limo seat, sipping champagne on her way to meet Eddie Bishop, Viola's mind was nowhere near Jasperville. She had left all thoughts about the Reverend, Nelvern, and Donald Hinson far behind. The ride was so smooth that Viola could barely feel the ground beneath her. Or perhaps it was the champagne. She kicked off her shoes, leaned into the empty seat beside her, and lit a cigarette. The smoke tasted better than usual tonight. Viola refilled her glass as the driver turned off the West Side Highway. The streets of midtown were empty, except for a few people entering or leaving restaurants. As they traveled toward the theater district, there was more activity. Her body was just beginning to relax when the car pulled up to PenWay Recording Studio. The small gray door was squeezed between an all-night delicatessen and a dry cleaner. A group of people stood outside, including two men who Viola recognized from Eddie's Quintet. They all jumped to attention when Eddie walked out of the building. The relaxed buzz she felt vanished when he squeezed into the backseat beside her. He leaned over and kissed her on the cheek. Then the entire group, and their instruments, all squeezed in.

"My place, Luth," Eddie said to the driver, patting the old man on the shoulder.

The sound of Louis Armstrong singing the "St. James Infirmary" played softly in Eddie's apartment. Only minutes before, the place had been filled with laughter and loud music: an Eddie Bishop gather. They'd been a party of seven, including Eddie, Viola, two men from the Quintet, a tech guy from the studio named Mohan, a fancy girl, and one bearded Japanese man who was convinced that Eddie could heal with his trumpet. There were drinks, reefer, a bowl of cocaine, and a spread of hard salami, raspberries, and cheese.

It was three A.M., and Eddie was showing the last of his entourage to the front door. Viola sat on the tan leather sofa, unsure whether to stay or go. He hadn't said a word to her about the meeting he had spoken of earlier. Viola got up from the couch, a bit dizzy from the champagne. She gazed out of the double glass doors. Only now could she really see the beauty of this twelfth-floor apartment with its ell-shaped balcony overlooking the Hudson River. A million city lights reflected off the water.

Viola walked through the place, looking into the kitchen and bedroom. Eddie's entire apartment was done in warm earth tones, each room a different shade of brown. But just like Eddie's personality, there was an occasional jolt to the senses. In the living room, the serenity of beige and rust was interrupted by four gigantic black spades painted on one wall. Alongside the oriental vases filled with delicate ficus stood a four-foot-tall cactus with large spikes.

Eddie walked back in from the hall with a cigarette in his hand. He poured himself a straight vodka and sat in a brown leather chair across from the couch. He lay back and stretched his long legs out in front of him. A cloud of smoke surrounded his head.

"What did you want to talk to me about?" Viola could hear the nervousness in her voice.

"Why not get to the point, Vee-ola?" he chuckled. He puffed again on his cigarette. Eddie kept his eyes on her when he spoke. "I just wanted to see you. That okay?" He smiled.

Viola felt nervous, recalling Miss Honeybee's warnings.

"I hear you been working out at the Parrot," he said. "Got to come by and hear you one day. Might have me another singer."

"I got a long way to go . . ."

"Maybe not," he said. "Sometimes you can't hear what other people hear. I came to trust my own opinion at an early age."

"How early?" she asked.

"I played my first club gig when I was nine. At sixteen, I recorded with Charlie Parker. The point is, don't be downplaying shit, Vee-ola. You got to jump in when the door open. And if you can't, then move the fuck out the way." Eddie took a silver cigarette case from his jacket. He pulled out another reefer and lit it. "The only way to get by in this business is to come to the stage with that fuck-everybody attitude." He threw his hands up. "Just fuck 'em," he yelled. "This is my voice, goddamn it! When you able to do that, you gon' have mu'fuckahs jumping off buildings trying to get to you. Just like they tryin' to get to Forestine." He moved to the couch beside her. Eddie smelled so good. It was a creamy musk that seemed to come from his pores.

"Damn!" he said, suddenly lurching forward in his seat.

"What?" Viola asked.

"I just remembered something. Muthafuckah," he spat.

"What's wrong?"

"I got this radio gig tomorrow and I don't know where the fuck it is."

Viola wasn't quite sure what to say. "Maybe . . . Bethanne knows."

"Bethy don't know shit about this." Eddie stared out like she wasn't even there. "Well, fuck it! They'll call me if they want me," he said, and then sat back again. "What you sayin' to yourself, Vee-ola?" he smiled. "You sayin', 'Eddie Bishop is a crazy muthafuckah,' right?" He laughed.

"No."

"It's okay," he said, sweeping a lock of hair from her cheek. "Forestine told me that you sing the shit outta 'Shadow of Your Smile,' " he whispered.

"It's my favorite song," she said.

"Sing it, Vee-ola."

"What?"

"Lemme hear some."

"Now?" She could barely talk with Eddie this close.

He got up and turned down the volume on the stereo, then sat back beside her.

Viola knew this was more of a seduction than an audition. It felt surreal sitting on Eddie's leather sofa in the middle of the night, his arm around her shoulder, trying to remember the words to a song. She managed to sing a few lines.

He stopped her by placing his finger on her lips. He nodded thoughtfully, then leaned forward to retrieve his cigarette from the ashtray. "You got some different shit happenin' up in there."

"Different?"

Eddie's demeanor became more businesslike. "Yeah."

"Different how?"

"Raw," he said.

Viola's face remained blank.

"Take Forestine," he said. "Aren't a lot of pure talents like hers. Ella, Sassy, Carmen McRae . . . like buttered bread. But there's another kind of singer. One that come at you different. Billie Holiday, Abbey Lincoln, Nina Simone. Come at you with an inflection that make you feel guilty for living. They might not have the cleanness of a Forestine

Bent or even the range, but they chill you to the fuckin' bone. That's you."

"You can tell that from what I just sang?" she asked.

"Don't take much, Vee-ola." He ran his fingers across her chin and then her neck. "Nobody expects that voice to come out somebody who look as sweet as you. That's gon' be your callin' card." He ran his hand across the top of her chest and kissed her softly. Then again until her head was light. "You gon' let me touch you?" he whispered into her cheek. Viola couldn't speak. "You gon' let me?" He slipped his hand into her dress and caressed her bare breast. She felt she should stop him, but his hands felt good on her skin. His touch was so light that she could hardly breathe. When he removed his hand, Viola prayed he'd put it back. He reached for the ashtray and relit the reefer. After he drew on it, he placed his lips on hers and slowly released the smoke into her mouth. Viola loved his power, his blatant sexuality, and his fingertips moving once again across the tips of her breasts.

Eddie lifted her from the couch and carried her into his bedroom. He pulled her dress over her head and she let him. He nuzzled her stomach and kissed the inside of her thighs and she let him. But when he moved the edge of her panty with his tongue, Viola jumped.

"What are you doing?" she demanded.

He looked up at her. "You mean, my man Att ain't never . . . moved on down the road?"

"Curtis is my friend," she insisted.

"And what's that make me?"

Betty Rawlins was singing "With the Dawn" when he lowered his head onto her lap again. This time Viola lay back, closed her eyes, and gave herself over to this painful pleasure. Every once in a while she had to push away. The sensation of being tickled all over her body was overwhelming.

> And with the dawn, the world still turns,
> The flame is gone, but the fire still burns,
> On my face, there's still a trace,
> Of the magic you left behind . . .

Eddie suddenly stood up. Just that quickly he moved away from her. Viola felt like she had been jerked out of a dream.

"I need to find out where that damn radio gig is," he said.

"But . . . it's four in the morning."

"I'll wake you when I come in, okay?"

He kissed her again, giving her back her own fleshy taste, then reached into his jacket for his silver case. Eddie quickly lit a cigarette as he walked into the living room. Seconds later, she heard the front door slam shut. Just like that, he was gone. Behind him a haze of smoke still lingered.

CHAPTER

15

Forestine had never noticed how many neighbors would sit waiting on their stoops somewhere around ten P.M. on a Friday night. They loitered outside to watch folks arrive at the Big House. Ed Edwards and his wife, Maxine, who lived directly across the street, sat on the top step of their brownstone and ogled the long, pretty cars gliding to a halt. Two doors down from the Edwards, Berle Coleman looked out from her first-floor window. Farther down the street, Forestine saw a bunch of teenagers watching the fancy men and women as they made their way up the steps to the door where Fred Nastor stood. Perhaps she hadn't noticed before because she was usually downstairs in the thick of the party.

Forestine stepped away from the pale yellow drapes and sat on the edge of her bed. In the dim lamplight she caught a vague outline of herself in the floor-length mirror across the room. Her dark silhouette, clad in only a black slip, sat hunched. Her chin raised just enough to see her melancholy reflection and the whites of her own accusatory eyes.

The last three weeks had seemed unreal. The trip to Brooklyn played in her mind over and over. That way of talking between Lilian and Benny reminded Forestine of people she had only seen on TV, grunting at each other while their hands thrashed about like hooked trout. She had considered going back to Lilian's house to see Benny. Perhaps if she talked clear enough, loud enough, or sang the songs that he liked most, he could hear her. But Forestine didn't go back. She would have had to admit that what she had seen was real and— even more frightening—that it was all her fault.

The platform room beneath her began to swell with music. Forestine could feel the drumbeat through the soles of her bare feet. Forestine had been crying for three weeks. She ate dinner and she cried. She sat in the kitchen or in the parlor with the three and she cried. She tried to sing and she cried. Tonight was no different. Through her tears, she glanced at the beige knit dress hanging on her closet door. Forestine had tried to go to the last gather but left after only thirty minutes. Most of that time she'd spent consoling the people who tried to console her, abiding the patting hands and the furrowed brows, as if she were the immediate family at a funeral. Forestine had figured she would be able to hide behind the music, but when she opened her mouth to sing, nothing came out.

"Got yo' priorities all messed up" was what Hattie had told her. Her mother's caustic voice echoed in her head. Forestine hated the sound of that voice, but Hattie Bent, with all her piss and vinegar, turned out to be right.

Forestine's tears fell against the carpet. She thought about Beck and wished she had the courage to find him and acknowledge that all he'd said was true. She wanted him to know she was truly sorry for ignoring his warnings time and again.

Forestine used the edge of the sheet to wipe her face dry. She could hear a muted singer and then the sounds of laughter. It had to be Shirley DeGrace. Then came a knock on her bedroom door. Miss Honeybee stood in the doorway, dressed in pink chiffon. The breeze blowing in from the hall was heavy with the smells of Willa's fried chicken and Vernon's coconut-laced peas and rice.

"Curtis is downstairs," she said. "He wanted to come up and say hey . . ."

Forestine shook her head no.

"Okay," Miss Honeybee replied.

"Is Viola with him?" Forestine asked.

Miss Honeybee's tone sharpened. "Ain't seen that gal in over a week. She call this morning to see how you were but . . . I told her that you still weren't seeing nobody."

After they'd returned from Brooklyn, Forestine had sat in her room for days, staring at the bare wall across from her bed. Without talking, Viola would comb Forestine's hair and massage her feet. Every once in a while she'd interject something like, "Can't blame yourself," or "This was just one of those things." Then came Eddie Bishop. If Forestine had even an inch of room in her heart to entertain thoughts of anyone but Benny, she'd be concerned for Viola.

"Yo' daddy called this mo'nin," Miss Honeybee said, standing in the door. "Just as worried 'bout you as the rest of us. Fred said you wouldn't take the call."

"Why?" Forestine asked.

Miss Honeybee pulled her head back in surprise. " 'Cause lately you ain't took nobody's call."

"Fred didn't tell me it was Willie," Forestine said.

"And if he did," Miss Honeybee said, "would that have mattered?"

"Maybe," Forestine admitted.

Miss Honeybee crossed the room to sit on the foot of the bed. The tuberose in her perfume masked the stale scent in the room. "You hell-bent on punishin' yo'self, ain't you?" she asked.

Forestine could hardly look at her.

"I hope you don't mind if I give you a piece of advice." Miss Honeybee's tone was gentle but firm.

"When have I ever minded, Honey?" Forestine smiled. "And if I did, would that stop you?"

"Prob'ly not." Miss Honeybee took Forestine's hand between her own two. She thought for a moment. "I throw one hell of a party, don't I?" she asked.

"Yes, you do," Forestine replied.

"I know how to make folks feel at home," Miss Honeybee went on. "That's *my* gift. That's what I do. And *you*—you s'posed to be out in the world singin'. That's *yo'* gift."

"I can't get there right now, Honey." Forestine released her hand. The floor vibrated with the sound of bass. Curtis was playing all by himself. A bass alone used to sound so forlorn, no color to lift the chords. These days it was comforting.

"You're outta yo'self right now, chile, I know," Miss Honeybee said. "But there are some things beyond yo' control and beyond mine. When you get back on yo' feet, I promise you'll be a stronger person. Then you can be a stronger mama."

Forestine chuckled bitterly. "A strong mama?"

"Maybe not right this minute," Honeybee said. "It hurts ... sho' it do, 'cause this is yo' baby we talkin' 'bout. Yo' lil' boy. But you cain't wallow in guilt too long, sugar, 'cause that won't do nobody no good. You had yo'self a plan, Forestine," Miss Honeybee went on, "and you got to get back to it. You come so far already ... folks is talkin' 'bout recordin' and such, settin' up yo' own tour ... then you could give Benny so much more ..."

"I can't give Benny anything," she said. "Never could. At least not what he needed."

"You only sayin' that 'cause you feel guilt. I understand, but ..."

"I need to get dressed, Honey," Forestine said, walking to the door.

"You gon' gather with us?" Miss Honeybee asked hopefully.

"No."

"I know you ain't goin' back to Lilian's. Not in this frame of mind."

"I'm not going to Lilian's," Forestine assured her. "But I am going back to Brooklyn."

"Fo' what?"

"Honey," Forestine said, opening her bedroom door. "I love you, I really do, but ... I need to get dressed."

Lester's Pub still had black crepe paper over the two windows on the door to block out the street light. Beneath a torn corner, Forestine could see the scales of a pink salmon painted on the glass, evidence of the old fish market that had occupied the space before the club. She walked in and stood at the back. Lester's Pub looked as small and shabby inside as it did out. Forestine wondered if it had always been this way and she had been too young to notice. Or perhaps singing in top houses made it look worse than she remembered.

The old rickety platform creaked and the mike squealed. Lester still hadn't bought anything new and barely even tuned the piano. Forestine did a double take at the woman singer who strutted across the stage. In the past, Lester had been partial to young, pretty girls. Though this older woman with her heavy makeup and page boy wig was just as tone deaf.

Forestine made her way down the center aisle to the bar. A handful of people sat at tables, mostly men in blue uniforms. She recalled that on Fridays the club filled with the guys from Brooklyn Union Gas. The bar stool that Willie had always sat in, the one with a clear view of the stage, was empty. She sat on Willie's stool and removed her overcoat.

"Dark rum, straight," she told the barmaid. The girl barely looked old enough to be in a bar, let alone to serve drinks.

Forestine didn't know any of the men in the small band. But then, the turnover for musicians had always been high. She suddenly saw herself standing on that stage at fifteen in pedal pushers and a clean white blouse, no makeup, her hair clinging to her scalp as tight as a wool cap. She remembered the way the audience had laughed when they first saw her. Forestine no longer felt sad about that. Now her regrets had only to do with Benny.

"Hold up here," Lester said, approaching the bar. "Just hold the goddamned phone so I can talk to Forestine Bent, y'all!"

"Hey there, Lester." She smiled.

"I'll be damned!" he said. "No," he corrected, "I'll be double goddamned!" Lester hugged and kissed her on the cheek. He had never kissed her before, and it took Forestine by surprise. "Girl, you look good as a Thanksgivin' turkey."

" 'Preciate it," she said.

"Ole Willie come in here every week talkin' 'bout all the big-ass folks you been singin' with. Say you even worked wit' Eddie Bishop." Forestine nodded humbly. "Well, fuck me." Lester laughed. "Look a h'yere," he called to the girl behind the bar. "This is Forestine Bent! *The* Forestine Bent. You give her anything she want . . . on the house."

"That's kind of you, Lester."

"You gon' sing fo' me, ain't you?"

"I'm here looking for Willie."

"He be in soon," Lester said. "Like clockwork, he come every Friday night after yo' mama's Bible study at the apartment."

"Bible study," she said in shock. "Willie Bent found the Lord?"

"Not lessen the Lord in the bottom of a shot glass," Lester replied. "Hattie say he need Jesus worser than any somebody on this earth. So she make him stay there and listen to them people quotin' scripture and everything."

Forestine laughed. "*My* daddy?" she asked.

"I ain't kiddin', neither. He leave the apartment every Friday and head straight fo' the club. Yo' daddy git a couple of belts of vodka in 'im and *then* he be ready to hold prayer service." Lester pointed toward the door. "Yonder come Reverend Willie, now."

Willie walked toward the bar, his hands deep in the pockets of his baggy pants and his hat tilted over his left eye. He strolled in like he was the most carefree fellow in the place. Carefree like it didn't matter that he worked more than sixty hours a week. Carefree like he didn't have a wife that constantly kept her foot in the crook of his neck.

Willie eased up to the bar, reluctant at first because someone was sitting on his stool. He sat down beside Forestine and nearly fell off the stool when he finally noticed who was sitting next to him.

"What the hell you doin' here?" he cried.

Until he hugged her, Forestine had no idea how much she needed it.

"Having a drink," she replied.

"Cain't believe you settin' here . . . you see this, Lester?"

Forestine suddenly felt shy around her father. Although she had talked to him on the phone and written him letters from the road, this was the first time she'd seen him in years. He looked at her from head to toe, smiling the whole time. Then he turned to Lester with that same proud expression that he always wore, the one that said this was his baby and the most beautiful girl in the world.

"Then again," Willie huffed, "you coming here is prob'ly the oniliest way I was gon' git to see you. Don't take folks' calls," he said, sitting beside her again. "What—you one of these movie stars that forget they own daddy?"

"You know that ain't true," she said.

"No, I don't neither," he said. The barmaid set down a drink in front of him. "You can do better'n that, Connie," he called. "My baby here. I can damn sho' get top shelf tonight."

"Bring Willie Bent some Stoli," Lester told her.

"Now, that's what I'm talkin' 'bout," Willie said.

"How 'bout I git you some ribs, Forestine," Lester offered. "You 'member I make the best ribs this side of Memphis."

"That would be fine," she said.

"Got some of them sweet rolls too," he said, coming from behind the bar. "They good fo' soppin' up the sauce."

"Thank you," she called as Lester walked toward the kitchen. "Things have sho'ly changed," she said to Willie.

"Lester tell anybody who listen how he discovered you," Willie said. "How he plucked this lil' homely gal from the projects and made her a star."

Willie could make her laugh like no one else. He took a sip from his glass, then looked directly into her eyes. His head started to quiver and Forestine knew that he was about to get serious.

"You gonna tell me too?" she asked. "You gonna tell me how I should get back out there and sing?"

"Didn't know you *weren't* singing," he said.

"It's just been three weeks. You'd think three weeks was a damn lifetime."

"Longer than I've known you to go," he said. "But ain't nobody got to tell you nuthin', Forestine. That's one of the good things about you. Always know what need to be done. Don't mean you always do it, but least you know."

"Why didn't you tell me, Daddy?" she asked. "About Benny, I mean. I talked to you plenty a times and you never said a word about Benny being . . . you know . . ."

"The boy is deaf, Forestine," Willie said, pointing to his ears. "He's *deaf* and you might as well say it."

"Why didn't you tell me?"

He took a gulp from his glass. "We found out just a couple of weeks after you left him with Lilian. If I told you . . . you'da prob'ly done one of two things . . . or both. You'da come and got him, and

Benny couldn't take another day of runnin' 'round out there. Or you woulda blamed yo'self and never made it to the big time." He shook his head with certainty. "I ain't got a single regret," he insisted. "Look at ya, Forestine. You somebody. And Lilian been a fine mama to Benny. She might be a lotta things, but she a good mama. Take him to the park, to the movies, the library . . . tuck him in bed at night, read to him . . ."

Forestine felt the tears coming again. All those mother-type things, simple things that every child deserved, she had never given her own son.

". . . and don't let the boy's nose get to runnin'," Willie went on. "Lilian right on it. Snot don't stand a chance 'round yo' sister."

Forestine laughed through her tears.

"So when's yo' next gig?" he asked.

"No gigs," she answered.

"Why?" he asked.

She shrugged. "Can't get a decent note out. My voice gets to shaking."

"Then let it shake," he insisted.

"Not so easy this time, Daddy."

"Hell, yeah it is," he replied. "How you think you got through yo' childhood? And look a h'yere, Forestine," he said, moving closer to her. "What happened to Benny was God's will. Wadn't nobody's fault. Could be that Benny woulda wound up that way if you stayed home every day, settin' by the fire. So you jes' get on away from thinkin' like that."

"I miss you, Willie Bent," she said. "I really do."

"Don't go startin' that stuff," he mumbled. "And where my damn Stoli?" he yelled to the barmaid.

"Daddy," she started hesitantly. "Do you think I could be a good mother . . . to Benny, I mean?"

"I know who the hell yo' chile is, Forestine. Lessen you got a whole tribe of 'em somewhere."

"No," she said with a laugh. She glanced at the stage. The woman on the platform was now singing "You Beat Me to the Punch." Her ballads were as off-key as her upbeat tunes. Still Willie hadn't answered. "Well?" she pressed.

"Damn it, Forestine," he whined. "You know the answer to these questions already."

"No, I don't," she said.

"Yes, you do," he insisted.

Forestine shifted on the stool. She nervously ran her finger around the rim of her glass.

"You got a proper place for a chile like him to stay?" Willie asked. "You got one of them special schools picked out? You got enough money to care for him? Do you even know how to talk to the boy?" Willie shook his head no. "It's what I been sayin' from day one, Forestine. Need to think fo' you act." Her eyes sunk into the bar glass again. "Look at me when I'm talkin' to you," he snapped. She looked up sheepishly. Willie's eyes were stone cold. "You done some things, that I ain't so proud of . . ."

"Daddy—"

"I was shocked when Lilian told me," he said.

"That's ancient history," she replied.

"The hell it is," he insisted. "You done had a chile from that *ancient history*."

"It wasn't like I was by myself," she said, sounding defensive. "Lucas was partially—"

"Ain't talkin' 'bout no damned Lucas," he barked. "Lucas ain't my chile! I'm talkin' 'bout you! You done set up here and asked me if you could be a good mama? The answer is hell, no, Forestine. Not lessen you take a good look at shit! Not lessen you take some responsibility."

Forestine cringed. She had wanted Willie's honesty, but it felt brutal.

"Yo' mama and I might not have been the best parents," he went on, "but we ain't never lied to you, Forestine, or to each other. Fo' fact," he mumbled, "Hattie mouth always been *too* damn honest. That's all I'm askin' from you. You need to set down and talk to yo' sister," Willie said. "Y'all need to talk like grown folks. Then see yo' boy. He still hollerin', 'When Forestine comin' back, when Forestine comin' back' . . ."

"He really asks fo' me?"

"All the time," Willie replied. "And why that boy be callin' you

'Forestine,' Forestine? Ain't no chile s'posed to be callin' his mama by her basket name."

"I don't know, Willie," she joked.

"I ain't in no teasin' frame a mind now," he said soberly.

Forestine cut her eyes away from his. "I do want to talk to Benny," she said, "but . . . he can't even hear me."

"He's deaf." Willie pounded again. "Gotta say that word sooner or later. In time, you'll learn how to talk to him. They got special classes fo' teachin' mamas how to do that hand jive. Lilian learned it good and I'm proud of her."

"You are?" Forestine asked.

"Come on, now," he consoled. "You my heart, you know that. But Lilian . . . she my baby too." Willie finished the last of the vodka in his first glass. Then he sipped the Stoli in the second glass and sighed, "There is a difference—damn sho' a difference. Now, this is what I call a blessin' from the Lord," he smiled.

"And you talk about *my* priorities," Forestine said, slipping on her coat.

"You got to go already?"

"I need to get back to the city."

"Back to the big time." He smiled.

"Willie Bent, you *are* the big time." She hugged him tight and Willie hugged her back.

"Enough of that nonsense," he said, shaking her off.

They walked to the front door of Lester's Pub, arm in arm. Forestine began to feel like she could breathe again.

"The boy gon' see you soon?" he asked.

"Yes, Daddy." Forestine kissed her father on the cheek again. Just then, Lester approached her with a brown paper bag.

"I saw you puttin' on yo' coat," he said. "Told 'em in the kitchen to pack Forestine ribs to walk with."

She could smell the vinegar rising from the warm package. "Smells good," she said.

"You take care of yo'self," he said, embracing her. "Go on out there and kick some mo' ass."

Lester and Willie waited outside the club while Forestine got into her car. She set the warm bag on the seat beside her and the vehicle filled with scent of Lester's Pub. The club would always be as much a part of her as the Kings County projects. Forestine waved at Willie and Lester as she drove off. No matter where she went or who she worked with, she would never forget the look of pride on those two men's faces. Especially Willie Bent's.

CHAPTER

16

At just past eleven P.M., Viola knew that the music at the Big House would be jumping, Willa and Vernon would be warming up the pots, and the gather would be in full swing. She had made up her mind upon waking this morning, that she had to get there. Then Eddie insisted on catching Dexter Gordon downtown at the Blue Note.

He was getting edgy. Eddie didn't have patience for opening bands, especially when he sat in the audience. Worse, he, Viola, and Squint, Eddie's bass player, had been waiting forty-five minutes for Dexter Gordon to arrive. Eddie sipped a straight bourbon loudly. His long legs hardly fit beneath the club's table. "This is fucked up," he muttered.

Squint shrugged his pudgy shoulders and drew on a Pall Mall. "Dex's playing is stupid," he said, "but the cat is in the zone sometimes."

"The shit is just plain unprofessional," Eddie said.

Viola fished a pack of Newports from her purse and lit the last one. After two months of being with Eddie Bishop, she knew that his words rarely matched his actions. She found his anger ironic because he was always late for his gigs, if he showed at all.

Eddie stood up, throwing his black leather coat across his shoulders like a cape. He headed through the club toward the front door.

"Bishop!" a deep voice in the crowd yelled.

"You ain't playing tonight, Eddie?" a woman called out.

His footsteps were heavy and deliberate as he walked out of the club. Viola and Squint had to run to keep up. He yanked angrily at the locked limo door until the driver jumped out and opened it. Squint and Viola slid into the backseat beside him. "Sweet Sue" was playing on the radio.

"Turn that shit off," Eddie yelled.

"Man, that's Miles," Squint said.

"Fuck Miles," he spat.

Eddie was constantly being compared to Miles Davis. Sometimes the yardstick for Eddie's playing on a particular night was how Miles blew the night before. When interviewers asked him what he thought of Miles, his ego wouldn't allow him to say much more than "the cat is proper." But when Eddie was alone, Viola saw him trying to imitate everything from Miles's fingering to his posture.

"Luther?" he yelled to the driver.

"Yes, sir?"

"My run, Luth."

"Yes, sir," he answered, and immediately headed east to 103rd Street.

Viola had made this stop with Eddie before. Usually he walked into the rundown building, tense, like he was now, but when he came out, his tone was mellow. She had seen similar transformations at least once a day since she met him. Viola understood that place inside of him where there wasn't enough music or enough love, and even God wasn't big enough to fill. Most women fell for the musician, but once they realized how self-destructive Eddie was, they made the fatal mistake. They tried to repair him. Viola never fussed about his disappearances or his bad mood swings. Hell, she'd grown up with a man who had an ego as big as Eddie's. Viola had learned from the master, Nelvern Bembrey, how to quickly and completely disappear behind it.

Eddie shifted in his seat and gnawed on the handle of his shades. He took out a reefer and lit it. After a few puffs, his tension began to subside. He then passed it to Viola. Just weeks ago it had burnt the insides of her cheeks, and she'd hated the smell of it in her clothes. Now the smoke tasted good and the buzz relaxed her.

The car drove up Sixth Avenue and then turned on Twelfth Street to the East Side. They stopped at a red light, and some of the people on the busy Greenwich Village sidewalk tried to peer through the dark limo windows. Viola had gotten used to the gawking. None were ever disappointed when the driver opened the car door and Eddie grandly stepped out with Viola by the hand. It was always exciting when he stopped to sign autographs on paper napkins or matchbook covers.

"Maybe we can go by the Big House for a minute," Viola said. "There's a gather tonight and I know Honey would love to see you. . . ."

"Ain't stoppin' at no damn Big House," he said, looking out of the window. "Can't deal with that shit tonight."

"What shit?" she asked.

"Honey lookin' at me like I'm some kinda monster," Eddie said. "And that damn Vernon . . . fuck that!"

"I haven't seen Forestine—"

"Ain't nuthin' wrong with Forestine," he chimed in. "Family shit, that's all it is. If I let that kinda thing stop me, I'd be beggin' for fuckin' quarters up there on a Hundred Twenty-fifth Street. 'Sides, what the hell can you do for Forestine? Need to take care of yo' damn self."

Viola had found it hard dating Eddie Bishop and living at the Big House. At first, the three had given Viola questioning glares whenever she left to meet him. Vernon sat with one pencil-drawn brow raised almost to the edge of his turban. Miss Honeybee talked about everything *but* what was really on her mind, and though Willa never wore a disapproving look, she seemed to get real busy whenever Eddie's name came up. Their silence spoke many conversations. After a month of this, Viola found it easier staying at Eddie's place. She got used to waking up beside him in the late afternoons. A sober Eddie Bishop was a different man indeed. He thrashed about his apartment like a new chick that had just come into the world. Sometimes Viola had to help him out of bed. She kept his appointments, maintained his home, and delivered him to shows and rehearsals. It felt good to be needed by a man as powerful as Eddie. Tonight, though, Viola's mind was on Forestine.

Viola had become so focused on Eddie that she'd let the weeks build up between them. Each day she had justified her absence by thinking that Forestine had the three to lean on, and there were no stronger shoulders in the world. Still, every day that she stayed away set them farther apart. Viola had talked to Miss Honeybee a few times on the phone, including this morning, and she could hear the concern in the woman's voice.

"Rose called me today," Miss Honeybee had said. "Say Cynthie Nettles had her fifth, a lil' girl named Roberta . . . say she also got some new dresses in the shop that I'd like . . . maybe you too."

"That's fine, Honey," Viola had replied.

"Rose asked to talk to you," she went on. "I told her you were out. When she asked me when you were coming back, I wasn't sure what to say."

"How's Forestine?" Viola had asked.

"Better," Miss Honeybee replied. "Finally got her to talkin' a bit. She even come to the last gather fo' an hour or two. I 'spect she'll stay the whole time tonight."

"I'm glad," Viola said.

"She lookin' to see you though. . . ."

"I'll try to get by tonight, Honey," Viola said.

"You *need* to get by," Miss Honeybee said. "And not jes' fo' Forestine's sake."

That was when Viola made her excuses and hung up the phone.

"You can leave me off up there at Seventy-sixth," Squint said to the driver. "Right there by that dry cleaner."

"We still got charts," Eddie reminded him.

The driver slowed the car and stopped by the curb.

"You wanna go into the studio *tonight*?" Squint asked, getting out.

"Yep," Eddie answered.

"It's already after eleven . . ."

"And?" Eddie asked.

"What kinda shape we gon' be in, startin' at—"

"You wanna work, mu'fuckah, or you wanna fuck around?" Eddie snapped. "Lot of niggahs out there lookin' for work. . . ."

Squint backed away from the car. "I'll drop by your pad later."

"Might wanna do that," Eddie said. He patted the seat, and the limo pulled off again. "Niggahs," he spat. Eddie took a cigarette from his silver case. Viola lit it for him, and then he settled back again. "Need to git me somethin' to eat," he said, as if suddenly realizing that he was hungry. "After my run, Luth?"

"Yes, sir."

"Willa made some oxtails tonight," Viola said hopefully. "I know how much you like oxtails . . ."

"I done told you, Viola," he said. "I ain't stoppin' at no Big House."

"Suppose *I* just run in for a minute . . . you can wait in the car . . ."

"I said no."

"But the gather'll be going on . . ."

Eddie pounded on the driver's headrest, and the car pulled to a stop with a loud screech. "Get the fuck out," he demanded. "Go'n take yo' ass back to the Big House."

"Don't yell at me," she said.

Eddie looked at her with an amused expression. "You tryin' to tell me what to do, Vee-ola?"

"No," she said.

"Don't you ever jump in my face like that." His voice was soft, but there was a sting to it that she was unused to. He nearly touched the tip of her nose when he pointed and said, "If you gon' stay on my back about some goddamned bullshit, then get the fuck out my car."

Eddie's deep brown eyes flashed a look that dared her. One that said that if she got out, she could never get back in. Viola was stunned. She didn't fear that he'd hit her or harm her, but that she'd cease to be a part of his life. These months with him had been as exciting a time as she'd ever spent, and Viola didn't want that to end. After a moment she sat back in the deep pile of the limousine seat. Eddie nodded, and the driver pulled off again.

The car barely came to a full stop on 103rd Street before Eddie jumped out. He hurried into the dim lobby of the building, and seconds later, Viola saw him step into a small elevator. Although she had been here several times, this was as close as she ever got to the place. It was a five-story brick apartment house with a small, dark lobby. It looked like people were supposed to be buzzed in, but the door was always open. Sometimes Viola would sit and watch men and women in clothes as expensive as Eddie's enter the building. Some came right back out, but others, like Eddie, stayed awhile.

Viola searched her purse and pulled out the empty pack of Newports. She crumpled it and stuffed it in the ashtray on the car door.

"How long you think he'll be tonight?" she asked the driver.

"Could be twenty minutes, could be two hours." Luther wasn't impolite, but maintained a cool distance.

"Must be hard driving Eddie sometimes," she said, trying to make conversation.

"It's my job," he replied.

"Eddie and all his cussin' . . ."

He shrugged.

"And . . . the 'runs' here?"

"I jes' drive," he said. He unwrapped a piece of Juicy Fruit gum and folded it into his mouth. He offered the pack over his shoulder, and Viola pulled out a piece.

"Think we'll have time to find a store for some cigarettes?" she asked.

His head tilted as if he were considering the question. "Sto' open down there on Ninety-sixth Street," he said.

"There's also one on One Thirty-ninth Street," she said.

He peered at her through the rearview mirror. "Up near that Big House?" he asked.

"Yes, sir."

He looked toward the building again. "You know I'd love to take you there, daughter, but Mr. Bishop come out and find us gone"—he shook his head sadly—"there'll be hell to pay. Cain't leave the man out there on the curb."

Viola smiled to herself. "You know, Luther," she said, "A year ago, I didn't even know what a curb was."

They sat again in silence. The street around her was quiet except for a few people who seemed to be setting off or returning from a night of partying. Viola tried to picture Eddie in this place. Perhaps he had now relaxed and gotten "straight." The straight that made the pain go away. The straight that made him hover in place, as if an angel had tapped his shoulder to keep him balanced. The one that made him easy to talk to and the one that made him agree to anything, perhaps even going to the Big House. She sat a few moments longer, then looked behind her down the dark and empty street. Viola unlatched the door and walked toward the building. Luther quickly slid out and stood by the car.

"I do believe you should wait here," he said.

"I'll be right back," she called to him.

Viola didn't feel as fearful entering the building as she knew she should. Eddie was somewhere inside, and she had seen all kinds of people go in, including women. Viola stood in the dim lobby wondering which way to go next. From outside, the bulb had seemed like it was just about to go out, but standing here, she saw that it was tinted a sickly amber color, as if to obstruct the view from the sidewalk. Viola could tell that this had once been a nice building, what Miss Honeybee called a prewar building, with detailed wood carving on the railings and tiling on the floors and walls. The pattern, several white squares, then a delicate gray fleur-de-lis, was often interrupted by a jagged chip in the tile or a splat of dried black gum. Viola stood helplessly. She had no idea which apartment Eddie had gone to, or even what floor. After a moment, the lobby door opened and a couple walked in. The tall white man, with dirty blond hair, wore jeans and an argyle sweater and tie. The rail-thin woman he was with, who appeared to be Hispanic, wore a red satin pantsuit. Viola knew they were going where Eddie was. She could tell by the way their eyes avoided hers and by how their chatter ceased when they entered the lobby, as it does when you begin a slow and steady rise to the top of a roller coaster. She followed them.

The elevator climbed to the fourth floor. When they stepped out, the landing was surprisingly bright. The long hall smelled of Friday night pork chops. The couple stopped at an apartment just right of the steps. The man gave the door one quick knock and waited. Seconds later the door cracked open and the couple entered. Although it was clear Viola was waiting too, the door closed again and she was left outside.

She waited a moment longer, and then gave the door one hard knock. It cracked open again, and a large brown woman answered.

"I'm looking for Eddie Bishop," Viola stuttered.

"Who's looking for Eddie?" the woman asked.

"His girlfriend," Viola said tentatively.

The woman chuckled. "Which one?"

"My name is Viola, ma'am."

The woman opened the door a little farther and looked at Viola from head to toe. "Well, Viola," she said sarcastically, "you just too sweet to be lying in my face."

The apartment was dim but roomy. They passed what looked like the living room, where a few people sat cross-legged on the floor or against the wall beside an open window. Smokey Robinson and the Miracles' "Shop Around" played from a radio. Yet another gather, Viola thought. Only here, there was far less joy, no food, and no one's eyes met her own. Had it not been for the odor of reefer, it might have reminded her of a dinner party at the Bembrey home.

The woman took her to the very back of the apartment. She knocked on a door, then opened it slowly. Eddie's song "Timeless" played inside. The woman covered the doorway with her body.

"Somebody named—" She quickly turned back to Viola. "What's your name, girl?"

"Viola."

"Girl named Viola," the woman announced inside. "Say she yo' steady."

The woman stepped behind Viola, shoved her in, and shut the door.

The room was even darker than the rest of the apartment. There was barely any furniture—only two armchairs and a small stereo. A beaded curtain hung in the doorway that led to an adjoining room, and there were several posters on the wall that Viola couldn't quite see. She could just make out Eddie sitting on a long cushion against a side wall. He hung in a dreamlike state.

She went to Eddie and shook him. He looked up with as much clarity as he could muster, then his head dropped to his chest again. This would have been at least a two-hour wait, Viola thought as she tried lifting him.

"Vee-ola," he said. "My sweet angel."

Eddie staggered to his feet, but then fell back to the cushion again, pulling her down beside him. Viola gathered her strength to try again.

"You come to get me, Vee-ola," he muttered. "Good, 'cause I'm hungry. I need you . . . I need you to cook something."

"Come on, Eddie," she said, trying to lift him again.

"Where my damn coat," he said.

"I have it," she said, picking up the leather coat from the cushion and slinging it over her arm.

"Solid," he said, trying to heave himself up. The large woman came into the room with a man even bigger than she was. With one swift pull, he yanked Eddie to his feet. As they walked through the hall toward the front door, the couple whom Viola had followed earlier patted Eddie on his back.

"That's Eddie Bishop," the man said. "I know that's Eddie Bishop."

"Everybody go'n back to what you was doing," the heavy woman said, clearing the hall. "Give the man his privacy." She unlatched the door and guided Eddie into the elevator. Viola took him the rest of the way to the car, where Luther helped him in.

Eddie was at peace now. No pain. No anger. He lay against Viola's shoulder, not quite asleep, but not awake either. When they reached home she helped him upstairs. Viola removed his jacket and his shirt and settled him on the bed. Then she made him steak and eggs.

Viola listened from the dining room as Eddie played his horn. She stacked her empty plate under his full one, on which lay a corn cob with a single set of teeth marks, two untouched scrambled eggs, and a porterhouse steak. He had cut a small piece of fat off the edge of the steak—that was a whole dinner for Eddie Bishop.

She stood for a moment and listened to Eddie blow "Gentle Is My Love."

Despair dotted the clean and simple melody, and he shaded the innocent love song with lustful strokes of red. This was Eddie Bishop. And this was why he was so revered.

Eddie's playing stopped midphrase. Viola looked into the bedroom and saw him lean over the night table to inhale a line from a tiny square of foil. It wasn't coke. She could tell by the way he sat back against the headboard and closed his eyes. Moments later the ghost took over. She could almost see this other person rise from his slackened body. The other Eddie Bishop who moved slowly and played sweeter. The Eddie Bishop who seemed so at peace, and anything she asked him was okay, and every sound in the room, including Miles, was music to him. He lifted his trumpet again and pointed it into his lap as he played. Viola stood curiously beside the bed. He opened his eyes just wide enough to see her, then stretched out his hand for her to sit beside him. She hated to admit it, but she liked the ghost of Eddie. He was warm and affectionate.

Eddie leaned over to the night table and inhaled with the other nostril. Viola drew the foil toward her.

"Hell, no," he said, pulling it back. "A little weed is fine but . . . this is a monster. I want you to leave it alone, okay?"

Viola didn't answer.

Eddie's laughter seemed to erupt in slow motion. "Honey would have a fit if she knew." His words sat on top of heavy breath. ". . . And Att . . . Att wouldn't allow you to . . . do no shit."

"Curtis doesn't even smoke a cigarette," she said.

"Att know the bitch personally," Eddie said. He sat against the headboard and pulled Viola into his arms again. His passion wouldn't go beyond this, because when Eddie was in a full bend, he had no nature at all.

The intercom rang. Viola went into the living room to answer, and when she looked back at Eddie sitting on the bed, his chin touched his chest.

"Squint is waiting downstairs," she called.

Eddie didn't move. She shook his arm.

"What?" he muttered.

"Squint is downstairs," she repeated.

"Forgot all about that mu'fuckah," he said, dropping his head. After sitting a few moments longer, he rose like a man still asleep. Eddie gathered the foil on the night table and shoved it into his pants pocket. He slipped on his shoes without his socks. He was still in a sleeveless undershirt, and his suspenders hung past his waist. "You need some money for shoppin' or somethin'?" he asked.

"In the middle of the night?"

"Whatever the fuck, Viola." Eddie hugged the top of her head, grabbed his horn, and stumbled out the door.

Viola walked with him to the elevator. Squint would be at the bottom floor waiting when Eddie got off. The Quintet was like a machine that fetched and delivered Eddie Bishop. She made sure the elevator doors closed before she went back into the apartment.

Viola gathered his socks and shirt from the bedroom floor. Eddie's jacket was slung over the back of a chair, and as she was about to hang it up, his heavy leather wallet fell out. Viola opened it, wondering if Eddie's wallet was as intriguing as his horn case, which he lined with Almond Joys, bits of clean flannel, and expensive pens. He had a couple of credit cards in his wallet, but she couldn't recall him using them. There were two hundred-dollar bills and a few twenties, but Viola knew that Eddie usually carried a lot of cash. In the clear sleeves were old pictures of a good-looking man holding a trumpet. His complexion was lighter than Eddie's, but his eyes slanted the same way. The fold of the wallet had another picture of the same man, surely years later, and he looked tired and worn-down. This had to be BoBo Bishop, she thought. Viola slipped the wallet back into his jacket and realized that Eddie had left his cigarette case behind. He usually traveled with it as religiously as his horn. Inside, Lucky Strikes were lined up as neatly as white sardines. She took one out, and under it was another tiny packet of foil.

This was what made Eddie Bishop leave home in the middle of the night. Made him show up late for a gig or not show up at all. Made him walk into run-down buildings at any hour. Viola set it on the night table. She opened the foil and stared at the beige powder. It also relaxed him to the point that he could play to a house of ten or ten thousand. Made him interesting, colorful, and made his shoulders large enough to touch both corners of the room. She couldn't imagine what it would be like to have the arrogance of Eddie Bishop or to converse with kings or queens at a gather without her hands trembling. Perhaps the high would be none of these things. But, at the very least, Viola wondered what it would be like to feel absolutely nothing.

It must have been early morning when the front door opened. The tiny bit of light from the hall caused her to squint. Viola tried to separate her lips, but a pasty film inside her mouth glued them shut. She wiped away the stickiness and started to pull herself up, but something pushed down on the top of her head. The door closed, and the room was dark again, except for the traces of sliced moonlight coming in through the blinds.

Eddie walked into the bedroom and clicked on the lamp. He seemed to stand there forever trying to make her out. Then he saw the half-emptied foil lying on the night table.

"Aw, hell no!" he said.

Viola pulled herself against the headboard but couldn't feel her legs.

He stood right over her. His body was a large dark shadow. "You done fucked up, Vee-ola," he said. "I swear fo' God."

"What?"

"I say, you fucked up!" He shook his head in disbelief. "I told you to stay out of it. I told you!" He walked quickly into the living room, his feet swushing angrily on the carpet. Then she heard his voice on the phone. Viola couldn't make out what he was saying, but she could hear the slither of his "s" and the angry pounding of his "t's." When he came back, he clicked off the bedroom light. The front door opened, then slammed shut. Once again the apartment was dark.

Viola sat in a weird stupor. She had no thoughts, really, just a calm void. Her chest was light, and she felt that if she breathed deeply enough, she might float away. She lay back on the bed for ten minutes, maybe an hour, before the front door opened again. He walked in and stood over the bed. Viola waited for more words. The Reverend's words. How disappointing she was. How much better than this she was. But the words didn't come. Viola felt a gentle hand lift her chin, the softness of a palm against her cheek, and then a long anguished breath. Forestine's forehead pressed against her own and then the breath was gone. Forestine rose to gather the bits of Viola scattered around the room. She put Viola's sweater over her shoulders, lifted her around the waist, and walked her out of the room.

Eddie was sitting on the couch. The light in the living room was so bright that Viola could barely make him out. But his voice was clear when he said to Forestine, "Tell her not to come back."

"She won't," Forestine said, leading Viola to the front door.

"I know you ain't mad at me, Forestine," Eddie chuckled.

Forestine didn't respond.

"Come on now," he said. "We got lots to do, you and me. This ain't got shit to do with us."

"I think it does," Forestine said, holding on to Viola.

"A lot of folks lookin' for work," he said.

"Like you're the only trumpet player in the whole damn city," Forestine returned.

"I'm the best," Eddie said.

Viola felt herself being lifted off of her feet. "Miles is the best," Forestine shot back. Then she took Viola home.

The three rarely strayed far from the Big House during the cold winter months. They remained snug and warm behind the heavy velvet drapes and sent Fred out to do the essentials. So clearly, when they saw Forestine and Viola sitting on the stoop of the brownstone on this nippy December day, they assumed the girls had lost their minds.

The curtains in the front window parted, and Willa's face appeared. Forestine couldn't quite make out what she was saying, but the words "crazy as hell" stood out. Then Willa disappeared into the house, and the drapes fell back into place again.

Forestine enjoyed layering herself in sweaters, tights, a hat, and gloves, and sitting outside. Much like the Kings County projects in the winter, Harlem was brisk and quiet, with few kids playing and even fewer adults coming and going. A perfect time to let the cold wind clear her head. Viola seemed to agree, for she too remained deep in thought as a hardy gust pulled strands of hair from the sides of her red wool hat. The girl had been getting stronger these past couple of days, her heart hurt more than any physical part of her. Forestine understood these feelings, especially the guilt and responsibility. Even now, she continued to struggle for answers. Forestine had promised Willie that she would think about singing again and that she'd sit down and talk to Lilian. Four weeks later, she had done neither.

The thin wool gloves did little to guard Forestine's hands from the chill. She shoved them into her pockets and felt them begin to thaw. As a child, she'd been able to sit out in the cold longer than anyone she knew. Willie would sometimes sit with her, but after less than half an hour, he'd limp back into the apartment on frozen feet.

Viola was still subdued, but she seemed to be doing better. The three treated her as gently as they had Forestine. But Forestine was relieved that Miss Honeybee hadn't seen them three nights ago, when she had picked Viola up and carried her home.

It had been difficult getting a cab. Drivers wouldn't stop when they saw Viola wobbling on her two feet, or bent over and vomiting in the middle of the street. Forestine couldn't blame them. After Viola's stomach had settled, Forestine held her upright around the shoulders, and they finally got a car.

They'd arrived at the Big House well after the gather had ended. The cleanup was over and everyone, including Fred, had retired. Somewhere around five A.M., just as the sky began to lighten, Forestine lifted Viola up the steps as quietly as she could. Though the three would have been glad to know that Viola was finally home, they would have been deeply upset to see her in this condition.

Forestine lay Viola across her bed and removed her shoes. Even in her drug-induced state, the girl was restless. Every once in a while, Forestine heard a sputter and a tiny gasp, as if Viola were having a nightmare. After filling a bowl with tepid water, Forestine set it on the night table beside the bed, dampened a cloth, and wiped Viola's face and hands. She slipped off her soiled dress, then pulled on a soft blue nightshirt from Viola's bureau drawer.

Viola allowed Forestine to move her about like a limp rag doll. She opened her eyes a bit, and they looked like two slits in the dusky room.

Viola whispered, "How you feelin', Forestine?"

Forestine smiled at the sound of her voice. "How am *I* feeling? I'm not the one laid out like a slab of concrete."

Viola didn't attempt to smile. "How's Benny?"

"Benny's fine," Forestine replied. She understood that, right now, Viola needed to focus on anything but her own bad judgment.

"Does Honey know I'm here?" she asked.

"No," Forestine replied

"I guess . . . Eddie spoke to you?"

"I answered the phone when he called."

"Good," Viola said. "I hope you answer the phone when he calls tomorrow," she went on. "I don't want Honey to have to talk to him. . . ."

"Tomorrow?" Forestine replied.

"He'll apologize for getting so angry," Viola explained. "He always does . . . apologize, I mean."

Forestine smoothed the covers over her friend. "I don't think so, Viola," she said.

"He's upset. . . ." Viola said.

"He won't call," Forestine said gently.

"Maybe not tomorrow," Viola said. "But . . . you know how moody he is. . . ."

"He won't call you anymore," Forestine said plainly.

Viola closed her eyes. A tear ran down the side of her cheek.

Forestine herself knew Eddie's appeal. The grandeur of the man and his lifestyle were as addictive as any drug. In the weeks Forestine had worked with him, she saw how women waited at the door of the club just to a catch a glimpse of him. But more than that, Forestine understood how easily Viola became enthralled by anything glamorous and new. She recognized Viola's desire to be something big, without a clue of how she'd get there or what to do if she arrived.

A gust of wind blasted down 139th Street, shaking Forestine from her thoughts. It rustled the trees and sent a garbage can clattering down the block. Viola's face was buried in a blue neck scarf pulled around her chin. She looked up at Forestine on the step right above her.

"I think I need warmth now," Forestine said, as if it were a confession.

"And plenty of it," Viola put in.

"Least you're smiling, baby," Forestine laughed.

" 'Cause my mouth is frozen this way," Viola said through quivering lips.

The drapes in the window moved again, and Vernon stood there with his hands on his hips and an irate look on his face. At the same time, the front door cracked open and Miss Honeybee stepped into the doorway, holding her white sweater closed with both hands.

"Enough is enough, y'all," she called. "I ain't about to be treatin' no pneumonia 'round here."

"Just a while longer," Forestine teased.

"Ain't no ladies s'posed to be sittin' out there on no cold stone," Miss Honeybee scolded. "Ha' that arthur-itis all up and down yo' legs." When Forestine rose from the step, Miss Honeybee went back inside.

Viola tried to pull herself up, but couldn't get her balance. Forestine reached out and with a strong bear hug, yanked Viola until her knees locked. The girl held Forestine tight around the neck and wouldn't let her go. Forestine could feel her friend's body quaking, and she began to rock her. Neither spoke. The swaying was just as comforting for Forestine. She took Viola by the hand and led her into the house.

The scent of stewing chicken filled the warm vestibule. Forestine could feel her cheeks and the tips of her ears tingle as she removed her sweaters and coat and piled them on the banister. When they entered the kitchen, Willa looked up from the stove and Miss Honeybee and Vernon turned from the beautifully set table. Floral cups sat on saucers at each place, along with the shining silverware. Quarter ham and cheese sandwiches with the crust cut away were piled on a platter. A bright red poinsettia adorned the middle. Before sitting, Willa brought over several bowls of homemade chicken and dumplings. The steam rushed out of each bowl and made a fragrant cloud above the table.

"I can almost understand Forestine settin' out in the cold like that," Miss Honeybee said. "Forestine was raised in this kinda weather. But Viola's from the heat—girl, you oughta know better'n that."

"Don't drop hardly below fifty where you come from," Willa said, setting down two more bowls in front of Forestine and Viola.

"Folks see snow in Jasperville," Miss Honeybee said, blowing the steam from a spoonful of amber broth, "even a flake or two, the whole damn town close up. Schools shut, shops close, and folks hunker down like a blizzard was ablowin' through." Forestine laughed. "Am I lyin', Viola?" Miss Honeybee asked.

"No, ma'am," she answered. She stabbed at a chunk of dough in her bowl.

"Don't look like you got around to eating much lately," Miss Honeybee said to Viola.

"Some," she replied softly.

"Such a life," Vernon said as he placed two of the sandwiches on a saucer beside his bowl. "What glamour . . ." he went on. "Cutler and I never knew anything but the poor side of the business. Very few musicians get to see that kinda lifestyle."

"Only the king of kings," Willa chimed in.

Willa and Vernon were being kind, Forestine thought. But the furrow in Miss Honeybee's forehead suggested that she might not be as delicate.

"Have you been singing at all, Viola?" Vernon asked.

"Not a lot," she answered.

"We were so close to you gettin' up there on that platform," Willa said.

"How many times, Viola?" Miss Honeybee cut in. "How many times did you do it?"

"Ma'am?"

"You know what I'm askin'," Miss Honeybee insisted.

"How many times have I sang—"

"Don't you bullshit me, young woman," Miss Honeybee said without wrinkling her brow.

Viola looked at Forestine as if she had been betrayed.

"You think Forestine had to tell us what you been up to?" Miss Honeybee asked. "You think the three of us just arrived on some damned turnip truck?"

Forestine had heard Miss Honeybee use cuss words before. Occasionally they added amusement to her anecdotes. Today they were biting.

"How many times?" Miss Honeybee repeated.

"Once," Viola answered.

"You sure?"

"First and last," Viola said.

Forestine continued to be floored by Honeybee McColor. The woman had a way of getting to the root of things with the least amount of words.

"It all looked good, didn't it?" Miss Honeybee's tone softened a bit. "We understand better than anyone how fine that kinda life feels. But comes a time when you got to trust what the old folks say."

"I've always trusted you, Honey," Viola said.

"Don't get me wrong," Miss Honeybee went on. "I didn't expect you to jes' walk away from someone as fine as Eddie Bishop because we told you to. It don't work like that . . . I know. Ne'er one of us ever walked away at yo' age. Yo' own mama didn't. But the trick is knowin' where to draw the line."

Viola kept her eyes focused on her bowl.

"And Eddie Bishop . . . Lord, but he was an easy one," Miss Honeybee confessed. "That's what worries me the most."

"I don't know what you mean," Viola said.

Forestine had seen Miss Honeybee wear that maternal expression before—it revealed how deeply she cared, but also hinted at her disappointment.

"It's like one of them traffic accidents," Miss Honeybee explained. "You know, where the alarms are screaming and red lights are blaring. That's Eddie. He lay his crap right at yo' feet, from day one. Ain't no guessin' or supposin' involved. He do this, he do that! And he do it like it's alright, too." Willa and Vernon chuckled. "That's what worries me, Viola," Miss Honeybee said. "It worries me, 'cause there'll be some men that'll come along and make Eddie look like a choirboy."

"Mercy," Willa said.

"And they'll be jes' as fine . . . jes' as shiny. But they'll sneak up on you with no alarms or red lights. Lord, gal, I'd hate to think where you'll be if you don't start drawin' a line."

"I guess we won't be seeing Eddie around here," Forestine said.

"He might stop in for a gather or two," Miss Honeybee said.

Forestine looked at the woman curiously. "And you'd let him in?"

"Yes, I would," she replied.

Willa and Vernon seemed to understand.

"But why?" Forestine asked.

"That's the whole point," Miss Honeybee said. "We can get rid of

Eddie, but sooner or later, another'n come walking along. Just like with you, Forestine," Miss Honeybee went on. "It ain't about yo' baby being deaf . . . not really. It's 'bout what you choose to do about it. If we disallowed every musician with a problem . . ."

"Lord, Jesus," Willa bellowed.

"Besides," Miss Honeybee went on, "I've yet to meet a woman that hasn't had an Eddie Bishop in her life. Someone that you *know* is trouble befo' you even start."

"For me it was K. C. Bates," Willa mused.

"Lucas Campbell," Forestine admitted.

"Joshua Mayfield," Miss Honeybee added.

"Sheila Thompson," Vernon said.

"Sheila?!" the women gasped at once.

"That's just it," Vernon sighed. "Folks do silly things when they're young." He waved the thought away with one of his pink manicured hands.

The women continued to talk as Forestine finished the soup in her bowl, then excused herself to the quiet parlor. She took the phone from the cabinet, set it on the end table, and dialed her sister's number in Brooklyn.

"Lilian?" she said.

"Forestine," she answered blankly.

"I . . . wanted to come by," Forestine said. "Maybe set down . . . see what we can see. . . ."

"Um-hm," Lilian replied absently. "When?"

"I don't know," Forestine said. "When's the best time for you?"

Curtis hung a chalkboard from a wooden peg on the door outside the Green Parrot. It announced the talent and the entree for the
evening. Viola wasn't sure who was more thrilled. Dolly, seeing the
words *"Dolly's Fried Wings and Buttermilk Biscuits"* written in Curtis's
scraggly penmanship, or Viola herself, seeing *"Featuring the Green Parrot Ensemble with Songstress Viola Bembrey."*

Curtis gave her two sets every Thursday and the early set on Friday nights. No waiting tables, no refilling peanut bowls. She even had
a tiny dressing room to change in. It was a storage closet that Curtis
had converted for his female singers. Viola shared the space with a
wall of rolled toilet paper and cans of brandless salted nuts. The room
was lit with a table lamp and could fit two, maybe three people. Small
people. The bulb was so dim that Viola could only see a shadow of her
face. But sitting in a dressing room after her own gig, she wouldn't
have minded if she had to sit in the dark.

Viola had just finished her Friday night set. The house ensemble
played "For the Good Times," as Viola rubbed away some of her heavy
stage makeup. Curtis had decidedly moved toward more R&B at the
Parrot lately. The community demanded it. It wasn't until now, 1962,

that Curtis obliged them by hiring local groups and moving some of the tables from the center of the floor so people could dance. The new club format gave the Parrot a different atmosphere. One that was hip, young, and less sophisticated, but also one that packed the house most every night.

Viola had wondered how well she would adjust to the informality of songs like "He's So Fine." She'd discovered that the sheer spunkiness of R&B suited her voice and personality better than jazz. Her body seemed to move more naturally, whether belting a dance song or something as angst-ridden as "Tonight's the Night."

There was a knock on the dressing room door. She knew it was Curtis. No matter how crowded the Parrot got on a gather night, Curtis insisted on going to the Big House. It was his only link back to jazz. His only time to be a part of a world that, for him, was slowly drifting away. He knocked again, and Viola moved her chair so the doorknob wouldn't slam into it. Curtis slowly opened the door, checking that the doorjamb was clear of chairs and people. A heavy-set girl entered behind him.

"You about ready to go?" he asked.

"About," Viola answered. She looked at the girl, who seemed to be taking in everything in the small room.

"This is Ellie," Curtis said. The girl stood over Viola's dressing table. Her brown face was impeccably made up, and though she was what Miss Rosalee called "a right healthy gal," her body looked sexy in its black satin dress. "You remember I told you about Ellie. Ellie and her cousin Sharletta," he said, trying to jog Viola's memory.

The big girl didn't seem a bit offended. She appeared to be completely in awe.

"Remember I told you that I went to the Community Center for the talent show they had a few weeks back? Ellie and her cousin were singing that night."

Viola vaguely remembered.

"Ellie just saw your set," Curtis went on.

"It was wonderful," the girl put in. "I mean . . . *you* were wonderful." Ellie's voice was light for someone so robust. Viola figured her to be in her early twenties, but it was hard to tell. "Sorry that Sharletta couldn't make it tonight—they put her man in jail yesterday and she had to go all the way out Rahway, New Jersey. Alonzo deserved it, though," she rambled. "I tole Sharletta that's exactly where he need to be because he's always into some stuff. . . ."

"I wanted you to meet Ellie," Curtis interrupted. "Maybe sit and talk about her and her cousin doin' some background work for you here at the Parrot."

"I could not believe it when Curtis told me about this," Ellie said. She squeezed into a chair beside Viola. "Us singing in a group and everything . . . is it true that you *live* at the Big House?"

"Yes."

The girl shook her head incredulously. "You ever meet Betty Carter?" Ellie asked. "My daddy love him some Betty Carter . . . also Maxine Sullivan and Abel Drake . . ."

"They've all been at a gather," Viola said. She couldn't believe how casual she sounded. A year ago, she had been just as wide-eyed as this girl.

"What about Nancy Wilson?" Ellie asked. "Ever see her at the Big House? She is so pretty, isn't she?"

"Yes, she is." Viola smiled. "And no, I haven't see her there myself. But I've heard that she's stopped by."

"More than once," Curtis confirmed.

"What about like . . . the Pickleman or Eddie Bishop . . . ?"

Viola could feel Curtis's eyes burn into her. "I've seen them both," Viola simply answered.

"You actually met Eddie Bishop?"

"You ever been to the Big House, Ellie?" Viola cut in.

"I've passed by . . . mostly in the daytime and twice on a Friday night. But I wouldn't have the nerve to even walk in the gate. . . ."

Viola slung her pocketbook over her shoulder. "We're about to head over now. You need to be someplace?" Ellie was dumbstruck. "You're welcome to come," Viola said.

"To Honey McColor's place, you mean?" she asked incredulously.

"We can talk about our group over some barbecue."

Ellie wore a look that Viola recognized. It made her recall her own first trip to the Big House, what seemed like a lifetime ago. Viola knew the sight of beautiful people gathering and kings and queens jamming would humble the girl. But like Viola, Ellie might someday become part of the grandeur of a Friday night. And if she was especially blessed, perhaps even part of the family.

EPILOGUE

The Big House was fragrant with short ribs of beef and stewed pigeon peas. The empty parlor was lined with dozens of folding chairs, extra coasters, and small paper plates with toothpicked chunks of cheddar cheese. In the platform room, the stage was set for the players. Two small spotlights caught the glint of red glass ashtrays, making them sparkle like garnets. It was a Friday night. A gather night.

Benny ran through at full speed and didn't stop until he'd leapt onto the empty stage. He pulled the silent mike from its stand and droned into it. His lankiness reminded Forestine of herself at that age. Only, Benny seemed to have a confidence, even at six years old, that she had never possessed. Forestine laughed as he danced across the stage like James Brown.

"Who say that child cain't hear," Willa said, arranging chairs against the wall. "Might not take the music in through his ears, but it's sho' 'nuff in his blood."

Forestine set a couple of bowls of pretzels on two end tables in the parlor room. After stuffing a pretzel in her mouth, she dusted flecks of salt from her navy pantsuit.

"You hear what I jes' said, Forestine," Willa called to her.

"Benny *does* have music in his blood," she said, parting the light summer drapes. "But he is still quite deaf."

"Folks hear in they own way," Willa said.

Vernon dragged more folding chairs from the basement. He held them away from his body, so as not to wrinkle his green satin tunic.

"Is Viola doing a song here tonight?" Forestine asked from behind the window's cream lace curtains.

"After she finish at the Parrot, I 'spect," Willa answered. "The chile been *working*..." She emphasized the word "working," but Forestine didn't bite. "So nice to see her on*stage*..." Willa called.

"Leave it alone," Vernon mumbled.

"Yes, do," Miss Honeybee said as she entered the parlor. She was breathtaking in a white dress that touched the tip of her knee. Gold sequins lined the neckline and the cuffs of her sheer white sleeves. Then Miss Honeybee grounded herself with a deliberate earthiness. "I'm 'bout to fall out this dress if somebody don't close it in the back."

"I don't know how you do it, Honey." Forestine zipped her, covering the white lace corset underneath.

"You too sweet," Miss Honeybee said graciously.

"How do you know, time after time?"

"Know what, sugar?"

"What you're gonna wear for a particular gather," Forestine asked.

"Depends on how I feel. Some nights a woman wanna look merely pretty. Other nights, nothing less than drop-dead stunning will do."

"This must be the latter," Forestine smiled.

"If I did it right," Miss Honeybee replied. She clipped on small diamond earrings. "Lilian ain't come yet?" she asked.

"Not yet," Forestine said, turning back to the window.

"I think your sister doesn't want to admit it," Vernon said, "but she'd like to come and listen to the music."

"I've invited her and Lucas to a gather more than a few times." Forestine sat on the couch beside Miss Honeybee "I've been inviting them for months, but Lilian say she can't be bothered with these hoity-toity people." Benny slid onto her lap, and Forestine held him around the waist. "Every other Friday, she wants to pick up Benny and be on her way."

"And always manage to get here *right* befo' the gather start." Miss Honeybee laughed. "She come with the same old story 'bout how the traffic was heavy coming in from Brooklyn and she don't mean to put nobody out *but*...and all the time her and Lucas is steady looking 'round here like they in an amusement park. I always tell her the same thing. I say, 'Come on in, baby. Set yourself down and have a plate.' "

"It makes Lilian's day to be able to pick Benny up on gather nights," Forestine said. She hugged him close. "You about ready to go to your Aunt Lilian's house?" she asked him. Before she could complete her sentence, Benny was up and about to dash toward the platform again. "Hey," she said, grabbing him and turning his head toward her. "I said, are you ready to go?"

"Sign it, Forestine," Vernon urged.

"He can read my lips."

"That ain't the point, sugar," Miss Honeybee said. "You payin' good money to learn, but the onliest way you gon' *really* know it is to use it."

Forestine sat Benny on her lap again, turned him toward her, and signed her words. She had started learning months ago, and only now could she actually put simple words together and talk to him. Miss Honeybee, Vernon, and Viola had gotten the knack of it earlier. Willa didn't bother at all. She just yelled everything.

"You pack your bag?" Forestine asked Benny, speaking and signing.

"Yes, Forestine," he answered.

"Did you pack your..." Forestine struggled with the word "pajamas," but Benny helped her.

"The ones with the baseball bats," he said. His tongue was thick in his mouth, but his words were clear.

"Well, go on and play 'til they get here," Forestine said.

Benny dove off of her lap and ran toward the platform.

"I'm proud of how you've handled things, Forestine," said Miss Honeybee.

"That goes for me too," Vernon put in.

"The boy is happy and Lilian's happy too, 'cause she gets to see him every other week. That's a fine thing you did..." Miss Honeybee's voice seemed to build toward a "but."

"Not tonight, Honey," Forestine said, reading her face.

"We ain't talked about this in a while," she said, "but it's not like we haven't been thinking about it."

"You won't even sing here at the gathers," Willa said. "And if there's anywhere you *can* sing, it's with us."

Fred Nastor shuffled down the hall. Someone had knocked on the front door.

"I know this ain't the right time," Miss Honeybee acknowledged. "But we'll come back to it."

"You always do," Forestine said.

"It's jes' that I cain't abide waste." Then the three rose ceremoniously and went out to the vestibule, ready to greet their guests.

The fact was that Forestine didn't quite know what stopped her from singing. Though it had started with guilt and heartache, perhaps now her reservations had nothing to do with Benny at all. She had always been so sure of her talent. But the longer she was absent from the stage, the less confident she became.

Forestine heard Lilian's high-pitched voice. From the archway, she observed her sister. Lilian's demeanor was always different at the Big House—less confident, almost shy. Forestine had once considered her a snappy dresser, but now Lilian's clothes looked modest and outdated. Her hair had always been in the latest styles when they were teenagers, but ten years later, her sister still wore the same flip.

"Sorry we a little late," Lucas said.

"That's okay, dahlin'," Miss Honeybee replied. "As you can see, ain't nuthin' quite started yet."

Lilian eyed Miss Honeybee from head to toe. Forestine knew that her clothes were surely a topic of conversation in the Campbell home.

"Smells so good in here," Lilian put in. "But then, it always does."

Vernon handed Lucas a bag. "I fixed you a couple of plates to take home," he said.

"Did you put some of that potato pie in there like the last time?" Lucas asked.

"Lucas Campbell," Lilian scolded.

"Apple," Vernon smiled.

"Awfully nice of you," Lilian said, stealing glimpses into the parlor.

Forestine knew that there was a part of her sister that didn't want to leave. Although the gather hadn't started, a sense of anticipation and gaiety already hung in the air.

"You ready, young man?" Lilian signed to Benny. "Give your mama a hug so we can get on."

Benny kissed Forestine, then Willa, Vernon, and Miss Honeybee.

"Maybe next gather," Forestine said as they walked out onto the stoop. "Hattie can take Benny and you and Lucas can stay for the party. . . ."

Lilian moved close to Forestine and whispered, "You know these ain't my kinda people."

Shirley DeGrace was coming up the steps. As usual, her arrival was loud and fun. Lilian actually turned Benny's face away from this woman in her frilly summer dress with its plunging neckline. She was with Betty Rawlins and three young male musicians. Benny trotted down the steps, curiously peeking behind him at the grinning men lugging instrument cases. The musicians went in and headed right for the platform. Before Lucas and Lilian had even gotten into their car, the Big House was jamming.

The parlor and platform rooms quickly filled. Soon there were five musicians playing and two waiting on the side. The younger players liked to arrive early before there was stiff competition to get on.

Forestine took a seat in the plush red armchair right below the stage. She settled in, and throughout the evening she watched the room fill, thin out, then swell again as the clubs downtown closed. All that time Forestine sat, sipping a dark rum that someone was always willing to freshen for her.

"You singin' tonight?" one of the musicians asked her.

Forestine didn't even know his name. There were always young players that she had never seen before.

"The man asked if you were singin' tonight." Viola slid onto the armrest of the chair and playfully leaned on Forestine's shoulder. Forestine responded by handing Viola her empty glass.

"It's been almost a year," Viola said, ignoring the glass. She talked into Forestine's ear. Her hair, now grown below her shoulders again, brushed against Forestine's cheek.

"Has it been that long?"

"I've tried to stay out of your business about this." Viola reached for Forestine's hand. "We've all tried. But this has gone on too long."

"I appreciate your opinion," Forestine said dismissively.

Viola ignored her. "You remind me of one of them little girls trying to skip double Dutch out there on the sidewalk."

"What?" Forestine laughed.

"You know how they stand at the edge of the turning rope, trying to jump in," Viola said. "They duck and they lean and they duck and they lean, but they too scared to get in there . . ."

Forestine looked into Viola's dark, pretty eyes and wasn't sure what surprised her most. The fact that Viola's analogy was so damn accurate or that the girl had acquired such sharp insight in the first place.

"Honey told me that Bobby Timmons offered you a three-month tour in Europe and you turned him down," Viola said. She was so close that Forestine could smell her perfume. "I'm singing my R&B," Viola said. "Occasionally a little jazz . . . but, you're the one, Forestine. There are singers and then there's you."

Forestine grasped Viola's hand tighter. She had heard similar words from her father, Miss Honeybee, Willa, and Vernon. Even Fred Nastor had brought a cup to her room full of clover honey and a dab of tea meant to soothe her throat.

"What in the world do you plan on doin' with yourself?" Viola asked. "You just gonna sit up here and get old? One thing I've yet to find in this house is an old person. . . ."

Forestine swirled the ice cubes in her glass as she stared at the players on the platform.

Viola moved even closer to Forestine and whispered, "I think I have a gig."

"Of course you have a gig," Forestine said, her eyes still on the platform. "You been at the Parrot—"

"I mean a *real* gig," she said excitedly. "The other night Curtis introduced me, Ellie, and Sharletta to a fella named Toland Murray."

"Toland Murray?" Forestine asked.

"He used to manage the Shirelles."

"You better shut up," Forestine said, looking directly at her.

"I'm not even kiddin', Forestine." Viola was hardly able to contain herself. "He told us he might be able to get us," she said increduously, "*us*, the Songbirds, to open the show for Jackie Wilson."

"Oh, sweetheart," Forestine said, hugging her. She was surprised when she felt a twinge of jealousy. "When?"

"Jackie starts his tour in September," Viola explained. "Jackie *Wilson*, I mean. . . ."

"That would be fantastic," Forestine said. "Did you tell Willa about this?"

"I wanted to tell you first."

"Girl, if she hears this from anybody but you," Forestine warned, "there'll be no end to the grief."

"You are surely right about that," Viola said. "And Curtis and Ellie are in the kitchen right now."

Viola was about to dash off, but then turned back. "*You're* the one, Forestine," she repeated. "You'll think about what I said?"

"Yes," Forestine replied. "But I have one question. . . ."

"Anything," Viola said.

"The Songbirds?"

Viola playfully rolled her eyes as she walked away. "I happen to like it."

Forestine made her way to the bar. She slid her empty glass to the edge and Vernon filled it. The crowd was light now. The Pickleman's tenor sax sounded like an old friend that Forestine had missed. He'd been touring a lot lately and hadn't been at the Big House for a few weeks. She took a seat on one of the red-topped stools and closed her eyes as he started to play "The Good Life." She couldn't help but imagine what it would be like if she couldn't hear these sounds. If she could never hear a Jimmy Smith organ solo or Toots Thielemans blowing a harmonica.

Forestine opened her eyes as Curtis walked onto the platform. He gestured for her to come up, but she quickly looked down into her glass. Curtis started to play, and she raised her head again. His bass grounded the song. Gave it a different soul. The ensemble jammed, and it was like watching the jump rope turn quickly. No one made a fuss when Forestine walked to the edge of the stage. She stepped onto the platform. Curtis looked up from his fingers and simply smiled.

Then, one by one, folks began to assemble. Miss Honeybee and Willa stood in the doorway. Viola and Vernon sat crossed-legged on the floor just under the stage. Fred Nastor looked in from the hall. No one urged. No one pushed. They sipped their drinks and stood quietly while Forestine sang. Just like that, she was gathering. Gathering good.

ACKNOWLEDGMENTS

My heartfelt gratitude to the Frederick Douglass Creative Arts Center (and 'specially Mr. Fred Hudson), the Mercantile Library, and the New York Foundation for the Arts.

I also wish to thank the following people: my editor, Susan Kamil and her fab associate Zoë Rice for their unflinching faith and enthusiasm as they made me change everything, my agent Ellen Levine for her guidance and kind ear, Steve Moyer, Kazutoshi Kojima, Gilbert "Tookie" Lewis, The Group (James Pelton, Rod Jackman, Sherland Peterson, Beatryce Nivens), Gary Stern (for the kernel), Kathleen Collins, Joan Cullen, Bettina Reichart, Corbin, Silverman & Sanseverino, Nancy Darmanin, and the lovely Miss Nora Cole.

I am greatly indebted to my mentor and friend, Arthur Flowers, who sometimes had to hurt my feelings so that I could grow, Mrs. "Stella B." Timmons for the first spark, my knight in shining armor, Steve Lewis (thanks for turning off the treadmill), the best family ever: my sister Dina Gavin, brother Kenny, my dearest Sybil Sunday Smith and Mom and Dad, Andrew and Barbara Smith. I love you all! And finally, thanks to my "lil' pumpkin seed," Andrew Smith Short. You are my heart, Drewie.